CHRONICLES OF DISORDER

CHRONICLES OF DISORDER

Samuel Beckett and the Cultural Politics of the Modern Novel

David Weisberg

State University of New York Press

Published by
State University of New York

For information, address State University of New York Press
90 State Street, Suite 700, Albany, New York 12207

Production by Dana Foote
Marketing by Fran Keneston

Library of Congress Cataloging-in-Publication Data

Weisberg, David, 1955–
Chronicles of disorder : Samuel Beckett and the cultural politics of the modern novel /
David Weisberg.
p. cm.
Includes bibliographical references and index.
ISBN 0–7914–4709–X (alk. paper) — ISBN 0–7914–4710–3 (pbk. : alk. paper)
1. Beckett, Samuel, 1906– —Political and social views.
2. Beckett, Samuel, 1906– —Fictional works.
3. Literature and society—History—20th century.
4. Modernism (literature) I. Title.

PR6003.E282 Z915 2000
848'.91409—dc21
00–034447

10 9 8 7 6 5 4 3 2 1

CONTENTS

ACKNOWLEDGMENTS / vii

INTRODUCTION
Beckett's Choice / 1

CHAPTER I
Entering the Literary Field / 10

Joyce and Proust: Involuntary Epics / 10
"It Is Not": Juxtaposition and Ethical Judgment
in "Dante and the Lobster" / 17
Versions of Modernism / 24

CHAPTER II
Contact with the Outside World / 28

Contesting "Social Reality" / 28
"Contact with Outer Reality" in Murphy */ 32*
Watt: *Novel of Resistance*
or Accident of War? / 41

CHAPTER III
Rewriting Modernism in the Nouvelles / 53

Primitivism in the Tone of Polite Conversation / 53
Writing and Begging in "The End" / 56
From the Metropolis to the "Text" / 64
Author or Writing Subject?
Beckett and Postmodern Fiction / 73

v

CHAPTER IV
Molloy (one): Molloy, the Subject / 83

Molloy's Class Consciousness / *83*
The Production of the Story / *88*
Molloy and the Police / *91*
Subjectivity as a Modernist Universal / *97*

CHAPTER V
Molloy (two): Moran, the Agent / 102

The Agent as Storyteller / *102*
"Strong Enough at Last to Act No More" / *107*
The Terms of the Story: Agent, Voice, Purpose / *110*
Structures without Agents:
Beckett and the Postwar Critique of Narrative / *116*

CHAPTER VI
A Contest of Nightmares: *The Unnamable* and *1984* / 124

"Incomprehensible Uneasiness" in the Void / *124*
The Flâneur in a Jar / *131*
The Reinvention of the New and the Aesthetic of Failure / *137*
Nightmare of Commitment: Orwell's "Inside the Whale" and 1984 / *149*

EPILOGUE
Engagement, Écriture, Autonomy:
The Displacement of Politics in Postwar Critical Theory / 161

NOTES / 169

WORKS CITED / 185

INDEX / 191

ACKNOWLEDGMENTS

Many people contributed to the writing of this book in many ways—my friends and colleagues who encouraged me, argued with me, pointed out both errors and strengths, and listened patiently to my complaints and flights of fancy. First, I would like to thank those who saw me through the earliest versions of this project, when inspiration overpowered perspiration and clarity: John Brenkman, Luke Menand, Gerhard Joseph, Anne Bowler, Sean McCann, and Fergal O'Doherty. I also extend gratitude to those who read portions of the revised drafts, and who guided me toward a finished book: Henry Abelove, Ann Ardis, Jed Esty, Jeff Hester, Tom Huhn, Noah Isenberg, Natasha Korda, Ellen Nerenberg, Osvaldo Pardo, Jeffrey Schiff, and Kach Tololyan. And then, there are those whose help cannot be measured in pages and chapters: my parents, Arnold and Rosalie; my big family of Bob, Elyse, Sam, Noah, Rachel, Ross, Lauren, Emily, aunts Martha and Blanche, and my grandmother Rachel Benson, who passed away, sadly, before I really understood who she was or what that mysterious, tattered copy of *L'Etranger* on her bedside table meant to her. Most of all, I thank Natalia, for whom this book is just a beginning, and Julius, for whom everything is just a beginning.

Introduction

Beckett's Choice

The idea that "all writing is political," axiomatic in much literary and cultural theory since the 1960s, would have seemed nonsensical to Samuel Beckett. Although, according to biographical accounts, Beckett held deeply felt political convictions (which led him to join the French resistance), he consistently denied that his works had any social or political significance. Beckett's apoliticism as a writer has been widely recognized, and just as widely misunderstood. Beckett would have thought the idea "all writing is political" nonsense not because he believed that literary art was intensively subjective or aesthetically "autonomous"; he would have thought it nonsense because he came of age as a writer in the 1930s and '40s, when every writer was under pressure to declare explicitly a political stand, a "tendency," a commitment or engagement. For Beckett's generation, writing was political because the writer consciously chose it to be. Beckett chose quite consciously against being a "committed" writer. While many writers of the '30s and '40s accepted, and in some cases promoted, the harshly divisive opposition between autonomous and committed art, Beckett did not. Beckett's rejection of politicized art was never an acceptance of its supposed antithesis. The consequences of this choice had an enormous and complex impact on the development of Beckett's career. What ultimately structures the innovative features of Beckett's best fiction is a struggle to reimagine a communicative literature beyond the choices of autonomy or commitment. If Beckett's writing is "apolitical" it is because, in the terms he was given, he really had no other choice.

While the literary politics of the '30s and '40s centered on the reductively defined choice of the writer, in the '60s and '70s there was a shift toward construing literary politics as a system of textual effects. No longer tied to political movements or specific social issues, the political implications of a work were now seen to reside in the degree to which writing resisted or reinforced "bourgeois" norms of communication and narrative authority. The progressive writer's goal (if such a phrase makes sense in this context) was to disappear into the discourse and allow the signifier free play. Since 1979, when Foucault framed his influential statement of this position, "What is an Author?" with a quotation from Beckett's "Texts for Nothing" ("what does it matter who is speaking"), the legacy of the 1930s and 1940s has been lost to Beckett criticism. Beckett's apoliticism, his denial of socially relevant meaning, was transformed into its opposite. The irony of this transformation seems lost as well: what had formerly been condemned as modernism's ideological retreat from the social and political world—its self-vaunted distance from everyday modes of communication and practical rationality—now constituted its political savvy. Instead of man-

1

darin elitism, impotent formalism, or bourgeois individualism, Beckett's reputed escape from the order of representation now stood, theoretically, for a radical, liberating indeterminacy.

A more credible account of Beckett's place in the cultural politics of the twentieth century lies somewhere between the harsh divisions of the 1930s, which he rejected, and their inversion in the fantasies of a writing free from the constraints of convention and representation; fantasies constructed by a generation of intellectuals whose ideas became fashionable years after Beckett had completed his major work. Subscribing neither to the prescriptions of commitment nor the effusions of the 1950s neo-avant garde from which theories of radical textuality emerged, Beckett crystallized his conflicted experience of the 1930s' culture wars in a series of fictions—written between 1945 and 1950—that compulsively challenge the assumptions and values of modernism, cultural vanguardism, and social commitment *in relation to one other.* If, as textualist critics claim, a defining feature of Beckett's writing is its indeterminacy, it is an indeterminacy specific to a midcentury, post–World War II instability in conceptualizing the writer's social function. What may, after all, constitute Beckett's importance for twentieth-century literary history is just how emphatically his work begs for an alternate way of configuring an aesthetics/politics nexus.

The view of Beckett that has dominated academic criticism in the last two decades—Beckett as poststructuralist or postmodernist *avant la lettre*—makes partial sense but is ultimately misleading. For while early proponents of textuality were, like Beckett, responding to the legacy of the 1930s (Barthes's 1953 *Writing Degree Zero* responds to Sartre's 1947 *What Is Literature,* itself an attempt to rescue the 1930s notion of tendency from didacticism) they were also reiterating the revolutionary poetics of an earlier "historic" avant garde. By 1945, however, Beckett no longer had faith in vanguardist claims for the transfigurative or revelatory power of art. The account of Beckett's postwar achievement that I offer neither harkens back to the high modernism of *Finnegans Wake* that Beckett once defended, in a most contradictory fashion, in his first published work in 1929, nor projects him forward into a poststructuralist aesthetic ideology that, I argue, reinvents the contradictory version of aesthetic autonomy that Beckett himself, by the end of the war, found inadequate. What the view of Beckett's fiction as a harbinger of poststructuralism actually signals is poststructuralism's own atavism—its incorporation of a set of early twentieth-century vanguardist values reinvested as academic-intellectual, rather than bohemian-artistic, capital. Beckett's work—irreverent, paradoxical, strikingly original, at times convulsively beautiful—was a valuable asset in such a transaction. By making Beckett a proponent of a theory of discourse that he never held, the poststructuralist appropriation of his work isolates one feature of his writing and turns it into its essence. From another perspective, it would be equally true to say that Beckett was a harbinger of the *critique* of poststructuralism, so vociferously does his fiction express the absurdity of confronting the self and the world as textually determined.

Compelling evidence for a reassessment of Beckett's fiction starts with Beckett's own statements about writing during the years he was completing the trilogy. In 1949, Beckett published a set of "Dialogues" with art critic Georges Duthuit. Rather obscure when they first appeared, the dialogues have since been republished and are now part of the Beckett canon. Although pervaded by a self-mocking irony, the dialogues nevertheless suggest a consistent, if convoluted, aesthetic position. Critics have seized on this short text, usually as evidence of Beckett's devotion to a formalist aesthetic autonomy (art is meaningful only in relation to itself) or his proto-deconstructionism (writing is a chain of signifiers, not a referent to a signified). One passage in particular has been cited, perhaps more than any other, as the credo of Beckett's entire career: "The expression that there is nothing to express, nothing with which to express, nothing from which to express, no power to express, no desire to express, together with the obligation to express" (*PTD* 103).

Almost a decade later, one of the first canonizers of Beckett's work, Alain Robbe-Grillet, published a foundational manifesto of a new literary movement, the *nouveau roman,* which played an important role in the formation of textualist cultural politics. Not only does *For a New Novel* (the claim to the new is, of course, quintessentially modern) enlist the then up-and-coming Beckett into the ranks of the movement, but it also offers an echo of Beckett's proclamation. "The genuine writer," writes Robbe-Grillet, "has nothing to say. He has only a way of speaking. He must create a world, but starting from nothing" (45). "Here," he continues, "is where the difficulty—one is tempted to say the impossibility—of creation resides: the work must seem necessary, but necessary *for nothing*" (46; emphasis in text).

At the level of vocabulary and phrasing there is some sense here in seeing an affinity between the two writers' positions. In most respects, however, the mature Beckett and the young manifestoist Robbe-Grillet seem the very antithesis of one another. Robbe-Grillet marshals negativity to proclaim the new novel's revolutionary power "to invent . . . the world and man of tomorrow" (9); he places unlimited faith in the "will," "rigor," and "patient labor" (11–12) of the experimental writer. Nothing could be further from Beckett's characterization of his own project: "I'm not master of my material," he claimed in a 1956 interview, "I'm working with impotence, ignorance. . . . I think anyone nowadays who pays the slightest attention to his own experience finds it the experience of a nonknower, a non-can-er" (qtd. in Shenker 148–49). Where Robbe-Grillet celebrates the "methodical" and "deliberate" force of an aesthetically autonomous "creative consciousness" (11), Beckett sees nothing but "a sense of invalidity, of inadequacy. . . . To be an artist is to fail, as no other dare fail" (*PTD* 124-25). "I'm not interested in stories of success," Beckett reiterated years later, "only failure" (qtd. in Bair 349).

Beckett's insistence on "failure" and his linguistic-expressive nihilism distance him from Robbe-Grillet's neovanguardism and the poststructuralist textual politics that succeeded it. Of course, Beckett's work (like that of most modernist writers) does *imply* ideas about linguistic expression that concur with poststructuralism, but Beckett never advances an idea of language per se. Rather, his comments on writing and his postwar novels advance an attitude, usually concerning the obligation of futile resistance, toward some imagined linguistic situation in which a faith in expression is severely damaged or impossible. A very similar attitude, and a similar imagined situation, appear in a work of Beckett's contemporary, Orwell's *1984*, written in the same years Beckett was completing the trilogy. Although in most literary-critical regimes Beckett and Orwell have been scrupulously detained within the respective borders of autonomy and commitment, they speak to each other in significant ways. Consider, for example, the character Syme from *1984*, the artistic, intellectual Newspeak philologist: "We're destroying words—scores of them. . . . We're cutting the language down to the bone. . . . It's a beautiful thing, the destruction of words. . . . After all . . . the whole aim of Newspeak is to narrow the range of thought. In the end we shall make thoughtcrime literally impossible, because there will be no words in which to express it" (200–201).

"I have not written a novel in seven years, but I hope to write another fairly soon," Orwell wrote in 1946; "It is bound to be a failure, every book is a failure" ("Why" 426). Failure, linguistic destruction, no words to express, the obligation to express: could it be that Beckett had more in common with Orwell than with Robbe-Grillet, or Joyce, or Kafka? Surely in the trilogy Beckett violates those precepts of engagement and plain-spoken communication (so important to Orwell) in favor of disruptive, modernist *écriture*. But the proximity of Beckett's declaration—"nothing to express"—to the propagandistic ideals of Newspeak indicates a cultural-political problematic that literary history has left unaddressed. To both Beckett and Orwell, a Poundlike injunction to make the novel "new" coupled with a faith in the (abstract) revolutionary power of autonomous art would have sounded hollow and naive, perhaps dangerously so. As my analysis of *The Unnamable* in the final chapter of this book shows, what the culminating novel of Beckett's trilogy expresses, more than anything else, is just how contradictory, disturbing, and inadequate the assumptions of high modernism, the avant garde, and committed writing had become by the late 1940s. Quite unlike Robbe-Grillet, Beckett and Orwell had experienced first hand the bitterly divisive cultural politics of the interwar years. Somehow Beckett, the apostle of autotelic apolitical art who defended Joyce's *Finnegans Wake* in 1929, and Orwell, champion of common sense and "democratic socialism" ("Why" 424), found themselves after the war at a similar juncture, crossing the ideological divide between autonomy and commitment.

Surprisingly, Beckett's fiction has received no sustained attention from a perspective informed by the history of the cultural politics of the modern novel. His development as a writer overlapped with a set of cultural agendas which explicitly sought either to sever or intensify a nexus among art, politics, nation, tradition, "personality," and everyday life. Beckett began to publish in the late 1920s, and his earliest works evince a conflicted engagement with British aestheticism, the traditions of bohemia, the project of the avant garde from futurism and dada to surrealism, the Irish cultural revival, and variants of Joycean and Eliotic modernism. His first novel, *Murphy*, was written in the mid-1930s amidst virulent polemics about (to paraphrase Walter Benjamin) the politicization of art and the aestheticization of politics. He served in the Resistance and wrote his second novel, *Watt,* while hiding from the Nazis in southern France. His first fiction published in French appeared immediately after the war in Sartre's leftist journal *Les Temps modernes.* His internationally famous works were almost all composed during the late 1940s when those modes of defining writers' relations to social and political processes constructed under the polarizing pressures of the interwar period ceased to have much meaning. The trajectory of Beckett's career calls for a historically contextualized critique of his writing in which considerations of art's political and social functions play a decisive role.

What has prevented such a critique of Beckett's fiction are the circumstances of its canonization. Poststructuralist critiques, based on an understanding of language (and all modes of signification) as a closed system, foreclose the recognition of the dynamic relationship between Beckett's work and the normative, social dimensions of narrative art. Critics informed by existential phenomenology view his work as a disruptive extraliterary exploration of the relation of language to perception, subjectivity, and knowledge. Theorists of postmodernist fiction see him as an avatar of the metafictional dissolution of the "writing subject." Whatever valuable light these views shed on one aspect or another of Beckett's work, they all obfuscate the cultural specificity of his fiction and implicitly place him in the 1920s of high modernism, or assimilate him into those explicitly neovanguardist movements whose principal figures, from Robbe-Grillet to Foucault, began their careers well into the 1950s. More problematically, however, they implicitly rearticulate—rather than examine—many of the polemical antinomies of the interwar period itself: formalism vs. realism; the irrational vs. instrumental rationality; passive vs. tendential; individual subjectivism vs. social objectivism; radical experimentalism vs. bourgeois art; a "Revolution of the Word" (*transition* editor Jolas's 1929 manifesto) vs. a revolution of the people, and so on. Beckett's formative entanglement with these contradictory cultural-political divides led him to reject the aspirations of both modernism and the avant garde. By the time he wrote *The Unnamable,* Beckett had created a narrative form out of nothing but contradictions generated by such oppositions; contradictions explicitly laid bare and carried out to exhaustion. As a self-conscious meditation on narrative art that takes as its starting point an awareness of the untenable polarizations of interwar cultural politics, Beckett's mature fiction cannot be understood by recourse to any single position within these polarizing attitudes.

Ultimately, it is in relation to the period's overarching antinomy—aesthetic autonomy vs. committed writing—that the culminating novel of Beckett's postwar project, *The Unnamable,* most closely resembles Orwell's last book. As Irving Howe noted, *1984* was both the culmination of the development of the modern political novel and its negation: "In a sense, it is a profoundly antipolitical book, full of hatred for the kind of world in which public claims destroy possibilities for private life" (239). *The Unnamable* holds an analogous position: it is both a culmination of the ideology of aesthetic autonomy and a profoundly antimodernist novel. To be sure, throughout their careers Beckett and Orwell made opposite aesthetic choices. But more significantly, both ended up struggling against the implications of the choices they had made. Both sensed failure as the inevitable outcome of the interwar polarizations and made aesthetic/political "failure" the focus of their postwar vision.

The arguments and analyses in this book have their bases in the perspectives of two very different critics of modern culture. One, T. W. Adorno, published in 1961 what might still be the best piece of criticism on a single work by Beckett, "Trying to Understand *Endgame*"; comments about Beckett appear throughout Adorno's writing on culture and aesthetics. The other, Raymond Williams, except for a few paragraphs on *Waiting for Godot* in his book on modern tragedy, made almost no mention of Beckett in his voluminous writings on English and continental modern literature. It was through the combined, mutually correcting writings of Adorno and Williams that I became convinced, at the end of my research for this book, of the deep-seated relation between Beckett's abstract, paradoxical, paratactic narratives and the realist traditions of the novel.

In his essay on *Endgame,* Adorno showed that the play's absurdity was neither an authorial preconception nor an existential motif but rather part of the play's "social content." For Adorno, the play interwove two central concerns: the social and political destruction of the autonomous individual, the ideology of which had sustained European culture since the Enlightenment, and the social function of modern art, which in its apolitical hypostatization of subjective freedom had contributed, knowingly or not, to the conditions leading up to the historical tragedies of the twentieth century. Through a deformation of the norms of classical and modern drama, the play transmogrified the role of the heroic individual into a mocking, frightening semblance of individualism. While the play's abstract, menacing backdrop of total catastrophe evoked, for its Cold War era audience, the irrational violence of World War II, Hamm's and Clov's fear "that they might mean something" evoked Beckett's own concern that his play be taken as a commentary on something essentially unrepresentable. As Adorno put it, "the violence of the unspeakable is mirrored in the fear of mentioning it" (245). For Adorno, the play was an exemplar of the post-Holocaust "antinomy of contemporary art" (249) because, while it protested against "the regression" of European humanism (248), it refused to put this protest into terms assimilable to the "instrumental" logic of domination and technocracy that had always shadowed the Enlightenment's promise of personal liberty.

Adorno established, brilliantly, that *Endgame* did indeed have a culturally specific "social content," but he understood Beckett's vision of society as restrictively encoded within an aesthetic rationality, a "counterlogic," that resisted the communicative norms of everyday life and protected serious art from capitulation to the "culture industry." The limitation of Adorno's view results from this overexaggeration of the oppositional "internal" logic of Beckett's work and his consequent underestimation of the aesthetic enterprise as a normative social process within modern civil society. Adorno actually made Beckett *more difficult* to understand, despite the title of his essay, because he wanted to ensure that Beckett remained unsullied by the popularity of mass-disseminated art. This may account for Beckett's bewildered annoyance (as reported in Knowlson, 428) when he met Adorno in 1961 and the "professor," disregarding Beckett's objections, regaled him with his "theory" about the relation of *Endgame* to *Hamlet*.

Like Adorno, Raymond Williams had a career-long concern with the social and political relations that underwrote, manifestly and latently, the forms of modern European culture. But whereas Adorno cordoned off the modernist aesthetic from everyday language and mundane rationality, Williams—perhaps more than any other literary theorist—sought to reestablish the connections between high culture and the lived culture of nations, classes, communities, and factions. Of the five works by Williams that figure prominently in this book, two in particular, *The English Novel from Dickens to Lawrence* and *The Politics of Modernism,* supply an account of the texture and pressures of artistic activity in democratic culture that led to the kind of aesthetic choices Beckett began to make in the late 1920s. From Williams's perspective, the integral but *negative* relation to the social world that Adorno attributed to Beckett's postwar writing takes on a positive, affirmative cast—not in relation to an abstract world of reified subjects, but in relation to other artists, writers, and intellectuals who were Beckett's first, primary audience. While Adorno's critical acumen was attuned to the semblance of the social world evoked through the tensions and contradictions of Beckett's work, Williams correctly located Romanticist, modernist, and avant-gardist expressions of opposition as crystallized articulations of the fears and aspirations of the rising and middle classes. In particular, it was in the genre of the novel, traditionally written by and for those classes, in which the modernist desire to stand outside social norms came into maximum tension with the various voices, expressions, and dissatisfactions of everyday, contemporary life that constituted the novel's core material. Ironically, although Adorno wanted to show that Beckett's work could not be folded back into the flow of the damaged social life from which it emerged, it was Adorno's unveiling of *Endgame's* "social content" that showed me just how much Beckett's experimental writing corresponded with the concerns of a postwar writer like Orwell, who was writing for the widest possible audience. Williams's critique of what he called the "selective tradition," that version of the modernist canon that separated out the "subjective" and "poetic" from the "social," set the stage for considering Beckett within, rather than opposed to, the common aspiration to communicate with and affect one's audience through an evocation of social life.

Like many works of literary interpretation, this book obeys certain limitations in order to present evidence for a sharply defined argument. I deal almost exclusively with Beckett's fiction, and his occasional critical writings about fiction. There are three simple reasons for this. First, Beckett saw himself as primarily a writer of fiction, and the majority of his work is in the form of stories, novels, and prose fiction "texts." Second, Adorno's essay notwithstanding, the cultural politics of Beckett's work has been taken up most systematically by critics and theorists of narrative. For obvious reasons, modern narrative—in the form of history, journalism, and fiction —bears the burdens of verisimilitude, communication, and social relevance in ways that lyric poetry does not. Of course, the narrative elements of drama are similarly burdened, but a discussion of Beckett's plays, and their performances, would have entailed a set

of issues beyond the purview of this book. Third, as literary historians have demon-
strated, the development of the novel and the development of the liberal, democratic
form of society in which modernism and the avant garde were born, are inseparable.
Considering Beckett's fiction as *novels,* rather than as abstract *texts,* automatically
involves the type of engagement with socially lived culture to which Williams devoted
his career.

This brings me to another, necessary limitation of this book. Rather than
consider all of Beckett's fiction, I have confined my analyses to the most characteristic
features of what I consider to be Beckett's representative, most important works.
Thus, while I give close attention to the *nouvelles,* especially "The End," I do not
consider *Mercier and Camier,* which I (and many other critics) consider an inferior,
minor work, and which, like the early, abandoned *Dream of Fair to Middling Women,*
was long considered unpublishable and only made available many years after Beckett
became famous. Nor do I consider, except for a few brief references, the fiction
Beckett wrote after the completion of *The Unnamable.* The reasons for these and
other, more debatable omissions (of the stories in *More Pricks than Kicks* I only
analyze the first, "Dante and the Lobster"; *Malone Dies* is given only a few paragraphs
of discussion) should become evident as my argument develops.

Another, related feature of this book warrants prolepsis: my argument rests on
accounting for substantive flaws in Beckett's early, interwar fiction (flaws Beckett
acknowledged, though in terms different from my own) and describing how Beckett
transformed these "failures" into artistic success in his postwar work. Obviously, some
readers will take issue with my characterization of *Murphy* as a seriously flawed work,
or of *Watt* as a static, transitional work whose value is more symptomatic than
substantive, or of *The Unnamable* as far superior to *Malone Dies.* My analyses try both
to explain these judgments and account for them in terms of Beckett's development as
a writer. While cultural context is vital to my argument, my attention is turned, first
and foremost, to the techniques and themes internal to Beckett's fiction, and to how
the actual workings of his fiction reflect the most enduring cultural and aesthetic
controversies of the century. My characterizations of cultural context are focused only
on points directly relevant for unraveling the paradoxes in the fiction and are not
intended to supply a cultural history of the period. Beckett himself once warned that
considerations of art's relation to its "occasion" too often led to a disquisition on the
occasion at the expense of the art. It is a warning I take seriously.

To describe briefly the contents of the book: Chapter 1 critiques the early essays
on Proust and Joyce, the story "Dante and Lobster," and takes up the issue of the
divergence and affinities among aestheticism, the avant garde, and so-called high
modernism, and how Beckett responded, in his work, to the conflicting aesthetic
agendas of the late 1920s. Chapter 2 critiques Beckett's well-known review of Denis
Devlin's poetry, and his first novel *Murphy,* to show how Beckett understood the
relation of literary language and form to the demand, in the 1930s, that art deal with
"social reality"; *Watt* is analyzed with a focus on the communicative function of
narrative, and how Beckett's isolation, during the war, is reflected in an apparent shift

in his attitude toward aesthetic autonomy. Chapter 3 deals with the postwar nouvelles and traces the technical innovations in these works, and their geopolitical placeless-ness, in terms of Beckett's transformation of key features of modern fiction, especially regarding the narrative order of the European metropolis; it also takes up influential theories of postmodern fiction and the one-dimensional manner in which Beckett's work has been subsumed into the "pomo" canon. Chapter 4 deals with part one of *Molloy* and explains how Beckett integrated the modernist "subjective" turn into his postwar work; it also offers a brief description, following the work of Williams and Peter Bürger, of the genesis of subjectivity as a literary value in the French and English modernist novel. Chapter 5 deals with part two of *Molloy* and takes up Beckett's representation of, and attitude toward, human agency; it also explains how the role of individual agency was the underlying issue of critical debates, beginning in the 1950s, about narrative ideology. Chapter 6 interprets *The Unnamable* and the "Dialogues" in the context of the *nouveau roman,* Orwell's criticism of interwar cultural politics, and *1984*. Finally, the epilogue contrasts three paradigmatic ideas about the relation of art and politics that emerged in the postwar period, and how the interpretations of Beckett I have offered measure up against them.

The overarching thesis of this book is that Beckett overcame his interwar ambivalence to the modernist ideal of aesthetic autonomy, not by taking up opposing ideals of commitment, but by fashioning a narrative form that consciously exploited contradictions inherent in the notion of an autotelic art. In practice, the modernist belief in aesthetic autonomy entailed a constellation of ideas and attitudes about individual agency, subjective knowledge and experience, the self-referential and com-municative features of language, the power of mass culture, universalism and cultural nationalism, and the hostility to middle-class norms that was itself rooted in the bourgeois institutions of modern life, from the metropolitan street to the university. Beckett's commitment to a vision of artistic integrity, formulated during two of the most turbulent decades of modern history, are a refraction of the more general struggle to define art's social function at a time when art seemed, to some, a super-fluous sphere of ideological endeavor, and to others, the last refuge of humane existence. To some extent, Beckett's work embodies both these beliefs; to some extent, this makes him a typical intellectual artist of his generation. For those who feel that uncovering Beckett's typicality diminishes his achievement, this book will seem of little value. It is my belief that such an understanding can only enrich it.

I

Entering the Literary Field

Joyce and Proust: Involuntary Epics

Samuel Beckett was a profoundly postwar writer. Although he began writing in the late 1920s, his major fiction—the *nouvelles,* the so-called Trilogy of novels, *Molloy, Malone Dies* and *The Unnamable,* and *Texts for Nothing*—was written in a remarkable five-year period immediately following Beckett's return to Paris in 1945. By the mid-1950s, he had become, as Kenneth Rexroth called him in a 1956 review of the Trilogy, an "international public figure like Lollobrigida or Khrushchev" whose reputation was (and still is) based almost exclusively on the critical success of the Trilogy and *Endgame* (1957) and the more popular success of *Waiting for Godot* (1953). While Beckett's cryptic declarations about an aesthetic of "failure" have been taken to refer to everything from the universal human condition to a postmodernist dissolution of the writing subject, the more mundane meaning of failure should not be overlooked. At the beginning of the 1950s, the two books of fiction Beckett had published in the 1930s, *More Pricks than Kicks* and *Murphy,* were virtually unknown, while his third novel, *Watt,* finished during the war, had been repeatedly rejected by publishers.[1] Put bluntly, Beckett had failed to establish himself as a recognized or economically self-sustaining writer.[2] After the war Beckett managed to take stock of this failure, chose a new language and audience (French), and developed both a new narrative point of view and a significantly different attitude toward writing as a communicative act. In so doing, he transformed failure into a stunning success.

Of course, it is hardly unusual for a great writer's youthful work to fail to measure up to mature masterpieces. Yet what strikes the reader familiar with the span of Beckett's career is the degree of sophistication and complexity of much of his interwar writing, not its immaturity. The failure of Beckett's interwar fiction is rooted in a particular form of artistic growing pains: his ambivalent and often self-contradictory attitudes toward the "literary field"; that is, the set of aesthetic and literary values of the early twentieth century in relation to which Beckett, as a young writer, shaped his own vision of literary art.[3] Beckett's earliest fiction reveals conflicting allegiances to a number of incompatible ideas about language and the social function of art. These wayward allegiances hold a key to understanding Beckett's development as a writer; for what appears as self-contradiction in Beckett's early writing becomes, in one way or another, explicitly thematized and incorporated into the narrative form of his postwar fiction. His early works are contradictory; his later works are intentionally "about" contradictions.

Criticism devoted to Beckett's oeuvre has dealt with the earlier work generally in two unsatisfactory ways. For some, the early writing reveals in embryonic form the themes and techniques of the postwar work, which is acknowledged as the ultimate achievement. Others take an approach analogous to the museum retrospective of an artistic genius: every scrap of writing is a unified and significant object in its own right and deserves extended admiration. The first approach distorts the early work by imposing upon it the necessity of leading up in a linear fashion to an inevitable telos; the second suspends critical judgment. My approach takes something from both.[4] My interest in Beckett's very first published works, written between 1929 and 1934 before his first novel *Murphy*, lies chiefly in how they reveal Beckett's attempt to negotiate the competing claims of the literary field, a mélange of beliefs and techniques which included: aestheticist notions of artistic genius and the autotelic work of art, a "Joycean" experimentation with radical stylistic diversity and the creation of a synthetic literary language, "Eliotic" ideas about the value of myth and literary tradition, the surrealist fascination with automatic writing and the creative resources of the unconscious, an avant-gardist hostility to the bourgeois institution of art and the commodifiable artwork, and various forms of anticapitalism, left wing and right, populist and aristocratic.[5]

Beckett's career got its first important push in 1929, when James Joyce asked the twenty-three year old literary scholar and aspiring poet, who had recently arrived in Paris to teach in an exchange program between Trinity College, Dublin and the Ecole Normale Supérior, to submit a piece to a collection of essays promoting the forthcoming publication of *Finnegans Wake* (then called *Work in Progress*). While both this piece, "Dante . . . Bruno . Vico . . Joyce" (*sic*) and an extended essay on Marcel Proust, commissioned by a London publisher and published in 1931, are significant works in the Beckett canon, they are difficult to read as serious attempts at criticism or aesthetic theory. Beckett makes little attempt to engage in a recognizable critical discourse—journalistic, scholarly, or belletristic. He exploits ellipticism, parody, provocation, and an idiosyncratic set of terms and allusions, in a mode much closer to the avant-gardist manifesto than to literary exegesis. Neither criticism distanced from its object nor direct declarations of his own artistic stance, these writings and their elliptical arguments demonstrate, more than anything else, Beckett's earliest attempts to smooth over a set of conflicting, contradictory ideas and claims about modernist literary art.[6]

The earlier essay discovers in Joyce's "Work in Progress" an ideal of aesthetic autonomy: "Here form *is* content, content *is* form. You complain that this stuff is not written in English. It is not written at all. It is not to be read—or rather it is not only to be read. It is to be looked at and listened to. His writing is not *about* something; *it is that something itself*" (*Disjecta* 27; emphasis in text). Joyce's writing has no communicative function; or rather, it only communicates self-referentially. In one sense, this statement echoes the philosophical tradition that defined the specifically aesthetic experience as that which transcends the cognitive or critical faculty's division between the general and the particular, or as that which fuses form and content. Joyce merely brings the aesthetic to its fruition. Yet Beckett goes on to specify "the formal structure raised by Mr. Joyce after years of patient and inspired labour" (31) in terms of the artistic material of *Work in Progress,* Joyce's created language. Beckett justifies Joyce's invention of a language no one else speaks or writes, an aesthetically autonomous language, through analogy with Dante's provocative innovation in literary language, the adoption of Italian over Latin:

> If English is not yet so definitely a polite necessity as Latin was in the Middle Ages, at least one is justified in declaring that its position in relation to other European languages is to a great extent that of medi- aeval Latin to the Italian dialects. Dante did not adopt the vulgar out of any kind of local jingoism nor out of any determination to assert the superiority of Tuscan to all its rivals as a form of spoken Italian. . . . His [Dante's] conclusion is that the corruption common to all dialects makes it impossible to select one rather than another as an adequate literary form, and that he who would write in the vulgar must assemble the purest elements of each dialect and construct a synthetic language that would at least possess more than a circumscribed local interest: which is precisely what he did. He did not write in Florentine any more than he did in Neapolitan. He wrote a vulgar that could have been spoken by an ideal Italian . . . but which in fact was certainly not spoken nor ever had been. Which disposes of the capital objection [to Joyce's work] . . . that at least Dante wrote what was being spoken in the streets of his own town, whereas no creature in heaven or earth ever spoke the language of *Work in Progress.* (31)

For Beckett, the creation of "a synthetic language" is a response to both an officially prescribed, dominant literary language—Latin or standard English—and the cor- rupted forms of spoken dialect. The ideal literary language also resists the regional and national identities encoded in everyday speech. Beckett views the process of "formal innovation" (31) in literature not so much in terms of an internal transfor- mation of technique, taking place from one literary generation to the next, but in terms of distinguishing the literary from ossified standardization or merely "local" spoken language.

Walter Pater, in his essay on "Style" (1888), had already made a similar case in defense of literary prose. Like Beckett's, Pater's defense of aesthetically autonomous prose described literary language as a unique type of discourse that distanced itself from science, history, "analysis," and the "vulgarity in the actual world" (Pater 14); the artist, wrote Pater, "opposes the constant degradation of language" (17). While science deals with "fact," and history is on the "border of science," artistic prose writing expresses "sense" (4–6). Language, for artists, is a raw "material," a medium like the "sculptor's marble" (9). Good writing aims at a "unity or identity of mind" (19). Music becomes "the ideal of all art . . . because in music it is impossible to distinguish the form from the substance or matter" (35). Yet the tone of Beckett's defense, and of Joyce's work, is far from Pater's aestheticist notion of art as a "cloistered refuge" for the "select few" (14): "Here is direct expression," Beckett exclaims, "and if you don't understand it, Ladies and Gentlemen, it is because you are too decadent to receive it" (26). Pater ends his essay with an appeal to the "matter" of art, the "dignity of its interests . . . devoted further to the increase of men's happiness, the redemption of the oppressed . . . the glory of God" (36). While Pater argues for the "beauties of prose" (2), Beckett argues for other qualities: "Shakespeare uses fat, greasy words to express corruption. . . . We hear the ooze squelching all through Dickens' description of the Thames. . . . This writing that you find so obscure [in Joyce] . . . is the savage economy of hieroglyphics. Here words are not the polite contortions of twentieth-century printer's ink" (28). The surprising reference to Dickens in itself marks, in relation to the tenor of the rest of the essay, an uneasy attachment to the autonomy Beckett espouses. While maintaining a concept of autonomy that shares much with Pater's aestheticism and its idealization of unity of form and content in the autotelic work, the appeal is to disruption rather than refuge, provocation rather than cloister, contortion rather than beauty. Beckett inflects his Pateresque defense of literary language with a surrealistlike antiaestheticism. "Beauty shall be CONVULSIVE," André Breton, the founder of the Surrealist movement, had claimed some years earlier, "or it will not be at all" (Breton 160).

This uneasy mixture of aestheticist purity and avant-gardist provocation is elaborated in the essay on Proust. Beckett describes Proust's writing as a break with rationality in terms similar to the surrealist program of automatic writing, which demanded that the writer cede all conscious effort in the process of composition. Chance, spontaneity, and the unconscious could then break through the barrier of social convention, to access a deeper poetic truth.[7] At the same time, Beckett's admiring interpretation of Proust centers on a set of oppositions—subject/object, fact/feeling, the real/the imagined, intellection/sensation, surface/essence, classical/romantic—that were common in theories of aestheticism and modernist impressionism, from Pater and Proust himself to Ford and Woolf.[8] Beckett generalizes these oppositions in terms specific to Proust's fiction: voluntary as opposed to involuntary memory. The devalued term is the first: "Voluntary memory (Proust repeats it ad nauseam) is of no value as an instrument of evocation, and provides an image as far removed from the real as the myth of our imagination or the caricature furnished by direct perception. There is only one real impression and one adequate mode of evocation. Over neither have we the least control" (*PTD* 15).

Voluntary memory is a form of conscious control that blocks the perception of the "real." It is similar to "habit":

> When the object is perceived as particular and unique and not merely the member of a family, when it appears independent of any general notion and detached from the sanity of a cause, isolated and inexplicable in the light of ignorance, then and then only may it be a source of enchant-

ment. Unfortunately Habit has laid its veto on this form of perception, its action being precisely to hide the essence—the Idea—of the object in the haze of conception—preconception. (23)

Like bourgeois morality, or the disenchanted rationality of the modern, industrial world, "Habit is a compromise between the individual and his environment, or between the individual and his own organic eccentricities, the guarantee of a dull inviolability" (19). Beckett's emphasis is not, however, on *conscious* innovation that dislodges knowledge or perception of the object from conventional thought, but on the cessation of rational control altogether:

Involuntary memory is explosive . . . in its flame it has consumed Habit and all its works, and in its brightness revealed what the mock reality of experience never can and never will reveal—the real. But involuntary memory is an unruly magician and will not be importuned. It chooses its own time and place for the performance of its miracle . . . the first [miracle of involuntary memory]—the famous episode of the madeleine steeped in tea—would justify the assertion that his entire book is a monument to involuntary memory and the epic of its action. The whole of Proust's world comes out of a teacup. (33–34)

Beckett further emphasizes the irrational by referring to the objects that spark off involuntary memory "by some immediate and fortuitous act of perception" as "fetishes"—the madeleine or "the noise of a spoon against a plate" (36–37). Yet this access to "the real" is also described by analogy to the technology of representation. Shocked out of his habitual mode of perception by the sight of his dead grandmother, Proust's narrator is given access to a vision of reality: "The notion of what he should see has not had time to interfere its prism [*sic*] between the eye and its object. His eye functions with the cruel precision of a camera; it photographs the reality of his grandmother" (27). Again, in reference to the image of Albertine: "Albertine is multiple, and just as the most modern applications of photography can frame a single church successively in the arches of all the others thus decomposing the illusion of a solid object into its manifold component aspects, so the short journey of his lips to the cheek of Albertine creates ten Albertines, and transforms a human banality into a many headed goddess" (49). Beckett presents the characteristic quality of Proust's writing as a direct recording of impressions without the imposition of rational thought or agency. He formulates this in several variations—"He is almost exempt from the impurity of will . . . will, being utilitarian, servant of intelligence and habit, is not a condition of the artistic experience" (90); "we are reminded of Schopenhauer's definition of the artistic procedure as 'the contemplation of the world independently of the principle of reason'"—(87) and develops it as a principle of narrative, contrasting it with "the grotesque fallacy of a realistic art" (76) and classicism. "The classical artist assumes omniscience and omnipotence. He raises himself artificially out of Time in order to give relief to his chronology and causality to his development. Proust's chronology is extremely difficult to follow, the succession of events spasmodic, and his characters and themes . . . are presented and developed with a . . . contempt for the vulgarity of a plausible concatenation" (81–82).

This view of Proust's writing, however, cannot be sustained, because the "involuntary" allows only a negative definition of the artistic work—"the artist is active, but negatively" (65)—instinctual, will-less, by accident, detached, inexplicable. The only positive element in Beckett's account is the distorting or interfering power of reason and will, the instrumental forces that involuntary memory overcomes. But Beckett is far too attached to the notion of the writer as the conscious creator of a new language—Joyce's "years of patient and inspired labour"—and of literature as an autonomous activity with its own set of rules and logic, to be satisfied with relegating art to the unconscious and the agentless. The similarity between his characterization of Proust and the surrealist notion of automatic writing suggests the contradiction in Beckett's argument. As Raymond Williams put it in his discussion of Surrealism,

> One can look back on "automatic writing," for all the meagerness of its actual results, with a certain respect for its ambitions of practice. . . . For language was being simultaneously identified with the blocking of "true consciousness" and, to the extent that it could emancipate itself from its imprisoning everyday forms and, beyond that, from the received forms of "literature," as itself the medium of the idealized "pure consciousness" . . . most writers stayed in the double position and then of course at once encountered the obvious and ominous question of "communication". . . . There [was] an emphasis . . . on the experience itself, rather than any of the forms of embodying or communicating it. (*Politics* 73)

In the Joyce essay, language was "the experience itself" rather than its communication. Yet Beckett's defense of Joyce's language through analogy with Dante's Italian implied, at the same time, an "ideal" communicability, a pure language assimilating "all the dialects of his country" (*Disjecta* 30). In the Proust essay the emphasis is not directly on language, but on involuntary memory which, like automatic writing, serves to access "real" consciousness. If, for the surrealists, language was both what blocked access to the real and the means of reaching it, for Beckett's Proust, the act of narrating—ordered, willed and active composition—blocks access to the real, but must also, somehow, be a means of representing the real. Beckett's solution to this double position follows a formulation from the last volume of *A la Recherche*:

> Now he [the narrator] sees his regretted failure to observe artistically as a series of "inspired omissions" and the work of art as neither created nor chosen, but discovered, uncovered, excavated, pre-existing within the artist, a law of his nature. . . . The conclusions of the intelligence are merely of arbitrary value, potentially valid. "An impression [writes

Proust] is for the writer what an experiment is for the scientist—with this difference, that in the case of the scientist the action of the intelligence precedes the event and in the case of the writer it follows it." . . . The artist has acquired his text: the artisan translates it. "The duty and the task of a writer (not an artist, a writer) are those of a translator." (84)

The opposing terms are familiar, though here not only is the artist distinguished from the scientist, but the artistic process is conceived as the reverse of the scientific, strengthening its claim of autonomy. Intelligence, formerly banished from the artistic in the essay, now reappears as a secondary feature. But the separation is maintained by the untenable dichotomies: art and artisan, artist and writer. The implication is that art itself is essentially an experience, while the actual work of art is a secondary phenomenon. Beckett's choice of "artisan" (in the place of Proust's "translator"), like his image of Joyce's labor, recalls Pater's vision of Flaubert as "the martyr of literary style" (24); as Flaubert himself put it, "my labour like a true working man, who . . . beats away at his anvil" (qtd. in Pater 26).

When Beckett reiterates the dichotomy a few pages later, contradictions within and between the avant-gardist and aestheticist attitudes becomes glaring: "For Proust the quality of language is more important than any system of ethics or aesthetics. Indeed he makes no attempt to dissociate form from content. . . . The Proustian world is expressed metaphorically by the artisan because it is apprehended metaphorically by the artist: the indirect and comparative expression of indirect and comparative perception" (88). Somehow, "quality of language" is separate from "aesthetics" (which now seems linked with "ethics"). The semantic distance between artist and artisan is maintained, but only by the further polarization of perception and expression, both of which are metaphoric, "indirect and comparative." Neither of these terms supports the claim for the nonrational or "involuntary" nature of the creative process and access to "the real." The oppositions that centered on the distance between "voluntary" and "involuntary" necessarily collapse when Beckett attempts to account for Proust as a writer.

The avant garde's stance against the constraint of rationality involved an antagonism to the *work* of art itself, the commodifiable object valued by the bourgeois institution of art. Ideally, dada and surrealism would not create artistic objects, but would break down the distance between art and life. Beckett takes a position close to surrealism concerning the constricting role of rational and conscious composition, but maintains a contradictory aestheticist emphasis on the work of art as an end in its own right. Toward the end of the essay, the pressure to account for Proust as an active creator of the "epic" of involuntary memory leads Beckett to situate him in a number of well-established literary roles: visionary romantic ("art is the apotheosis of solitude" [64]; "He is a Romantic in his anxiety to accomplish his mission. . . . He does not seek to evade the implications of his art such as it has been revealed to him" [81]); amoral aesthete ("Proust is completely detached from all moral considerations" [66]; "his complete indifference to moral values and human justices" [89]); symbolist

("Proust's point of departure might be situated in Symbolism" [80]); impressionist ("By his impressionism I mean his non-logical statement of phenomena in the order and exactitude of their perception" [86]). The last paragraph evokes the Pateresque trope of music as the aesthetic ideal: "Music is the Idea itself, unaware of the world of phenomena, existing ideally outside the universe . . . untouched by the teleological hypothesis. . . . Music is the catalytic element in the work of Proust" (92).

While devoid of the argumentation that the essays provide, Beckett's often-referred-to "German letter of 1937" concerning his own work stages the same instability:

> It is indeed becoming more and more difficult, even senseless, for me to write an official English. . . . As we cannot eliminate language all at once, we should at least leave nothing undone that might contribute to its falling into disrepute. . . . Or is literature alone to remain behind in the old lazy ways that have been so long ago abandoned by music and painting? . . . so that through whole pages we can perceive nothing but a path of sounds suspended in giddy heights. . . . At first it can only be a matter of somehow finding a method by which we can represent this mocking attitude towards the words, through words. . . . An assault against words in the name of beauty. (*Disjecta* 172–73)

Language is both the "veil" and the means of tearing it apart; words must be "mis-used" so that "literature" may approach "music and painting"; words are both non-communicative and nonrational, "a path of sounds" which nevertheless need to "represent this mocking attitude," and all of this "in the name of beauty." The letter demonstrates an apparently urgent attempt to define a position within a set of attitudes that cannot cohere.

"It Is Not": Juxtaposition and Ethical Judgment in "Dante and the Lobster"

Like his early critical writing Beckett's earliest fiction reveals an attempt to reconcile a set of conflicting cultural attitudes. As its title suggests, Beckett's second published story, "Dante and the Lobster," which appeared as the leading story in his first published book of fiction, *More Pricks than Kicks*, employs the surrealist technique of juxtaposition. Breton had advocated a poetic image based on Lautréamont's jarring juxtaposition of objects from divergent spheres of everyday life—"the fortuitous encounter of an umbrella and a sewing machine on a dissecting table" (qtd. in Lippard 2).[9] Beckett's juxtaposition depends on a different type of contrast that the story goes on to exploit: the young hero's immersion in translating Dante is disrupted by his obligation to run an errand for his aunt, buying a lobster for dinner. The two sides of the contrast—the study of classical literature and the "obligations" (10) of everyday life—are for the hero antithetical; however, by the end of the story—a collagelike parodic presentation of an afternoon in the life of the juvenile, artistic-bohemian protagonist in Dublin—the omniscient narrator attempts to mediate high art and mundane life with a third element: a moral or ethical judgment about suffering and justice.

The story begins with the hero's head in a book: "It was morning and Belacqua was stuck in the first of the canti in the moon. He was so bogged that he could move neither backward nor forward. Blissful Beatrice was there, Dante also, and she explained the spots on the moon to him" (9). The first paragraph extends this motif. Belacqua (the protagonist's name is an allusion to a character in Dante, canto four of the *Purgatorio,* and his "legendary torpitude" [Kenner 18]) is immobilized by a literary problem. "He pored over the enigma, he would not concede himself conquered, he would understand at least the meanings of the words" (9). Literature appears as a closed system: just as the story assumes the reader's familiarity with Dante, understanding *The Divine Comedy* is presented as internal to Dante's work itself. Belacqua the reader is presented on the same plane with the figures in the poem, the poet Dante and Beatrice. Yet the third-person narration breaks the hermeticism of the literary realm. The storytelling voice, although focalized here through Belacqua, is on a separate diegetic plane. While the story represents literature as a unidimensional, closed-off realm, Beckett's omniscient, parodic narration—which relies on distance, on one perspective reflecting on and contrasting with another—emphasizes a discontinuity between literary tradition and the world from which the story is narrated.

The theme of literary culture as an hermetic system is expanded in the next two paragraphs, which also delineate the story's controlling juxtaposition:

> He was still running his brain against this impenetrable passage when he heard midday strike. At once he switched his mind off its task. He scooped his fingers under the book and shoveled it back till it lay wholly on his palms. The *Divine Comedy* face upward on the lectern of his palms. Thus disposed he raised it under his nose and there he slammed it shut. He held it aloft for a time, squinting at it angrily. . . . Nothing could be done until his mind got better and was still, which gradually it did and was. Then he ventured to consider what he had to do next. There was always something one had to do next. Three large obligations presented themselves. First lunch, then the lobster, then the Italian lesson. (9–10)

Belacqua "switched his mind" from Dante to "obligations," from literature to everyday life. While the transition is presented as absolute, as "switch" implies, his mind needs to become "still" before the transition can be effected. The literary landmark, *The Divine Comedy,* becomes materialized as an object, which he slams shut and considers "angrily." The transition between art and life involves a hostile gesture toward one realm or the other. The narrative style also registers the switch, from an allusive beginning in which the protagonist is viewed as inside the literary system, along with Dante and Beatrice, to the quotidian list: lunch, lobster, lesson.

In modernist visual art the collage achieves its effects by linking diverse materials usually considered functionally distinct—a painted surface and a scrap of newspaper, for example, in a work by Picasso. In the story, however, the controlling contrast seems not only to juxtapose culture and everyday life, or art and obligation, but to reverse their functions. The hero's frustration and immobility when immersed in Dante unsettle his mind. Yet "lunch," first appearing as the disruptive "obligation," is presented in the terms of isolation, sensation, and passion usually associated with a romanticist aesthetic:

> He must be left strictly alone, he must have complete quiet and privacy, to prepare the food for his lunch. (10); Toast must not on any account be done too rapidly. . . . Otherwise you only charred the outside and left the pith as sodden as before. If there was one thing he abominated more than another it was to feel his teeth meet in a bathos of pith and dough. (11); He would snap at it [the sandwich] with closed eyes, he would gnash it into a pulp, he would vanquish it utterly with his fangs. Then the anguish of pungency, the pang of the spices, as each mouthful died, scorching his palate, bringing tears. (13)

Of course, this is parody. But the lunch of charred toast, "Savora, salt and Cayenne" (12) and "Gorgonzola cheese" (13) is also another juxtaposition and an affront to bourgeois taste, in its most literal sense: "He didn't want fragrance, he wasn't a bloody gourmet, he wanted a good stench" (14). Nor is it free from literary allusion: "gorgonzola" is the petit bourgeois Leopold Bloom's lunch as well. The story emphasizes both a separation of art and life, Dante and the lobster, and a parodic type of unification. The humor of the lunch comes from the aestheticistlike emphasis on sensation over a trivial and definitely antiaestheticist object: "a good stench." In *Molloy,* Beckett will pose culture (in the sense of the cultivation of manners and taste) as the source of both the hero's suffering and the effective articulation of his misery. Here, however, there is neither suffering nor causal identification. Instead, there is bohemian indignation.

The figure of Belacqua is himself a juxtaposition of art and social life, both an allusion to Dante and, as he is referred to in another story from *More Pricks than Kicks,* a bohemian "dirty lowdown Low Church Protestant high brow" (172). Since the middle of the nineteenth century the figure of the bohemian in European culture symbolized an attempt to make the celebration of everyday life the focus of art; Belacqua's aesthete-bohemianism emphasizes this attempt and, at the same time, the distance between the everyday and the properly artistic.[10] While he devotes his attention to Dante and the sensations of his grotesque lunch, his indignation is directed at domestic life. He burns a hole in the wallpaper of his cheap room—"This was hooliganism pure and simple. What the hell did he care? Was it his wall?" (12). His walk to the grocer stresses his isolation: "Now the great thing was to avoid being accosted. To be stopped . . . and have conversational nuisance committed all over him would be a disaster" (13). He despises his connection to family, "his lousy old bitch of an aunt" (16). He is antibourgeois, bohemian poor, an aesthete of the grotesque, but like Pater a lover of Dante.

When focalized through Belacqua, the omniscient narrator shares with him the clashing attitudes of the aesthete, bohemian, and classicist. However, there are moments when the narrative focus shifts and the voice has no apparent relation to the characters, especially when there is an ethical evaluation made or suggested. On one hand, there seems to be an attempt to portray the juxtaposition of attitudes and tastes as itself an ethical stance. On the other, the ethical suggestions cannot be made through the techniques of collage, nor through Belacqua's contradictory assemblage of attitudes and tastes. In order to suggest, as the story does, that the bohemian-aesthete is somehow superior to his surroundings and sensitive to suffering and injustice, Beckett needs another type of narrative voice and a more integrative story structure. An aesthetic resolution or epiphany that would bind the elements in the story seems at variance with the principles of collage, though not in any absolute sense (a good collage is harmonious regardless of its disparate, "nonorganic" character), but as a matter of degree and emphasis. Thus, Beckett tries to resolve the juxtapositions through a nonfocalized (i.e., independent from the consciousness of the characters) ethical realization at the end of the story. This attempted resolution is set up through the story's minimal, but necessary, plot.

The plot revolves around a trivial problem. The story takes place in Dublin and begins with Belacqua alone in his room, immersed in a translation problem in Dante. He hears "midday strike" (9) and mechanically switches his mind to the "three large obligations" (10) that will take up the rest of his afternoon. While making his grotesque-aesthete lunch, he notices a photo in the *Herald,* which he is using as a tablecloth. "The rather handsome face of McCabe the assassin stared up at him." He makes his toast with "real skill" to ensure the desired "bathos of pith and dough" (11). The narration of the toast making is interrupted by a brief reflection, relating back to the passage in Dante, but allusively presented: "The spots were Cain with his truss of thorns, dispossessed, cursed from the earth, fugitive and vagabond. The moon was that countenance fallen and branded, seared with the first stigma of God's pity, that an outcast might not die quickly" (12).

The "outcast" in Dante is structurally related to the condemned assassin Mc-Cabe in the newspaper, but Beckett does not make the connection explicit. The connecting evaluation is embedded in the reflection on Dante and the disapproving attitude toward a religious morality that exalts suffering over forgiveness. Belacqua continues to make his toast, and then ventures out to the grocer to buy his cheese. He is careful to avoid others, since the enjoyment of his lunch depends on isolation. He enters "a little family grocery. In the shop they were not surprised. Most days, about this hour, he shot in off the street in this way" (13). Although the action is habitual, and Belacqua feels that the family "were very decent obliging people" (14), there is no personal interaction between the customer and the grocer. Because the cheese is not the "stenching rotten lump" Belacqua desires, he becomes indignant, but storms out with the cheese anyway, while the grocer remains impassive. Significantly, for the first time in the story there is a shift in narrative point of view:

> The grocer, without closing his eyes or taking them off the receding figure, blew his nose in the skirt of his apron. Being a warm-hearted human man he felt sympathy and pity for this queer customer who always looked ill and dejected. But at the same time he was a small tradesman, don't forget that, with a small tradesman sense of dignity and what was what. Thruppence, he cast it up, thruppence worth of cheese per day, one a tanner per week. No, he would fawn on no man for that, no, not on the best in the land. He had his pride. (15)

The portrait of the grocer is isolated. It seems both sympathetic and condescending. His "sympathy and pity" for the "ill and dejected" Belacqua is neutralized by his "small tradesman sense of dignity." This paragraph is closer to the Dublin of Joyce's *Dubliners*—a book that rendered the paralysis and indifference of a rigidly moralistic, petit bourgeois Dublin community in an almost naturalist tone, usually focalized through the consciousness of its isolated characters—than to the rest of the story.[11] The narration immediately shifts back to Belacqua, the grotesque aesthete who is equally isolated, but willfully so. The problem of the plot, in all its triviality, is explicitly stated as Belacqua sits alone in the pub eating his lunch. It revolves (like a plot from Dickens or Balzac) around time, money, and the city:

> At a quarter to three he was due at the [language] school. Say five to three. The public closed, the fishmonger reopened, at half-past two. Assuming then that his lousy old bitch of an aunt had given her order in good time that morning . . . so that her blackguard boy should on no account be delayed . . . it would be time enough if he left the public as it closed, he could remain on till the last moment. Bennissimo. He had half-a-crown. That was two pints of draught anyway . . . he would still be left with coppers enough to buy a *Herald* and take a tram if he felt pinched for time. Always assuming, of course, that the lobster was all ready to be handed over. God damn these tradesmen, he thought, you can never rely on them. He had not done an exercise but that did not matter. His Professoressa was so charming and remarkable. (16)

Beckett needs to lay out the plot explicitly because the collagelike presentation does not allow the reader to infer relations among characters, motives, or actions. Dublin and the "tradesmen" appear as an obstacle course between Dante, beer, and the charming Italian teacher. While, in *Dubliners,* moral obligations take on tragic dimensions, here moral obligation itself appears unimportant. For Belacqua, struggle takes place only over cultural mastery (Dante) and an antiaesthetic (slamming the book closed angrily, making lunch). The rest is blind necessity, measured in minutes, coppers, and pints.

Morality, however, is not absent from the story, but rather has no integral relation to the narrated events. A moral psychology of character necessitates a more integrative structure than juxtaposition, which does not allow for the cause-and-effect relations of ego formation. The plot confirms the story's impersonal moral homelessness. After musing on his "professora" in a passage full of a male-adolescent's aesthete judgments ("Manzoni was an old woman . . . Pellico was another . . . the 19th century in Italy was full of old hens trying to cluck like Pindar" [16–17]), he heads to the school. He is surprised that the cheese was, after all, to his liking:

> Also his teeth and jaws had been in heaven. . . . It was like eating glass.
> His mouth burned and ached with the exploit. Then the food had been
> further spiced by the intelligence . . . that the . . . murderer's petition for
> mercy, signed by half the land, having been rejected, the man must swing
> at dawn in Mountjoy and nothing could save him. . . . Belacqua, tearing
> at the sandwich and swilling the precious stout, pondered on McCabe in
> his cell. (17)

The earlier moral suggestion, embedded in Dante, concerning mercy and suffering, and the photo of McCabe glimpsed in the paper, are now narratively joined. Yet these elements do not combine into a moment of meaning or judgment. This juxtaposition of narrative data neither invites the reader to make an evaluation (as Jauss [42–45] claims for the function of modernist free indirect discourse) nor expresses an avant-gardist contempt for the hypocrisy of bourgeois morality through images of cruelty (as in Artaud or Lautréamont, or even later Beckett). The earlier moral suggestion is sincere, but the conflicting styles and aims in the story give it no functional or coherent role.

There is a complex relation of culturally and morally inflected themes: Dante's purgatory and McCabe's prison, prolonged suffering and execution, divine and democratic (the petition "signed by half the land") mercy. This complexity is built up through juxtaposed moments, not a series of interrelationships. The last pages of the story, however, attempt to integrate the themes, to create a kind of epiphany. The conflicting styles and intentions, however, defeat any symbolic resolution, and the ending is simultaneously sincere and parodic. Following the structure of the controlling juxtaposition, the moral-social problem of purgatory that begins in Dante and moves to McCabe ends up with the lobster. Despite Belacqua's fears, the lobster is ready, and the man at the fish market assures him it's "'Lepping fresh . . . fresh in this morning.' Now Belacqua . . . supposed the man to mean that the lobster had very recently been killed" (18). This sets up the story's mock-epiphanic ending.

The lobster in a bag, he goes to his Italian lesson, where he asks the *Professoressa* about the difficult passage in Dante. She suggests that for practice he "might do worse than make up Dante's rare moments of compassion in hell" (19). As he walks to his aunt's house he sees in the "yellow light" of early evening an injured horse, and then a "poorly dressed couple . . . in the bay of a pretentious gateway, she sagging against the railings, her head lowered, he standing facing her . . . his hands dangled by his sides" (20–21). These images, like the momentary image of the grocer, have the feeling of a naturalist study. They compel the walking Belacqua to reflect: "Why not piety and pity both, even down below? Why not mercy and Godliness together? A little mercy in the stress of sacrifice, a little mercy to rejoice against judgment. . . . Poor McCabe, he would get it at the neck at dawn" (21). He reaches his aunt's and they go to the kitchen, where he gives her the lobster and is shocked to discover that it is still alive. The story ends with a judgment:

> It [the lobster] shuddered again. Belacqua felt he would be sick.
>
> > "My God" he whined "it's alive, what'll we do?". . . .
> > "Boil the beast" she said, "what else?"
> > "But it's not dead" protested Belacqua "you can't boil it like
> >   that.". . . .
>
> "Have sense" she said sharply, "lobsters are always boiled alive. They must be." She caught up the lobster and laid it on his back. It trembled. "They feel nothing" she said.
>   In the depths of the sea it had crept into the cruel pot. For hours, in the midst of its enemies, it had breathed secretly. . . . Now it was going alive into the scalding water. It had to. Take into the air my quiet breath.
>
> > Belacqua looked at the old parchment of her face, grey in the dim kitchen.
> > "You make a fuss" she said angrily "and upset me and then lash into it for your dinner."
> > She lifted the lobster clear of the table. It had about thirty seconds to live.
> > Well, thought Belacqua, it's a quick death, God help us all.
> It is not. (21–22)

The ending is perhaps the least parodic part of the story, and the moral-ethical problem of mercy and pity is given a blunt objectification. Yet the surrealist juxtaposition, the bohemian antiaestheticism, the high cultural allusions, and even the naturalist moments, are simply left behind. There are moments of lyricism—"In the depths of the sea . . ." "her face, grey in the dim kitchen"— which suggest an epiphanic mood, but epiphany would require that the lobster (like, for example, Michael Furey at the end of Joyce's "The Dead") be a multivalent symbol. But symbolism is an aesthetic strategy that most of the story seems to reject. The story ends in juxtaposition, even though the mood seems the opposite of avant-garde provocation.

The contradiction of aesthetic modes is most strongly revealed in the last line: "It is not." It is the only line of the story that is purely omniscient narration. It expresses a moral stance: pain must never pass unexpressed. The relative unimportance of the pain, in relation to McCabe's (or his victim's, or Cain's), strengthens the absolute refusal to ignore even the smallest signs of unfeeling. Rabinovitz, in his study of Beckett's early fiction, concludes that the story's ending shows that "Beckett's main concern is his protagonist's moral equivocation" (47), but the last line is not a judgment directed at the hero. Rabinovitz accounts for this by claiming that "Beckett's method in these episodes [in *More Prick than Kicks*] is to introduce recurring details which call attention to subjects that the narrator tries to avoid" (43). The question this raises is directly related to the story's contradictory structure: how can an author supply details in a third-person narration that "the narrator tries to avoid"? The voice that delivers the last line does not fit well with either the parodic omniscient narrator who hovers above the narrative material, nor with any character's consciousness: a third voice—the author's point of view?—must be introduced because the story has no organizational structure to integrate such a judgment. Nevertheless, the judgment is made.

This judgment out of nowhere is a sign of Beckett's conflicting attitudes and concerns. In fact, the appearance of an attempt toward some kind of unification or epiphany is perhaps the only thing that holds the story together and prevents it from becoming an indeterminate collage of contradictory aesthetic modes. But the last line merely suggests an overarching intention. That the suggestion is made through an ethical judgment seems to indicate an overall aesthetic confusion. The only thing that could bring "Dante" and the "lobster" together in a meaningful way is the very thing that the parodic and juxtapositional structure of high culture and crustacean cannot create: a meaningful judgment.[12]

Versions of Modernism

Beckett's first professional recognition arrived not on the crest but in the wake of the modernist and avant-garde movements that have come to define our ideas of innovation and experimentation in the modern arts. *Finnegans Wake,* in defense of which Beckett propelled himself into the literary arena, was itself one of modernism's most eccentric and problematic works. The contradictory clash of aesthetic values I have described in Beckett's earliest writing was, in part, a consequence of the accumulated iconoclastic effects of the modernist era that had peaked in the 1920s. By the 1930s, the innovations of successive modernist and the avant-garde modes—from Zola's "experimental" naturalist novel, futurist paeans to speed and violence, and dada's celebration of nonsense, to Woolf's intense depictions of intersubjective identity formation—along with the rapidly growing technologies of mass-disseminated culture, had created an historically unprecedented plurality of aesthetic possibilities and combinations. While arguments for an overarching singular aesthetic, like those advanced at the end of the nineteenth century (for example, Zola's argument for naturalism or Pater's for aestheticism), no longer held much force by the end of the 1920s, the political urgency of the 1930s would soon inaugurate a new set of cultural prescriptions.

Although I have claimed that the attitudes Beckett inherited from various modernist movements implied contradictory cultural-political positions, more often than not the basic tenets of high modernism and avant-garde experimentation have been viewed as congruous, not contradictory. Cultural critic Franco Moretti's essay "The Long Goodbye: *Ulysses* and the End of Liberal Capitalism," an incisive account of the cultural politics of high British modernism, offers a somewhat alternative account of the plurality of conflicting values at the end of the modernist decade.[13] Central to Moretti's argument is a duality in the modernist use of myth. While T. S. Eliot's famous essay on Joyce's use of myth in *Ulysses* claimed a congruence between Eliot's own project and Joyce's, Moretti convincingly argues the opposite:

> In Eliot['s discussion of the "mythic method"], there is a clear distinction: on the one hand myth ("controlling, ordering, giving a shape and a significance"), on the other, history ("immense panorama of futility and anarchy"). Myth must mold history: it is the active agent of the pair, *form* to history's *content*. In Joyce, myth and history are *complementary:* they presuppose and neutralize each other, and it is impossible to establish a formal or ideological hierarchy between the two. In Joyce, myth is not identified with the aesthetic *form* (as in Eliot), and therefore cannot be the starting point for a new *cultural hegemony*. (192; emphasis in text)[14]

Eliot's agenda is constructed on a conservative premise: it locates value in the cultural icons of the past, and devalues his own social present. Joyce's position, in contrast, is "structurally ambiguous: neither an 'apology' for nor a 'criticism' " of liberal, capitalist society (190–91).

According to Moretti, Joyce used the world of the present and the cultural landmark which the *Odyssey* represented in his own cultural milieu as counterparts— "to parody Bloom with Ulysses and Ulysses with Bloom" (192). Contra Eliot's description of the mythic method, Joyce's use of myth did not—could not—argue for any form of "cultural hegemony." In fact, Moretti argues that the lack of any hierarchically ordered principle of organization in *Ulysses* is its most significant feature:

> The most peculiar aspect of Joyce's novel is that it uses a plurality of aesthetic forms that lie at opposite extremes. . . . In *Ulysses,* then, the world goes to pieces not because it is a text prolific in apocalyptic visions, but, rather, because in it every idea of a cultural system goes awry. Joyce's

novel is irreducibly opposed to the hierarchical principles of the great
bourgeois culture of his time. By rendering any "organic" pretension of
the work of art vain, Joyce also declares the impossibility of "deducing"
from it an idea of a cultural system capable of restoring order to society.
(204)

Moretti's description provides a relevant framework for understanding Beckett's relation to the literary field at the end of the 1920s. Given Beckett's personal and
professional ties to Joyce, the preeminence of *Ulysses,* as well as the excitement
generated by the portions of the very different *Finnegans Wake* being published in
transition (where Beckett also published, discussed in the following chapter), the very
idea of what constituted literary prose must have appeared radically indeterminate.
Already in *Ulysses,* as Moretti argues, the "plurality of styles" precludes the possibility
that any one style dominate. "In Joyce, when one episode is presented in two or three
or fifty different styles, the procedure is not based on any codified literary motiva-
tion," as it is in James's or Conrad's use of multiple point-of-view, motivated by the
shifting psychological states of their characters. "It is pure technical exploration." All
the styles in the novel "therefore, are equally *irrelevant* as interpretations of reality or
formalization of literary language." Because of this, "Joyce does not found a school
. . . [to] imitate one of *Ulysses* many styles betray[s] the fundamental intention of his
novel: the systematic refusal to assume *one* style as the privileged vehicle of expression" (206).
    The juxtaposition of aesthetic modes and intentions in Beckett's early work is,
in part, due to the enormous influence of Joyce's experiment, and also to the conflicting values that appeared, at the time, complementary, as evinced in Eliot's remarks on
the mythic method. But while Moretti's analysis is exemplary when untangling the
ideological strands of Eliotic and Joycean myth, he falters when he then attempts to
take the implications of Joyce's ambivalence toward cultural hegemony outside the
realm of high modernism. Having distinguished, correctly, between the implications
of Eliot's and Joyce's use of myth, Moretti conflates Joyce's project with that of the
avant garde. It is worthwhile to examine Moretti's claims, because they help clarify the
diversity of the literary field.
    Moretti asserts that in *Ulysses* "Joyce dismantles the ideology of 'organic' art"
(205); that "there is no qualitative distinction between 'elite' and 'mass' culture" in
the novel (206); and that "Joyce's indifference to any criterion of functionality or
truth in cultural forms brings him close to Dada" (206). All of these claims are
interrelated, since the organic work of art, with its unity of form and content, was a
self-defining feature of high art, and avant-garde movements such as dada and cubism
had already created the collage and juxtaposition techniques that exploited discontinuity of themes and materials, thereby violating the norms of aesthetic organicism.
As Peter Bürger has argued, the specificity of the "historical" avant garde resided in
the attempt to transform the *function* of art. Reacting to aestheticism's heightened
value of aesthetic autonomy, the avant garde was the first art movement that was able

to understand art as an *institution* functionally divorced from everyday life and therefore unable to effect social transformation. Williams concurs: "almost the only distinguishing feature, and even then incompletely, is less a matter of actual writing than of successive formations which challenged not only the art institutions but the institution of Art, or Literature, itself, typically in a broad programme which included, though in diverse forms, the overthrow and remaking of existing society" (*Politics* 67).

From this perspective, Joyce's project, like that of Eliot or Woolf, seems much closer to an "aestheticism [that] merely rejects the means-end rationality of everyday life" (Bürger, *Theory* 49) than to dada, Surrealism, Italian futurism, Brecht, Constructivism, etc. While "elite" art and "mass" culture may be *represented* in *Ulysses* without "qualitative distinction," the book's own status as an autonomous art object, meticulously brought to perfection by an artistic genius and to be interpreted and appreciated by a classically educated elite, is not at issue. It was modernist novels such as *Ulysses*—following a development that traced its beginnings to Flaubert in France, and Pater, James, and Conrad in England—that gave the novel, a genre always associated with popular literary culture, the status of high culture. As Ernst Curtius put it, *Ulysses* was a novel dependent for the unfolding of its layered meanings on the "entire wealth of philosophical and theological knowledge, [the] power of psychological and aesthetic analysis, [and the] culture of the mind educated in all the literatures of the world" (qtd. in Moretti 204).

At a moment when the European novel, in the search for a universal, aesthetically autonomous language, had ironically severed itself from all but the most specialized readership, as Joyce did in *Finnegans Wake,* Beckett found himself in his earliest fiction and critical writing responding uncertainly to the conflicting agendas of modernist art and literature. By the time he wrote his first publishable novel, a very different situation was influencing the task of the writer. In *Murphy* Beckett attempts to fuse a novel about a "mind" striving to shut out the outer world with the story of a man and a woman failing to communicate or to find love and companionship. Most other writers of the time, however, were crying out that the literary exploration of the inner mind was a game that, for better or worse, had played itself out: the outer world—from the agitation for socialist revolution to the rise of fascism—could no longer be ignored.

II

Contact with the Outside World

Contesting "Social Reality"

1938 marks an important beginning, and an important end, in Beckett's career. After having been rejected by no fewer than forty-two publishers, Beckett's first novel *Murphy* was finally released by Routledge in March of that year. His previous book, the collection of stories *More Pricks than Kicks,* published by Chatto and Windus in 1934, had done miserably: only two copies had been sold in 1935.[1] The publication of *Murphy,* a more developed work than the earlier collection, would presumably establish Beckett as a serious novelist. The book received a brief, moderately favorable notice in the March 12 *Times Literary Supplement.* Beckett was now a publicly recognized, if still relatively obscure, young Anglo-Irish novelist.

In 1938 Beckett also published a review of a volume of poetry by Denis Devlin, a friend from Ireland, in the journal *transition (sic)*. In contrast to the frustration he had experienced finding a place for *Murphy,* he had always had a friendly forum for his shorter pieces in the international, Paris-based journal whose literary importance was closely tied to the serial publication of installments from Joyce's "Work in Progress." In fact, Beckett's first published piece, the commissioned essay on Joyce, appeared in one of the earliest numbers of *transition,* in 1929; he went on to publish over twenty-five stories, poems, translations, and reviews in the journal between then and 1938. More so than any other literary publication or group, the contributors and readers of *transition* constituted Beckett's practicing literary milieu.

Beckett's review in 1938 most concretely marks an end for Beckett because it appeared in the very last issue of *transition*.[2] Beckett's artistic circle was about to undergo a radical transformation. As *transition* editor Eugene Jolas explained many years later, summing up both the journal's self-proclaimed purpose and the reason it ceased publication, the "by then inevitable approach of World War II made it no longer possible to concentrate on abstract laboratory problems, or to daydream about new forms in art and language. The totalitarian menace was looming on the horizon, and I came more and more to feel that the writer could defend the spirit only by participating actively in the battle against the enemy" (14).

Beckett's difficulty in finding a British publisher for his first novel and his decade-long association with *transition* are, when viewed from the perspective of the cultural politics of the 1930s, mutually determining. To put the matter in terms current at the time, *transition* maintained a formalist, abstract apolitical aesthetic that by the midthirties was no longer fashionable or, for many writers, sensible or ethical.

In many respects *Murphy*—with its arcane allusions and vocabulary, its concerns with metaphysics, the occult, the life of the "mind," its convoluted syntax and purposively trivial yet overly complex plot structure—too closely resembled the writing of the out-of-date literary experiments of the twenties.[3]

Jolas's belief that by 1938 "abstract" experimental literature was pointless can be justifiably interpreted as a belated confession of artistic failure; years earlier, authors such as Auden, Orwell, Malraux, Gide, and Aragon (the list goes on) had already decided that writers should abandon this aesthetic "daydream" and actively take a stand in their writing against fascism, capitalist imperialism, and totalitarianism.[4] By 1935 *transition* stood for many writers as a symbol of a dangerously apolitical literary hermeticism. Like many of the surrealist poets it published, it became a target of attack in journals such as *Left Review,* which considered Jolas's aesthetic not only irresponsible but "near-Fascist" (qtd. in Cunningham 5). If publishers were reluctant to take on *Murphy,* it was because, like *transition* itself, it seemed a remnant of the modernism of the previous decade, irrelevant to the urgently communicative, politically charged tendential writing of the thirties. Even the staunchly belletristic reviewer in the *TLS* wagged a politely accusing finger at Beckett's irresponsibility: "one feels that the talent and knowledge [*Murphy*] reveals deserve a theme of more depth and substance" ("Murphy").

The harsh oppositions of 1930s' cultural politics were usually presented as a set of interrelated choices: communism or fascism, the proletariat or the bourgeoisie, concrete communication or abstract formalism, active participation or passive observation, the collective of humankind or the bourgeois individual, the literature of socialist realism or the literature of a dying capitalism.[5] Inevitably, within actual literary works these oppositions manifested themselves inconsistently. For example, Malraux, one of a number of French writers most closely associated with the Soviet Union and socialist realism, was vilified by other leftist intellectuals for portraying the Chinese revolution in his 1934 *La Condition humaine* not as a vast class struggle but as an opportunity for individual acts of heroism in an essentially irrational world.[6]

In many respects, Jolas's 1929 *transition* manifesto "the Revolution of the Word" marks the end of the interwar avant-gardist attempt to make consciousness or language itself the locus of political and social transformation. What Jolas implicitly hoped to yoke together—a dedication to the "pure," "autonomous" word/ imagination with the excitingly antibourgeois cachet of "revolution" (173)—is precisely what the political pressures of the decade were ripping apart. Just as *transition* was beginning its publication in 1929, the founders of surrealism, Breton and Aragon, were quarrelling over the question of how closely artists dedicated to a revolution in language and consciousness should involve themselves in party politics and the international antifascist, proletarian movement. As one chronicler of the decade's divisions put it: "Henceforth [from 1930] surrealism pursued its course on two parallel paths: that of political Revolution, that of the ever widening exploration of the unknown forces of the unconscious" (Nadeau 175).

The interpretation of Beckett's work is still caught up in these difficult oppositions. In most cases, we have now put the divisive evaluations of the decade in historical perspective; by and large they are no longer operant in our own critical vocabulary. Aside, perhaps, from those "formalist" (the scare quotes indicate an historical usage) writers of the period who explicitly embraced various aspects of a regressive political ideology (like Pound or Lewis), we are no longer willing to judge the writers of the period by applying the period's own damning oppositions. Similarly, we now know how politically blind much of the "alliance" between left-leaning intellectuals, the communist party, and the Soviet Union actually was.[7] Nevertheless, the overarching opposition between socially indifferent formalism and socially responsible writing, as it was constructed throughout the period itself, has remained a controlling perspective in regard to Beckett's work. If we accept this polemical logic, Beckett's writing appears simply antithetical to that of explicitly leftist writers; antithetical, in fact, to the entire trend, quite diverse in itself, of socially engaged literature, from the surrealist Aragon to the plain-spoken Orwell. But once the *evaluative* oppositions of the period have been rendered historical and viewed as polemically driven, then the still accepted *analytical* oppositions need to be worked through as well, rather than implicitly upheld.

The often-cited review Beckett published in the final number of *transition* is a case in point for viewing his work within, rather than antithetical to, the explicitly political literary trends of the thirties.[8] The review rehearses a struggle on the part of the just-published young novelist to find terms of connection between art, politics and, in his own words, "social reality." Defending his friend Devlin—as he already had Joyce and others—against the charge of obscurity, Beckett begins with a dig at explicitly political literature. Devlin's work, "with himself on behalf of himself . . . is a relief now that verse is most conveniently to be derided (or not) at the cart-tail of faction. . . . The relief of poetry to be derided (or not) on its own terms and not in those of politicians, antiquaries . . . and zealots" (*Disjecta* 91).

While the phrase "antiquaries and zealots" might refer to the Celtic Revival and the cultural conservatism of Irish nationalists, the defense of Devlin's autonomous art, his "profound and abstruse self-consciousness," is made in reference to a pan-European cultural prescription: the doctrine of socialist realism.[9] Devlin's best work depends "on a minimum of rational interference" which overrides any concern for unambiguous messages: "art has nothing to do with clarity, does not dabble in the clear and does not make clear." Art can only be judged in

> terms of need, not of opinion, still less of faction; opinion being a response to and at least (at best) for a time an escape from need, from one kind of need, and art, in this case these poems, no more (!) than the approximately adequate and absolutely non-final formulation of another kind. Art has always been this—pure interrogation, rhetorical question less the rhetoric—whatever else it may have been obliged by the "social reality" to appear, but never more freely so than now, when social reality (*pace* ex-comrade Radek) has severed the connexion. (91)

The oppositions are present, but they are not static. Beckett's concern is with the "terms" in which poetry is judged, not with denying the relation of art to "social reality." The typical critical take, that in the review Beckett "sides with the self against society" (Cohn 12), is locked in the ideology of the period it presumes to examine. In fact, "social reality" and "connexion" are active, operative terms here. Other phrases, like "terms of need," "escape from need," "obliged by the 'social reality' to appear," are as vaguely political and materialist as they are vaguely aesthetic and psychological. By the end of the paragraph, however, Beckett's loose logic takes on a definitive target. "Social reality" appears twice in the concluding sentence: once in scare quotes, indicating a usage Beckett distrusts, and once as a political fact. The rights to this "term" are being contested, not conceded (this same begrudging refusal to concede the importance of the social situation of art will appear, with a change of emphasis, ten years later in the "dialogues" with Georges Duthuit).

If for Beckett art is "pure interrogation," it is nevertheless "obliged" to be other things as well, to have an impure manifestation in social reality. Beckett's mistrust, in this first usage, signals a disparity between the artist's aspiration and the work of art's contingent nature in an historical world of "need." More specifically, Beckett addresses the cultural politics of the period by making social reality the dominant concern. The doctrine of socialist realism, as defined by Karl Radek, one of the principal speakers at the influential First Soviet Writers' Congress of 1934, put forth a monologic definition of "the position of man on this planet" to which all progressive writers must subscribe (Radek 158). Beckett wanted to point out that this same, officially sanctioned social reality had seen it necessary, by 1938, to purge "ex-comrade Radek" from its ranks and send him into exile.[10] Acceptable versions of social reality were contingent on political expediency.

For Beckett, it is the operant social reality which has "severed the connexion" between a "need" best addressed in art and a "need" in political terms. Radek had argued that writers like Joyce—*Ulysses,* he declaimed, was "a heap of dung, crawling with worms, photographed with a cinema apparatus through a microscope" (153)—falsified the representation of the social world "under a cloak on impartiality" (158). Radek's charges against Joyce and other modernists were echoed in leftist journals in England and France: Joyce's realism was too narrow, both elitist and petit bourgeois, when what needed to be portrayed was the totality of social relations (as in Marx, Balzac, and Tolstoi); his language was mandarin when it was necessary to speak to a mass audience; his preoccupation with the "irrational" and the "subconscious" precluded him from a "conscious" engagement with "the fate of humanity" (158).[11] Beckett's response reverses the charges: it is politicians and zealots who have corrupted art's necessary function of "interrogation." For Beckett, Radek's fate was a compelling sign of how the attempt to define, politically and authoritatively, "social reality" was itself a fatal severing of cultural expression from actual social life.

As with Beckett's earlier criticism, it is difficult to identify anything more definite here than a struggle, in his idiosyncratic syntax, to maintain a connection between art and social reality, even while he argues for the clear separation of the terms of aesthetic judgment and political or sociological judgment. The topical, biting reference to Radek, as well as Beckett's punning allusion to Auden (Devlin's fusion of form and content is "extraaudenary" [94]) are signs of engagement, at an ironic distance, with questions of tendency and political art. What does the contested, active, and yet also ideological (with scare quotes) phrase "social reality" mean from a writer like Beckett? His first published novel, written while Beckett was living in London and Dublin in 1935–36, and which takes place during the "postwar recovery" (*Murphy* 50), does not really answer the question: rather, it expands the terms and scope of Beckett's struggle with the idea of social reality itself.

"Contact with Outer Reality" in *Murphy*

The brief notice on *Murphy* in the *TLS,* which viewed the book as a "curious . . . elaborate parody of the world we know," cited a passage from the novel as best describing the protagonist Murphy's "attitude toward life" ("Murphy"). The passage refers to Murphy's job as an attendant at a hospital for the insane, his feeling for the patients there and

> his loathing of the textbook attitude towards them, the complacent scientific conceptualism that made contact with outer reality the index of mental well-being. . . . All this was duly revolting to Murphy, whose experience as a physical and rational being obliged him to call sanctuary what the psychiatrists called exile and to think of the patients not as banished from a system of benefits but as escaped from a colossal fiasco. (100–101)

"Contact with outer reality" is the key phrase here. On one hand, it recapitulates a persistent aporia of modernism, that an inner reality and an outer reality exist separately, and can be evaluated and gauged as such, as on an "index." On the other hand, it expresses the choice facing the artist in the 1930s: respond to the "colossal fiasco" either by engaging it, by making "contact," or by escaping into the freedom of the imagination, even if the escape courts madness. Murphy is clear about his choice: rather than fight against scientific conceptualism and an ideological "system of benefits," he chooses to side with a passive withdrawal into his mind. "His vote was cast. 'I am not of the big world, I am of the little world'" (101). This is, more or less, the major conflict in the novel: Murphy's struggle to escape the exigencies of the "big" or "outer" world so that he might enjoy the "sanctuary" of the little, inner one. But does this correspond to the author's struggle as well, to Beckett's choice?

Murphy's struggle to "come alive in his mind" (6) and Beckett's struggle to reconcile his ambivalence toward social reality with his insistence on the purity of aesthetic judgment resemble each other in a complicated way. What stands most in

Murphy's way are the contingencies of practical, everyday life whose ultimate priority he challenges; for Beckett, the struggle is to find a mode of narration that resists a stable depiction of social reality without conceding the concept itself. The ambivalence is thematized and gently parodied as a philosophical problem:

> The nature of outer reality remained obscure. The men, women and children of science would seem to have as many ways of kneeling to their facts as any other body of illuminati. The definition of outer reality, or of reality short and simple, varied according to the sensibility of the definer. But all seemed agreed that contact with it, even the layman's muzzy contact, was a rare privilege. On the basis of this the patients were described as "cut off" from reality, from the rudimentary blessings of the layman's reality. . . . The function of treatment was to bridge the gulf. (101)

This phenomenological description of outer reality and the "sensibility of the definer" helps Murphy justify his identification with the patients. For Murphy, they symbolize "that self-immersed indifference to the contingencies of the contingent world which he had chosen for himself as the only felicity and achieved so seldom" (96). From this perspective, to be "cut off" from "layman's reality," the mind "a closed system . . . self-sufficient and impermeable" (64) is only exchanging one definition of reality for another. Yet Beckett's compulsion to justify, rationally and communicatively, Murphy's choice of rejecting "layman's reality" in favor of the psychotics' reality is itself an indication of an outer reality, the definition of which is never questioned by the omniscient narrator. It is to this outer, social reality that the problem of Murphy's quest to "come alive in his mind" (6) is always referred, even though "outer reality" is presented, pseudophilosophically, as a contingency, no more or less primary than Murphy's mind.

This ambivalence—outer reality as an operant force that motivates the struggle to escape into the mind, or outer reality as a contingent phenomenon that varies with each individual mind—creates a problem in the construction of the novel and, in turn, a problem in interpreting it. As the narrator explains, "Murphy felt himself split into two, a body and a mind. They had intercourse apparently, otherwise he could not have known that they had anything in common. But he . . . did not understand through what channel the intercourse was effected nor how the two experiences came to overlap" (64). Body and mind are associated in the novel with outer and inner realities: the big world of money, motion, work and other people whose "sight and sounds . . . detained [Murphy] in the world to which they belonged, but not he, as he fondly hoped" (6), and the little world of internal stillness, the imagination "cut off" from everything but itself. For Murphy, "the problem [of intercourse between body and mind] was of little interest" (64). The omniscient narrator also displays a lack of understanding this channel of overlapping experiences of world and mind, of social reality and autonomous art. What is a matter of indifference for Murphy appears, I argue, as an underlying problem in the construction of the novel itself. Like Murphy's mind, the novel is split into two closed systems between which intercourse is always apparent: it is the means of their interaction that Beckett the novelist fails to understand. .

The opening chapters evince the two "systems" of the novel, the apparent connection between them, and the failure to understand how they relate. Beckett sets up the plot as a parody of modernist melodrama centering on Murphy, who "belonged to no profession or trade; came from Dublin" and lived on "small charitable sums" (14). Murphy is an elaboration of the Anglo-Irish bohemian-aesthete protagonist of "Dante and the Lobster." His occult studies with Neary and his quest to self-sufficiently "come alive in his mind" (6) correspond to the avant-gardist attempt to aestheticize everyday life. But this will to withdraw into the mind conflicts with his attraction, physical and emotional, to Celia, a working-class woman compelled by economic necessity into prostitution, whose only real friend is her old, infirm grandfather. Murphy can only "come alive in his mind" when alone, his body at rest and "appeased" (6). When he wants Celia to quit working the streets and live with him— gender roles in the novel remain locked into norms of monogamy and male dominance, despite the overall disdain for middle-class values toward career, religious morality, or nation[12]—he is confronted with the "question of economy" (16): "When there was no money left . . . Celia said that either Murphy got work or she left him and went back to hers. Murphy said that work would be the end of them both" (16).

Despite the eccentric details, the story begins with a set of novelistic cliches void of psychological character development (the narrator refers to all the characters, except Murphy, as "puppets" [71]), including a convoluted but conventional subplot involving the love interest of Murphy's former teacher, Neary. What is not conventional is the writing. Parody, while relevant to Beckett's intentions, does not adequately describe the relationship between plot and presentation. The novel is full of intellectual jokes, punning references to high, occult, arcane, and contemporary culture which function primarily to display the narrator's easy and clever command of a "Joycean" range of knowledges. The sentence structures vary from simple declarations that sketch out the plot to self-conscious, mannered arabesques of rhetorical inversion, chiasmus, and oxymoron. Many of these features are remnants of Beckett's allegiance to a modernist stylization that the most effective parts of *Murphy* leave behind. The essential thing is not the word games, played at a level that cuts most readers out of the competition. Rather, the active, omniscient game with words, constructed outside the experience of the characters, attempts to compensate for—to ride over rather than address—the failure to understand the interaction between systems of mind and reality, words and world; an interaction that the conventional but necessary plot repeatedly makes apparent.

When Celia confronts Murphy for breaking his promise to find work, his response is constructed in one of the novel's basic modes of narration:

> He closed his eyes and fell back. It was not his habit to make out cases for himself. An atheist chipping the deity was not more senseless than Murphy defending his courses of inaction, as he did not require to be told. He had been carried away by his passion for Celia and by a most curious feeling that he should not collapse without at least the form of a struggle. . . . To die fighting was the perfect antithesis of his whole practice, faith and intention. (26)

"Inaction" must be defended, actively and with a struggle. Even withdrawal into the mind involves a struggle as long as there is an outside world against which the withdrawal takes place. Individual agency, impassivity, and physical paralysis, important in all of Beckett's fiction, are presented here as objective, as not affecting the mode of narration. The oxymoronic logic, as in the phrase "courses of inaction," allows the omniscient narrator both to sympathize with Murphy's reaction to the "colossal fiasco" and maintain an active, communicative link to a world outside the mind. There is, in Beckett's compositional technique, an ambivalence toward inaction—silence, withdrawal, the self-sufficient mind—that conflicts with, almost contradicts, the thematic pseudophilosophical valuing of impassivity, inner self-sufficiency, and the devaluing of interconnecting communication.

In one sense, the last line of the above passage is a rebuke to a directly political aesthetic whose ideal practitioner would be willing "to die fighting" for a cause. In this same scene of conflict between Murphy and Celia, Beckett suggests a congruence between his own aesthetic beliefs and Murphy's "senseless" defense of himself:

> She looked at him helplessly. He seemed serious. . . . She felt, as she felt so often with Murphy, spattered with words that went dead as soon as they sounded; each word obliterated, before it had time to make sense, by the word that came next; so that in the end she did not know what had been said. It was like difficult music heard for the first time. (27)

Here are the two systems: on one side, an autonomous language, like "difficult music," that is semantically void, from which communicative sense is withheld; on the other, a description in the clearest, communicative language of a woman and man failing to understand. Both of the systems are linked in the act of communicating their separation. But it is the story of their separation, of Murphy's withdrawal from outer reality, of the game with words unrelated to the experience of the characters, that Beckett emphasizes. While the figure of Murphy is in many ways an image of the "antithesis" of the committed writer, the novel as a whole expresses Beckett's ambivalence toward this cultural-political image; it is an attempt to defend and describe—omnisciently, parodically, oxymoronically—what Beckett himself does not accept as a definition of his own "practice, faith and intention." It is, in practice, a rejection of one side of the opposition—the revolution of the word, the formalism cut off from the social reality—but without an acceptance of the other side.

The struggle to keep these two systems separate when their overlapping is apparent becomes manifest, at the most general level, in the juxtaposition of the two middle chapters. Chapter 5 traverses the familiar terrain of the modern novel—a man, alone, moving through an alienating, hostile urban world, while his woman waits for him at home. Chapter 6 is an ironic description of an entity called "Murphy's mind" (63). Both chapters are characterized by word play, parody, and intellectual gamesmanship. While each chapter makes apparent the "contact" between inner and outer worlds, each exemplifies the separation. As Raymond Williams observed about a key innovation in the Bloom sections of *Ulysses,* "there is no longer a city, there is only a man walking through it. . . . The substantial reality, the living variety of the city, is in the walker's mind" (*Country* 243–44). Joyce's portrait of modernity is an interaction of objective city—as both potential community and alienating urban space—and observing mind. The emphasis is on the interaction from the perspective of an individual consciousness; its own sense of individuality and inwardness is presented as a product of, and a reaction to, the complex status of Dublin, part metropolis, part provincial colonial city. It is this type of interaction that the two central chapters of *Murphy* separate out: the novel of the man, the woman, and the metropolis of London in chapter 5, and the novel of the mind, as isolate object, in chapter 6.

Compare the opening lines of each. From 5:

> The room that Celia had found [for her and Murphy] was in Brewery Road between Pentonville Prison and the Metropolitan Cattle Market. West Brompton knew them no more. The room was large and the few articles of furniture it contained were large. The bed, the gas cooker, the table and solitary tallboy, all were very large indeed. (40)

London is a set of proper nouns that signify manufacture, labor, the force of law, slaughter, and commerce. This is the outer reality, definitive and stable. Its nature is not dependent on the "sensibility of the definer." The cheap furnished room, between prison and market, a "cage" (5), is likewise a hard, alienating reality. Within it the lone woman feels lost.

In contrast, chapter 6 begins:

> It is most unfortunate but the point of this story has been reached where a justification of the expression "Murphy's mind" has to be attempted. Happily we need not concern ourselves with the apparatus as it really was—that would be an extravagance and an impertinence—but solely with what it felt and pictured itself to be. (63)

When the narrative is focused inward, the voice must point to itself, to its own need for "justification." There is a double inwardness—a picture of "what it pictured itself to be"—yet the passage is in essence objective, outside the working of the "apparatus," looking in. Perhaps it is only from the perspective of Beckett's postwar fiction—with his creation of an inner voice so intense that its own contradictory functioning is a powerful expression of the connection between mind and world—that we can see how inadequate this is, even as a joke. Yet, even though the separation is made so complete that each side, outer and inner, needs its own separate chapter, within each chapter itself connections become apparent, become inescapable.

In chapter 5, the outside reality, the "laymen's reality," is characterized by a damaging utilitarianism. Murphy goes to look for work so that Celia does not have to go back "to walking the streets . . . or wandering in the Market, where the frenzied justification of life as an end to means threw light on Murphy's prediction, that livelihood would destroy . . . life's goods" (42). Murphy "on the jobpath" is hopelessly awkward, antisocial, anxious "to cultivate the sense of time as money which he heard was highly prized in business circles" (43); he passes through a city scarred by "those malignant proliferations of urban tissue known as service flats" (47), perceiving places of possible employment as "slave-markets" (47). He is met with an "attitude of derision" by those from whom he ineffectually seeks employment. This is outer reality: "for what was all working for a living but a procuring and a pimping for the money-bags, one's lecherous tyrants the money-bags, so that they might breed" (47). In response, weary and defeated, afraid of the consequences if he cannot manage to earn a living, he fantasizes a Dantesque image of escape and withdrawal, sitting on a hill against a rock in

> embryonal repose, looking down at dawn across the reeds to the trembling of the austral sea and the sun. . . . he actually hoped he might live to be old. Then he would have a long time lying there dreaming, watching the dayspring run through its zodiac. . . . This was his Belacqua fantasy and perhaps the most highly systematized of the whole collection. It belonged to those that lay just beyond the frontiers of suffering, it was the first landscape of freedom. (48)

Inwardness and the literary tradition are joined in the fantasy; this is the transcendent moment of the chapter, "just beyond the frontiers of suffering." The inwardness is a response to the outward reality, so much so that it must be "systematized" in order to stand up to the hierarchical exchange-value system of London. The emphasis falls on the antithesis between Dantesque "Paradise" and the "miasma of laws" (48), the "mercantile gehenna" (26). There is no interaction between mind and outer reality; subjectivity, like the hermetic view of literature, is a systemized, closed withdrawal. Yet the expression of the withdrawal is not within the closed system; it is active, responsive, as though a "landscape of freedom" is made visible by the negative force of London. The omniscient narrator does not imaginatively enter Murphy's subjective response, but presents it as yet another image of the separation between inner and outer, literature and reality, though outer reality is the compelling horizon against which the inner appears.

The negative view of outer reality—an attitude shared by character and narrator—leads to a narrated conflict: enervated by this "vision" Murphy decides to sit down and take his "fourpenny lunch." He finds "a branch of the caterers he wanted" and begins the "ritual" whereby "he defrauded a vested interest" out of a penny or two. He drinks half his tea, then complains so vociferously to the waitress that she has brought him the wrong kind, that she brings him another. The narrator describes this petty "swindle" in heroic and political terms:

> No matter how the transaction were judged from the economic point of view, nothing could detract from its merit as a little triumph of tactics in the face of the most fearful odds. Only compare the belligerents. On the one hand a colossal league of plutomanic caterers, highly endowed with the ruthless cunning of the sane, having at their disposal all the most deadly weapons of the post-war recovery; on the other, a seedy solipsist and fourpence. (50)

The trivial action is made humorous through hyperbole. This is not an image of class struggle, but a case of Beckett exploiting the terms of struggle to give a parodic dignity to the "solipsist"'s plight. In order to do so, the "plutomanic" outer reality must be represented as existing outside the mind of the solipsist. The hero may be a solipsist, but the narrative perspective is closer to the "cunning of the sane."[13]

Later in the chapter, Murphy goes to Hyde Park to eat the packet of assorted biscuits he buys in the restaurant where he enacts his swindle. Like Molloy with his sucking stones, Murphy's attention turns to the question of form:

> They were the same as always, a Ginger, an Osborne, a Digestive, a Petit Beurre and one anonymous. He always ate the first-named last, because he liked it the best, and the anonymous first, because he thought it very likely the least palatable. The order in which he ate the remaining three was indifferent to him and varied regularly from day to day. On his knees now before the five it struck him for the first time that these prepossessions reduced to a paltry six the number of ways in which he could make this meal. But this was to violate the very essence of assortment. . . . Even if he conquered his prejudice against the anonymous, still there would be only twenty-four ways in which the biscuits could be eaten. But were he to take the final step and overcome his infatuation with the ginger, then the assortment would spring to life before him, dancing the radiant measure of its total permutability, edible in a hundred and twenty-ways. Overcome by these perspectives Murphy fell forward on his face in the grass, besides those biscuits of which it could be said as truly as the stars, that one differed from another, but of which he could not partake in their fullness until he had learnt not to prefer any one to any other. (57)

Toward what end is this preoccupation with form and "total permutability" narrated? In *Watt* and *Molloy*, similar permutations are carried out in the language itself: sucking stones and words are equally permuted according to Molloy's destitute desire for symmetry. The modulated repetition of phrases in the later fiction breaks the flow of narrated action—the action is equally in the permutation of language and in the distribution of simple objects or actions. But here Murphy's concern with form is not refracted in the mode of narration. Rather, "total permutability," the desire for "fullness," is related to the principle of distinction. Only by relinquishing the priorities and pleasures of taste and sensation can a fourpenny lunch of five biscuits become, imaginatively, satisfying. Murphy's poverty, a result of his desire for inner self-sufficiency in response to the instrumental outer world, leads him to an awareness that links aesthetic pleasure to social hierarchy. Because his impoverished lunch lacks "fullness" in a material sense, questions of taste and sensual preference become damaging. Conversely, for Murphy to act upon his likes and dislikes means foregoing the relative fullness that indifference would bring. This choice—trivial if the game with words and biscuits is the sign of an indifferent art, but serious if the game with words is covering up Beckett's ambivalent struggle to make words and world interact—is indicative of an artistic problem relevant to Beckett's subsequent fiction: how to reconcile a conscious, rational rejection of hierarchies of taste and judgment with a literature that manages to create an aesthetically pleasing and effective "fullness" out of semantically and rationally impoverished material.

The schisms in the novel—inner and outer, word and world, omniscient narrative game and "puppets" whose words fail to hold their meanings—do not allow novelistic development of the implications of Murphy's choice. In Beckett's later fiction, critiques of the social hierarchy of taste are expressed, in spite of the paradoxes inhering in the "closed systems" of language and "inner" self, through poignant aphorisms; as Molloy bitterly learns, "to him who has nothing it is forbidden not to relish filth" (*Molloy* 30). In *Murphy* there is no subjective realm through which such an awareness becomes integral to the story. Instead, in the following chapter, Beckett presents the "justification of the expression 'Murphy's mind'" outside of a concern with "this apparatus as it really was." While it is chapter 5—the seedy solipsist dreaming and wandering alone through a hostile environment—that implicitly expresses the problem Beckett's successful postwar fiction would center on and transform, it is in chapter 6 that Beckett most explicitly attempts to merge mind, word, and art and oppose them to "outer reality."

Beckett makes Murphy's mind an arena for arguments about aesthetic autonomy: "Murphy's mind pictured itself as a large hollow sphere, hermetically closed to the universe without. This was not an impoverishment, for it excluded nothing that it did not itself contain." Aware that this is a tautology, not a productive paradox, the narrator needs to point out that "this did not involve Murphy in the idealist tar. There was the mental fact and there was the physical fact, equally real if not equally pleasant" (63). The "justification" of the expression "Murphy's mind" becomes a justification of a division between inner and outer that, from an omniscient perspective looking in, that Beckett cannot sustain. In turn, the division is belabored in terms of "criteria" reminiscent of the review of Devlin: "The mental experience was cut off from the physical experience, its criteria were not those of the physical experience, the agreement of part of its content with physical fact did not confer worth on that part. It did not function and could not be disposed according to a principle of worth" (64).

As in Beckett's review, here there are two realms of experience that cannot be judged with a single "principle of worth." While in the review it was "social reality" that ultimately severed the connection between aesthetic and social worth, here it is inner reality, Murphy's mind, that determines the cut off. Contributing to the loss of expressive language which this "justification" entails is Beckett's replacement of concrete images of the material world—so important to the power of Beckett's inner voices, because they make palpable the pain of the separation of self from society, of language from signification—with pseudophilosophical abstractions. Aware of this loss of narrative tension, Beckett tries to recover a sense of material struggle by animating his abstractions with vaudevillian variables: "He neither thought a kick because he felt one nor felt a kick because he thought one. . . . Perhaps there was, outside time and space, a non-mental non-physical Kick from all eternity. . . . But where then was the supreme Caress?" (64). The language becomes comically expressive in reference to blows and caresses, conflict and reconciliation, but the pseudo-Platonism remains sterile and self-contradictory. While Murphy believes that "his mind was a closed system, subject to no principle of change except its own, self-sufficient and impermeable to the vicissitudes of the body," it is the vicissitudes of the body that are primary: "But motion in this [mental] world depended on rest in the world outside" (64).

Murphy's goal, withdrawing into the inner world of his mind, is to feel "sovereign and free" (65), but the withdrawal, characterized by physical impassivity, is described as compensation for the lack of agency in the outer. There are "three zones" of Murphy's mind.

> In the first . . . the pleasure was reprisal, the pleasure of reversing the physical experience. Here the kick that the physical Murphy received, the mental Murphy gave. . . . Here the whole fiasco became a howling success. In the second were the forms without parallel. Here the pleasure was contemplation. . . . Here was the Belacqua bliss and others scarcely less precise. The third, the dark, was a flux of forms . . . the world of the body broken up into the pieces of a toy . . . without love or hate or any intelligible principle of change . . . Here he was not free, but a mote in the dark of absolute freedom. (65–66)

Of the three zones—fantasies of reprisal, contemplation, and darkness—it is the last that Murphy ultimately desires: "in the dark, in the will-lessness, a mote in its absolute freedom" (66). As in the surrealist's uneasy union of communism and pure automatism (a union broken by politics at the beginning of the 1930s) it is in the dark of the will-less, formless unconscious that freedom becomes not merely an individual experience but a condition of existence. This freedom is attained, at the end of the chapter, through rational "justifications" built on a series of oppositions that Beckett cannot maintain. The private, subjective realm in which such freedom becomes visible is antithetical to the narrative perspective, which can only look in at a mind, an "apparatus," looking at itself. Doubly removed from the most complete image of freedom in the novel, the omniscient game with words (Murphy's mind is ultimately only an "expression") is locked outside the transcendent dream. As if Beckett realizes the ineffectual manner in which these sincere utopian moments of freedom are achieved, he ends the chapter by reminding the reader of the "colossal fiasco" which, after all, seems to be the only reality that counts, the reality to which the novel as a whole is addressed: "This painful duty [of justifying the expression 'Murphy's mind'] having now been discharged, no further bulletins will be issued" (66). The "mind," as Beckett has strained to imagine it, is a lost cause.

Beckett's ambivalence toward the terms social realism offered, and toward political definitions of the outer world, lead him, in his first novel, to an impasse. Aesthetic autonomy, imagined as a closed, self-sufficient system of mind and language, blocks rather than provides access to the liberation of the "real" (as he put it in "Proust") from habituated modes of perception. Chapter 5, Murphy in London, suggests that only from a perspective which clearly defines the outer world as an instrumental rationality can a withdrawal into the mind be justified. Chapter 6 mocks subjectivity by making the mind not, as in stream-of-consciousness, an active observing voice, but a static, contradictory set of oppositions between inner and outer, viewed from the outside. Beckett's choice of omniscient point of view and his allusive, oxymoronic game with words points to the impasse. On one hand, the novel implies that language cannot refer seriously to anything but its own functioning; on the other hand, narrative—the story of withdrawal from community and meaning— cannot function without a relation to the outer reality. Beckett would need either to extend one of these propositions or find a linguistic and narrative method that could reconcile them. *Murphy* shows the signs of Beckett's struggle with these divergent impulses, but it fails to make a convincing case for either.

Watt: Novel of Resistance or Accident of War?

However ambivalent Beckett was toward the idea of a socially relevant literature, as an Anglo-Irish intellectual traveling between Germany, Paris, London, and Dublin in the 1930s, he was far from ambivalent toward the social reality he witnessed all around him. Unlike the older Joyce, who according to Richard Ellmann presented to his friends a "cultivated disengagement" concerning the threat of German fascism, Beckett openly expressed his anti-Nazi sentiments.[14] In September of 1939, when Hitler invaded Poland and France and England declared war on Germany, Beckett, who at the time was staying in officially neutral Ireland, quickly returned to Paris. By the end of October of the next year, he had joined the French Resistance. His first biographer Deirdre Bair vividly relates the drama of Beckett's involvement in the war, the day-to-day dangers he faced, the discovery of his intelligence-gathering activities by the Gestapo, his nearly tragic escape from Paris in August 1942 and his isolated existence in the small village of Roussillon in southeast France where, for two-and-a-half years, living and working under the deprivations and anxieties of the war, he wrote his second novel *Watt.*

The story of Beckett's life and the interpretation of *Watt* have been oddly interrelated: oddly, because while in most cases the events of an author's life are evoked in order to shed light on his or her artistic practice, in Beckett's case it seems that the events in his life have been explained in light of his reputed aesthetic beliefs. For example, Bair gives this account of Beckett's decision to join the Resistance, which she calls his "abandonment of neutrality":

> All around Beckett senseless arrests and killings were commonplace. Even more devastating was the knowledge that *numerous friends were either openly collaborating with the Germans or indirectly toadying to them.* He found himself unable to remain neutral any longer. Now that the war touched his friends, it was no longer *a philosophical exercise.* . . . [His friend Paul] Léon's incarceration was just one of the events which led to Beckett's abandonment of neutrality: "I was so outraged by the Nazis, particularly by their treatment of the Jews, that I could not remain inactive," he said. Long after the war, when an interviewer asked Beckett why he had taken an *active political stand,* he replied, "I was fighting against the Germans, who were making life hell *for my friends, and not for the French nation.*" He was being consistent in his *apolitical behavior.* (308; emphasis added)

Just as the ideology of aesthetic autonomy insists that political or moral values are irrelevant to artistic values, here, dominant ideas about Beckett's writing lead to a similar insistence about his life. Beckett's Resistance work was "apolitical," his attitude toward the war "philosophical." His motives are personal. Neither politics nor history is admitted as a meaningful context for his actions.[15] The same holds true for standard interpretations of *Watt:* "an academic exercise for a vital mind hemmed in by the accident of war" (Bair 329); "the principal theme of the novel [is] the need to know and the difficulty and indeed impossibility of knowing. . . . Pure form . . . takes over, and meaning evaporates" (Harvey 95; 99); "Watt's journey metaphorically represents an inner experience" (Rabinovitz 125); "it probes the precarious foundations of meaning by showing clarity and stability to be provisional effects of a larger network of inconsequence, arbitrary coincidence and self-defeating discontinuity" (Hill 20). In these views, the novel Beckett wrote during the most devastating and transformative historical event of the twentieth century bears no mark of the world around it. Like an "accident of war," its relation to its history is an "arbitrary coincidence."

Watt was Beckett's most radical attempt to put into practice his interwar notions of aesthetic autonomy. It is in this choice, in the specific form Beckett gives it, that the novel's relation to Beckett's experience of the war resides. The paragraph cited above from Bair's biography suggests, in its contradictions, the formative context. Beckett's friends—intellectuals and artists, many Jewish, many associated with *transition* and other small literary journals—were also his most important (in some cases his only) audience. His relation to them was both professional and personal. It was within this circle, in creative response to it, that Beckett's ideas about art and his own work evolved. Fascism crystallized ideologically around a politics of nation and race. Most of the international artistic circle of immigrants and exiles to which Beckett belonged abjured these values. In this context, to reject a politics of *nationalism,* as Beckett says he did, was de facto a political act. Beckett's choice—a conscious, difficult choice; not all of Beckett's friends or fellow artist-intellectuals were willing to, or even wanted to, actively oppose the Nazis—was not apolitical.[16] It was based on the values of an international community that refused fascist and nationalist French, Irish, and English norms of culture, identity, and inclusion.

As Raymond Williams has argued, there was a formative relationship between literary innovation and the cross-cultural status of many modernist and avant-garde artists, those who during the first half of the century came to London, Paris, or Berlin from "colonized or capitalized regions [within Europe] . . . linguistic borderlands . . . [or] as exiles . . . from rejecting or rejected political regimes."[17] For Beckett—who in 1929 had praised Joyce's "synthetic language" for transforming a reified English into a purified aesthetic medium—artistic innovation was carried out in a context where language became detached, in various ways, from nations or peoples.[18] Fascism attempted to destroy the set of social groupings in which, for Beckett and others, artistic innovation was also a means of communication, even though in extreme cases innovation meant severing communication with everyone but the most select intellectual community. Actively taking a stand against fascism entailed a defense of the lines of communication that linked Beckett's aesthetic beliefs and practices, his identity as an international artist, to a whole way of life—a way of life that since the inception of an artistic bohemia in the midnineteenth century had provided a social arena where the sons (and, in different ways, daughters) of the bourgeoisie could express, in creative works and behavior, the contradictory implications of modernization, capitalism, and imperialism.[19] Fascism not only threatened Beckett's friends, it threatened the only social matrix in which his writing might make sense.

In itself, a commitment to aesthetic autonomy has no particular political meaning. During the rise of fascism and Stalinism, however, the idea that art should serve no external purpose took on heightened urgency, both negative and positive. Both fascism and Soviet totalitarianism necessitated the destruction of cultural freedom in order to consolidate social control and maintain the repression of democratic dissent. What offended the cultural prescriptions of Nazi and Soviet doctrine alike—even more than direct attacks on beliefs about the German "race" or the heroism of the proletariat, which could be directly refuted—was ambiguity. Cultural control means not only the suppression of "degenerate" artists and works, but the assurance that the public see the "correct" meaning of a work, clearly and unassailably.[20] Even in democratic societies, attacks on artistic decadence, from the trials of Flaubert, Wilde, and Joyce to the travails of Finley and Mapplethorpe, ultimately have as much to do with the difficulty in pinning down the artist's attitudes and intentions, or the artist's attitude toward "art" itself, as with controversial subject matter.[21]

It is under these twin pressures, the breakup of Beckett's crosscultural literary community and the renewed urgency of aesthetic freedom and autonomy, that "meaning evaporates" in *Watt*. The extreme ambiguity and communicative break-down in *Watt*, so different in form from the intellectual puzzles of *Murphy*, are signs of a shift—as uncertain in direction as the extreme conditions in which he was working—in Beckett's understanding of narrative writing. While the changes in Beckett's life were forced by the fascist occupation and war, the changes in his writing were chosen from within the range of already existing alternatives. It is change within continuity that must be accounted for first. Take the most basic example, the novelistic necessity of creating a protagonist. This is Celia, describing Murphy to her grandfather, Mr. Kelly:

> Celia replied that Murphy was Murphy. Continuing then in an orderly manner she revealed that he belonged to no profession or trade; came from Dublin—"My God!" said Mr. Kelly—knew of one Uncle, a Mr. Quigley, a well-to-do ne'er-do-well, resident in Holland, with whom he strove to correspond; did nothing that she could discern; sometimes had the price of a concert; believed that the future held great things in store for him; and never ripped up old stories. He was Murphy. He had Celia.
> Mr. Kelly mustered all his hormones.
> "What does he live on?" he shrieked.
> "Small charitable sums," said Celia. (14)

This is an explanation, full of references to the outer world, in a clipped and clever style, almost jaunty; Murphy the bohemian, dependent on the loose change of the affluent class. Compare this to an early passage in *Watt*, where Mr. and Mrs. Nixon and Mr. Hackett, sitting on a bench in an unspecified town, observe Watt getting off a bus. At first, seeing Watt from a distance, they are "not sure whether it was a man or a woman. Mr. Hackett was not sure that it was not a parcel, a carpet for example, or a roll of tarpaulin, wrapped up in dark paper and tied about the middle with a cord" (16). Discovering that Mr. Nixon had once been acquainted with Watt and had loaned him some money, Mr. Hackett, burning with curiosity, insists that Nixon tell him more about the "solitary figure."

I really know nothing, said Mr. Nixon.

But you must know something, said Mr. Hackett. One does not part with five shillings to a shadow. Nationality, family, birthplace, confession, occupation, means of existence, distinctive signs, you cannot be in ignorance of all this.

Utter ignorance, said Mr. Nixon.

He is not a native of the rocks, said Mr. Hackett.

I tell you nothing is known, cried Mr. Nixon. Nothing.

A silence followed these angry words, by Mr. Hackett resented, by Mr. Nixon repented.

He had a huge red nose, said Mr. Nixon grudgingly. (21–22).

The change, within the continuity, is both thematic and formal. Rather than explanation, there is enumeration, a list of the criteria of identity that the "figure" Watt lacks, a protagonist who has no "distinctive signs." The geopolitical is reduced to a scant synecdoche: "the rocks." The language is likewise reduced, the dialogue given a rhythmic simplicity. Instead of a character sketch there is stark ambiguity, trivial and mocking. And while to know "nothing" becomes an epistemological limit in the novel, there stands in contrast the "five shillings" and the "huge red nose"— nothingness with the broadly sketched face of a clownish tramp. Other attributes accrue, according to Mr. Nixon: "no fixed address"; "truthful, gentle and sometimes a little strange"; "to be seen in the streets"; "a university man" who only drinks "milk" (22–23). The function of the attributes, however, is not to create a character but to fill a narrative space, to make a minimal but specific "figure," to give the narrative just enough semantic material to create a situation and a question: "What does it matter who he is?" (25) asks Mrs. Nixon. "He is setting out on a journey" (17) says Mr. Nixon. Who? Where? This is enough to get the novel on the way.

The nature of the change from *Murphy* to *Watt* is difficult to characterize without understanding where the change will lead Beckett. In the most important sense, *Watt* is a transitional work. It has almost no significance—no mode of signifying—except as a transition, a change in directions. This is part of its radical autonomy and a consequence of the conditions under which it was created. If we jump ahead to the first lines of *The Unnamable*, one thread of development becomes evident: "Where now? Who know? When now? Unquestioning. I, say I. Unbelieving. Questions, hypotheses, call them that. Keep going, going on, call that going, call that on" (3). The action is entirely in the questioning, the urge to tell a story becomes the narrative impetus, the existence of words is tied in with the struggle to define them, there is a compulsion to continue narrating, as if someone is there, behind the voice, threatening. In *The Unnamable* the narrative questions are raised explicitly within the voice itself; there is no pretense to make them questions from outside, from a Hackett and a Nixon.

The change within continuity is also starkly evident in Beckett's obsession with "total permutability," presented in *Murphy* as a communicated concept and part of the bohemian-intellectual response to the "plutomanic" instrumentality of modernity. In *Watt,* permutation becomes a method of automatic composition:

> Here he stood. Here he sat. Here he knelt. Here he lay. Here he moved, to and fro, from the door to the window, from the window to the door; from the window to the door, from the door to the window; from the fire to the bed, from the bed to the fire; from the bed to the fire, from the fire to the bed; . . . [thirty-three lines later !] from the fire to the door, from the door to the bed. (203–204)

The simplest words, the simplest actions: nothing is expressed, no psychic depths are probed, there is only a filling of pages with a minimal variety of literary material or invention. Such permutations appear in almost every scene in the central sections of the novel, and in different forms, such as Watt's inversions of spelling and word order (164–68). Just as no creative thought is required on the part of the writer once the four concrete nouns—window, door, fire, bed—are chosen, no effort is required on the part of the reader. This is the novel's gesture toward radical autonomy. Language is neither narrative, expressive, nor conceptual: its function is to take up the material space and duration-time of writing, with no intent of generating the reader's interest. Language becomes like a code of dots and dashes arranged in a mechanical fashion; a code without a key, because there is no longer an interpretive community. This is the ideal or limit style in *Watt.* The break with the outer world is no longer justified in a language that makes "contact" even as it rejects it. Rather, the break is with communication itself. Loss of community means loss of communication.[22]

Literary aesthetic autonomy, as Beckett had described it in 1929 in reference to Joyce's "synthetic language," entailed aspirations to both universalism and self-contained meaning, a pure "closed system" purposely fashioned with patient artistic labor; in Murphy there was the analogy to "difficult music heard for the first time." But in *Watt,* autonomy becomes the antithesis of artistic effort: a mechanical static enumeration. Every spiritual or philosophical suggestion of meaning—like "absurdity" or "necessity"—is subjected to this noncommunicative formalist ideal. Thus, when Watt ponders the conditions under which he serves his master Knott:

> But he had hardly felt the absurdity of those things, on the one hand, and the necessity of those others, on the other (for it is rare that the feeling of absurdity is not followed by the feeling of necessity), when he felt the absurdity of those things of which he had just felt the necessity (for it is rare that the feeling of necessity is not followed by the feeling of absurdity). (133)

The very last line of the novel in the author's "addenda"—"no symbols where none intended"—reiterates this overall schema: there is no denial of meaning (symbolic or otherwise) because, ideally, the language is a result of neither the creative work (conscious or "automatic") nor the intentionality necessary to make a meaning in the first place.

It would be tempting to link *Watt*'s radically impoverished, labor-less autonomy directly to the scarcity of war; to see it as an attempt to make something out of nothing, an effort totally cut off from meaning that reflected total irrationality and the destructiveness of historical chaos. Yet its continuity with Beckett's other fiction makes this inadequate—true enough perhaps on its own terms, but not really the novel's essential quality. For, as in the works Beckett wrote in French directly after the war, the contradictions inhering in the implications of a radically autonomous art, which revolve around the need for communication and conscious creative effort, begin to become thematized, tentatively and statically, despite the extremes of formalism. Ambiguity, constructed in concrete, simple sentences and phrases, becomes part of a story, told from a perspective outside the experience of ambiguity, about the difficulty of communication.

Perhaps the overall sign of the novel's relation to the destruction of artistic community during the war is *Watt*'s placelessness.[23] While in *More Pricks than Kicks* and *Murphy* the sense of the outer world of Dublin and London was a necessary contrast to an aesthetic and "mental" inner world, in *Watt* the scant parodic references to England or Ireland are empty ciphers. Just as Watt has no psychological or inner existence as a character, the novel has no need to create a corresponding sociological or outer existence. But the novel's aspirations toward total geopolitical dislocation pose a problem in narrative form. The central scenes of radical ambiguity and verbal permutation—the incident of the Galls, the naming of the pot, the feeding of the dog, and so on—are not quite free floating, not quite the "logographs" that Beckett once considered as a possible description of his own artistic project.[24] Two of the concrete terms propping up this narrated ambiguity are *master* and *servant*, reductive emblems of social hierarchy that fill in, barely, for the novel's geopolitical void.

The condition of servitude described in the novel, Watt's life as a servant in master Knott's country manor, and the condition in which language loses its ability to refer to things and events, are intertwined. Watt's "need of semantic succour" (83) is illustrated through his inability to understand the relationship between the word *pot* and the object he cooks with in Knott's kitchen and into which his "tears of mental fatigue" and physical "exertions" fall (88). The mechanistic verbal manipulations describing how Watt follows Knott's instructions to feed leftovers to the famished dog is played out with a similarly reductive social imagery. The enumerated possibilities lead to the speculation that Knott maintains at his own "expense on some favourable site . . . a kennel or colony of famished dogs," while he gives small sums of charity to "a suitable large needy local family" whose impoverished children will lead a famished dog to the back of the mansion every night (99–100). The novel's suggestion of society consists of the stable "superior existence" (50) of the master, Knott; a series of replaceable servants, including Watt; and "immense impoverished families . . . miles around in every conceivable direction" (100). What denies this image (no doubt Beckett's skeletal description of rural Ireland) the status of a social content is Beckett's commitment to extremes of ambiguity and autonomy.[25] Unlike Murphy, the willfully passive bohemian-aesthete, or the narrator-protagonists of the nouvelles and the trilogy, Watt has no class consciousness, no internal adversarial voice. His only function is to signify, and be subsumed in, a pervasive ambiguity.

In *Murphy,* passivity required a vigorously narrated defense of "inaction." In *Watt,* the theme of agency or action is usually presented in counterpart to the mechanist, passive mode of composition. "Too fearful to assume the onus of a decision, said Mr. Hackett," about Watt's seemingly meaningless behavior, "he refers it to the frigid machinery of a time-space relation" (21). His speech is likewise detached from rational control or volition: "Watt spoke also with scant regard for grammar, for syntax, for pronunciation. . . . The labour of composition . . . had here no part, apparently. But Watt spoke as one speaking to dictation, or reciting, parrot-like, a text" (156). Ambiguity is the conjunction of a willed will-lessness—as in automatic writing—and an outside determination, a mindless servitude. The long, central passages describing Watt's attempts to understand "incidents" that transpire while he is a servant in Knott's mansion likewise present ambiguity as a two-sided content, the expression of which necessitates a "labor of composition" that the novel always resists.

When Beckett attempts to reconcile the two impulses—one toward the formal ideal of radical autonomy, one toward a story about Watt's immersion in extreme ambiguity—he inevitably turns to the theme of communication, as if this, ultimately, is the only possible goal. Like the naming of the "pot," the "incident of the Galls" (70–79) is often cited by critics to demonstrate how Beckett undermines meaning by demonstrating the "arbitrary" nature of signification. The Galls are piano tuners. Their visit to Knott's house is narrated in the simplest terms: "While Watt looked round, for a place to set down his tray, Mr. Gall Junior brought his work to a close, put back his tools," and so on. The father and son have a short, enigmatic conversation and then leave. The narrator refers to this as "the principal incident of Watt's early days in Mr. Knott's house." The next several pages are then taken up with Watt trying to understand "what had happened." At first, this is given a purely formalist emphasis: the incident "continued to unfold, in Watt's head, over and over again. . . . It developed a purely plastic content, and gradually lost . . . all meaning, even the most literal" (72–73). The loss of literal content "caused him to seek for another, for some meaning of what had passed, in the image of what had passed" (73).

The ambiguity does not center on the incident's missing significance, but on the need to reconfigure experience into a communicable, narrative form: "Watt did not know what happened. But he felt the need to think that such and such a thing had happened then, the need to be able to say . . . Yes, I remember, this is what happened then" (74). The aesthetic value placed on the incident of the Galls—"of great formal brilliance and indeterminable purport"—seems to reflect and parody Beckett's own aesthetic ideal in the novel. For Watt, however, the incident is a source of anxiety. While the omniscient perspective up to this point is wholly outside the narrated action, the theme of communication forces the distinction between Watt's anxiety and Beckett's aesthetic ideal to break down. The ambiguity, now formulated as a question, is neither an epistemological nor hermeneutic problem, but an inter-subjective problem in narrative communication. As such, the outside perspective must be broken:

> But what was this pursuit of meaning, in this indifference to meaning? And to what did it tend? These are delicate questions. For when Watt at last spoke of this time, it was a time long past, and of which his recollections were, in a sense, perhaps less clear than he would have wished. . . . Add to this the obscurity of Watt's communications, the rapidity of his utterance and the eccentricities of his syntax, as elsewhere recorded. Add to this the material conditions in which these communications were made. Add to this the scant aptitude to receive of him to whom they were proposed. Add to this the scant aptitude to give of him to whom they were committed. And some idea will obtain of the difficulties experienced in formulating . . . the entire body of Watt's experience. (75)

The constant term here is *meaning*, while the antithetical terms of *pursuit* and *indifference* simply and statically cancel each other out. This impasse leads to a transformative change in perspective, a transformation—situated between the earlier omniscient, mandarin game with words and the testimonial voices of the trilogy—which begins to appear in this key passage. There is a consciousness struggling to understand. It as yet has no place in the narrated actions, it's simply there: on one hand, "the obscurity of Watt's communications," on the other, "the scant aptitude to receive of him to whom they were proposed." Between Watt and the receiving consciousness stand the difficult "material conditions"; between the narrating voice and the reader stands "the scant aptitude to give." This is one way that Beckett's own "material conditions," cut off from his literary community with no way of knowing what the outcome of the war would be, is embedded in the novel: because there is no communicative context, the chain of transmission is broken. Ambiguity remains the thematic focus, but it is around the explicitly raised problem of communication that the pursuit of, and indifference to, meaning is raised.

In the second part of *Watt*, Beckett strains to incorporate fully this concern with communication, despite the novel's commitment to pure formalism. On one hand, there is the awareness that the more the conditions that make communication possible are destroyed, the greater the need for a narrative reconfiguration of what "happened" into transmittable form. On the other, the aesthetic ideal, the "closed system" of language, severely delimits the awareness. As the "incident of the Galls" continues, there is a new, troubling realization: "a thing that was nothing had happened, with the utmost formal distinctness. . . . [But] Watt could not accept . . . that nothing had happened, with all the clarity and solidity of something" (76; I have severely redacted these quotes to save space; multiple permutations and repetitions subsume the content within the limit style). While Watt "could not bear" this ambiguity, he somehow finds it possible to communicate it to the receiving, narrating intelligence:

> To elicit something out of nothing requires a certain skill and Watt was not always successful. . . . No, he could never have spoken at all of these things, if all had continued to mean nothing, as some continued to mean nothing, that is to say, right up to the end. For the only way one can speak of nothing is to speak of it as though it were something, just as the only way one can speak of God is to speak of him as though he were a man . . . and as the only way one can speak of man, even our anthropologists have realised that, is to speak of him as though he were a termite. (77)

The abstract terms which are shifted around, *something* and *nothing*, are meaningless because they simply refer to each other; they tend toward the radical ideal. But the narrator finds a meaningful analogy for these abstractions. The reduction of man to termite is a metaphor for the inadequacy of a totalized outer perspective; to speak of "man" as a whole, either from the perspective of God or positivist social science, is already a loss of human value. Watt cannot "affirm" an identity between his own sense of being and the word *man*, in this sense. Nevertheless, he "continued to think of himself as a man, as his mother had taught him" (83). Likewise, while Beckett does not refer his writing to *man* in a social sense, he nevertheless feels the need to forge a link between radical autonomy and the ultimate communicative referent of any narrative, the social world. To refuse to call oneself a "man" or write about "man" takes on, ironically, a humanist value; as with the term *social reality* Beckett is contesting the rights to a concept he views as intellectually debased.

The reference to "*our* anthropologists" is one of the few moments in *Watt* where Beckett violates the game of mechanistic self-sufficiency, and directly addresses his intellectual peers. Of all the modern human sciences, anthropology has had the closest relation to modernism. In the early twentieth century, the ethnographer, like the artist, saw himself in a position to recognize the relative, conventional nature of social norms and Judeo-Christian morality within his own social world; both modernist art and ethnography saw in premodern "primitive" life, and its artifacts, an originary link among the unconscious, morality, and aesthetics that could justify, quite rationally, modern art's controversial antipathy to late Victorian ethics, both religious and utilitarian.[26] While Beckett mocks the positivist arrogance of the science of man, it is the ethnographer who supplies the model for the figure of the receiving, narrating voice in section three of *Watt*. "It was about this time," the section begins, "that Watt was transferred to another pavilion, leaving me behind in the old" (152). The appearance of the first-person, implicit in the earlier references to a receiving consciousness, is not motivated by a plot, nor is there any attempt to render plausible the narrator's claim that Watt "told" him the entire story. The "I" appears, apparently, as the only way to work the extremes of ambiguity and autonomy into the problem of communication. As such, the "I," given the authorial name "Sam" (153), is constructed not as a character, but merely as a means of transmitting the story.

Sam and Watt meet in the fields behind their masters' mansions, fields crisscrossed with barbed wire fences (156). They meet on "a rustic humpbacked bridge in a state of extreme dilapidation" which, one day, almost collapses under Watt. "And he would certainly have fallen, and perhaps have been carried away by the subsequent flood, had I not been at hand to bear him up." Sam receives no thanks for his help. Instead, he and Watt begin to repair the bridge, lying on their stomachs, arms outstretched "until our task was done. . . . Then, our eyes meeting, we smiled, a thing we did rarely, when together. . . . And then we did a thing we seldom did, we embraced. . . . We were attached, you see, to the little bridge" (154–55).

While the bridge and the embrace, provisional signs of an eccentric parable of brotherhood in a time of war, point toward an incipient plot, the ideal of autonomy compels the focus back to the problem of communication. No longer one who experiences ambiguity, Watt is now the producer of ambiguity. Along with its "scant regard" for norms of spoken speech and its automatic quality, Watt's mode of speech is linked, parodically, to anthropological concerns, as if he belongs to some hitherto undiscovered tribe: "When Watt spoke, he spoke in a low and rapid voice. . . . That there ever issued from the mouth of man . . . except in moments of delirium, or during the service of the mass, a voice *at once* so rapid and so low, is hard to believe" (156). Although Watt is supposedly the source of the novel's mangled story, here his speech is presented as an object to be analyzed. What becomes important is the active attempt to decode and record Watt's increasingly cryptic communications. The novel begins to mimic an analytic report, as if Sam were an ethnographer who engages personally with the inscrutable native other—"Often my hands left his shoulders, to make a note in their little notebook" (165)—in order to study him. Watt's direct speech is laid out in italicized "examples" from each "period" (164–68) of their relationship. Sam describes the rules of Watt's "manner" of talking, citing "inversion," "ellipse," "reversal of discourse," and the like.

As soon as Sam begins to understand Watt's system of communication, however, Watt modifies his manner of speaking, as if to thwart him. Thus, the recording of Watt, which begins in an ethnographic mode, takes on the character of an aesthetically unassailable resistance to rational speech:

> So all went well until Watt began to invert, no longer the order of the words in the sentence, but that of the letters in the word. This further modification Watt carried through with all his usual discretion and sense of what was acceptable to the ear, and aesthetic judgement. Nevertheless to one, such as me, desirous above all of information, the change was not a little disconcerting. (165)

Watt's increasingly inverse speech (and behavior, as he also begins to walk backward) is a deadpan, parodic image of the "aesthetic judgment" guiding the modernist opposition to corrupt everyday language and instrumental logic. The relationship between Sam and Watt expresses, as in the bridge scene, the hope of human compassion; but communication, the most essential social interaction, is presented, finally, as the ludicrously mechanistic incommensurability of art and "information," aesthetic and purposive rationalities.

Lacking both the passive, but vigorously narrated, struggle against the outer world, as in Beckett's first books of fiction, and the struggling inner voices of his later ones, *Watt* is a static, transitional work. While the values of the international artistic circle to which Beckett belonged during the interwar years compelled him to take an active political stand, the loss and threatened annihilation of that community compelled Beckett to take his commitment to aesthetic autonomy to an extreme. Beckett's choice in *Watt*, the mechanistic shuffling of simple terms and phrases, lay at the far end of the spectrum from both Proust's multilayered dispersion of habituated perception and Joyce's heroic labor in creating a "synthetic" language. The self-contradictory impasse of Beckett's earlier beliefs about the conscious effort of the writer and the closed system of language, his antiaesthetic provocations and his unwillingness neither to concede "social reality" nor redefine it—all are brought into stark relief. The intellectual games with syntax and learning in *Murphy* are reduced to a set of irreconcilable antinomies: master and servant, things and the names of things, observer and observed, meaningless art and artless information. *Watt* is the record of Beckett's discovery that what compelled this logic of oppositions, and what in effect rendered it superfluous, was the force of narrative communication. The discovery is clear in both the limpid language and the aborted story about Sam and Watt. It was with a new awareness about the communicative function of art—an awareness in part an accident of the war, in part conscious choice—that Beckett, upon the reconstitution of the literary world in postwar Paris, began to transform failure into success.

III

Rewriting Modernism in the Nouvelles

Primitivism in the Tone of Polite Conversation

Despite his efforts, Beckett never really had a chance at becoming a good modernist. By 1929, the year he began his literary career with an essay praising of one of high modernism's most problematic swan songs, Joyce's *Finnegans Wake,* demands for ceaseless artistic innovation—Pound's injunction to "make it new"—were starting to sound old.[1] Beckett's first published book, a 1931 monograph on Proust, praised the creative power of "involuntary memory" almost a decade after surrealism had established chance and the unconscious as the ultimate sources of poetic truth. Indeed, by 1931 the founding members of the surrealist group, one of the most influential avant-garde movements of the century, were breaking up over the question of whether revolution should be fomented through unleashing the power of the unconscious or consciously committing the poetic imagination to the cultural prescriptions of the Communist Party.[2] The literary aspirations of the thirties—the decade during which Beckett published his first two books of fiction—toward an accessible, directly political writing had cast serious doubt on the viability of maintaining many of the modernist ideals and techniques which Beckett, in his own fashion, had adopted. Beckett's failure both to accommodate the divergent, waning aesthetic values of the early twentieth century and still be "new" and innovative seems, in retrospect, inevitable. If in his early writing Beckett was a failed modernist whose work went largely unnoticed, it was not because he tried unsuccessfully to move beyond the modernisms of his immediate past, but because he tried too hard to incorporate too many conflicting modernist values all at once.

During the war, after the Nazis had discovered his involvement in the Resistance and he had been forced to flee Paris, Beckett wrote his third book of fiction, *Watt.* In certain respects, its stylized obsessive repetitions and its thematics of extreme ambiguity form an eccentric homage to earlier, pre-World War I avant-gardist concerns, recalling both Gertrude Stein's "logographs" (as Beckett had called them) and dadaist nonsense. While the childlike simplicity of syntax and vocabulary in *Watt* also reflects a desire for a totally accessible writing, the novel's incessant separation of "things" and "words for things" reduces the promise of communication to an absurdist joke. If, in *Finnegans Wake,* Joyce's attempt to create a universal literary language had resulted in a polysemous code whose multiple meanings were accessible only to a small, highly educated coterie, in *Watt* Beckett created its mirror opposite: a language almost anyone could understand but that signified nothing. *Watt* is Beckett's most meaningless book because in writing it he realized that the values of modernism—as he had experienced them in Paris, London, and Dublin of the interwar years—could no longer generate meaning of any kind.

The process of experimentation carried out in *Watt* led Beckett to two somewhat incongruent places. On one hand, his fiction had regressed, from sophisticated language games and bohemian satire of Dublin in *More Pricks than Kicks* and London in *Murphy,* to the mindless permutations and neutralized feudalistic no-place of *Watt.* On the other hand, Beckett's experimentation with a style at once accessible and meaningless, and with a static narrative that linked images of social hierarchy, semantic chaos, and the receiving, reportorial consciousness of "Sam," had already moved him beyond the contradictory games with language, beyond the impasse of trying to justify, from the outside, the primacy of "inner" reality. With astonishing success, Beckett was able to shape this simultaneous regression-progression into a startlingly direct mode of narrative in the first fictions he wrote after his return to Paris in the fall of 1945, a group of stories written in French as the nouvelles and translated into English as the first three stories in *Stories and Texts for Nothing.*[3] The first of these, published in partial form in Sartre's journal *Les Temps modernes* in 1946 and titled in English "The End," is an episodic tale that sets a pattern for Beckett's major postwar fiction.[4] The unnamed first-person narrator recounts, in a voice that ranges from an affectless childlike simplicity to an ironic lyricism, how he was released after an unspecified but apparently lengthy stay at a hospital-like "charitable institution." He wanders "lost" through unnamed city and countryside, isolated, fiercely antisocial, physically deteriorating, objectlike and unfeeling toward everything except the most distant memories of his childhood. In this haunting, intensely focused fiction, Beckett evokes an anonymous storytelling figure whose primitive, objectlike existence signals a yearning for stories incompatible with literary modernism and its generative social matrix, the modern metropolis.

This transformation in Beckett's writing is powerfully evoked in a central image from "The End." Midway through the story the narrator tries to make his way back to the city where he can beg for coins:

> Soon there were carts, but they all refused to take me up. In other clothes, with another face, they might have taken me up. I must have changed since my expulsion from the basement. The face notably seemed to have reached its climacteric. The humble, ingenuous smile would no longer come, nor the expression of candid misery. . . . I summoned them, but they would not come. A mask of dirty old hairy leather, with two holes and a slit, it was too far gone for the old trick of please your honor and God reward you and pity upon me. It was disastrous. What would I crawl with in the future? I lay down on the side of the road and began to writhe each time I heard a cart approaching. That was so they would not think I was sleeping or resting. I tried to

groan, Help! Help! But the tone that came out was that of polite conversation. (62)

The first-person voice, telling the story of his life through the beggar's "mask," will become Beckett's single most important narrative technique, the signature feature of his postwar fiction. Interwoven in this direct, expressive image of the inexpressive face, unable to smile or show pain, and the inexpressive voice, unable to cry out, are the thematic and communicative strands of Beckett's rewriting of modernism. The narrating figure appears premodern, like an archaic or primitive artifact, "a mask of dirty old hairy leather, with two holes and a slit." Because it is not individuated, it gives no clue to the narrator's public or private self. The mask is also the face itself; there is nothing behind it that is more expressive, it hides no authentic self, no real identity. The narrator is thus presented not as a poetic persona through which the arch-modernist Beckett speaks, but rather as an explicit and experimental aesthetic choice. What had been separated out, in contradictory fashion, in much of Beckett's interwar writing is inextricably bound together. Writing, for Beckett, is now relegated to a single voice, a lyrical instrument which gains emotive power in proportion to its represented inability to express. "I tired to groan, Help! Help! But the tone that came out was that of polite expression." While the face cannot be contorted into a pathetic expression, in order to "please your honor," the voice is incapable of everything but genteel chatter. The contradictions built into the narrating figure play havoc with the antinomies of modernist autonomy: entirely self-referential (it is only authentically itself) yet yearning to communicate; a grotesque affront to bourgeois standards of propriety and self-respect, yet locked into the "tone" of "polite conversation."

In the nouvelles Beckett breaks away, clearly but with difficulty, from one of the controlling attitudes of modernism, the distancing disdain for the middle classes and the norms of bourgeois existence. The interwar figure of the bohemian involved a principled rejection of liberal, capitalist civil society and implied the belief that there was somewhere outside society—be it the inner mind or the insane asylum—from which to substantiate such a rejection. But in the nouvelles, and the fiction that follows, Beckett aspires to rid his writing of any positive notion of identity whatsoever, including the disdainful antibourgeois posture. To this end, Beckett must turn the modernist fantasy of autonomy on its head: identity and the self, it turns out, are completely dependent on the socioeconomic order. The voice of the nouvelles, Beckett is at pains to remind us, is always a beggar's voice. Its lack of expressiveness comes with a cost: "It was disastrous." To create a pathetic expression, false or otherwise, is the beggar's only hope of eliciting sympathy: "What would I crawl with in the future?" The story that the nouvelles begin to tell is this disastrous disengagement from the social world, but without the vanguardist presumption that there is an alternative realm.

If modernists were attracted to the "primitive" and "savage" urges that they presumed lay beyond the boundaries of an overcivilized, effete Western Europe,

Beckett's primitive face-mask is resolutely and explicitly bound to the bourgeois world. Beckett does, to be sure, pose his narrator as an emblem of "otherness," but because he explicitly constructs this image within, rather than against, bourgeois values, he insures that no recuperation is possible. The coordinates of identity that have come to constitute our understanding of socially institutionalized difference— race, ethnicity, gendered sexuality—have all, to some extent, been reinvented in a positive light within contemporary capitalist, global culture. The reason we now find so many modernist images of the "primitive" or culturally "other" offensive, even when embedded within critiques of empire or racism, is because they presumed to speak *for* the other, when typically their concerns were with the wounded psyche of the disaffected European intellectual.[5] In the wake of decolonization and the various civil rights movements of the last four decades, both high and popular culture can now boast (no matter how sincerely or disingenuously) the inclusion and affirmation of previously marginalized voices. The only "difference" that cannot be celebrated, even hypocritically, is poverty. Confronting, rather than eschewing, the conventions of realist mimesis, in the nouvelles Beckett begins to unravel the novelistic require- ment of coherent psychological and culturally specific character by stripping his hero of all but the most minimal inclusion in the socioeconomic order. Beckett's striking postwar innovations in narrative form are inseparable from this choice, from Beckett's compulsive iterations of material dispossession.

If Beckett's major work has anything to contribute to the emergence of feminist or postcolonial perspectives, or to the politics of cultural identity, it is only to the degree that his commitment to moving beyond the modernist values that dominated his early work engages the self-contradictory nature of those values.[6] While he creates no new perspective outside the tradition itself, his reformulation of modernist and avant-gardist attitudes toward the norms of liberal civil society allowed him to rework the narrative and linguistic strategies of high modernism in a nonregressive manner: his "primitivism" (as Lukács called it; his critique of Beckett is discussed below) shares nothing with conservative or reactionary calls to return to more primal forms of solidarity, racial or otherwise. In his first postwar fictions, Beckett fashions a narrating device whose attributes of nonauthenticity, premodernity, bourgeois gentility, and aesthetic self-consciousness are formed in conjunction with a "story in the likeness of [a] life" about a homeless, dispossessed, wandering beggar. The contradictory voice functions to preclude any possible reading of the nouvelles as realistic portraits of poverty-stricken outcasts. The narrator-protagonist's position is unreal but neverthe- less depends on a sociological premise: without the minimal requisites of membership in a socioeconomic order, no self, no affirmative identity, is possible.

Writing and Begging in "The End"

The first pages of "The End" describe the hero-narrator's expulsion from an institu- tion of social welfare into the city street where he wanders "lost" and disoriented. This expulsion, repeated in various forms in the nouvelles (in "The Expelled" the narrator-hero is thrown out the front door of his family's middle-class home; in "The Calmative" the narrator asks, "Was I being thrown out?") is the paradigmatic origin of Beckett's postwar narrators. Its consequences reverberate throughout the trilogy, in Molloy's diatribes "against the charitable gesture" and "the social worker" (30), in Malone's institutionlike sickroom, and in the closing phrases of *The Unnamable*—"I can't go on, I'll go on"—which are already being formulated in the first sentences of "The End":

> They clothed me and gave me money. I knew what the money was for, it was to get me started. When it was gone I would have to get more, if I wanted to go on. The same for the shoes, when they were worn out I would have to get them mended, or get myself another pair, or go on barefoot, if I wanted to go on. (47)

The institution imbues the narrator with a liminal social identity. He is the passive recipient of charity, already an incipient beggar, soon to be barefoot and moneyless. The narrator is aware that the institution is the only context in which he has a modern identity; that is, an identity that requires both a sense of individuated independence and what Max Weber, in reference to the expulsion of Adam and Eve from paradise in one of modernity's earliest definitive works, *Paradise Lost,* called the individual's "acceptance of his life in this world as a task" (88). Forced to leave after an apparently lengthy stay, the narrator has a parting conversation with the bureaucratic administrator, Mr. Weir:

> I am greatly obliged to you, I said, is there a law which prevents you from throwing me out naked and penniless? That would damage our reputation in the long run, he replied. Could they not possibly keep me a little longer, I said, I could make myself useful. Useful, he said, joking apart you would be willing to make yourself useful? . . . If they believed you were really willing to make yourself useful they would keep you, I am sure. . . . This is a charitable institution, he said, and the money you receive is a gift. When it is gone you will have to get more. . . . Never come back here, whatever you do, you would not be let in. (49)

Beckett's rejection of the novelistic mimesis of the social world, even in its modernist form of subjective perception, is presented here as the social world's final rejection of the narrating figure. The hero's desperation to maintain his liminal identity is already a sign of what he has lost. He recalls fondly his publicly administered, objectlike existence: "I saw the familiar objects, companions of so many bearable hours. The stool, for example, dearest of all. The long afternoons together. . . . At times I felt its wooden life invade me, till I myself became a piece of wood" (49). It was modern art's functional uselessness, theorists of modernism from

Wilde to Adorno have maintained, that gave it value in a world increasingly prone to judge everything in instrumental terms of exchange.⁷ Beckett fuses this idea into the narrating figure itself: he is incapable of being useful, of exchanging himself for anything.

At first, the narrator is stirred back into a sensate existence simply because his material needs are no longer taken care of: "I longed to be under cover again, in an empty place, close and warm. . . . From time to time someone would come to make sure I was all right. . . . It was long since I had longed for anything and the effect on me was horrible" (52). With this renewed longing, and with the money he has been given, the narrator is tempted to create a social identity for himself, outside of the minimal one he has acquired in the institution: "In the days that followed I visited several lodgings. . . . They usually slammed the door in my face. . . . It was in vain I put on my best manners, smiled and spoke distinctly. . . . It was at this time I perfected a method of doffing my hat at once courteous and discreet, neither servile nor insolent" (53).

Beckett describes the narrator's descent into primitive facelessness as a process in which the hero himself has little control. No matter how he tries, his "method" of mimicking civility fails him. When his money runs out, the narrator must give up his quest for lodgings and begins to beg. Begging too necessitates a method, one that requires that the hero present himself in terms of the class-conscious world from which he is excluded. Writing and begging, as public acts, become metaphorically linked at this juncture in the story: the further the narrator is pushed away from the social world, the less his ability to appeal to the public, to beg for his existence. Individuated expressiveness fades away with social marginality, and the narrator's face has now become locked in its grotesquely primitive affectlessness. Figuring out how to beg under such conditions becomes a methodical search for a new mode of expression:

> So I covered the lower part of my face with a black rag and went and begged at a sunny corner. . . . I couldn't use my hat because of my skull. As for holding out my hand, that was quite out of the question. So I got a tin and hung it from a button . . . of my coat, at pubis level. It did not hang plumb, it leaned respectfully towards the passerby, he only had to drop his mite. But that obliged him to come up close to me, he was in danger of touching me. In the end I got a bigger tin . . . and I placed it on the sidewalk at my feet. But people who give alms don't much care to toss them, there's something contemptuous about this gesture which is repugnant to sensitive natures. . . . There are those, to be sure, who stoop, but generally speaking people who give alms don't much care to stoop. What they like above all is to sight the wretch from afar, get ready their penny, drop it in their stride and hear the God bless you dying away in the distance. . . . In the end I got a kind of board or tray and tied it to my neck and waist. Some days I strewed it with flowers. . . . They must

have thought I loved nature. . . . I leaned against the wall, but without nonchalance, I shifted my weight from one foot to the other and my hands clutched the lapels of my coat. To beg with your hands in your pockets makes a bad impression, it irritates the workers, especially in winter. (63–65)

In the tone of polite conversation, Beckett sketches out a reception theory of begging. The audience includes aesthetes and romantics—those with "sensitive natures" or a sentimental attachment to "nature"—as well as the disaffected "workers." Beckett takes into account the perspectives of a class-stratified society and presents the beggar as an objectified vision of the random passerby loath to come too close but equally unwilling to ignore this sign of social decay. The beggar's strategy for making a good "impression" is presented as a reaction-formation to both genteel and working-class notions of propriety and justice. His attempt to elicit a response from his audience is nothing but a reflection of the fear or shame he inspires in others, and it reflects the change in Beckett's idea of art. Beckett's interwar modernist opposition to both polite bourgeois taste and popular culture is turned inside out. Unlike the manner in which he positioned his earlier bohemian-aesthete heroes and arch-intellectual omniscient narrators above and outside the "colossal fiasco" (*Murphy* 101) of the everyday world, Beckett now shapes the narrating figure's voice and self-understanding as a manifestation of the tastes and attitudes of the social world modernism opposed.

In one respect, the beggar speaks from the position of the modern individual. The city street is the modernist's typical vantage point; yet the more he adopts the perspective of the crowd, the more he becomes objectified and primitive. Physical sensation, bound up in early modernism with the intensely private, ultimately tragic attempt to expand the range of exquisite sensual pleasure (as in Huysmans's *Au Rebour* or Wilde's *The Picture of Dorian Gray*), here entails the regression to an infantile, presocialized state beyond distinctions of public and private. "I unbuttoned my trousers [on the street corner] discreetly to scratch myself" he proudly asserts. "It was in the arse I had the most pleasure. I stuck my forefinger up to my knuckle. Later, if I had to shit, the pain was atrocious. . . . Often, at the end of the day I discovered the leg of my trousers all wet. That must have been the dogs. I personally pissed very little" (65). These primly correct descriptions of self-gratifying degradation purposively mock the contradictory modernist aspiration both to outrage the proprieties of official culture and claim the institutional status of high art.

At the same time, Beckett directly counters the possibility that his satire will be read as anticapitalist. The story's counterpart to the bourgeois "charitable institution" is the radical leftist reformer, who equally turns the narrator into a passive, identityless primitive:

One day I witnessed a strange scene. . . . It was a man perched on the roof of a car and haranguing the passers-by. That at least was my interpretation. He was bellowing so loud that snatches of his discourse reached my ears. Union . . . brothers . . . Marx . . . capital . . . bread and butter . . . love [ellipses in text]. It was all Greek to me. . . . All of a sudden he turned and pointed at me, as at an exhibit. Look at this down and out, he vociferated, this leftover. . . . Old, lousy, rotten, ripe for the muckheap. And there are a thousand like him. . . . Every day you pass them by . . . and when you have backed a winner you fling them a farthing. . . . It never enters your head . . . that your charity is a crime, an incentive to slavery, stultification and organized murder. Take a good look at this living corpse. You may say it's his own fault. Ask him if it's his own fault. . . . Then he bent forward and took me to task. . . . Do you hear me, you crucified bastard! cried the orator. Then I went away, although it was still light. But generally speaking it was a quiet corner, busy but not overcrowded, thriving and well-frequented. He must have been a religious fanatic, I could find no other explanation. Perhaps he was an escaped lunatic. He had a nice face, a little on the red side. (66–67)

The beggar's self-definition as untouchable wretch, fashioned from the responses of the stratified crowd passing by, is confirmed by his objectification as a political exhibit, an edifying spectacle for the masses.

The scene of the Marxist orator serves Beckett's purpose in two ways. First, it intensifies the narrator's identitylessness by denying him any oppositional stance to his social origin, the charitable institution. The more the narrator's social degradation is presented, mockingly, from a leftist political perspective, the more the narrator mimics the middle class's aversion to a political interpretation of poverty. Conversely, when elsewhere in the story the narrator catches a glimpse of his own son, archetypically capitalist-bourgeois, "striding along with a briefcase under his arm . . . bowing and scraping and flourishing his hat," he is quick to utter a judgment—"The insufferable son of a bitch" (58)—that neutralizes his role as father of a solid, charitable citizen. While the parodied Marxist extremist consigns him to a lumpenproletariat oblivion, the narrator himself inveighs against every sign of his own contribution to the reproduction of the social order. Beckett makes his beggar reject every chance to develop or signify a political identity.

Secondly, Beckett both invites and mocks a political reading of his own work. Beckett knew quite well that no parody of a communist, no matter how broad, would be taken lightly in Parisian literary circles just after the war.[8] The story's publication history suggests this was the case. Only the first half of "La Suite" (the original French title of "The End") was published in the explicitly leftist *Les Temps modernes;* the second half, which contained the satire of the orator, was omitted. Beckett later claimed that the omission was due to a misunderstanding, but one of the editors, Simone de Beauvoir, claimed that the second part was rejected because it did not fit the general tone of the journal.[9] More significantly, in the late fifties, when Beckett's postwar fiction and drama had garnered international acclaim, the primitive, perverse, animallike existence of the narrating figure came under attack by Marxist critics of modernism. Lukács's critique of *Molloy*—"Beckett presents us with an image of the utmost human degradation—an idiot's vegetative existence" ("Ideology" 292)— echoes the orator's description of the beggar. But Lukács, Beckett's most strident critic, understands something about the social genesis of Beckett's fiction that many of Beckett's admirers miss altogether. For Lukács, Beckett's work was the "*ne plus ultra*" of a literary modernism whose "frank glorification" of "the purely subjective," of "perversity" and "psychopathology," was an honestly intentioned but ultimately empty "moral protest against capitalism" (290). While realism (for Lukács, quite distinct from naturalism's observational determinism) presents man as "*zoon politikon,* a social animal," "the ontological view governing the image of man in the work of leading modernist writers is the opposite" (280).

> Man, for these writers, is by nature solitary, asocial, unable to enter into relationships with other human beings. . . . Man, thus conceived, is an ahistorical being. . . . This negation of history takes two different forms in modernist literature. First, the hero is strictly confined within the limits of his own experience. . . . Secondly, the hero himself is without personal history. He is "thrown-into-the-world": meaninglessly, unfathomably. He does not develop through contact with the world; he neither forms nor is formed by it. The only "development" in this literature is the gradual revelation of the human condition. Man is now what he has always been and always will be. The narrator, the examining subject, is in motion; the examined reality is static. (280–82)

Beckett's fiction is without doubt part of this larger development, ascribed by Lukács to both nineteenth-century naturalism and high modernism. But is Beckett's primitivism an acritical intensification of modernism's subjective, existential rejection of history, of man as a social actor? Or is it a critical exploration of the consequences, for the individual and for literature, of such a vision? Although Lukács's static oppositions of realism and modernism, perspective and distortion, typical and pathological, do not allow him to perceive variation within the works of modernism themselves, his insight into the profound "negation of history" in Beckett's fiction well describes the manner in which Beckett aspires to create a narrating figure without a social identity. Lukács could only pose, as an alternative to modernism, a return to the realism of Balzac or Tolstoy (in the "new realism" of Solzhenitsyn, for example). Beckett sought to undermine that part of the modernist vision that posited individualism as essentially asocial. Beckett's primitivism, rather than merely presenting a more absolute ontological view of character, reflects back on the modernist values that Lukács critiques. If Beckett mocks the leftist view of "pathological" modernism, he equally derides the literary hypostatization of an autonomous inner self.

Social connectedness, the loss of which Lukács bemoans, returns in "The End" as the missing element that would promote a strong self of sense in the first place. Taking up residence in a rotting, rat-infested boatshed on the grounds of an abandoned "private estate" (67), the narrator gradually gives up his "work" (67) on the corner. At first, Beckett presents this as an ironically humble triumph of the will:

> It seemed to me I had grown more independent of recent years. That no one came anymore, that no one could come any more, to ask me if I was all right and needed nothing, distressed me then but little. I was all right, yes, quite so. . . . As for my needs, they had dwindled as it were to my dimensions and become, if I may say so, of so exquisite a quality as to exclude all thought of succour. To know I had a being, however faint and false, outside of me, had once the power to stir my heart. (70)

What imbued the narrator with a sensation of self, what once stirred his heart, is the connection to charity and begging he has now lost. "Being" is a social phenomenon; to have no "outside" manifestation of self means a loss of interiority, not an intensification of subjectivity in the face of an alienating social world. Independence, the sign of a healthy modern ego, is achieved negatively, as though it were an affliction. Typically, though, Beckett ensures that the narrator's radical negation of self is never too far, in "tone," from the polite conversation of the middle-class world; in this case, he evokes the wistful sigh of a mildly regretful, lonely pensioner: "You become unsociable, it's inevitable" (70).

Beckett locates the extremes of the narrator's regression at the limits of life, at senility or infantilism when the fulfillment of needs is beyond one's control. He has taken to lying for days on end in a coffinlike boat:

> There were times when I wanted to push away the lid and get out of the boat and couldn't, I was so indolent and weak, so content deep down where I was. . . . So I waited till the desire to shit, or even to piss, lent me wings. I did not want to dirty my nest! And yet it sometimes happened, and even more and more often. Arched and rigid I edged down my trousers and turned a little on my side, just enough to free the hole. To contrive a little kingdom, in the midst of the universal muck, then shit on it, ah that was me all over. (70)

Lying in his own shit, defiling the isolated independence of his "little kingdom," having neither social identity nor inner being, Beckett's narrator is now the primitive, helpless creature suited only for the institution of charity from which he was originally expelled and to which he is forbidden to return. The narrator's regression is also a regression of the principles of narrative. Just as the narrator can no longer "go on" without money, as he was warned from the very beginning, Beckett's episodic story structure, far from the interwoven, shifting perspectival intricacies of modernism, comes to a halt with the narrator's physical paralysis. As if to compensate for the inevitable narrative debility that results from the narrator's loss of both physical and emotive viability, Beckett terminates the story with a form of closure that retains a vestigial, positive notion of identity. Unable to move from his boat-coffin, the narrator begins to have "visions" that resuscitate the temporal dynamic of retrospective, first-person narration.

> I knew they were visions because it was night and I was alone in my
> boat. . . . I was neither cold nor warm and all seemed calm. Now the sea
> air was about me, I had no other shelter than the land. . . . I saw the
> beacons, four in all, including a lightship, I knew them well, even as a
> child. It was evening, I was with my father on a height, he held my hand.
> I would have liked him to draw me close with a gesture of protective love,
> but his mind was on other things. (71)

As the unloved son (who, earlier in the story, renounced his own role as father), the narrator at last acquires the lyrical, psychological depth that his regression into objectlike selflessness denies. The individuated expressiveness absent from the beggar's mask returns as the distant memory of repressed emotion. But this return to a psychological notion of self and identity is accompanied by an interference in the resuscitated narrative communication. The story ends with the narrator's apparent suicide, "in my boat and gliding on the waters" (71), embedded within the vision itself. In the final lines of the story, Beckett makes this violation of narrative mimesis both dramatic and emphatically metatextual:

> There I was down on my knees prying out the plug with my knife. The
> hole was small and the water rose slowly. . . . Back now in the stern-
> sheets, my legs stretched out, my back well propped against the sack
> stuffed with grass I used as a cushion, I swallowed my calmative. The
> seas, the sky, the mountain and the islands closed in and crushed me in a
> mighty systole, then scattered to the utmost confines of space. The
> memory came faint and cold of the story I might have told, a story in the
> likeness of my life, I mean without the courage to end or the strength to
> go on. (72)

The narrator, who has neither courage, strength, nor a sense of being, is ultimately deprived a textual stability. The psychological depth is flattened out, made into the "trick" that the narrating hero takes all expression to be. This metatextual aspect of the narrative—a feature which becomes increasingly pronounced in Beckett's fiction and which has become the focus of postmodern and poststructuralist readings of his work—was already implicit in the face of the expressionless beggar and the methodical descriptions of begging. While the story operates on the premise that socioeconomic status is the ultimate determinate of individual identity, Beckett works out a narrative mode that renders the premise of the story paradoxical. Just at the moment when the narrator appears as a psychologically valid character, Beckett exploits those features of narrative discourse that emphasize language as a closed, self-referential system. What is denied the narrator by the rejecting social world is equally denied him by the "tricks" of language. Both the social exclusion and the rhetorical foreclosure are linked to an integral, generative element of all modern fiction: the metropolis. Beckett's first postwar fictions take place in, and are structured by, the dissolution of the city as the ordering, social matrix of narrative mimesis.

From the Metropolis to the "Text"

"Death," Walter Benjamin wrote, "is the sanction of everything the storyteller can tell. . . . Just as a sequence of images is set in motion inside a man as his life comes to an end . . . suddenly in his expressions and looks the unforgettable emerges and imparts to everything that concerned him that authority which even the poorest wretch in dying possesses for the living around him. This authority is at the very source of the story" (*Illuminations* 94).

"I don't know when I died," begins "The Calmative," one of Beckett's 1946 nouvelles. "It always seemed to me I died old, about ninety years old, and what years, and that my body bore it out, from head to foot."

> For I'm too frightened this evening to listen to myself rot, waiting for the great lapses of the heart, the tearings at the caecal walls, and for the slow killings to finish in my skull, the assaults on unshakable pillars, the fornications with corpses. So I'll tell myself a story, to try and calm myself, and it's there I'll feel old, old, even older than the day I fell, calling for help, and it came. Or is it possible that in this story I have come back to life, after my death? No, it's not like me to come back to life, after my death. (27)

For Benjamin, writing between the wars, storytelling was an art whose decline was directly tied to modernity's destruction of the bonds of community; for Beckett, writing in the wake of World War II, the need to tell stories returns, grotesquely deformed by the loss of any authoritative vantage point from which to narrate meaningfully. Without death, without the ritual of dying as a "public process in the life of an individual" (*Illuminations* 93) to serve as a boundary, neither space nor time is stable. "I'll tell my story in the past none the less," claims the narrator of "The Calmative," "as though it were a myth, or an old fable" (28). The narrator hopes to mimic an epic form, but his "fable" lacks the most basic feature of the mythic: the monologic voice of authority.[10] Indeed, the narrator knows his act of telling is the antithesis of epic stability. "All I say cancels out, I'll have said nothing" (28). This is the ultimate failure of the storyteller. Instead of purveying wisdom and experience, there is only the futility of language—a closed system of self-referential signs—and a death, in isolation, that bestows neither meaning nor order.

For a writer whose early fiction strained to incorporate the most sophisticated and alienating techniques of modernism and the avant garde, this explicit, deeply felt longing for stories marks a significant departure. What emerges in the postwar nouvelles is an image of the storyteller whose primitive, suffering, deathless existence is itself an emblem of the ruins into which stories, for Beckett, had collapsed. While the narrator longs for a story like an "old fable," Beckett constantly plays this longing against the absence of narrative authority and stability, the absence of a long-vanished, authoritative human bond:

> But it's to me this evening something has to happen, to my body as in myth and metamorphosis, this old body to which nothing ever happened, or so little, which never met with anything, loved anything, wished for anything, in its tarnished universe, except for the mirrors to shatter . . . and to vanish in the havoc of its images. Yes, this evening it has to be as in the story my father used to read me, evening after evening, when I was small, and he had all his health, to calm me, evening after evening, year after year. (29–30)

"Story" stands for the authoritative, stable, death-bound fixity of a tellable life and a paternal, community-bound purveyance of wisdom. For Beckett, "story" stands in contradistinction to the narrator's desire for the shattered mirror and the "havoc of its images." The longing for the premodern fable is put into productive tension with modernist, tradition-shattering writing. Employing the simplicity of a storytelling voice, Beckett's first postwar writing hovers between the modernism he rejects and the return to stories that he insists is impossible.

This longing for stories amidst the deathless "havoc" has a necessary counterpart in the haunting absence of the geopolitical world that the nouvelles evoke. Both the chaotic but crafted shape of Beckett's postwar narratives of isolation and wandering, and their increasing emphasis on the paradoxical "tricks" of narrative language, have the same determinant source: the rejection of the metropolis as an organizing narrative principle. In *More Pricks than Kicks* and *Murphy* Beckett had taken a typical modernist urban perspective. Murphy's retreat into the "apparatus" of his mind, a process metaphorically linked to the autonomy of art, is a reaction to the "malignant proliferations of urban tissue" (47), the "closed system" of modern life, the "mercantile gehenna" (26) of interwar London. In *Watt* Beckett constructed a feudallike nowhere zone, but the novel's static structure, and static metaphors of communication, resulted not in a reworking of modernist concerns but rather a demonstration of their meaninglessness when taken to such extremes. In contrast, the nouvelles unfold in the abstract series of empty rooms, refuges, forests, ditches, and barely glimpsed towns that will also characterize the novels of the trilogy. What Beckett establishes in the nouvelles is not only a new, dynamically effective storytelling voice which breaks sharply from the high modernist omniscience of his earlier fiction, but a new social content whose articulation is developed in contradistinction to the metropolitan structure of modern narrative.

Since the bourgeois revolutions of the eighteenth century, the industrial, imperial city has served as the center of politics, education, art, fashion, and finance to which intellectuals and artists were increasingly drawn, in which they were able to live and work. As Raymond Williams has pointed out, by the nineteenth century even the defining contours of the countryside (or the sea, or the world beyond Europe) became dominated by the perspective of the urban dweller. Georg Simmel's turn-of-the-century analysis of urban consciousness, "The Metropolis and Mental Life," described the "objective culture" of the late-nineteenth-century technological city not only in terms of an unprecedented set of impersonal, highly organized economic relations, but also in terms of the intensified sense perception and subjective orientation of the metropolitan individual. It was the highly stratified social life of the capitalist city, its unpredictable, alienating, and exhilarating transformation of individual lives, which provided the themes and forms of the modern novel: both the organization of the plot of everyday life as a sequence of time-space relations subject to sudden change and reversal, and the flowing, multifaceted, individualized observations of the detached narrator. As Franco Moretti put it in relation to Balzac, "the urban narrative environment makes it possible, for the first time, to create an enthralling plot without having to resort to the freak [of the gothic novel]. . . . What engages the reader is no longer the 'state of exception' . . . but the unpredictability harboured in ordinary administration and everyday life. . . . With Balzac the 'prose of the world' ceases to be boring" (115). The metropolis is the decisive social formation guiding modern European fiction; in many respects, it is the theme-form of the city which accounts for the continuity evident in realist, naturalist, modernist, and "postmodernist" narrative techniques.[11]

In "The End," both the wandering beggar's psychic deprivation and his longing for stories seem activated by the city's inability to provide temporal or spatial drama. Expelled from the cloistered institution, the narrator finds himself in a place hostile to storytelling, a place which is also an image of a transformed, postwar world:

> In the street I was lost. I had not set foot in this part of the city for a long time and it seemed greatly changed. Whole buildings had disappeared, the palings had changed position, and on all sides I saw, in great letters, the names of tradesmen I had never seen before and would have been at a loss to pronounce. There were streets where I had remembered none, some I did remember had vanished and others had completely changed their names. The general impression was the same as before. It is true I did not know the city very well. Perhaps it was quite a different one. I did not know where I was supposed to be going. I had the great good fortune, more than once, not to be run over. My appearance still made people laugh, with that hearty jovial laugh so good for the health. (51)

The characteristic modernist responses to the city street, from alienation to exhilarating stimulation, are replaced by the blandest of observations: despite the obvious great changes, "the general impression was the same as before." Just as "The End" is strewn with fragmentary references to the war (the narrator mistakes the receipt Weir gives him for a "safe-conduct" (48) and his hat for a "kepi" [53]), the narrator's benumbed emergence from the hospital-like institution into the city street echoes the psychic trauma of the shell-shocked veteran returning home. But for Beckett the postwar city does not function as a representation of social chaos or personal dislocation. Rather, Beckett presents the "greatly changed" city as a space of narrative debility. Unimpressed, at a loss to pronounce the names of tradesmen (names that are crucial to the reader's ability to follow Joyce's meticulous, interiorized mapping of Dublin in *Ulysses*), without a goal, and uncertain of whether the change has occurred within himself or in his surroundings, the narrator is detached from any ordering principle inhering in the urban space. Even more, the narrator can only register continuity and emotion in respect to his own objectification: "My appearance still made people laugh." While the city street provided the modernist narrator with the stimulating "shock" and spectacle of modernity itself, it conversely deprives Beckett's narrator of the basic coordinates of modernist fiction, not least of which is his status as the subjective recorder of his own experience.

Individual action, the minimal narrative requirement, fades away with the loss of the modern public space. The simplest activity—walking down the sidewalk— takes on the greatest weight. In "The Expelled," the narrator walking in the city is the parodic negation of the modernist *flâneur:*

> The weather was fine. I advanced down the street, keeping as close as I could to the sidewalk. The widest sidewalk is never enough for me, once I set myself in motion, and I hate to inconvenience strangers. A police-man stopped me and said, The street for vehicles, the sidewalk for pedestrians. Like a bit of old testament. So I got back on the sidewalk, almost apologetically, and persevered there, in spite of an indescribable jostle, for a good twenty steps, till I had to fling myself to the ground to avoid crushing a child. . . . I would have crushed him gladly, I loathe children, and it would have been doing him a service, but I was afraid of reprisals. . . . I fell then, and brought down with me an old lady. . . . Her screams soon drew a crowd. . . . I took advantage of the confusion to make off, muttering unintelligible oaths, as if I were the victim, and I was, but I couldn't have proved it. They never lynch children, babies, no matter what they do. . . . I personally would lynch them with the utmost pleasure, I don't say I'd lend a hand, no, I'm not a violent man, but I'd encourage the others and stand them drinks when it was done. (15–16)

If the narrator of "The End" experiences the city as a place of narrative debility, the narrator of the "The Expelled" can neither navigate urban space nor separate feelings of alienation from a mob mentality. Beckett makes him no less victim than victimizer, both the ultimate outsider and the anonymous man of the crowd, the silent supporter of the lynching party. Like the narrator of "The End" his presence in the street and his compulsion to "go on" are linked to his dwindling ability to define himself as a member of the socioeconomic order: "The great disadvantage of this condition," he says when his money runs out, "which might be defined as the absolute impossibility of all purchase, is that it compels you to bestir yourself" (18).

In "The Calmative," the dissolution of the city and the loss of narrative order is intertwined from the outset. If in "The End" and "The Expelled" Beckett was constructing the voice of the beggar in relation to the rejecting/rejected social reality, in "The Calmative" (written after the other nouvelles) the primitive narrating figure has lost the liminal social identity of passive victim. The most immediate difficulty, in the absence of a form-giving death, is the disposition of the narrative space:

> What possessed me to stir when I wasn't with anybody? Was I being thrown out? No, I wasn't with anybody. I see a kind of den littered with empty tins. And yet we are not in the country. Perhaps it's just ruins. . . . I have changed refuge so often, in the course of my rout, that now I can't tell between dens and ruins. But there was never any city but the one. It is true you often move along in a dream, houses and factories darken the air, trams go by, and under your feet wet from the grass there are suddenly cobblestones. I only know the city of my childhood, I must have seen the other, but unbelieving. All I say cancels out, I'll have said nothing. (27–28)

The geopolitical city, the city of distant memories or dreams, "cancels out." From the nouvelles on, much of Beckett's fiction will reenact this paratactic, associative wandering through spaces that refer to a social world left behind, in ruins, rejected, forgotten, unbelievable, canceled out. Without the metropolitan perspective, without an observing intelligence describing the objective social world and the impressions that it evokes, all that is left is abstract movement, to "go on." This theme-form of perpetual movement is Beckett's alternative to the paradigmatic figure of modernism, the walker in the city. The deathless, goal-less, place-less movement provides only a skeleton of a narrative order. In turn, the skeletal schema always refers back to the originating moment of expulsion, to the tension between the desire for stories and the "havoc of images." Compare, for example, the openings of the "The End" and "The Calmative" (quoted above) with the opening of "Text 1" written almost a decade later, after the novels of the trilogy:

> Suddenly, no, at last, long last, I couldn't anymore, I couldn't go on. Someone said, You can't stay here. I couldn't stay there and I couldn't go on. I'll describe the place, that's unimportant. The top, very flat, of a mountain, no, a hill, but so wild, so wild, enough. (75)

While the fusion of the story and the chaotic act of narrating is more extreme in the "Texts" than the nouvelles, the continuity is striking. The voice, lost in time and rooted in space, still registers its identityless existence as the passive object of a "someone." The need to go on is motivated by an expulsion outside the control of the "I." The "place," while unimportant, must nevertheless be described in order for movement—narrative movement—to occur: an unnamed wild fragment, not nature but simply a space where there are no signs of social existence. This space will find a counterpart, equally outside of social life but free, as well, of reference to the natural world, in the "flattened cylinder" (7) of "solid rubber" (8) which forms the setting, as it were, of the 1971 novella *The Lost Ones*. The more severe the diminution of the social world and the metropolitan narrative order, as in the "Texts," the more every narrative utterance is an explicit manifestation of the difficulty of storytelling.

In an important sense, Beckett's turn toward the text is also a conscious, strategic choice against constructing an alternative narrative space outside the definitive social matrix of urban modernity. Many postwar writers responded, in various ways, to the tradition of modernism by seeking such alternatives, all of which, like Beckett's textual turn, were already present or latent, in one form or another, in the modernist novel. Some, like Camus in *The Stranger* or Bowles in *The Sheltering Sky*, refigured modernism's ethnographic fantasies of a precivilized world beyond Europe. Others, like Márquez in *One Hundred Years of Solitude*, presented the historical annihilation of older forms of communal identity as bound up with literacy and writing, constitutive features of modernization that went hand in hand with the destructive effects of European colonialism. Or writers such as Robbe-Grillet, in *The Erasers* and later novels, greatly intensified the alienating effects of the city, to the point where the postwar metropolis appears as a seamless structure of inexorable time-space relations which negate individual will or agency. But Beckett turns neither to a premodern or non-European world, nor to a representation of the late capitalist world whose technocratic metropolis engulfs all. For Beckett, the "text" replaces social modernity as the principle of narrative movement; the text becomes, in effect, a narrative space and is never without content. This move toward the text is motivated, just as the longing for stories appears as a response to the havoc of images.

In "The Calmative," this movement—from city to text, from the expulsion from socioeconomic status to the struggle to tell stories—is given explicit expression. It is no longer the need for money but the compulsion to tell stories that provokes the minimal series of narratable events. The city, as we have seen, is canceled out as a narrative possibility. There is no sign of connection between the narrator and the modern world: "of my last passage no trace remained" (30). There is, however, no place else to go. The narrator recounts a foray from the "refuge" into the city as a paratactic series of symbols, images, and encounters that both evoke and negate modernity and aesthetic modernism. The entrance to the town is antiquated, with "ramparts . . . Cyclopean and crenellated. . . . I entered the town by what they call the Shepherd's Gate without having seen a soul" (30–31); the mood, though, is one of extreme alienation. "I felt the houses packed with people, lurking behind the curtains" (30–31); "All the mortals I saw were alone and as if sunk in themselves" (38). The hauntingly attenuated town, where "the trams were running, buses too, but few, slow, empty, noiseless, as if under water" (30), is a place that inspires narrative anxiety. "What would, what could happen to me in this empty place?" In response, the narrator heads toward the harbor—the ancient source of epic and fable—as if it might provide the barest elements of a story: "Then all the bustle of the people and the things of the sea. . . . it would be a sad state of affairs if in that unscandalizable throng I couldn't achieve a little encounter that would calm me a little, or exchange a few words with a navigator, for example, words to carry away with me to my refuge, to add to my collection" (31–32).

On one hand, the writing moves further away from epic stability toward self-reflexive text. "For we are needless to say in a skull, but I have no choice but to add the following few remarks" (38), Beckett announces in the middle of the tale, reminding us that the only reality here is language. On the other, the images become archaic and evoke the longing for communication. Sitting by the harbor the narrator has his first encounter. "I found facing me a young boy holding a goat by a horn. . . . He was barefoot and in rags. Haunter of the waterfront he had stepped aside to see what the dark hulk could be abandoned on the quayside." The narrator's desire "to exchange a few words" is thwarted by his own contradictory existence as both primitive, inexpressive mask and self-conscious bourgeois. At first, it is his distance from the social world (and the world of literature, as signaled by the allusion to Dante) that silences him:

> I resolved to speak to him. So I marshalled the words and opened my mouth, thinking I would hear them. But all I heard was a kind of rattle, unintelligible even to me who knew what was intended. But it was nothing, mere speechlessness due to long silence, as in the wood that darkens the mouth of hell, do you remember, I only just. (33)

When the boy is about to leave, the narrator is inspired:

> With a great gesticulation of my whole body I motioned him to stay and I said, in an impetuous murmur, Where are you off to, my little man, with your nanny? The words were hardly out of my mouth when for shame I covered my face. And yet they were the same I had tried to utter but a moment before. (34)

Beckett imbues the grotesque old man with a naturalist urban pathos. The boy offers him "a sweet out of a twist of paper such as you could buy for a penny. . . . The sweets were stuck together and I had my work cut out to separate the top one, a green one, from the others, but he helped me and his hand brushed mine" (33). When the silent boy walks away after the narrator's shamefully banal words, the narrator is full of regret: "If I had had a penny in my pocket I would have given it to him, for him to forgive me, but I did not have a penny in my pocket, nor anything resembling it. Nothing that could give pleasure to a little unfortunate at the mouth of life" (34). The city hovers between the world of the storyteller, both urban and archaic (from a distance the narrator thinks he "might have taken [the boy] for a young centaur") and the nowhere zone beyond the metropolis. The narrator's search for words yields images from the modernist repertoire and pits them against both the contradictory primitivism and the space of the text. His sensation of self is the opposite of his reflection in the physical surface of the city: "My legs were paining me, every step would gladly have been the last, but the glances I darted towards the windows, stealthily, showed me a great cylinder sweeping past as though on rollers on the asphalt" (35). The pain of going on, the old, slow "dark hulk" of the grotesque body, is juxtaposed to a Legerlike cubo-futurist image of speed.

"The Calmative" contains another image of modernist man, an image made famous in critic Hugh Kenner's comments on "the Cartesian centaur": a cyclist "pedalling slowly in the middle of the street, reading a newspaper which he held with both hands spread open before his eyes. Every now and then he rang his bell without interrupting his reading. I watched him recede until he was no more than a dot on the horizon" (38). Kenner sees this image, along with the broken-down bicycles and bodies throughout Beckett's writing, as emblematic of Beckett's obsession with the body-mind duality and the "muddle" (Kenner 121) that Descartes's radical separation of cognition from physical being bequeathed to the Enlightenment tradition. But more specifically, the bicycle and the newspaper appear in Beckett as cultural icons of staid bourgeois existence. For Beckett's narrator, modern European man appears as an anonymous, mechanized cog mediating the physical and intellectual devices of ordinary modern life. In *Molloy* it is the narrator's painful difficulties with his bicycle at the gate of the city that draw the attention of the authorities, while the *Times* serves as his blanket when he sleeps on a public bench. As the grotesque walker through the city in "The Expelled" comments when exhorted by the policeman to clear the walkway, "He pointed out to me that the sidewalk was for everyone, as if it was quite obvious that I could not be assimilated to that category" (16). "Man" is "everyone" who commands the space and information of the city, everyone that the narrator is not. Descartes's "muddle" is, in fact, triumphant. In Beckett, it is only the mind separated from the social body of liberal civil society that is plagued by its own perverse functioning.[12]

As the narrator of "The Calmative" sits on a bench and dozes off, he experiences his final encounter with modern man and his last chance for an exchange of words—an encounter in which Beckett parodically confronts the modernist linkage of narrative action, love, sex, and chance meeting in the metropolis of romantic possibility.[13] The encounter is random: "the next thing was a man sitting beside me." The narrator's first impulse, to fix himself in time and space by asking directions and the time of day, is pointless: "He said a time, I don't remember which, a time that explained nothing, that's all I remember, and did not calm me. But what time could have done that?" (40). Nor can the man, who claims to be a traveler "not from these parts," help the narrator find his way out of the city. But he might, instead, fulfill the narrator's desire for an exchange of words. In fact, the man himself solicits a story: "But tell me," he says to the narrator, "the story of your life." The narrator is horrified—"My life! I cried." Modern man, however, has no fear of self-definition. "Shall I tell you mine, then you'll see what I mean. The account he gave was brief and dense, facts, without comment. That's what I call a life, he said, do you follow me now? It wasn't bad, his story, positively fairy-like in places" (41).

"Facts, without comment," the opposite of the narrator's own tortuous self-reflexivity, is an ironic reflection of the narrative stability he longs for. The man lets the narrator know right away what kind of story he wants to hear in return: "Are thighs much in your thoughts," the man asks him, "arses, cunts and environs. I didn't follow. No more erections naturally, he said. Erections? I said." Seeing that the narrator cannot respond to his request, the man tries to sell him one of the "phials" he has in his black bag:

> I told him I had no money. No money! he cried. All of a sudden his hand
> came down on the back of my neck, his sinewy fingers closed and with a
> jerk and a twist he had me up against him. But instead of dispatching me
> he began to murmur words so sweet that I went limp and my head fell
> forward in his lap. Between the caressing voice and the fingers rowelling
> my neck the contrast was striking. But gradually the two things merged
> in a devastating hope. (42)

This final encounter in the city registers the failure of male sexual desire to generate an ordered narrative. Beckett mocks a common impetus of the modern plot, the chance urban encounter between the independent male observer and a female figure of desire, replacing it with the primitive narrator's sexless acquiescence to a travelling salesman, the quintessential figure of so many joking, sexist stories. The contrast between the "caressing voice" and the threatening hand around his neck arouses a "devastating hope" that comes to nothing: "I have reached this point (in my story) without anything having changed, for if anything had changed I'd think I'd know" (42) the narrator comments in the midst of the man's violent embrace.

While "The End" closes with a metatextual device that distances the reader from the lonely memories of the narrator, foreclosing a psychological reading of the story, "The Calmative" closes with the emasculated narrator passing through the emptied-out image of the city, his longing for words and myth unfulfilled. He tries to find his way back to the Shepherd's Gate, whence he had come:

> At first nothing, then little by little . . . a kind of massive murmur
> coming perhaps from the house that was propping me up. That re-
> minded me that the houses were full of people, besieged, no, I don't
> know. . . . I thought of ringing at the door and asking for shelter and
> protection till morning. But suddenly I was on my way again. But little

by little, in a slow swoon, darkness fell about me. . . . I found myself admiring, all along the housefronts, the gradual blossoming of squares and rectangles, casement and sash, yellow, green, pink, according to the curtains and the blinds, finding that pretty. Then at last, before I fell, first to my knees, as cattle do, then on my face, I was in a throng. I didn't lose consciousness, when I lose consciousness it will not be to recover it. They paid no heed to me, though careful not to walk on me, a courtesy that must have touched me, it was what I had come out for. (45)

Amidst the cubist-impressionist house fronts, alienated beyond redemption among the anonymous throng, the narrator still refuses to doubt the reality of his pathetic, paradoxical condition. One of the most pervasive aesthetic ideals of the interwar period, the primacy of the unconscious in artistic creation, to which Beckett had been so attracted, is derided here in two ways. The narrator, whose paratactic monologue mocks rational order, clings resolutely to his consciousness. It is the modernist affirmation of the unconscious that he most detests: "But it's the end. Or have I been dreaming? No no, none of that, for dream is nothing, a joke, and significant what is worse" (43). Not even the unconscious, creative work of dreams—unraveled in Freud's Vienna, novelized in Proust's urbane involuntary memories, automatically inscribed in the surrealists' aimless Parisian wandering—can help restore him to stories and fables. "But reality, too tired to look for the right word, was soon restored," the narrator concludes; "the throng fell away, the light came back and I had no need to raise my head from the ground to know I was back in the same blinding void as before" (45). The resigned acceptance of the word *reality* signals the end of one central strand of Beckett's modernist struggle against both realist mimesis and social commitment. From the nouvelles on, the placeless void that Beckett's narrator-heroes encounter does not serve, as was contradictorily proposed in *Murphy*, as a space in which to resist the social world and recover the autonomous workings of self and mind. Both the void and the text are the consequences of an aesthetic choice that eschews the formative ground of modern narrative, while still refusing to replace it.

Author or Writing Subject? Beckett and Postmodern Fiction

In the nouvelles Beckett began to find solutions to the failure of his earlier fiction. Beckett addressed his postwar audience in a language and style that replaced the mandarin sophistication of his interwar writing with a direct storytelling voice whose dynamic qualities arise in tension with the evocation of a severely attenuated social and psychological identity. For Beckett, communication is no longer caught up in an antagonism between an aesthetically advanced writer and an "ignorant" public (as Beckett charged in his essay on Joyce). Communication is now imagined as a problem situated between the narrator and "stories" for which there is no authoritative ground, no shared social context. The difficulty of communicating now implicates author, storyteller, and reader alike. The turn toward "text," as it is worked out in conjunction with the rejecting-rejected social world, is the vehicle of this newly imagined relationship.

Does Beckett's postwar struggle with modernist modes of writing make him a late modernist, a postmodernist, or merely the "non plus ultra" (Lukács's term) of certain tendencies prevalent in modernism since Flaubert? Is his work transitional, a link between two cultural paradigms that belongs wholly to neither? To a degree, the question is tautological: it all depends on how we characterize these unstable categories in the first place. But the question is revealing when considered in light of the broader cultural issues underlying the category of postmodernist fiction. Theories of postmodern fiction (as Raymond Williams observed about the "selective tradition" of the modernist canon) are already effacing the "internal diversity of methods and emphases" (*Politics* 43) that characterized the development of postwar literature. Unraveling Beckett's entanglement in the postmodern canon helps isolate and clarify the issues that shaped the emergence of his postwar aesthetic.

The works of Brian McHale, Foucault, Barthes, and Andreas Huyssen provide paradigmatic statements about the meaning of postmodern fiction. There are three main themes around which theories of postmodern fiction have developed: the first concerns the "ontological" status of fictional discourse (McHale) and techniques of metatextuality and intertextuality; the second concerns "the writing subject" (Foucault, Barthes) and the relation between author, reader, and text; and the third concerns the "great divide" (Huyssen) between "high" and "low" (popular, mass) culture. A full account of Beckett's postwar writing needs to bridge the gaps between these themes.

Brian McHale's *Postmodernist Fiction* (1987) remains one of the most influential accounts of a shift in narrative art during the postwar period. McHale takes into account earlier attempts at defining postmodern literature (Lodge, Hassan, and Wollen, for example [7]) and his work is cited as a definitive statement about postmodern narrative in major sociological, feminist, and postcolonial analyses of postmodern culture.[14] Given its influence and the pivotal role Beckett plays in his argument, it is worth looking at McHale's discussion in some detail. For McHale, modernist fiction "as a whole" is organized by what he calls an "epistemological dominant": "modernist fiction deploys strategies which engage and foreground questions such as . . . How can I interpret this world of which I am part? . . . How is knowledge transmitted from one knower to another, and with what degree of reliability? . . . What are the limits of knowledge? And so on" (9). Corresponding to these concerns are a number of characteristically modernist formal devices: "the multiplication and juxtaposition of perspectives, the focalization of all the evidence through a single 'center of consciousness' . . . virtuoso variants on interior monologue," and so on. Modernism thus "transfers the epistemological difficulties of its characters to its readers; its strategies . . . *simulate* for the reader the very same problems of accessibility, readability and limitation of knowledge that plague" the represented and narrating characters (9–10; emphasis in text).

Postmodern fiction, in contrast, is organized by an "ontological" dominant. It "deploys strategies which engage and foreground questions like . . . Which world is this? What is to be done in it? Which of my selves is to do it?" Such questions "bear either on the ontology of the literary text itself or on the ontology of the world it projects. . . . What happens when . . . boundaries between worlds are violated? . . . What is the mode of existence of a text?" (10). McHale underscores the fact that, when pushed far enough, epistemological questions inevitably become ontological questions, and vice versa. But he claims that postmodern writing self-consciously foregrounds ontological questions and puts epistemological ones in the background (11). The best way to see this shift, says McHale, is to look at "writers who in the course of their careers travel the entire trajectory from modernist to postmodernist poetics" (11). Beckett, he argues, is one of these writers.[15]

McHale isolates the increasing metatextual and intertextual features in the novels of the trilogy as the sign of this "travel" from modernism to the postmodern. Thus, while on one hand the juxtaposition of the two separate narrators in *Molloy* resembles "a minimal structure of modernist perspectivism," the "internal contradictions" inhering in the two narratives and the "blurring of identities" between the two narrators already begin "to destabilize the projected world and . . . foreground its ontological structure." This destabilizing is taken further in *Malone Dies* through intertextuality and a conflation of diegetic levels. First, "Malone's claim to authorship of *Molloy* has the effect of foregrounding the act . . . of fictionalizing. . . . Malone's stories of Macmann . . . constitute a second, embedded ontological level." But the novel ends with "the text breaking off while we are still at the level of the secondary world" thus "leaving us to wonder which was the 'more real' world." This second novel of the trilogy evinces a "limit modernist . . . hesitation between an epistemological . . . and an ontological dominant." This limit is exceeded in *The Unnamable* where the narrator claims to have been the author of "all the worlds of Beckett's earlier fictions." Like Malone, he "projects worlds, but he displays greater freedom of ontological improvisation than Malone ever did, constructing, revising, deconstructing, abolishing and reconstructing his characters and their worlds." Even more, the narrator is aware of his own status as a fiction and "tries to imagine himself as the character of someone else," a "they" or "master" who must inevitably be a construct of yet someone even more "ontologically superior." The narrator "can never get outside of his own imaginings to the reality of his ultimate creator." The novel radically "foregrounds the fundamental ontological discontinuity between the fictional and the real" (12–13).

McHale's analysis implies, then, that while modernism retained a continuity between social reality and fiction by focusing on epistemological problems about knowing the world, Beckett moves beyond modernism and this continuity by proclaiming, with every resource of narrative discourse, that fictional worlds only relate to other projected, fictional worlds. McHale makes this aspect of his argument explicit when he accounts for *why* this ontological emphasis becomes dominant during the last half of the century. Following (partially and implicitly) Baudrillard's vision of a contemporary world of "simulacra," McHale claims that, in the final analysis, postmodern fiction employs the logic of a transhistorical mimesis:

> What postmodern fiction imitates, the object of its mimesis, is the pluralistic and anarchistic ontological landscape of advanced industrial cultures. . . . One of the features of this ontological landscape is its permeation by secondary realities, especially mass-media fictions [newspaper, radio, sports, holidays, a James Bond adventure movie] and one of the most typical experiences of members of this culture is that of the transition from one of these fictional worlds to the paramount reality of everyday life, or from paramount reality to fiction. (38–39)

Ultimately, McHale's account of postmodernism relies on notions of literature, culture, and mimesis that recapitulate key modernist values. For McHale, there is a strict separation between postmodern fiction and mass culture (which is postmodernism's subject matter, its "object of mimesis"); popular culture constitutes a "secondary reality" that is neither the "reality of everyday life" nor has the aesthetic power of postmodern fiction, whose textual ingenuity reveals ("foregrounds") the fictionality of this secondary reality. The mimetic logic McHale describes (which he likens to a "mirror of reality" [39]) does not really differ from modernist notions of mimesis which claimed that fiction presented the image, perception, "impression," or "sense" of things and facts, rather than objective things or facts. McHale's focus on metafiction and intertextuality clearly leads to a neomodernist concept of aesthetic autonomy. What distinguishes the canonical works of postmodernism from the "secondary reality" of "mass media fictions" is their formal emphasis on being self-consciously fictional, "discontinuous" from the real world and its "anarchistic" second reality. Postmodernism's importance is established by separating itself from the illusions ("secondary reality") of mass and popular culture. The ontological dominant of postmodernism is to the anarchy of popular images and representations what the epistemological dominant of modernism was to the naivete of realism and positivism. The shift in emphasis is not really a shift in its "underlying systematicity" (7), as McHale claims, nor a shift in its social function or values. The "discontinuity" McHale emphasizes is not, in effect, between metafiction and the world, but between the works of Beckett, Pynchon, or Robbe-Grillet, and the world of mass and popular culture.

The underlying logic of McHale's argument was already present in Roland Barthes's 1966 essay "Structural Analysis of Narratives." While not yet directly championing, as he was to do in *S/Z*, the "writerly" text (a category that resembles McHale's postmodernist fiction and includes the works of Beckett and Robbe-

Grillet), Barthes nevertheless sets the writerly (or, here, "avant-garde") text in opposition to the mass cultural narrative:

> Every narrative is dependent on a "narrative situation," the set of protocols according to which the narrative is "consumed." In so-called "archaic" societies, the narrative situation is heavily coded; nowadays, avant-garde literature alone still dreams of reading protocols. . . . Generally, however, our society takes the greatest pains to conjure away the coding of the narrative situation: there is no counting the number of narrational devices which seek to naturalize the subsequent narrative by making it the outcome of some natural circumstance and thus, as it were, "disinaugurating" it. . . . The reluctance to declare its codes characterizes bourgeois society and the mass culture issuing from it: both demand signs which do not look like signs. (*Image* 116)

On one side, there is a mass culture that functions like McHale's "secondary reality": it strives to naturalize itself and cloak the "discontinuity" between fiction and reality. On the other side, there is an avant-gardist text (Barthes cites Michel Butor, who also appears in McHale's canon) which "declare[s] its codes" in order to emphasize its ontological status and its distance from nature. Barthes's later formulation of the ideal writerly text as "a galaxy of signifiers, not a structure of signifieds" (*S/Z* 5) repeats the opposition in a more abstract language. "The enormous mass of our literature," Barthes claims, are "readerly" texts which present themselves as "a structure of signifieds," a set of organized meanings—this is McHale's "secondary reality" of "mass-media" fictions. The writerly, avant-gardist text, however, explicitly emphasizes the "signifier," writing not as meaning but as the constructing of meaning, "production without product" (4–6). This is the mimesis of postmodernist fiction— it discloses the secondary reality as fiction, the world of signifieds as signifiers. If, in McHale, postmodernist fiction turns out to be not an alternative to modernism but to mass culture, for Barthes the writerly text is nothing but the negation of the "mass of literature": "for the plural [writerly] text, there cannot be a narrative structure, a grammar, or a logic" (6). There are only signifiers as signifiers, fictions foregrounded as fictions.

One of Barthes's most interesting points (though one of his least convincing) is that somehow writerly texts change the relationship between literature and reader. For Barthes, the readerly (bourgeois, mass-cultural) text is a "product"; it makes the reader a consumer. But the writerly text is "produced" by the reader him- or herself, because, as nothing but a galaxy of signifiers, it creates indeterminate ("plural") configurations of meaning. It is not a reified product whose meaning can be used up or exchanged for something else (i.e., for an interpretation). Aside from some of his terminology, it is difficult to distinguish the substance of Barthes's claims from modernist claims for innovation and difficulty. Any novel that breaks with existing conventions of narrative representation, that makes the reader work at reading, might be characterized as "writerly." The writerly and the postmodernist are, it seems, trapped in the logic of modernist writing. If there is a difference, it is one of degree or variation, not of function or composition.

Closely related to Barthes's writerly, and equally influential, is Foucault's description of the disappearance of the "writing subject" in "contemporary writing," expressed in paradigmatic form in the essay "What Is an Author?" Both McHale (who cites him throughout his book) and Foucault stress how the new writing breaks down distinctions between author and narrator, author and character, story and metastory, fiction and other types of writing. For Foucault, the new writing resists notions of "individualism" and advances a "proliferation of meaning" that the bourgeois category of the "author" ideologically limits (118–19). Beckett is his first and most important example of the new writing:

> Beckett nicely formulates the theme with which I would like to begin: "'What does it matter who is speaking,' someone said, 'what does it matter who is speaking.'" In this indifference appears one of the funda-mental ethical principles of contemporary writing (*écriture*). . . . Today's writing has freed itself from the dimension of expression. . . . It is an interplay of signs arranged less according to its signified content than according to the very nature of the signifier . . . a question of creating a space into which the writing subject constantly disappears. (101–102)

At the most general level, Foucault is advocating a type of postmodernism in the sense that he intends to deconstruct and move beyond key categories of modern literature, from realism to modernism: the "author" as genius, writing as representa-tion or meaning (as signified rather than signifier), literature as a form of "expres-sion," the autonomous individual, and so on.[16] At a performative level, however, Foucault's authoritative citing of a famous author at the beginning of his own deconstruction of the ideological "author function" is an internal contradiction of the type that poststructuralism, as a whole, cannot seem to avoid.[17] Much of Foucault's argument about the historical particularity of institutions of knowledge articulates, albeit in an original fashion, a Weberian view of the differentiation of the spheres of science, culture, and religion in modernity. Historically, writes Foucault, "it has not always been the same types of texts which have required attribution to an author"; in the seventeenth or eighteenth century it became necessary for literary texts to be attached to an individual author while scientific discourse became detached from the authority of the individual (Hippocrates, Pliny, etc.) and instead became "autho-rized" through experimentation and empirical evidence. Foucault's explanation of the author function employs a sociological form of intellectual history that Foucault's philosophy rejects. The problem arising when Beckett's work is assimilated into theories of postmodernist fiction are similar to the problems implicit in poststruc-turalism's reputed break with the modern human sciences.[18] What claims to be postmodernist or a break away from modernism is in effect a working out of ideas, problems, and oppositions already a part of the modernist intellectual imagination.[19]

The problems, however, are instructive. Foucault cites "Text for Nothing 3," a posttrilogy work in which Beckett's turn toward textuality is most pronounced. Like McHale and Barthes, he notes how Beckett's work stresses the signifier rather than the signified. This results, Foucault claims, in a move away from "expression," it releases a positive "plurality of meaning" (119), and serves to deemphasize the importance of the individual "writing subject," the individual author, which for Foucault is a sign of power and control, "a certain functional principle by which, in our culture, one limits, excludes and chooses; in short, by which one impedes the free circulation . . . the free composition . . . of fiction" (119). Thus, Beckett's work consciously (Foucault calls it an "ethical principle" of the new writing [101]) strives to foreground its own status as nonexpression, as signifier rather than signified, as "indifferent" to representing historically situated individuals. While Foucault imparts to these features an abstract democratic quality (he advocates the "free circulation" of fiction), he also avoids articulating any vision of the social good premised on the normative democratic value of individual rights. That the writing subject and the author function dissolve into "the anonymity of a murmur" (119) emerges as a precondition of a more democratic, pluralistic social world.

These aspects of Foucault's essay add something missing from both McHale and Barthes. Its more historical dimension implies a significant, reciprocal relationship between the rise, in the modern era, of the ideological, restrictive "author function" and this new writing in which "the writing subject cancels out the signs of his particular individuality" (102). But it is exactly this type of causal relationship that Foucault's antimodernist mode of argumentation can't make—or rather, resists making. As Foucault recognizes from the very outset, "this indifference [to questions of individual authorship] is not really a trait characterizing the manner in which one speaks and writes" (101). There is a gap between the historically situated notion of the author and the more amorphous poststructural notion of the writing subject, an unexplained divide between the modernity Foucault analyzes ("our era of industrial and bourgeois society, of individualism and private property" [119]) and the creative response of writers like Beckett. This gap, signalled by Foucault as something quite concrete ("the manner in which one speaks and writes"), can only be described historically, as a development within modernity itself, a question not of the "writing subject" but of the relation of the writer to the modern institutions of culture through which the author function operates. In other words, it is a question of the relationship between Beckett's consciously chosen project of dissolving, in fiction, the writing subject and the cultural-political situation of postwar writing.

This type of historical-institutional question is raised in Andreas Huyssen's account of postmodernism. Indeed, he begins by questioning what McHale and many others take for granted, "whether this transformation [in the arts] has generated genuinely new aesthetic forms or . . . mainly recycles techniques and strategies of modernism itself, reinscribing them into an altered cultural context" (181). In many respects, Huyssen's analysis is intended as a corrective to both formalist (like McHale's) and poststructuralist accounts of the avant garde, modernism and post-modernism. While McHale and Barthes construct their definitions of the postmodern or the writerly through a neomodernist opposition with popular culture, Huyssen places the relationship between postmodernism and mass culture at the center of his argument. Working through an analysis of the cultural politics of the avant garde between the wars and a critique of Adorno's view of modernism as a "reaction formation" to the culture industry and commodification (57), Huyssen reconstructs a model of modernism which views the works of Flaubert, Kafka, and Joyce as themselves shaped in a dynamic relationship with everyday cultural experiences. "Contrary to the claims of champions of the autonomy of art, contrary also to the ideologists of textuality," he writes, "the realities of modern life and the ominous expansion of mass culture throughout the social realm are always already inscribed into the articulation of aesthetic modernism. Mass culture has always been the hidden subtext of the modernist project" (47).

Huyssen wants to understand how (or if) postmodernist literature makes an attempt at bridging or dismantling the institutionally maintained divide between high and low culture. "At stake in this debate about postmodernism is the great divide between modern art and mass culture, which the art movements of the 1960s intentionally began to dismantle in their practical critique of the high modernist canon" (59). In many respects, Huyssen's argument has little to do with the immediate postwar fiction of writers like Beckett. While his contention is that "the most significant trends within postmodernism have challenged modernism's relentless hostility to mass culture" (188), by "modernism" Huyssen is explicitly referring to "a certain austere image of 'high modernism' as advanced by the New Critics and other custodians of modernist culture" (189). Thus, "the revolt of the 1960s [in pop art, Beat literature, Donald Barthelme, John Cage, for example] was never a rejection of modernism *per se,* but rather a revolt against that version of modernism which had been domesticated in the 1950s, become part of the liberal-conservative consensus of the times. . . . In other words, the revolt sprang precisely from the success of modernism. . . . Modernism had been perverted into a form of affirmative culture" (190).

"Against the codified high modernism of the preceding decades" (the decades in which Beckett wrote his major fiction), Huyssen contends, "the postmodernism of the 1960s tried to revitalize the heritage of the European avant garde" (188) (like Peter Bürger, Huyssen distinguishes the avant garde from canonical, "high" modernism). It did so in four ways: first, it displayed "a powerful sense of the future and new frontiers, of rupture and discontinuity, of crisis and generational conflict, an imagination reminiscent of . . . Dada and surrealism rather than high modernism" (191); second, it "included an iconoclastic attack on . . . the 'institution art' . . . the ways in which art's role in society is perceived and defined . . . produced, marketed, distributed, and consumed" (191–92); third, as with the 1920s avant garde's excitement about photography and film, it embodied an uncritical "technological optimism" in the "new media" of television, video, and computers (193); and fourth, it was characterized by a "largely uncritical attempt to validate popular culture as a challenge to the canon of high art, modernist or traditional" (194). Huyssen relates this understanding of the emergence of postmodernism in America to a European context. "The ethos of artistic avantgardism as iconoclasm, as probing reflection upon the ontological status of art in modern society . . . was culturally not yet as exhausted in the U.S. of the 1960s as it was in Europe. . . . From a European perspective, therefore, it looked like the endgame of the historical avantgarde rather than like the breakthrough to new frontiers it claimed to be. . . . American postmodernism of the 1960s was both: an American avantgarde *and* the endgame of international avantgardism" (195).[20]

As for Beckett's place within these transformations, Huyssen agrees with John Barth, quoting his 1980 claim that Beckett's *Stories and Texts for Nothing*, a "late modernist marvel," "was the effective exhaustion not of language or of literature but of the aesthetic of high modernism" (qtd. in Huyssen 189). Within Huyssen's schema, Beckett's most intense period of fiction writing, from *Murphy* in the mid-1930s to the *Texts* in 1955, falls into a gap, between the works of literary high modernism and the reaction, beginning in the late 1950s primarily in the United States, to canonical modernism, and the attempt to revive an avant-garde sensibility. Huyssen describes this gap in reference to the pressures that led to the canonization of high modernism in terms of an "austere" aesthetic autonomy. "The primary place of what I am calling the great divide was the age of Stalin and Hitler when the threat of totalitarian control over all culture forged a variety of defensive strategies meant to protect culture in general. . . . It is surely no coincidence that the Western codification of modernism . . . took place during the 1940s and 1950s, preceding and during the Cold War. . . . The age of Hitler, Stalin, and the Cold War produced specific accounts of modernism, such as those of Clement Greenberg and Adorno, whose aesthetic categories cannot be totally divorced from the pressures of that era" (197). If, for Huyssen, the postmodernism that emerged in the 1960s has enduring importance, it resides in the move beyond the cold-war logic of modernism "codified in the various classical accounts" of twentieth-century art, a logic which "no longer seems relevant to postmodernist artistic or critical sensibilities" (197).

None of these accounts of the new writing of the postwar period, by itself, adequately describes Beckett's response to the modernisms he had experienced in Dublin, London, and Paris between the wars. When taken together, however, they suggest how Beckett's innovations, beginning with the nouvelles, emerged from a set of aesthetic and cultural values already in a process of transformation. The "ontological" emphasis of his fiction links, rather than separates, Beckett's fiction to modernist aesthetics. From Foucault's perspective, this turn toward the signifier, like the author function itself, is tied to an historical process in which literature becomes bound up with institutional mediations among reader, writer, and text that delimit the "proliferation of meaning." Beckett's narrator, the beggar whose face is also a mask, and the ironic failure of the beggar's voice—"I tried to groan, Help! Help! But the tone that came out was that of polite conversation"—is a startling image of inexpressiveness and the effacement of the writing subject. But while Foucault posed the disappearance of expression and the autonomous subject as a solution or corrective to the restrictive author function, Beckett poses this dissolution as a problem in aesthetic communication, as an explicit contradiction thematized throughout his postwar fiction. The writing subject never disappears, but is forced to take up an untenable, paradoxical position, both inside and outside the bourgeois institution of "polite conversation" it hopes to escape.

The techniques Beckett developed in the nouvelles evince a narrative mode quite distinct from interwar high modernism. As Huyssen has convincingly argued, the postwar period saw the consolidation of a canon of modernism; under the auspices of academic criticism, "modernism" became the very thing against which both modernists and avant gardists had promoted their own, difficult, at times intentionally unreadable and offensive work: official bourgeois culture. Beckett's postwar fiction occupies a cultural-historical space in which the tensions between the actual aesthetic practices of the interwar years—among aestheticism, Joycean modernism, avant-gardist provocation, and the tendentious literature of the thirties—were still in the process of being flattened out, reduced to a linear, teleological narrative of an austere formalism. For Beckett, however, the antinomies of the past were still operant, his failure to negotiate them a formative pressure. If Beckett continued to write from what Huyssen calls modernism's "pedestal of high art," it is a pedestal whose foundations Beckett makes contradictory and whose pretensions are vociferously mocked by the two narrator-heroes—one, a hapless victim of decorum, the other an "agent" and exemplar of bourgeois propriety—of his first and perhaps most successful postwar novel, *Molloy.*

IV

Molloy (one): Molloy, the Subject

Molloy's Class Consciousness

I had a certain number of encounters in this forest, naturally,
where does one not, but nothing to signify.

The reader even minimally acquainted with Beckett's trilogy immediately recognizes in this sentence from the first section of *Molloy* a set of Beckettian constants: the ubiquitous "I," the nameless forest, the parodic obeisance to formality, the philosophical twist that negates the apparent announcement of a significant event: "but nothing to signify." The next sentence, typically, negates the negation: "I notably encountered a charcoal burner" (112).

Which takes precedence? Will the encounter be notable and interpretable or "nothing to signify," a fragment inscribed in the universal text of the absurd? Beckett intends that his narrator produce paradox, not certainty. Whatever Molloy claims in prolepsis, in the next few pages Beckett gives us in detail the notable, nonsignifying encounter, only to have Molloy conclude: "I have delayed over an incident of no interest in itself, like all that has a moral" (115).

These are the parameters of many episodes in *Molloy:* it does not signify, but it is notable; it has no interest in itself, but it has a moral. What is the function of this self-reflexive mode of narration? Does it affect the reader's understanding of the encounter in the forest? Or is the hermeneutic paradox a comment on Molloy-the-narrator's difficulty in understanding an event from his own life? What relevance, if any, do such questions have to the action vividly described between the framing sentences?

> I might have loved him, I think, if I had been seventy years younger. I never really had much love to spare, but all the same I had my little quota, when I was small, and it went to the old men, when it could. . . .
> He was all over me, begging me to share his hut, believe it or not. A total stranger. Sick with solitude probably. I say charcoal burner, but I really don't know. . . . A long dialogue ensued, interspersed with groans. . . . I asked him to show me the nearest way out of the forest. I grew eloquent. His reply was exceedingly confused. Either I didn't understand a word he said, or he didn't understand a word I said, or he knew nothing, or he

wanted to keep me near him. It was towards this fourth hypothesis that in all modesty I leaned, for when I made to go, he held me back by the sleeve. So I smartly freed a crutch and dealt him a good dint on the skull. (113)

The paradox about the hermeneutic status of the encounter itself—notable, meaningless, uninteresting, moral—is echoed in the narrated action: Molloy trying to understand and communicate with a stranger. Another set of Beckettian constants is evident: isolation, sickness, poverty, confusion, the thwarted need for companionship and love, and a blow to the head. The humor of the "fourth hypothesis" depends on the contrast between the vocabulary of logic and the pathetic content: it signals the fact that intellectuals and "charcoal burners" never converse, except perhaps in jokes.[1] As the encounter continues, the humor turns cruel:

> That calmed him. The dirty old brute. I got up and went on. But I hadn't gone more than a few paces . . . when I turned and went back to where he lay, to examine him. Seeing he had not ceased to breathe I contented myself with giving him a few warm kicks in the ribs, with my heels. This is how I went about it. I carefully chose the most favourable position, a few paces from the body, with my back of course turned to it. Then, nicely balanced on my crutches, I began to swing, backwards, forwards, feet pressed together, or rather legs pressed together. . . . in an ever widening arc, until I decided the moment had come and launched myself forward with all my strength and consequently, a moment later, backward, which gave the desired result. . . . The shock knocked me down. Naturally. . . . I rested a moment, then got up, picked up my crutches, took up my position on the other side of the body and applied myself with method to the same exercise. I always had a mania for symmetry. (114)

"Symmetry" is an aesthetic value. Violence is parodied though artifice. Molloy is an aesthete as well as a crippled vagrant. His rendering of how he "went about it" is a discourse on artistic "method," an "exercise" in style. The last line might apply to the narrator or Beckett himself, formalist craftsman of the famous sucking stone scene in *Molloy,* with its compulsive attention to problems of "circulation" and "trim" (93–100). But Beckett never lets an emphasis on aesthetic form become detached from the material content through which form becomes manifest. From Murphy's dilemma deciding the order in which he will eat the assorted biscuits of his impoverished lunch, to the mathematical permutations of Watt feeding the famished dog, to Molloy's need to suck his stones in an aesthetically pleasing manner, the "mania" for an artful order, for a principle of distinction, is always contrasted with a condition of poverty and privation. We laugh because we know starving people aren't concerned with aesthetic form; we know that Beckett's characters don't seriously signify suffering because of the heightened attention to artifice in their pathetic attempts to overcome misery. Such explicitly self-conscious writing, so distant from the concerns of realism or naturalism, mingles uneasily with realism's attention to the margins of liberal society. Is Molloy's well-wrought beating of the charcoal burner a refraction of Beckett beating down and parodying any sympathetic identification the reader might experience with his storytelling vagrants, as if to render senseless any resemblance between his own abstract art and the prosaic messages of socially engaged literature? Is Beckett's purpose in letting Molloy, for once, give the blows instead of receive them, an attack not on social injustice but on literature's presumption to take the side of the powerless victim against an alienating, unjust social world?

The end of the encounter drives the questions home:

> But I must have aimed a little low and one of my heels sank into something soft. However. For if I had missed the ribs, with that heel, I had no doubt landed in the kidney, oh not hard enough to burst it, no, I fancy not. People imagine, because you are old, poor, crippled, terrified, that you can't stand up for yourself, and generally speaking that is so. But given favourable conditions, a feeble and awkward assailant, in your own class what, and a lonely place, and you have a good chance of showing what stuff you are made of. And it is doubtless in order to revive interest in this possibility, too often forgotten, that I have delayed over an incident of no interest in itself, like all that has a moral. (114–15)

The aesthetics of violent symmetry becomes a lesson about a law of social existence: Molloy has a reactionary class consciousness. He knows he can only assert his autonomy—show his stuff, stand up for himself—by crushing someone equally low but a little more vulnerable. If Molloy is vicious, his cruelty is justified by both the formalist-aesthetic need for symmetry and the psychological need of the victimized vagrant—"I am full of fear," Molloy cries, "I have gone in fear all my life, in fear of blows" (28)—to exact vengeance on whomever is weaker than he. Which takes precedence? Is Beckett balancing Molloy the victim with Molloy the victimizer to provide formal symmetry, as he does by breaking the novel into paradoxically corresponding Molloy/vagrant and Moran/bourgeois sections, or to provide a "moral" about how the social hierarchy reproduces itself by pitting victim against victim? Why are the formalist techniques in Beckett's fiction so often presented in conjunction with images, parodic and exaggerated, of the "poor, crippled, terrified" remnants of social decay?

The paradox of the framing sentences might, it seems, bear a significant relation to the questions raised by the narrated action in the encounter. If the episode simultaneously is "nothing to signify" and contains a moral intended to correct what people imagine about the powerless vagrant, then Beckett is both a formalist unconcerned with intentional messages and a social critic. Such divergent cultural roles, however, are hard to imagine as anything but opposites, not least because, as the encounter itself suggests, an overriding concern with experiments in form seems to militate against or even suppress the reader's sympathy for or serious engagement with Molloy as a meaningful symbol of anything at all outside the text.

The antinomies embedded in Beckett's metanarrative play with meaningless-ness, morals, and class-conscious cruelty have led admiring commentators on *Molloy* to reproduce, rather than untangle, the hermeneutic puzzles that the novel itself stages. Since its initial reception in 1951, the novel has received a curious roundelay of nonsignifying summaries, from cultural and literary critics alike: "everyone sees in it what he wants to see" (Nadeau, quoted in Abbott 92); "it discloses no more than what it literally means" (Sontag 29); "[its] technique results in a total devaluation of language by accentuating the arbitrariness with which it is applied to the objects it seeks to grasp" (Iser 164–65); "[its] characteristic quality . . . has less to do with the expression of ideas than the manipulation of verbal forms. . . . There exists no intentional message that may be extracted from the verbal motions of the text" (Hill 120). Not surprisingly, academic critics have proclaimed that the effort to interpret *Molloy* is exhausted; it can now only be regarded as a dispersion of textual effects.[2]

The turn away from interpretation, which began to gain prestige in academic literary criticism in the decade following *Molloy's* publication, is both insightful and shortsighted.[3] It makes sense that, if *Molloy* itself foregrounds problems of under-standing, then criticism of the novel should foreground similar problems. Interpreta-tion, as a fixed instance of one understanding of a text which leaves the problem of meaning itself unaddressed, avoids the explicit hermeneutic issues at the center of such fiction. The insight of the anti-interpretive stance recognizes that the novel compels the reader to consciously experience meaning, as constructed through narra-tive and language, as a problem.

This insight, however, has a serious drawback. The anti-interpretive stance replaces interpretation with a demonstration of how the text creates a plurality of indeterminate meanings, none of which is privileged over others. Meaning, from this perspective, is viewed as a textual effect rather than an intentional message. But *Molloy* does undeniably incorporate a specific intention, forcefully and completely worked out: to make the understanding of its own content paradoxical, both within the novel, as the narrators' confusions attest, and for the bemused reader. In light of this, the anti-interpretive stance seems self-invalidating. As a critical *response* to the intentional construction of textual paradox in the novel, the analysis of textual effects actually depends on the very thing it claims the text does not have: an overarching intention. If this too is a paradox, it is not a meaningless one. Like Molloy's anti-worldly class consciousness, the intentional cross-circuiting of narrative sense is part of Beckett's quite serious play with the cultural politics of the modern novel.

In Beckett's fiction, the "significance of a paradox is never the paradox itself, but what it is a symptom of. For a paradox demonstrates that our understanding of some basic concept or cluster of concepts is crucially flawed, that the concepts break down in limiting cases" (Barwise 4). *Molloy* is such a limiting case; it demonstrates the inadequacy of understanding narrative as *either* textual effect *or* communicative message. On one hand, in *Molloy* Beckett plays havoc with the conventions of narrative structure and literary language to such an extent that positive meaning is denied value. On the other hand, Beckett's foregrounding of these hermeneutic problems is sustained through the novel's communicative, culturally symbolic content. The two narrators' extreme socioeconomic difference, Molloy's violence and moral transgressions, his self-deprecating awareness of hierarchies of taste and decorum, Moran's middle-class "horror of the body and its functions," the heightened emphases on interiority and subjectivity, the paralyzing sense of alienation and dissolution of civic bonds, the conflict between private inner freedom and public coercion: all these aspects of the novel bespeak its relation to the literary critique of social modernity. The hermeneutic problems arise from the interplay of, and mutual interference between, these two conflicting intentional features: *Molloy* is a novel that evokes protest against the debasement and suffering of its eponymous hero and, at the same time, textually disrupts the narrative conventions through which this critical attitude is sustained. Unlike many of the great works of modernism, *Molloy* holds no key to the puzzles it presents, there is no master schema or mythic parallels, no intricate imbrication of perspectives, no encoded lexicon or symbolic tapestry. The novel is compulsively readable, compulsively suggestive, the better to frustrate compulsively its reception. In this sense, the paradox in narrative communication is also a paradox about the social function of art, about what it means for a novel to critique or disclose an engagement with the world.

In his essay on *Endgame*, Adorno observed that Beckett's distortion of the traditional elements of tragedy gave the play a structure that sustained and determined its protesting "unintelligibility."[4] Similarly, underlying the nonsignifying encounters narrated by Molloy and Moran are the skeletal remains of narrative form, from epic imitation of action to the impressionist interior monologue. In the *nouvelles* Beckett had resurrected a storytelling voice poised tensely between a longing for stories like "my father used to read me" and a rejected-rejecting social world whose "havoc" of images was devoid of narrative authority (30). In *Molloy* Beckett exploits the voice of the storyteller much more thoroughly, and juxtaposes its implicit narrative stability and authority against one of the modernist novel's most characteristic features, the intensively subjective point-of-view. Adorno once remarked that Beckett's principle concern in his novels and plays was with the "abdication of the subject" ("Commitment" 314). But Adorno's polemic entanglement with both Lukács and Sartre led him to overstate the case.[5] What *Molloy* expresses is not a negation of subjectivity, but a pervasive ambivalence about the individual as speaking, knowing subject. Through parody and compulsive exaggeration, Beckett makes explicit the contradictions inherent in the modernist literary aspiration to articulate the autonomous voice of individual existence. Beckett's self-absorbed storyteller, both victim and victimizer, ironically boasts of his sense of autonomy at the troubled conjunction of a "moral" and "nothing to signify."

The Production of the Story

The problem of understanding *Molloy* and its relation to the traditions of novelistic mimesis is writ large in Beckett's division of the book into two first-person narratives. Molloy is presented as a pathologically withdrawn, penniless vagabond with a grotesque physical appearance; Moran, in contrast, is a church-going Catholic property owner, a slavish follower of bourgeois decorum. Molloy, whose narrative in part one tells of his encounters as he wanders in search of his mother, becomes the subject of Moran's "report" in part two. The obvious philosophical joke, that Molloy and Moran are counterparts in the phenomenological dynamics of perception and knowledge, is complicated by the suggestive, undecipherable network of similarities between the two narrator-heroes, as if in fact they are, or become, the same person. Various interpretations of their relationship—id and ego, body and mind, child and father—are plausible enough, but none actually cover the full extent of Beckett's division of the book in this way.[6] What seems undeniable is that two forces are at play here. First, Beckett makes the contrast between the narrators explicitly in terms of social status, regardless of whether the representation of social status is intended to be taken seriously or realistically. Molloy or Moran may, after all, only be textual constructs, and their self-enclosed "I" may be nothing but a rhetorical game. But the only way the reader can get to this, the way that Beckett gets to it (if that's indeed where Beckett means to go), is through the initial contrast, which is a contrast in social content. Thus, no defendable interpretive choice can be made between, first, Molloy and Moran as vagrant and bourgeois, or, second, as arbitrary textual constructs that merge into each other. If, as the views of the novel quoted above imply, the social content of the novel is negated in favor of the play of signifiers, nevertheless the social content is there, as the thing to be negated. The point is simple; I belabor it only because it seems so overlooked in the critical literature. Beckett might have made the central contrast through purely psychological or philosophical vectors. But as a novelist, he chose to make it through socioeconomic attributes.

As part one of *Molloy* begins, well before the reader comes up against the contrast in social difference and the textual network of similarities, Beckett embeds the figure of Molloy in a narrative structure that complicates the idea of self-expression implicit in first-person narration. The modernist convention of the narrative frame contextualizes an act of storytelling as a transaction among author, speaker, and audience; paradigmatic modernist examples are Marlow aboard the yacht in *Heart of Darkness,* or the female figure meeting Jim Burden aboard the train in *My Antonia.*[7] The opening of *Molloy* exploits the convention of the frame by making the storytelling act a literal image of novel writing:

> I am in my mother's room. It's I who live there now. I don't know how I
> got there. . . . I was helped. I'd never have got there alone. There's this
> man who comes every week. . . . He gives me money and takes away the
> pages. So many pages, so much money. Yes, I work now, a little like I

used to, except that I don't know how to work any more. That doesn't matter apparently. What I'd like now is to speak of the things that are left, say my good-byes, finish dying. They don't want that. Yes, there is more than one, apparently. . . . When he comes for the fresh pages he brings back the previous week's. They are marked with signs I don't understand. . . . When I've done nothing he gives me nothing, he scolds me. Yet I don't work for money. For what then? I don't know. The truth is I don't know much. (7–8)

Molloy seems to be a caricature of the alienated modern writer, his audience an anonymous "they" who care nothing for the writer's wishes but simply treat the "pages" as a commodity. Molloy, like a true artist, does not write for the money. His wish "to speak of the things that are left, say my goodbyes, finish dying" is both lyrical and spiritual, in contrast to the representative "man" and his businesslike editorial attitude. The short sentences and the conventional feeling of alienation, expressed in a resigned mood, give the first page of *Molloy* the quality of a confession, written under compulsion, of a defeated, sensitive soul. Interspersed between the simple statements, however, are phrases indicating a disruption of understanding and communication: "I don't know how to work any more"; "signs I don't understand"; "the truth is I don't know much." As the framing paragraph continues, the series of declarative, rather elemental sentences about Molloy's situation in his mother's room—"I sleep in her bed. I piss and shit in her pot" (8)—become imbued with an increasing futility:

> Here's my beginning. Because they're keeping it apparently. I took a lot
> of trouble with it. Here it is. It gave me a lot of trouble. It was the
> beginning, do you understand? Whereas now it's nearly the end. Is what
> I do now any better? I don't know. That's beside the point. Here's my
> beginning. It must mean something, or they wouldn't keep it. Here it is.
> (8)

Beckett inverts the cliche of the misunderstood artist who persists in writing despite the unwillingness or inability of the public to accept his art. Rather than explain Molloy's motives for telling his story, the narrative frame represents him in the situation of writing without knowing what his writing means or why he does it. When he declares, "It must mean something, or they wouldn't keep it," he resigns the understanding of his story to "them," and at the same time recognizes that his story *does* have a meaning, even if he can only surmise this from someone else's response. It is precisely the commodification of his work by the anonymous "they" that allows Molloy to write without knowing why.

The ironic contradiction here is difficult to characterize because it works so well: the effect is not to relay some observation about how an individual can never grasp the enigma of his own existence, but rather to reveal that no matter how much the production of the story depends on some agency outside the individual author, the story is nonetheless posed as an extremely personal self-expression, a confessional first-person narration. The content that is easily understood because it clearly refers to a cultural icon, the alienated writer in his room, is subject simultaneously to reversal and reaffirmation. The more Molloy realizes his position is false, the more alienated he feels: he will go on to tell the story of his life as a self-originating act, knowing all along that the story's meaning isn't really his. The force of the first-person narrative form, as it is worked out in the confessional, victimized mood, implies that the occasion and aim of Molloy's story will be self-understanding, an exploration of how Molloy got "there," to his mother's room, both physically and psychically. Molloy's confusion, about how his writing acquires meaning and how he came to the retrospective point from which he narrates, is refracted through both the social content and the innovative form. The experiment in narrative Beckett carries out in part one is predicated on an explicit contradiction drawn from the legacy of modernism. Writing is a product of the autonomous self, but it's meaningless without the "man" who buys it; the narrated world is a construct of an individual consciousness, but to adopt this perspective means never knowing how one "got there," to the place of narration, in the first place.

The metanarrative self-reflection Molloy delivers near the end of part one, just before he resumes the journey to his mother's room, indicates how this contradiction is played out throughout the novel:

> And yet it might have been better for me to try and stay [in the forest]. But I also said, Yet a little while, at the rate things are going, and I won't be able to move, but will have to stay, where I happen to be, unless someone comes and carries me. Oh, I did not say it in such limpid language. And when I say I said, etc., all I mean is that I knew confusedly things were so, without knowing exactly what it was all about. And every time I say, I said this, or, I said that, or speak of a voice saying, far away inside me, Molloy, and then a fine phrase more or less clear and simple . . . I am merely complying with the age old convention that demands you either lie or hold your peace. For what really happened is quite different. And I did not say, Yet a little while, at the rate things are going, etc., but that resembled perhaps what I would have said, if I had been able. In reality I said nothing at all, but I heard a murmur, something gone wrong with the silence. . . . And then sometimes there arose within me, confusedly, a kind of consciousness, which I express by saying, I said etc., or . . . by means of other figures quite as deceitful, as for example, It seemed to me that, etc., or, I had the impression that, etc., for it seemed to me nothing at all, and I had no impression of any kind . . . and that I might doubtless have expressed otherwise and better, if I had gone to the trouble. . . . So I said, Yet a little while, at the rate things are going, and I won't be able to move, but will have to stay. . . . (118–19)

Molloy attempts to explain the disjuncture between the "limpid language" of his narration and the confusion surrounding what "really happened." At one level, this is a parody of classic statements of novelistic impressionism, from Proust to Woolf, that isolate the subjective impression as the appropriate subject matter of fiction.[8] But the passage goes further than parody. The acuity of the narrating voice, which seems the opposite of the confusion and helplessness it describes, breaks apart the unity of narrator and character that the convention of the first person is intended to convey. It achieves this not by dispelling any illusions about the referential function of language or the relation of the "I" to the self. On the contrary, the passage reasserts the necessity of a subjective point of view in spite of the awareness that its "impressions" are false. Literary impressionism, in one of its varieties, argued for the subjective truth of the aesthetic impression over the "facts" of science or history.[9] But here, the subjective impression is ultimately irrelevant: "I had no impression of any kind." The passage turns impressionism on its head, and what is finally asserted, "So I said, Yet a little while, at the rate things are going, and I won't be able to move" is exactly the "lie" that Molloy's metanarrative reflection was supposedly going to correct. The tension between the two emphases—Molloy's confusion in the woods and his awareness of the "conventions" which communicate his confusion and helplessness—is also a tension between contrasting aesthetic logics. While mocking impressionism's privileging of subjective experience, the blunt recognition that "you either lie or hold your peace" argues that the subjective voice, the interior "murmur," is the only one possible for Molloy. As Molloy's eloquent chronicle of his own disordered speechlessness, part one of the novel presents the use of the first-person voice as both a necessity and a tragically inadequate perspective.

Molloy and the Police

Beckett's ambivalence toward the modernist emphases on interiority and subjective knowledge is never expressed through an alternate, objective view of the world. Much of the comedy and pathos in the encounters described by Molloy are driven by the vertiginous disjuncture between the hapless wandering of the terrified, grotesque vagrant and the unknowing testimonial eloquence of the narrator who writes from his mother's room. In one sense, this disjuncture signals an absolute discontinuity between experience and literary expression: the more alienated the writer Molloy feels, the more his story conjures up images of social and physical degradation, and the more he makes rhetorical moves to signal that the words and impressions of Molloy-the-vagrant are nothing but lies. But Beckett builds into the novel a satirical, running commentary on power, authority, and identity that reflects back critically on Molloy the writer. If in the nouvelles the beggar-narrator was ultimately denied a psychological self by both the rejected-rejecting social world and the rhetorical foreclosure on narrative communication, in *Molloy* the contradictory disunity of the first-person voice allows Beckett to develop this social-rhetorical theme episodically, within the retrospective narrative itself. This development, and the type of self-critical comic pathos it creates, is clearly evident in Molloy's encounter with the police, when he is ordered to produce his identity papers.

The episode begins with Molloy's approach to the unnamed town. Although Beckett's hero has a bourgeois sensibility, he is denied the social requisites of family and education that might allow him a bourgeois existence. He follows the imperative "to go and see my mother," as if the knowledge of his birth might explain his right to exist; likewise, he enters the town, goaded by a "craving for a fellow," a simple desire to be sociable (19). Much more so than with the hero of the nouvelles, Beckett makes Molloy's psyche in the likeness of the expectations of the social world from which he is excluded. The town, too, is reminiscent of the hollowed-out modernity of the first postwar fictions:

> I covered several miles and found myself under the ramparts. There I dismounted in compliance with the regulations. Yes, cyclists entering and leaving the town are required by the police to dismount, cars to go into bottom gear and horsedrawn vehicles to slow down to a walk. The reason for the regulation is I think this, that the ways into and of course out of this town are narrow and darkened by enormous vaults, without exception. It is a good rule and I observe it religiously. (25)

The image of the "narrow and darkened" passage evokes the hero's difficulty in entering anything even remotely indicative of the social world. This passage may also stand for the birth canal, as some critics have suggested, given the maternal object of Molloy's journey, his infantile physical helplessness, and Beckett's occasional enthusiasm for Jungian philosophy.[10] The bicycle on which he is mounted, however, is Beckett's archetype of the quaintly modern, just as the passage seems like a checkpoint at a border. Molloy must expend great effort to negotiate these "difficult straits" because "of the difficulty I have in advancing on my crutches and pushing my bicycle at the same time" (25). As in the nouvelles, physical and narrative movement is always debilitated in relation to the rejected-rejecting social world. In this case, the rejection is heightened to a confrontation, as Molloy immediately runs up against an administered public realm:

> But a little further on I heard myself hailed. I raised my head and saw a policeman. Elliptically speaking, for it was only later, by way of induction, or deduction, I forget which, that I knew what it was. What are you doing there? he said. I'm used to that question, I understood it immediately. Resting, I said. Resting, he said. Resting, I said. Will you answer my question? he cried. So it always is when I'm reduced to confabulation, I honestly believe I have answered the question and in reality I do nothing of the kind. . . . It ended in my understanding that my way of

resting, my attitude when at rest . . . was a violation of I don't know
what, public order, public decency. (25–26)

The powerless outsider's confrontation with the forces of law and order, like the
motif of the alienated artist, is a familiar cultural icon. The joke here, Beckett's
contribution to the art of burlesque, is that Molloy's existentially honest reply of
simply existing, of "resting," is never a valid one, because to demand to know "what
are you doing?" is the prerogative of authority, not philosophical speculation. As
Moran remarks later in the novel: "If there is one question I dread, to which I have
never been able to invent a satisfactory answer, it is the question what am I doing"
(237). If in *Murphy* philosophical repose from the mercantile world held a sincere
transcendental promise, in *Molloy* activity of any kind, including the act of doing
nothing (see the discussion of Moran in the next chapter), is held to a strict worldly
logic: everything Molloy thinks or does or does not do is ultimately referred to the
excluded social world.

Instead of opposing aesthetic and worldly modes of communication, as Beckett
had done in his interwar writing, in *Molloy* communication and coercion are entirely
intertwined. To say anything at all is to give way to a deluding bad faith in the
liberating effects of self-expression. For Molloy, no amount of searching self-reflection
will ever yield a coherent identity. What replaces a psychologically autonomous
identity is an entirely political one. The hypostatized self of modernist interiority has
its counterpart in the reified self of the police state:

> Your papers! he cried. Ah my papers. Now the only papers I carry with
> me are bits of newspaper, to wipe myself, you understand, when I have a
> stool. Oh I don't say I wipe myself every time I have a stool, no, but I like
> to be in a position to do so, if I have to. . . . In a panic I took this paper
> from my pocket and thrust it under his nose. (26)

This misunderstanding over the demand for "papers" would certainly have had
a potent resonance in Paris in 1951, when the novel was first published. More
generally, of course, both having one's papers in order and wiping oneself "every time"
are forms of socialization.[11] The dynamic between Molloy's antisocial body and the
mimetic havoc of his story, a result of the attenuation of the socially ordered narrative
space, is emblematized in one of Beckett's many double-edged jokes: "Hole" is both
the name of a town (193) and "the symbol of those passed over in silence . . . a link
between me and the other excrement . . . the true portal of our being" (107). Molloy
acquiesces, but his good intentions have no meaning. For Molloy, both resisting and
giving in to authority amount to the same thing; the radical rejection of the world
staged in Beckett's fiction is quite purposely intended to signal capitulation. Thus,
when Molloy is dragged to the police station, all he wants to do is comply, like a good
citizen:

He [the police sergeant] listened to his subordinate's report and then began to interrogate me in a tone which, from the point of view of civility, left increasingly to be desired, in my opinion. Between his questions and my answers, I mean those deserving of consideration, the intervals were more or less long and turbulent. I am so little used to being asked anything that when I am asked something I take some time to know what. And the mistake I make is this, that instead of quietly reflecting on what I have just heard, and heard distinctly, not being hard of hearing, in spite of all I have heard, I hasten to answer blindly, fearing perhaps lest my silence fan their anger to fury. I am full of fear, I have gone in fear all my life, in fear of blows. (27–28)

The contrasts here are revealing: the tone mimics a refined, almost genteel conversation, but in the service of explaining why the terrified Molloy can't converse. Molloy is confused and antisocial in the presence of others because he is afraid of being beaten. In turn, it is the fear of being beaten that makes him unable to "reflect" or answer. In the end he realizes it is his fear-induced silence that will lead to yet another beating. Molloy's solipsism follows a law of self-fulfilling injustice. Whether he answer blindly or remain silent, he is bound to fail. There is no way outside the circle; his inwardness is not a philosophical stance, it is a disastrous defense. In its literal clarity, this passage offers a plausible explanation for the hermeneutic problems Molloy (as vagrant) encounters and (as narrator) produces throughout the novel. He is a beaten-down beggar, cringing before the authorities who have made him what he is. The demand for common sense, like the demand to know "what are you doing," always appears as a threat that destroys the hope of the sufficient reason necessary for intersubjective communication in the first place.

After "turbulent" intervals of miscommunication in the face of the police's demand to identify himself, Molloy finally has a flash of enlightenment: "My name is Molloy, I cried, all of a sudden, now I remember. Nothing compelled me to give this information, but I gave it, hoping to please, I suppose" (29). Commanded to give his name, he can only remember it when the outer compulsion is internalized and the sense of his own freedom is restored. Beckett presents Molloy's moment of autonomy as servile condescension, "hoping to please": "But they only have to be a little gentle, I mean refrain from hitting me, and I seldom fail to give satisfaction" (28). Freely given under compulsion, the name Molloy contains the contradictory play of inner autonomy and outer compulsion, of social negation and social determinism, characteristic of the novel as a whole. Its unavoidable reference to anglicized Irish ethnicity contrasts sharply with the novel's equally unavoidable lack of reference to historical time and place. As an Irish name its status is paradoxical, since it signals both an Irish "authenticity" and a stereotyped, derisive image of an Irish peasantry. References to Irish cultural politics, so specific in *Murphy* that Beckett was sued by an Irish poet parodied in the novel, are here reduced to nominative ciphers. Like the emptied-out images of modernity he began to construct in the nouvelles, the cryptic fragments of

Anglo-Irish cultural context that Beckett builds in to his postwar fiction function to signal the impossibility of divorcing narrative from the geopolitical world, even when the world is refused as an object of representation.[12]

In the nouvelles, as we have seen, Beckett staged the expulsion from social identity that predicated his turn toward the "text" as the space of narration. In *Molloy*, the hero is so thoroughly invested in the text from the very beginning, disengaged and writing in his mother's room, that any oppportunity to return to the liminally social world is violently rejected. The source of the invitation to rejoin civil society is, typically, in Beckett, the institution of welfare:

> But suddenly a woman rose up before me. . . . I still wonder today if it wasn't the social worker. She was holding out to me . . . a mug full of a greyish concoction which must have been green tea with saccharine and powdered milk. . . . Between mug and saucer a thick slab of dry bread was precariously lodged, so that I began to say, in a kind of anguish, It's going to fall. . . . A moment later I myself was holding, in my trembling hands, this little pile of tottering disparities . . . without understanding how the transfer had been effected. Let me tell you this, when social workers offer you, free, gratis, and for nothing, something to hinder you from swooning, which with them is an obsession, it is useless to recoil, they will pursue you to the ends of the earth, the vomitory in their hands. . . . Against the charitable gesture there is no defense, that I know of. You sink your head, you put out your hands all trembling and twined together and you say, Thank you. . . . To him who has nothing it is forbidden not to relish filth. (29–30)

The detail in the description of the proffered "filth" is reminiscent of more journalistic literary accounts of social welfare—Orwell's evocation of poorhouse tea and bread in *Down and Out in Paris and London,* for example. The aphoristic moral—"to him who has nothing it is forbidden not to relish filth"—like the "moral" of the encounter with the charcoal burner, is bound up with Molloy's class consciousness, his status as a grotesque vagrant with the sensibility of an outraged bourgeois. Whenever an episode in *Molloy* settles into a positive statement, Beckett immediately undercuts it, as if to deny the hero any dimension of dissent, no matter how ineffectual. Thus when Molloy is later released from jail, he is "conscious of my wrongs, knowing now the reasons for my arrest, alive to my irregular situation as revealed by the inquiry" (31). The encounter leads only to inwardness and fawning self-accusation. Indeed, Molloy's asocial, antirealist qualities are the means of his salvation: "To apply the letter of the law to a creature like me is not an easy matter. . . . If it is unlawful to be without papers, why did they not insist on my getting them. Because that costs money and I had none?" (31). If in "The End" it was the Marxist orator who supplied the beggar with the totally objectified vision of his own degradation, here it is liberal civil society. Shame replaces revolutionary invective.

Regarding himself "a deplorable sight, a deplorable example," and resigned to "never rest in that way again" (31), Molloy slinks away from the town, back into the forest and the space of the text, with its permutations, negations, and other tactics of mimetic foreclosure.

In the encounter with the police, Beckett builds up the requisite social content against which the devaluation of narrative mimesis takes place. But even more, there is a satiric edge that Beckett aims at himself, or least at the implied image of the author behind the writing, unknowing Molloy. The erudition that was so archly on display in the omniscient narratives of *More Pricks than Kicks* and *Murphy* becomes, for Beckett, the ultimate source of shame. If in the transitional novel *Watt* Beckett numbly banned intellectual effort from the narrative procedure, in part one of *Molloy* he makes the social distribution of knowledge and taste the decisive social content. Because the autonomous inner self and aesthetic autonomy were fused values in the modernist enterprise (see the discussion in the following section), Beckett's ambivalence toward one is always an ambivalence toward the other. Molloy's banishment from the norms of the psychological self and civil society is also his banishment from the institutionalized values of discrimination, personal and cultural.[13] The most blatant sign of the disjuncture between writer and vagrant within the single figure of Molloy is his consummate knowledge of his own ignorance:

> I have only to be told what good behaviour is and I am well-behaved, within the limits of my physical possibilities. . . . And if I have always behaved like a pig, the fault lies not with me but with my superiors, who corrected me only on points of detail instead of showing me the essence of the system, after the manner of the great English schools, and the guiding principles of good manners, without going wrong, from the former to the latter, and how to trace back to its ultimate source a given comportment. For that would have allowed me, before parading in public certain habits such as the finger in the nose, the scratching of the balls, digital emunction and the peripatetic piss, to refer them to the first rules of a reasoned theory. On this subject I had only negative and empirical notions, which means I was in the dark, most of the time, and all the more completely as a lifetime of observations had left me doubting the possibility of systematic decorum, even within a limited area. (32)

The controlling contrasts here are between "the great English schools" and Molloy's "lifetime of observations," between "reasoned theory" and the "scratching of the balls," between the accusation against Molloy's "superiors" and his self-characterization as "a pig."[14] The function of the contradictory first-person voice is essential to Beckett's purpose, because it allows him to speak of Molloy's suffering and isolation from both within and outside experience, to parody both the pretence of high learning in a world where material deprivation makes nonsense of systematic philosophy and the pretence of trying to make social suffering the occasion for high art. In this sense, Beckett's use of the vagrant motif recalls Joyce's use of myth in *Ulysses*. If, as Moretti argued, Joyce's parody was double edged, bringing myth down to earth while playing mythic grandeur over and against demotic everyday life, in *Molloy* philosophical art and social suffering mock one another equally. The major innovation in Beckett's postwar aesthetic ethos, in this regard, lies in the way he represents the strain of keeping within the mind of the vagrant, of the "long confused emotion" (32) of Molloy's life. In part one of *Molloy*, the narrating intelligence, although clearly capable of repeating the lessons of "the great English schools," is pathetically confined to Molloy's mother's room. This is one reason why we never find out how Molloy "got there." What Molloy's sociologically astute critique of the hierarchy of decorum demonstrates is how much Beckett's concern with the ethics of writing now weighed on his devotion to aesthetic autonomy. The self-contradictory, storytelling voice of Molloy, the nonsignifying writer, the fearful speaker, proved a powerful technique for refiguring the relation between inner mind and outer reality, between an art that refused, on principle, to communicate and a story about the confused suffering of those who dwell in silence.

Subjectivity as a Modernist Universal

One of the more meaningful outcomes of debates about postmodernism and the culture of late capitalism has been the concomitant reassessment, during the last few decades, of the category of modernism itself. As Raymond Williams has argued, the critique of the established view of high modernism entails the rejection of a self-validating "selective tradition" that has singled out features like formal innovation or the representation of individual consciousness as "modernist universals." What Williams seeks to account for, instead, is the modernist period's "internal diversity of methods and emphases: a restless and often directly competitive sequence of innovations and experiments, always more immediately recognized by what they are breaking from than by what, in any simple way, they are breaking towards" (*Politics* 43). Similarly, modernist "universals" themselves need to be reinterpreted outside "the context of a literary ideology created by modernism itself" (Menand 6). Following the work of Williams and sociologist of literature Peter Bürger, I would like to offer a brief view of the genesis of modernist "subjectivity" relevant to Beckett's innovation in first-person narration in *Molloy*.[15] Assimilated into the selective tradition, Beckett's work has too often been interpreted within a narrow conception of modernism's subjective turn, within one extreme side of what Williams refers to as the "split" in the British novel originating at the turn of the century.

The split that Williams analyzes was both theoretical and practical, a divisiveness that manifested itself in explicitly laid-out aesthetic programs and, to varying degrees, in "a new situation in the English novel" in the decades preceding World War I. At issue was "the relation between what separates out as 'individual' or 'psychological' fiction on the one hand and 'social' or 'sociological' fiction on the other" (*English Novel* 119–20). Two of the most representative statements of this split were formulated by H. G. Wells and Henry James in their critical quarrel over the function of the novel. James advocated an idea of fiction organized around a "center" of individual consciousness, and considered the art of the novel an autonomous field defined only by a set of literary "methods." "What really matters in James," says Williams, "is that act of signifying in which the novel becomes its own subject. . . . Consciousness in James . . . is the almost exclusive object and subject of consciousness" (135). In contrast, for Wells, the novel has "inseparable moral consequences" (Wells 143); literature is a "vehicle" for addressing the social consequences of class relations and technology. Not only does Wells reject "intense self-consciousness" (153) as the novel's exclusive domain, but he argues that the novel should function as a "social mediator," as a form of broad social critique, an "instrument of self-examination . . . . [providing] criticism of laws and institutions and of social dogmas . . . . business and finance and politics and precedence and pretentiousness" (154–56).

As Williams so aptly put it, "at this new frontier, the writer can seem to be required to present himself with a clear identity paper: is he poet or sociologist? interested in literature or in politics?" (132); this "is no choice at all: the terms, the questions, are just records of a failure" (138). Even in James "the wrenching-apart of 'individual' and 'society' comes in to confuse us. . . . Since consciousness is social its exploration, its rendering as a process, is connecting, inevitably" (135). While Williams sees the interwar period of high modernism as entailing a responsive renewal of fiction, he complains, justifiably, that "literary history hasn't really caught up" (139).[16] The "split" was, and to a certain extent, especially in regard to a writer like Beckett, is still taken "as a sort of prescription—actually a biased prescription, a symptom—when the real sickness is the separation into classes, into categories, into mutually hostile preoccupations and methods: the individual *or* society; public *or* private; social *or* literary studies" (139). Thus is true of those half-interpretations of Beckett's writing that pose as definitive descriptions: a search for the self, an exploration of disembodied consciousness, a meditation on narrative discourse itself, a descent into solipsism, a tour de force of pure textuality. What needs to be explained is the connecting logic, evident throughout Beckett's entire career as a novelist, of subjectivity, autonomy, and the norms of communicative narrative mimesis—a connection that becomes central in Beckett's major postwar fiction.

Peter Bürger, in his essay "Naturalism, Aestheticism and the Problem of Subjectivity," examines a similar "split" in the turn-of-the-century French novel, a vital context for Beckett's bilingual fiction. The debate between naturalism and aestheticism—Zola and Maurice Barrès are the representative figures—ultimately centered, as Bürger demonstrates, on subjectivity: both the literary representation of subjective experience and the status of the writer's own subjectivity in the process of writing. Although Zola was attacked by critics for his violation of classical norms of beauty and unity, "the critique of naturalism which was mounted by aestheticism was not directed against the violation of . . . norms. On the contrary, it put the whole naturalist project of reproducing social reality into question" (*Decline* 95). At issue was "the institutionalization of literature in bourgeois society . . . those general ideas about literature which serve to define its social function" (96).

Zola attempted to ground literature in the methods of the natural sciences: "the experimental novel," he wrote, "is a consequence of the scientific evolution of the century . . . it substitutes for the study of the abstract and the metaphysical the study of the natural man, governed by physical and chemical laws, and modified by the influences of his surroundings" (Zola 23). Zola's aim, as Bürger points out, was complex: to legitimate his writing in a competitive literary market, "establish a new concept of literature which will liberate it from the taint of romanticism" and provide "useful insights into the social and biological conditioning factors of human behavior" for a large number of readers (100).

Inspired by positivist claims for scientific objectivity, Zola's model of the literary process presented the writer as an observer and recorder whose own subjective views would ideally be excluded from the construction of the novel. "His observation," wrote Zola, "should be an exact representation of nature. . . . He listens to nature and writes under its dictation. But once the fact is ascertained and the phenomenon observed, an idea or hypothesis comes into his mind, reason intervenes, and the experimentalist comes forward to interpret" (Zola 7). While he insists on "the impersonal character of the method" (43) Zola also feels the pressure to distinguish literature from science, to legitimate the novel as an important social institution in its own right. "A contemptible reproach which they heap upon us naturalist writers," he complains, "is the desire to be solely photographers. We have in vain declared that we admit the necessity of an artist's possessing an individual temperament and a personal expression" (11). Inevitably, he falls back on quasi-romanticist notions of personality and genius. "Since feeling is the starting point of the experimental method, since reason subsequently intervenes to end in experiment, and to be controlled by it, the genius of the experimentalist dominates everything" (34).

Importantly, Zola reverts to these ideas not by making a qualifying contrast between the scientist and the writer, an analogy he needs to maintain, but between the significant writer and the hardworking but lesser one who is, at best, a modestly gifted craftsman. He conjures up a picture of the great writer as part egalitarian scientist, part isolated romantic genius. On one hand, he claims that in naturalism there is "nothing but a vast movement, a march forward in which everyone is a workman, according to his genius" (Zola 44–45); on the other, that "form is sufficient to immortalize a work; the spectacle of a powerful individuality reproducing nature in superb language will interest all ages" (49). As Bürger put it, in Zola's attempt to defend the naturalist novel as art, he "appeals to the traditional concept of the genius which is actually quite incompatible with his attempt to render literature more scientific. . . . Zola is unable to explain the position of the productive subject within his own concept of literature" (102).

Bürger demonstrates that the "same sort of contradiction" about subjectivity appears in much of Zola's fiction. The primacy of representing individuals as socially and genetically determined contrasts with a "psychologization of the action" (108), the technique that most likely accounted for the popularity of his novels. According to Zola's positivist-grounded theories, "individual subjects simply possess a functional role" but within the novels themselves they are given "a determining part to play." He "thus tends to fall victim to the very ideology of the autonomous individual which he otherwise contests. . . . Within Zola's concept of the representation of the social lifeworld the subject only occupies the place of a functional role-bearer and does not appear as intrinsically problematic. The subject serves to present social conditions in a vivid way, not to thematize the problems of subjectivity as such" (110–11)

Bürger's most interesting point is that "the problematic [concerning subjectivity] which leads to the aestheticist turn to the subject is already implicit within naturalist literature" (113). Just as aestheticism directly attacked naturalism and sought to legitimize its own conception of literature, it also attempted to resolve the contradiction about subjectivity raised in the naturalist project. What is involved is threefold: a heightened emphasis on the authorial subject; the primacy of the representation of subjective states, personality, and the autonomous self; and the autonomy of artistic fiction and its absolute differentiation from both positivism and popular culture.

In the preface to his trilogy of novels, *The Cult of the Self* (1889–1891), Barrès directly opposes Zola's project: "Reality changes along with the observer for it is the totality of our habitual ways of seeing, feeling and thinking. . . . This [novel] is no logical investigation concerning the transformations of sensibility; rather I am directly reproducing visions and emotions profoundly felt" (qtd. in Bürger 114).[17] Using the first-person and "alternating the presentation of felt subjective experience with the process of reflection," Barrès composed a fragmentary narrative in which the clearly autobiographical narrator "opposes the purposive orientation of instrumental rational action with his infinite susceptibility to different impressions and experiences. . . . The problem of discovering a unitary self becomes the central issue of the work" (Bürger 115–16). Instead of trying to solve the problem by accounting for the role of the individual in relation to social and biological determinants, Barrès creates the aestheticist counterpart to Zola's contradictory exclusion of subjectivity. Not only is his narrator entirely preoccupied with his inner self-development, he actually pursues estrangement from others and from society. As Bürger puts it, in Barrès "alienation is . . . almost elevated into a principle according to which one should attempt to live. . . . If naturalism had grasped reality [only] as objectivity . . . the anti-naturalist novel . . . only address[ed] the problem on the condition that reality is construed in turn as the production of the subject itself. . . . These two movements correspond to one another, even if only by way of reciprocal negation" (118–19). In turn, while Zola "struggles against romanticism in the name of truth and science precisely because he is convinced that his conception of literature is the one which is really appropriate to a democratic-egalitarian society," Barrès "ties the process of literary evolution to the abstract principle of [personal] renewal" (124).

As Williams and Bürger have convincingly argued, the social-objective and psychological-subjective strands of modernism had always developed in dynamic relation, and are in fact inseparable. Some modernists actually made the "split" their main concern. This is obvious in a novel like E. M. Forster's *Howards End,* with its injunction "to connect" the perspectives of public and private, economic and aesthetic, moral and sexual, although, typically and lamentably, Forster's devotion to liberalism has led defenders of canonical modernism to exclude him from the high modernist canon.[18] In relation to a work like Joyce's *Dubliners,* the oppositions make no sense at all, there can be no measure as to whether these stories are more naturalistic or aestheticist, more interested in critically analyzing a specific set of social and moral problems (from Irish nationalism to alcoholism) or in pursuing the depiction of consciousness through symbolist techniques and transcendent epiphanies. As I have tried to show, in the nouvelles and the first part of *Molloy,* Beckett created a unique form of narrative perspective that took one feature of modernist ideology, centering on the link between subjectivity and the socially grounded ordering principle of modern novelistic mimesis, and exaggerated it to the point where its inconsistencies and absurdities acquired tragic dimension. If in the first part of the novel Beckett eschews narrative momentum for an episodic meditation on class consciousness and writing in a socially voided world, in the second part, narrated by the gentleman-agent Moran, the problem of subjectivity is refigured in a manner specific to *narrative*—not just novelistic narrative, but all narrative. Every theory of plot, story, epic, and narrative discourse, from Aristotle to Propp to Ricoeur, has had to confront the ontology of "action" and "agents" (actors, actants, protagonists, etc). It is the constitutive link between action and narration "itself" that provides the dynamic interplay of mimesis and textuality in the bourgeois half of *Molloy.*

V

Molloy (two): Moran, the Agent

The Agent as Storyteller

The second part of *Molloy*, narrated by Jacques Moran, is marked "II" in the text. The schema of the novel is ingenious and deceptively simple: two apparently separate first-person narratives, one following the other, in which the second narrator begins his story by recalling "the day I received the order to see about Molloy" (125). Molloy, of course, is the hero (anti- or otherwise) who narrates "I." The suffering, irreverent, and paradoxical subject of the first part becomes the object of Moran's search. Since Moran fears what may befall him should he fail to find Molloy, Molloy is also the focal point of his increasing anxiety. As Moran's report, as he calls it, of his ill-fated search for Molloy continues, Beckett sets up an abundance of suggestive details, a network of similarities between the two sections that simultaneously provokes and frustrates the reader's attempt to relate them in a meaningful way. Moran may or may not be Molloy himself, or a version of Molloy; "II" may take place after "I," before "I," or at the same time; Moran's son may be the son to whom Molloy alludes, or Moran might be Molloy's son, or Moran's son an incipient Molloy, and so on. There is ample but inconclusive textual evidence for each supposition.

This binary structure allows Beckett to experiment with the fundamental elements of narrative. While Beckett's later fictions seem to do away altogether with a coherent story, *Molloy* retains the clear contours of traditional, modern, and popular narrative forms (the tale, the first-person impressionist confession, espionage fiction) in order to exploit readers' expectations about the kind of information, pleasure, and meaning a good plot provides. The overall effect of the carefully constructed duality in *Molloy* is to short-circuit the stable coordinates by which we orient our reading of a narrative. It is this *narrative* feature of *Molloy* which, according to theorists of the postmodern novel, marks the novel's importance in the transition from the "epistemological" concerns of high modernism to the "ontological" concerns of the contemporary novel. In other words, the new novel no longer emphasizes, in its formal structure, questions of knowledge or perception, as did the high-modernist experimentation with point of view (Conrad, Faulkner, Woolf, Joyce, etc.). Rather, the emphasis falls on the status of fictional discourse itself, as a rhetorical construct that creates the illusions of character, action, value, and reference to "reality."[1]

Among literary theorists of the novel, it has become commonplace to claim that Beckett's novels are concerned only with the "nature of fiction" or "the act of narration itself" (Brooks 215). As Gerard Genette put it, Beckett's fiction "challenges the notion of how (where) to locate *narrative* discourse in its specificity as narrative" (135). In *Molloy,* however, Beckett not only raises ontological questions about narrative mimesis or the referential function of language; concomitant with these reputedly postmodern concerns, there is a concern, perhaps a more emphatic one, with the *value* of narrative. Take, as a simple example, Moran's exclamation, about midway through his report:

> Oh, the stories I could tell you, if I were easy. What a rabble in my head, what a gallery of moribunds. Murphy, Watt, Yerk, Mercier and all the others. I would never have believed that—yes, I believe it willingly. Stories, stories. I have not been able to tell them. I shall not be able to tell this one. (189)

Moran expresses both a willed refusal to narrate ("if I were easy") and an almost nostalgic desire to do so. The subjects of the stories he could/cannot tell are the characters of Beckett's earlier fiction. The stories are already there for the telling: the emphasis is not on the ontological status of fiction, but on the capability and desire to tell stories, one of which Moran is already (and uneasily) in the midst of recounting. Moran's ambivalence centers on a relation between stories and an ability or willingness to tell them.

For Moran, storytelling is an action. Behind the ontological mystery of narrative mimesis, there is a more fundamental question of agency. Moran's ambivalence is built upon a distinction analogous to the analytical division between *story* and *discourse,* a cornerstone of narratology since Propp.[2] "Story" refers to our everyday understanding of narrative as a set of significantly interrelated characters, actions, and circumstances; "discourse" refers to the set of rhetorical devices ("codes," as Roland Barthes called them) through which a story is constructed. Discourse, as a rhetorical term, always refers to an action—speaking or writing—with an intention to persuade or evoke a particular response. As part of the *story* in "II," individual action is represented in two closely related ways: just as Moran is ordered to search for Molloy, he is also ordered, by the same authority, to write the report; in turn, the report is the occasion to tell the story about both the thwarted search for Molloy and Moran's reflections on what has befallen him. Moran's anxiety over his life as an agent compels him to express his complaints in his report to the "Chief." Thematically, individual agency is a concern because Moran is forced to act against his will:

> Here are your instructions, said Gaber. . . . When at last he had finished I told him the job did not interest me and that the chief would do better to call on another agent. He wants it to be you, God knows why, said Gaber. . . . He said . . . that no one could do it but you. . . . In that case it's hard for me to refuse, I said, knowing perfectly well that in any case it was impossible for me to refuse. Refuse! But we agents often amused

ourselves with grumbling among ourselves and giving ourselves the air of free men. (128–29)

The tension between Moran's wish to consider himself free and the requirements of his existence as an agent plays an important role in the novel. Beckett's broad characterizations in "II"—agent and chief, employer and employee, father and son, master and servant—are all suggestive of social hierarchy and conflict. Moran's admission that he cannot refuse, that he knowingly acts against his own wishes, unfolds within a larger relation, between himself and what he calls a "vast organization":

> And when I speak of agents and of messengers in the plural, it is with no guarantee of the truth. For I had never seen any other messengers than Gaber nor any other agent than myself. But I supposed we were not the only ones and Gaber must have supposed the same. For the feeling that we were the only ones of our kind would, I believe, have been more than we could have borne. . . . That we thought of ourselves as members of a vast organization was doubtless also due to the all too human feeling that trouble shared, or is it sorrow, is trouble something, I forget the word. . . . But to me at least . . . it was obvious that we were perhaps alone in what we did. . . . At times I came even to doubt the existence of Gaber himself. . . . And . . . I might have gone to the extreme of conjuring away the chief too and regarding myself as solely responsible for my wretched existence. (146–47)

What was first posed as a problem concerning freedom of action is now posed in terms of taking responsibility for one's actions. The structure of relations is the same, whether or not Moran acts alone: he understands his actions as mediated through some source outside of himself, be it a "vast organization" or the chief. Moran cannot account for the events in his story, or even bear to think about them, without two conflicting views of himself—as an individual responsible for his own actions and as an agent of an "anonymous" cause:

> For what I was doing I was doing neither for Molloy, who mattered nothing to me, nor for myself, of whom I despaired, but on behalf of a cause which, while having need of us to be accomplished, was in its essence anonymous, and would subsist, haunting the minds of men, when its miserable artisans should be no more. It will not be said, I think, that I did not take my work to heart. But, rather, tenderly. Ah, those old craftsmen, their race is extinct and the mould broken. (156–57)

While one set of terms is broadened—from chief and organization to simply a "cause"—another is narrowed, from "what I was doing" to "work." Work is both

Moran's search for Molloy and his telling/writing of the story, two actions which are thematically unified since Moran has also been ordered to write the report. While many critics, following Genette, claim that in Beckett's fiction, "the action [i.e., the story] . . . is reduced to the condition of simple pretext, and then abolished" (219), it is more accurate to say that Beckett creates a tension between *story* and *discourse,* between work as a story event, and work as the discursive construction of narrated events. For a novelist, narrating is work, artistic activity and career. If, as I am proposing, the narrative experimentation in *Molloy* is centered on the question of individual agency, then the dialectic of individual agent and anonymous cause that "II" constructs might be read as an aesthetically mediated image of Beckett's self-understanding of his own agency, as a novelist. The nostalgic tone of the passage quoted above, out of keeping with the cynical and mannered style of most of "II," with its lament for the "old craftsmen," expresses a sense of loss for an historically "extinct" mode of narration. A similar sense of loss was expressed, in 1936, in Walter Benjamin's essay "The Storyteller."

Both the storyteller's subject, "communicable experience" (84), and the social stratum in which he flourished, "the artisan class" (85), Benjamin argues, had nearly vanished from European life after World War I. In contrast to the storyteller stands the now-dominant form of narrator, the novelist:

> The storyteller takes what he tells from experience—his own or that reported by others. And he in turn makes it the experience of those who are listening to his tale. The novelist has isolated himself. The birthplace of the novel is the solitary individual, who is no longer able to express himself by giving examples of his most important concerns, is himself uncounseled, and cannot counsel others. To write a novel means to carry the incommensurable to extremes in the representation of human life. In the midst of life's fullness, the novel gives evidence of the profound perplexity of the living. (87)

In Benjamin's account, it is the absence of a mediating realm between the individual and an abstract, isolating society, the absence of a class or community, that affects both the decline in storytelling and the rise of the novel, from creation to reception: "A man listening to a story is in the company of the storyteller; even a man reading one shares this companionship. The reader of a novel, however, is isolated, more so than any other reader" (100).[3]

The same absence of any mediating community, between individual will and anonymous cause, between the "solitary" man (156) and the invisible "vast organization" of agents, is the decisive social content that compels Moran's ambivalence, in the *story,* about telling stories. Beckett's emphasis on the *discourse,* in Moran's metafictional comment on his own narrating work, points to a correspondence between agent and novelist. A similar correspondence is suggested by Beckett's emphasis on the theme of voice. To some extent, Beckett compensates for the abstract quality of

Moran's report through the intensity of Moran's anxiety and angry resistance, which are directed at the compulsion to act and, consequently, to write his report. As in part one, Beckett puts an internalized voice into uneasy proximity with complicity, resignation, and an external, fear-inducing authority; a proximity that casts doubt on the potentially liberating effect of self-expression. Midway through his report, Moran registers this ambivalent but deeply felt attachment to voice:

> And if I submit to this paltry scrivening which is not of my province, it is for reasons very different from those that might be supposed. I am still obeying orders, if you like, but no longer out of fear. No, I am still afraid, but simply from force of habit. And the voice I listen to needs no Gaber to make it heard. For it is within me and exhorts me to continue to the end the faithful servant I have always been, of a cause that is not mine, and patiently fulfill in all its bitterness my calamitous part, as it was my will, when I had a will, that others should. And this with hatred in my heart, and scorn, of my master and his designs. Yes, it is rather an ambiguous voice and not always easy to follow, in its reasonings and decrees. But I follow it none the less. . . . And I feel I shall follow it from this day forth, no matter what it commands. And when it ceases, leaving me in doubt and darkness, I shall wait for it to come back, and do nothing, even though the whole world, through the channel of its innumerable authorities speaking with one accord, should enjoin upon me this or that, under pain of unspeakable punishments. . . . Does this mean I shall one day be banished from my house, from my garden, lose my trees, my lawn, my birds . . . all those things at hand without which I could not bear being a man, where my enemies cannot reach me, which it was my life's work to build, to adorn, to perfect, to keep? I am too old to lose all this, and begin again, I am too old! (180–81)

With Moran, Beckett turns the internal disjuncture of Molloy's voice inside out. In possession of all those things that Molloy lacks—home, family, the command of a "systematic decorum"—he unconsciously shifts his sense of unfreedom from external to internal causes. Beckett builds irony most effectively into the voice of Molloy by having him forfeit his justification to protest just at the moment his complaint reaches its most incisive expression, in his peroration against the "great English schools." By eloquently expressing the objective conditions of his own debasement, Molloy loses his status as silent, fearful, confused vagrant. In "II," however, Beckett creates a narrating figure explicitly in possession of the knowledge and resources necessary to reflect critically upon the conditions of his own existence. If Moran protests, it is through the perspective of his social status, not, as Molloy does, in spite of it.

The most salient difference that structures the binary schema of the novel is a socioeconomic one: Molloy's isolate vagabondage in contrast to Moran's home, gardens, son, servant, church, and career. It is when Moran's sense of endangered class identity—"well-shaven and perfumed and proud of my intellectual's soft white hands" (233)—intersects with his anxious reflection on the source of his narration, both the external compulsion and the internal voice's "reasonings and decrees," that the *story* most strongly reflects on the *discourse* as an intentional, rhetorical act. Moran's increasing anxiety and anger, his will to narrate, his desire for freedom, and the prerogatives of his endangered social status are inextricably intertwined. The terms Beckett uses to represent Moran's dilemma, *agent* and *voice,* are, not coincidentally, terms that refer as well to narrative discourse (every narrative has an agent or actant and is told in a voice). The suggested correspondence between Moran's work and the novelist's work proliferates through Beckett's use of these abstractions: just as Moran worries about his rational will and social identity, so too are questions of conscious volition and class consciousness embedded in the self-understanding of the modern novelist. To what extent do these authorial concerns—concerns that are evident, in contradictory ways, in Beckett's interwar writings—shape Moran's story of agents, voices, and the compulsion to report?

"Strong Enough at Last to Act No More"

One of the most persistent motifs in Beckett's fiction in the undesirability or difficultly of physical mobility, which becomes increasingly acute in the novels of the trilogy. In Beckett's interwar fiction, characters like Belacqua (the name alludes to Dante's personification of sloth) in *More Pricks than Kicks* and Murphy protest, in the manner of the bohemian aesthete, against norms of rational and purposive activity through their ironically willful adherence to principles of laziness and antisociability.[4] In these works, immobility and withdrawal are compensated for by both an energetic, allusive, punning omniscient narrator and a purposively convoluted (though minimally engaging) plot. Thus, while *Murphy* begins with an image of the hero's self-immobilization, ritualistically bound to his rocking chair, in the second chapter, as Murphy listens to Celia's demand that he get a job, his response is described in an oxymoronic paragraph that contrasts action with inertia:

> He closed his eyes and fell back. It was not his habit to make out cases for himself. An atheist chipping at the deity was not more senseless than Murphy defending his courses of inaction. . . . He had been carried away by his passion for Celia and by the most curious feeling that he should not collapse without at least the form of a struggle. . . . To die fighting was the perfect anti-thesis of his whole practice, faith and intention. (26)

The oxymoron is sharpest in the phrase "Murphy defending his courses of inaction."[5] Murphy's problem is how actively to resist activity. In the early fiction this conflict is only thematic. The omniscient narration and the plot line seem inordinately complex and precociously deliberate, requiring on the reader's part an attentiveness disproportionate to the rewards gained by following the story. Beckett's letter in response to a publisher's request that he cut parts of *Murphy* indicates as much: "I do not see how the book can be cut without being disorganized," he wrote. "Do they not understand that if the book is slightly obscure it is because it is a compression and that to compress it further can only result in making it more obscure? . . . And of course the narrative is hard to follow. And of course deliberately so" (*Disjecta* 103).

In *Molloy,* as well, the problem of action centers on an antagonism toward instrumental thought and behavior. What is different is that, in *Murphy,* the ironic distance between slothful character, on one side, and convoluted plot and archly intellectual narrator, on the other, undercuts the thematic antagonism to purposive effort. The hero's will to inaction is neutralized, rather than effectively expressed, by the narrative's too-eager compensatory activity. In *Molloy,* the rhetorical blockage—created in part by the novel's binary structure, in part by the crystal clarity of the prose—makes the novel impossible, rather than difficult, to follow. The deliberate obscurity of the plot in *Murphy* is created in order to be deciphered; in *Molloy,* the aesthetic effect is to solicit and then block the reader's expectations about basic narrative features of action and agency, such as causal and temporal relations of events, or consistent identity of the narrating characters. When Moran, awaking in the forest and finding himself crippled and abandoned by his son, contemplates a course of inaction, the theme of agency and the mode of narration are fused into a single expression:

> And I remained for several days, I do not know how many, in the place where my son had abandoned me, eating my last provisions (which he might easily have taken too), seeing no living soul, powerless to act, or perhaps strong enough at last to act no more. For I had no illusions, I knew that all was about to end, or to begin again, it little mattered which, and it little mattered how, I had only to wait. And on and off, for fun, and the better to scatter them to the winds, I dallied with the hopes that spring eternal, childish hopes, as for example that my son, his anger spent, would have pity on me and come back to me! Or that Molloy, whose country this was, would come to me, who had not been able to go to him, and grow to be a friend, and like a father to me, and help me do what I had to do, so that Youdi would not be angry with me and would not punish me! Yes, I let them spring within me and grow in strength, brighten and charm me with a thousand fancies, and then I swept them away, with a great disgusted sweep of all my being, I swept myself clean of them and surveyed with satisfaction the void they polluted. And in the evening I turned to the lights of Bally, I watched them shine brighter and brighter, then all go out together, or nearly all, foul little flickering lights

of terrified men. And I said, To think I might be there now, but for my misfortune. (221–22)

The thematic shift from the earlier fiction is clear: from a defense of inaction to a paradox about agency. The paralyzing logic—"powerless to act, or perhaps strong enough at last to act no more"—is raised in the context of the dialectic of solitary agent and vast organization, with its themes of isolation, compulsion, and the longing for companionship and community, despite Moran's disdain for the distant "lights of terrified men." In contrast to the problem of action in *Murphy*, Moran's course of inaction is expressed not through an oxymoron, but as an hermeneutic impasse: there is no way to distinguish inaction as a lack of capability, "powerless to act," from inaction as an exertion of capability, "strong enough . . . to act no more." This is not a *defense* of inaction, but a problem in understanding that is rooted in Moran's anxiety over the disposition of his will-to-act, situated between the poles of solitary self and unknowable, abstract organization.

When read as an event within the *story*, Moran's reflection upon being abandoned by his son does, in fact, evoke, through temporal references and the themes of hope and fear, the presence of a coherent, overarching narrative. At the same time, however, the event's status as part of an overall configuration of events is disrupted. The disruption is controlled by the paradox about agency: unable to understand the meaning of inaction—where doing nothing is a sign of either powerlessness or capability, passivity or strength—the narrator is equally uncertain about the parameters of the story he is telling: "For I had no illusions, I knew that all was about to end, or begin again, it little mattered which, and it little mattered how, I had only to wait."

One way this disruption works is through the isomorphism between syntax and plot, between sentence elements and story elements.[6] In *Murphy*, with its complex, twisting and turning sentences, syntax, like the plot itself, becomes an exercise in the reader's willingness to follow. Here, however, the opposite occurs. The short phrases that make up the sentences stand on their own: I was therefore alone; eating my last provisions; and grow to be a friend; I watched them shine brighter and brighter. At the level of the sentence the style offers no resistance to understanding. But the accretion of simple words and phrases creates the expectation that the narrated events, like the phrases themselves, fit together in an intelligible order. Thus, while the problem of agency is explicitly expressed at the level of the sentence and the single event within the *story*, at the level of the configuration of events this explicitness is denied. The plethora of commas which separate each autonomous phrase and break down the narrative into hundreds of simple statements indicate how far the first-person narratives in *Molloy* are from the Joycean stream of consciousness (in Molly's soliloquy in *Ulysses*, for example) where an associative logic orders the configuration of a life story. In *The Unnamable* the single comma-bound phrase becomes the monad of meaning; even the attempt to fit together the phrases within a single sentence becomes a problem in configuring single events into a meaningful whole. In Beckett's later works, especially *How It Is*, the commas are removed but the phrase-by-phrase construction is retained; reading becomes a constant struggle to recognize unmarked units of meaning and relate them in coherent, variable configurations.

Moran's reflection on the paradox of inaction invokes what Paul Ricoeur refers to as the "semantics of action," the ontology of human agency that prefigures any narrative act.[7] Along with the sense of overall conflict—the father with the son, the agent with the organization, the haughty but pathetic Moran with the town of "terrified men"—there is reference to a range of concepts which express action in terms of reason and will: deliberation, premeditation, hope for help and friendship, fear of punishment, and so forth. Yet if, in "II," the meanings of actions are blocked, and beginnings cannot be differentiated from ends, then neither can hopes and fears be realized or alleviated, nor even comprehended as a relation of cause and effect. Rather, hope is raised as if only in order to be blocked: "And on and off, for fun, and the better to scatter them to the winds, I dallied with the hopes that spring eternal, childish hopes . . . and then I swept them away . . . and surveyed with satisfaction the void they polluted." The idea of hope contains an inherent narrative temporality which Moran negates, not only psychologically, in the manner of the nihilist, but also by reducing it to cliché: "hopes that spring eternal."

Moran's dismissal of hope does not, however, negate the imagined set of reconciliations: "my son would have pity on me and come back to me . . . Molloy . . . would come to me . . . and grow to be a friend . . . and like a father . . . Youdi [the chief] would not punish me." The transcendent moments in Beckett's postwar fiction always revolve around this sense of hope and imagined reconciliation between symbols of hierarchy, like father and son, but only at the level of the sentence or the single event. There is no way to represent reconciliation without the mimesis of individual action. In the trilogy, actions and hopes are already undermined because the overarching narrative progression from prior to present to after, from cause to effect, is effectively blocked. The controlling paradox of agency—of the meaning of individual action in relation to the vast organization, to the anonymous cause, to external compulsion or inner voice—renders hope and reconciliation "void."[8]

The Terms of the Story: Agent, Voice, Purpose

The term *agent* in part two of *Molloy* has three references. First, as I have discussed, there is the question of Moran's agency in the sociological sense. Moran is uncertain of how or why he acts because the context that mediates his will is beyond—or hidden from—his understanding. Secondly, Beckett plays with and exploits the plot of the espionage novel; much of the narrative expectation evoked, and then frustrated, stems from the parody of a popular cultural form, a genre often viewed as a paradigm for modern narrative in general.[9] Third, there is an experiment with basic narrative elements: an agent (actor or actant) is simply a functional role in the *discourse*, an element of narrative mimesis.

This tripartite pattern of reference—social, popular-cultural, and narratological—is evident from the beginning of "II." The plot begins with Moran receiving "the order to see about Molloy. It was a Sunday in summer. I was sitting in my little garden, in a wicker chair, a black book closed on my knees. It must have been about eleven o'clock, still too early to go to church. I was savouring the day of rest, while deploring the importance attached to it" (125–26). Socially, Moran is a complacent, "slightly libertarian" (125) bourgeois; the narrative parodies the convention of novelistic expectation ("All was still. Not a breath" [126]). But these specific social and cultural references are immediately made abstract:

> I've always loved doing nothing. And I would have gladly rested on weekdays too, if I could have afforded it. Not that I was positively lazy. It was something else. Seeing something done which I could have done better myself, if I had wished, and which I did do better whenever I put my mind to it, I had the impression of discharging a function to which no form of activity could have exalted me. But this was a joy in which, during the week, I could seldom indulge. (126)

On one hand, Moran's enjoyment of "doing nothing" is a prerogative of his social status. On the other, "doing nothing" complicates the relationship between "function" and "activity." Moran's love of doing nothing refers just as much to his class status as it does to the logic of narrative discourse. Beckett's abstractions articulate with those of narratology because narrative and action cannot be separated: the paradox about agency is always also a paradox in the narrative form. The effect of the simultaneous social-cultural and metanarrative references is to create a tension between *story* and *discourse,* between the specific cultural meanings out of which the story is constructed and the act of narration itself. This tension is most strongly at play whenever agency or action is thematically explicit.

The disruption of bourgeois complacency at the beginning of the plot suggests a narrative logic typical of the modern novel: order—disruption—restoration of order through transformation. In Fredric Jameson's influential theory of the novel, which employs Lévi-Strauss's method of myth analysis, this logic reveals the ideological function of novelistic plot, to provide an "imaginary resolution of a real [social-historical] contradiction" (Jameson 77).[10] But here the formula is apparently invoked only in order to be violated. Unified only by the overarching narrative function of the search for Molloy, the episodic plot moves from this initial order to increasing disorder, signaled most strongly by Moran's growing anxiety and physical deterioration. After the messenger Gaber destroys Moran's peaceful Sunday of doing nothing with the order to find Molloy, Moran is forced to act. The tension between compulsion and freedom, as I have discussed, unfolds within a set of larger abstract relations between Moran and the "vast organization." Thus, to put the matter in Jameson's terms, the social-political contradiction that the novel expresses, and the expectation of its resolution, concern the illusory individual freedom to which Moran clings.

However, just as the order-disorder-restoration formula is evoked and then violated, so too is the contradiction-resolution formula. The thematic contradiction in the plot is not resolved; rather, it becomes increasingly pronounced, both in the *story* and in the narrative structure, the *discourse*.

Narrative analysis places a great emphasis on endings because it is only in retrospect that the various strands of a story can be recognized as a sequence of events that cohere (or, in a bad story, inadequately cohere) into a configured whole. One of the most remarked features of part two of *Molloy* is the metanarrative negation Beckett builds into the framework of Moran's report. Thus, "II" begins: "It is midnight. The rain is beating on the windows. I am calm. . . . My report will be long." Since the chronology of the plot (i.e., the chief's order and Moran's search for Molloy) leads up to the time of the narrating act (Moran writing the report in retrospect), then the end of "II" should seamlessly close the narrative. When, in the last pages of the novel, Moran returns home, abandoned by his son, crippled, in debt, his garden in ruins, his house deserted, he announces the close of his tale: "Now I may make an end." Recalling the reiterated order to write the report, Moran reflects on the conditions under which his narration has been undertaken:

> I have spoken of a voice telling me things. I was getting to know it better now, to understand what it wanted. It did not use the words that Moran had been taught when he was little and that he in his turn had taught to his little one. So that at first I did not know what it wanted. But in the end I understood this language. I understood it, I understand it, all wrong perhaps. That is not what matters. It told me to write the report. Does this mean I am freer now than I was? I do not know. I shall learn. Then I went back into the house and wrote, It is midnight. The rain is beating on the windows. It was not midnight. It was not raining. (241)

Like the term *agent,* the category of voice in "II" has three simultaneous references. Socially, it is a marker of individual autonomy or freedom of expression, especially in regard to the connection between writing and coercion. In the culture of the modern novel, it signals interiority, private conscience, or psychic irrationality (i.e., hearing voices). Narratologically, voice describes the relation of the narrated events to the time, place, and origin of the narrating act. Barthes and Genette both consider the disposition of voice the most important marker of a narrative's sociopolitical status: traditional and bourgeois narrative is bound up with the third person absolute past tense. In the new "writerly" mode (with which Beckett is so often associated), the closer the time, place, and origin of the narrating act to the narrated events, the more the emphasis is on the *discourse,* while the *story* appears, as Genette puts it, as merely a "pretext."

This complete rhetorical foreclosure of *story,* however, is not evident in *Molloy.* Instead, what Beckett does is block the possibilities of resolution inherent in the theme of voice, in all its implications: the tensions between freedom and compulsion, between internal and external voices, and between *story* and *discourse,* are left in heightened suspension. Moran begins to understand the voice, but the positive meaning of understanding is undercut: "I understand it, all wrong perhaps." While the report has already been demanded by the authority of the organization—once in a letter from the chief and again by the messenger—now the voice itself becomes the authority behind the narrating act. The question, "does this mean I am freer now?" elicits another epistemological doubt and indicates a final but ambivalent transition from external to internalized coercion. The famous last two lines of the novel, however, do seem to throw the entire *story* into the realm of mere "pretext." Iser points to the end of the novel as a "total negation . . . which results in a total devaluation of language by accentuating the arbitrariness with which it is applied to the objects it seeks to grasp" (164–65). But this "devaluation" is not only, as Iser implies, an instance of the *discourse* negating the signified of the *story;* it is also a sign of an irresolvable tension between *story* and *discourse.*

The negation produced by the final lines is constructed through a *linguistic* paradox which exploits the contradictions inherent in language, but only when language is understood *as a formally closed system.*[11] It follows the form of the well-known paradox "everything I say is a lie." Thus, when considered as *discourse,* "II" cancels itself out, or rather, it short-circuits, since the chain of negation would logically continue, switching from affirmation to negation and back again ad infinitum. But the *thematic* paradoxes in the *story* are just as pronounced as the *linguistic* paradox in the *discourse.* The protest against external coercion signaled by the ambivalent voice manifests itself in Moran's refusal to give the chief the kind of report he wants. The thrice-repeated "He asked for a report he'll get his report" (164, 165, 240) is a rallying cry against the enforced narrating act. The negations in the last lines are clearly part of Moran's refusal to narrate under duress and are motivated by the events in the *story,* even while the linguistic paradox short-circuits their ontological status. The rhetorical foreclosure of narrative mimesis is just as much an event in the *story* as it is a sign of the story's existence as pure *discourse.*

Unlike the second novel of the trilogy, *Malone Dies,* which terminates in a series of fragments that conflate diegetic levels, "II" has a coherently organized closure that strengthens the thematic contradictions about writing, acting, and voice. As Peter Brooks observes, postwar experimental writers like Beckett created and exploited "an altered situation of plot, which no longer wishes to be end determined" (314). Closure, however, does not refer only to how a plot is ultimately resolved. As Ricoeur describes it, the dynamic of emplotment transforms a sequence of actions or events into a configured, temporal whole by providing some type of end point from whose perspective the events cohere. Thus, in "II" this end point makes a set of contradictions cohere by *not* resolving them. Another way of putting this is in terms of Hayden White's description of the transition in early European historical writing, from *chronicle,* a listing of events that simply lead up to rather than inform or explain the chronicler's present, to history as *narrative,* which depends upon the organizing presence of a retrospective ethical, ideological, or rational-scientific perspective. In narrative historiography, a *sequence* of events becomes a *relation* of events whose clearest manifestation is in the historical occurrences with which the historian chooses to close the narrative. Thus, another way of describing the tension between *story* and *discourse* in "II" would be as a tension between chronicle and narrative forms. Just as a chronicle cannot (or does not aim to) account for the present as an outcome of the past, the narrative cannot account for the past except as a leading-up-to the present, even if this leading-up-to is open to endless hermeneutic speculation.[12] The paradoxical form of closure in "II" not only leaves the thematic contradictions in place, but also points to the function of narrative closure itself as, simultaneously, a manifestation of coercion and an act of protest. The ethical or moral standpoint that would legitimize the narrativizing retrospective—the reclamation of one's own voice—is presented too ambivalently to make the sequence of events in "II" cohere, but at the same time is too strongly expressed (like "hope") to be discounted entirely as the possible end (i.e., moral) of the story. Like Beckett's ambivalence toward interiority in part one, his ambivalence toward *story* requires that the resolution of the symbolic conflict be presented as a possibility that is blocked or held in suspension but never ignored.

The end of a story is also an end in the sense of a purpose, even if it is the absence of any goal that creates an intended aesthetic effect of evoking futility. In our practical understanding of agency, what differentiates an action from an occurrence (accident, randomness, natural disaster, etc.) is, in fact, the presence of some immediate or long-range purpose.[13] Beckett exploits the abstract idea of purpose in the same manner as he does agent and voice. Moran's attempt to understand the purpose of the search for Molloy is one of the central motifs of the story. The need for a purpose first appears as Moran's reluctance to face the task ahead of him:

> The fact is I had not yet begun to take the matter seriously. And I am all the more surprised as such light-mindedness was not like me. Or was it in order to win a few more moments of peace that I instinctively avoided giving my mind to it? Even if, as set forth in Gaber's report, the affair had seemed unworthy of me, the chief's insistence on having me, me Moran, rather than anybody else, ought to have warned me that it was no ordinary one. And instead of bringing to bear all upon it without delay all the resources of my mind and my experience, I sat dreaming of my breed's infirmities and the singularities of those about me. . . . I stirred restlessly in my armchair, ran my hands over my face, crossed and uncrossed my legs, and so on. The colour and the weight of the world were changing already, soon I would have to admit I was anxious. (131–32)

Moran knows he must expend the conscious effort "to grasp the Molloy affair" in order to succeed (133). The sense of coercion is accompanied by pride at being singled out for the extraordinary mission. This ambivalence is consistent with the ambivalence concerning voice as both freedom and internalized authority. At first, the purpose of the search for Molloy is connected to Moran's status as an agent, both socially and within the parodied espionage plot. These social and cultural references are then articulated in reference to the narrative meaning of purpose. Moran retires to his room to think. "My concern at first was only with its [the Molloy affair's] immediate vexations and the preparations demanded of me. The kernel of the affair I continued to shirk. I felt a great confusion coming over me." In order to avoid the "kernel," the purpose of the search, Moran begins with practical matters:

> Should I set out on my autocycle? This was the question with which I began. I had a methodical mind and never set out on a mission without prolonged reflection as to the best way of setting out. . . . But if I was in the habit of first settling this delicate question of transport, it was never without having, if not fully sifted, at least taken into account the factors on which it depended. For how can you decide on the way of setting out if you do not first know where you are going, or at least with what purpose you are going there? . . . To try and solve the problem of transport under such conditions was madness. Yet that was what I was doing. I was losing my head already. (134)

"Purpose," generalized within the problem of transport, becomes abstract: how can the narrative proceed without the requisite goal or purpose that configures the actions and episodes? Moran's failure to understand the purpose of his mission is equally a moment in the *story* and a narrative problem affecting the ordering principle of the *discourse*.

In a long paragraph in which Moran attempts to understand the essence of his mission, Beckett weaves together the themes of isolated agent, anonymous organization, loss of community, and purposeless action. Even the conditions necessary for reflection seem disrupted by the agent-organization paradox:

> Far from the world, its clamours, frenzies, bitterness and dingy light, I pass judgment on it and on those, like me, who are plunged in it beyond recall. . . . The blood drains from my head . . . my eyes search in vain for two things alike, each pinpoint of skin screams a different message, I drown in the spray of phenomena. It is at the mercy of these sensations, which happily I know to be illusory, that I have to live and work. It is thanks to them I find myself a meaning. . . . And yet it is not unpleasant, before setting to work, to steep oneself again in this slow and massive world . . . where, of course, no investigation would be possible. . . . For it was only by transferring it to this atmosphere, how shall I say, of finality without end, why not, that I could venture to consider the work I had on hand. . . . And though this examination prove unprofitable and of no utility for the execution of my orders, I should nevertheless have

established a kind of connexion, and one not necessarily false. For the falsity of the terms does not necessarily imply that of the relation, so far as I know. (151–52)

Moran admits that he can only understand the purpose of his work by "transferring it to this atmosphere . . . of finality without end," a state of illusory sensations and chaotic fragments of indeterminate meaning which, though imbued with a form of closure, imply no resolution. Moran's abstract proposition, that "the falsity of the terms does not necessarily imply that of the relation," well describes the essence of fictional narrative mimesis. Understanding the purpose of one's actions is like configuring the elements of a story: it is not the truth (or ontological fictional status) of the particular events that is at issue, but the way in which they relate as a whole. This relation of terms, and not their ontological status, is what is blocked for Moran, and, through his report, for the reader. The overarching relation—of individual agent to anonymous organization, of the "being apart" to the "masses" and the "vast conglomerate"—remains an irreducible paradox and renders any provisional understanding of agency, voice, or purpose a self-contradictory source of anxiety. In the network of terms through which Beckett constructs Moran's report, the individual-social paradox is reproduced at every blocked intersection of action and meaning, at every disruption of *story* by *discourse*.

Structures without Agents: Beckett and the Postwar Critique of Narrative

The discovery of narrative as an isolatable, distinct discursive entity—transhistorical and transcultural, as Roland Barthes put it—has its roots in Propp's search for the synchronic "deep structure" of narrative forms in *Morphology of the Folk Tale* and the research of the Russian formalists (1915–30). By the 1960s, many theorists of the novel began to take for granted that a typology of plots derived from the deep structure of myths and folktales was necessary to understand the development of the genre. Northrop Frye (1963) assumed that this interest in the structure of narrative was also shared by the modern novelist: "Folk tales tell us nothing credible about the life or manners of any society. . . . [They] are simply abstract story-patterns, uncomplicated and easy to remember. . . . Writers are interested in folk tales . . . because they illustrate essential principles of storytelling" (27). Frye's references to folk tales and myth recall the whole development of the structural study of narrative, from Propp to Lévi-Strauss. By the 1960s, theorists' concern with narrative involved a firmly established belief: narrative had become a quasi-anthropological category, a timeless, ahistorical structure empty of social or psychological content.

For critics and literary historians who attempted, in various ways, to incorporate the structural study of narrative into their analyses of the novel—among them, Frye, Barthes, Genette, Goldmann, Jameson, and Brooks—it became necessary to describe how narrative, a seemingly universal structure, becomes filled with the social specificity and aesthetic intentionality of the novel; how an abstract pattern is transformed into an historically situated set of meanings. In general, the study of narrative has no concern for the role of individual agency, because the folk tales, myths, and other anonymous stories from which narratology derived its model of narrative structure were taken to be traditional, collective entities: in effect, they have no author. Yet, as I shall argue, the structural critique of narrative actually depended on a belief in the transformative power of the individual agent—both author and reader—even though the individual was discredited as a constitutive factor in the production of narrative. I would like briefly to describe this deep-seated, contradictory account of individual agency implicit in the critique of narrative mounted in the postwar period. As with Beckett's experiments in narrative form, the decisive social content informing the critical methods of Barthes, and others, was a perceived crisis in the status of meaningful human agency.

The terms of the postwar critique of narrative mimesis were already in place in Georg Lukács's 1936 essay "Narrate or Describe." For Lukács, as for the later theorists, no writer better represented the archetype of the modern novelist than Flaubert. Lukács linked the narrative perspective of Flaubert's novels to his position as a writer entrenched in a newly consolidated bourgeois society. For Flaubert (and Zola), "the only solution to the tragic contradiction in their situation [as writers who expressed revulsion toward the values of the political and social order of their time] was to stand aloof as observers and critics of capitalist society. At the same time, they became specialists in the craft of writing, writers in the sense of the capitalist division of labour" (119). In Lukács's account, this position as "observer" and "specialist" led to an emphasis away from "narration," always rooted in action, toward detached "description." "Men's words, subjective reactions and thoughts are shown to be true or false . . . in practice—as they succeed or fail in deeds and actions," he argued. "Primitive poetry [fairy tales, ballads or legends] . . . is always based on the primacy of action. This poetry has continued to have a profound meaning because it depicts the success or failure of human purpose in the test of practice. . . . When the artistic literature of a period does not provide actions in which typical characters with a richly developed inner life are tested in practice, the public seeks abstract substitutes. Such was the case with literature in the second half of the nineteenth century. Literature based on observation excludes this interaction to an ever-increasing extent" (123–24).

Lukács's partitioning of the nineteenth-century novel into narration (Balzac and Tolstoy) and description (Flaubert and Zola) is analogous to the structuralist-based analytical division of *story* and *discourse*. What distinguishes Lukács's argument from narrative theory are the opposing values: his critique of the discourse-emphatic modernist novel is matched by the later theorists' praise of the liberating effects of Flaubert's, Proust's, or Robbe-Grillet's reputed rejection of narrative conventions. Like Lukács, Peter Brooks—writing in 1985, in the wake of structuralism's influence—similarly links the representation of action and agency to the modernist emphasis on the *discourse,* though with a different verdict. "If *L'Education sentimentale* claims to be the history of Flaubert's generation," Brooks argues, "it appears to pass its severest judgment on that generation's belief that change is within the grasp of human agency. . . . The promise that the novel seemed to tender its readers, that Frédéric's hitherto aimless career might take on meaning when 'the moment' finally came . . . comes to naught. . . . *L'Education sentimentale* . . . appears to counsel passivity, the knowledge that action is futile" (203). For Brooks, this negative lesson is countered by the novel's discourse-emphatic quality. "The achievement of *L'Education sentimentale* does not reach us as a direct commentary on life, but rather as a commentary on the narrative forms in which life has traditionally been rendered. This commentary . . . works toward bringing into the foreground the place from which all commentary proceeds, the act of narration." Brooks goes on to link this development to Beckett; the attenuation of the "commentary on life" leads ultimately to "the situation of Samuel Beckett's narrators." The impulse to narrate now comes not from the relation between the author and the social world, but from "the act of narration itself" (215).

I have taken these arguments about Flaubert somewhat out of context (Lukács's Weberian-Marxism and Brooks's psychoanalytic model) in order to highlight a continuity spanning several decades of criticism addressing the value of narrative mimesis. Both Lukács and Brooks link Flaubert's position as a writer in modern bourgeois society to the *representation* of the futility of individual action, and both link his belief in the futility of human agency to the formal innovation in his work, whether characterized negatively as an emphasis on observation and description or positively in terms of a metanarrative "commentary." What this suggests is that the formal innovation in narration, and the thematic defense of inaction, are two aspects of a single expression; a single, complex response to the consolidation of bourgeois society in the midnineteenth century.

It is around the question of agency that the postwar critique of narrative, and the structural analysis that informed it, became self-contradictory. While Flaubert stood as the archetype of the modernist author of the bourgeois age, in postwar debates about the relation of the novel to contemporary society, Robbe-Grillet occupies an analogous position. Both Lucien Goldmann and Barthes hold him up as an exemplary writer whose work addressed a newly entrenched social order. In his 1964 *Towards a Sociology of the Novel,* in which he attempted to fuse Marxist and structuralist methods, Goldmann argued that Robbe-Grillet's novel *Les Gommes* involved a strategic reconfiguration of mythic narrative structure. "The kinship [between this novel and the Oedipus myth] resides in the fact that, in each case, there is a concatenation of events unfolding in accordance with an ineluctable necessity, quite unaffected by men's intentions and acts." While there is a great difference between ancient tragedy's view of destiny and "the mechanical and inevitable process" described by Robbe-Grillet, the myth provided a structure in which to disclose a contemporary crisis in human agency. "The content of the work is precisely this mechanical and ineluctable necessity that governs both relations between men and relations between men and things in a world that resembles a modern machine deprived of self-regulatory mechanisms" (142). Similarly, the content of *Le Voyeur* concerns "the disappearance of any importance and any meaning from individual action" (145). It is this thematic concern which, according to Goldmann, "explains the [innovative] style of the work" (144). What Robbe-Grillet's work addresses, concludes Goldmann, "is the great social and human transformation brought about by the appearance of two new, extremely important phenomena . . . the self-regulations of society and . . . the increasing passivity, the character of 'voyeurs', that individuals are gradually assuming in modern society, the absence of any *active* participation in social life" (146).

The contradiction about agency becomes evident in Goldmann's analysis: the novelist (and the critic) appear as conscious, critical, self-reflexive actors, even while Goldmann argues that Robbe-Grillet's characterization of a totally passive world is sociologically accurate. Unlike Lukács, Goldmann cannot account for the relation between the agency of the writer within the bourgeois institution of letters, on one hand, and the representation of total passivity on the other. While Roland Barthes agrees that Robbe-Grillet is a "radically realistic writer" (as Goldmann put it; 149), Barthes emphasis falls not on what Goldmann refers to as "the simple level of the story" (148), which is where Goldmann locates his own analysis despite the attention to mythic structure; rather, Barthes's defense of Robbe-Grillet and his attack on "Narrative" refigure the understanding of agency through a more formalist, discourse-based analysis and a broader concern with the institution of art.

There are two key concepts in Barthes's analysis of narrative. First, in *Writing Degree Zero* (1953), Barthes argues that narration, "a form common to both the Novel and to History" is "the expression of an historical moment [the nineteenth century]." Narrative invokes the timeless quality of myth and religion; it "presupposes a world which is constructed, elaborated, self-sufficient, reduced to significant lines." The "function" of the narrator of the bourgeois novel "is to unite as rapidly as possible a cause and an end." Because narrative is "the image of an order," presented as immutable and coherent, it "is part of a security system for Belles-Lettres . . . it is one of those numerous formal pacts made between the writer and society for the justification of the former and the serenity of the latter" (29–32). The function of narrative is thus ideological, because "it involves giving to the imaginary the formal guarantee of the real" (33). Posing an opposition between the nineteenth-century narrative-based novel (Balzac) and other works in which "narrative is rejected" in favor of other literary genres (Flaubert) (32), Barthes claims that there begins "an art which in order to escape its pangs of conscience either exaggerates conventions or frantically attempts to destroy them" (38). Because narrative is a set of ordering conventions that "guarantees" a particular social order, those works, from Flaubert to Robbe-Grillet, that reject the conventions of narrative constitute a revolt against that order and its typical artistic institutions.

The second key concept, in "Introduction to the Structural Analysis of Narratives" (1966), is equally polemical. Here, the underlying opposition is not between bourgeois realism and innovative modernism, but rather between "mass culture" and "contemporary writing." Significantly, the concept of narrative, characterized in the earlier essay as "the expression of an historical moment," becomes properly structural and quasi-anthropological: "narrative is present in myth, legend, fable, tale . . . [it] is international, transhistorical, transcultural: it is simply there, like life itself" (79). Although the ostensible purpose of the essay is to delineate narrative's "implicit system of units and rules" (81), the earlier polemic is refigured to disclose the ideological ordering principle of story-emphatic mass culture. Barthes uses Ian Fleming's espionage novel *Goldfinger* (and the movie made from it) to illustrate "that the mainspring of narrative is precisely the confusion of consecution and consequence, what comes *after* being read in narrative as what is *caused by.*" Narrative, in this sense, is "no more than the 'language'" of "Destiny" (94).

This definition of narrative makes the intention of Barthes's essay clear: the mass-culture novel is the modern form of myth, while contemporary experimental writing is the demythification of narrative and its ideological compact with the social order. Integral to his argument is the link, as he sees it, between the ideological function of narrative and the agency of both writer and reader. Agency is represented in fiction through a "code by which the narrator and reader are signified throughout the narrative itself" (110). "In fact," he explains, "narration strictly speaking . . . knows only two systems of signs: personal and apersonal." Barthes describes the "traditional mode of narrative" as entirely apersonal, "designed to wipe out the present of the speaker. As Benveniste puts it: 'In narrative, no one speaks'" (112). For Barthes, what characterizes modern mass-culture narrative, as distinct from purely apersonal traditional narrative, is the "dishonest tourniquet of the two systems," the mixing of the personal and the apersonal. Thus, in the popular crime novel it is "as if in a single person there were the consciousness of a witness, immanent to the discourse, and the consciousness of a murderer, immanent to the referent" (113). Barthes asserts that the dominant type of popular fiction, the first-person "psychological novel," while claiming to represent a purely locutionary act that originates from an individual consciousness, "usually shows a mixture of the two systems, successively mobilizing the signs of non-person and those of person."

This represents, for Barthes, the manner in which popular narrative naturalizes or guarantees the bourgeois ideal of the autonomous individual, and the manner in which the new, contemporary writing seeks to demythologize this ideal. "The psychological person (of referential order)," Barthes claims "bears no relation to the linguistic person, the latter never defined by states of mind, intentions or traits of character but only by its (coded) place in the discourse." By conflating the "psychological person" (who has a will, who acts intentionally) with the "linguistic person," popular narrative dishonestly forges its rhetorical image of the individual in the name of the "real." In contrast, "it is this formal [linguistic] person that writers today are attempting to speak and such an attempt represents an important subversion (the public moreover has the impression that 'novels' are no longer being written)." This act of demythification "aims to transpose narrative . . . whereby the meaning of an utterance is the very act by which it is uttered: today, writing is not 'telling' but saying that one is telling and assigning all the referent ('what one says') to this act of locution; which is why part of contemporary literature is no longer descriptive, but transitive" (114).

It is this quality of being transitive that allows the new, experimental writer to engage actively the agency of the reader, but only by devaluing agency within the work itself. "Our society," writes Barthes, "takes the greatest pains to conjure away the coding of the narrative situation: there is no counting the number of narrational devices which seek to naturalize the subsequent narrative by feigning to make it the outcome of some natural circumstance. . . . The reluctance to declare its codes characterizes bourgeois society and the mass culture issuing from it: both demand signs which do not look like signs" (116). It was from this point that Barthes develops, in *S/Z,* the idea of the writerly: "Why is the writerly our value? Because the goal of literary work (of literature as work) is to make the reader no longer a consumer, but a producer of the text" (4).[14] Underlying the logic of Barthes's critique is a curious reversal: the more that "contemporary writing" declares its narrative codes, emphasizing the *discourse* by transposing the personal mode into the purely apersonal, the more active or productive the reader. This leads to another reversal. The more that *story*—the representation of meaningful individual action—is deemphasized in favor of *discourse,* the more the reader's agency is activated. Thus, for Barthes, it is the intentional demythification of narrative in, for example, Robbe-Grillet's work—dismantling sequence as causality, disclosing its own codes through an emphasis on *discourse,* and removing those narrative conventions whose function is to depict action as motivated and intentional (i.e., the representation of the "psychological" person)—that allows writing to regain a nonideological relation to an actual social world. In *Le Voyeur,* Barthes argues, there is a "tendentious destruction of the story. Plot recedes under the weight of objects. No motives or crime or events, only isolated description of materials denied any intentionality" (*Critical* 53); "the novel becomes a direct experience of man's surroundings" (23).

Paradoxically, by actively removing the representation of agency from narrative, the experimental writer activates the reader's individual productive capability. The contemporary writer transforms the abstract structure of narrative, which is rooted in the premodern genres of myth and folk tale, by extracting narrative's apparent originary focus, individual action. The writer thus consciously, actively, contests his or her membership in the bourgeois order, in which narrative passed from the anonymous-collective to the professional-individual. As I have discussed, it was this problem of active-passivity—of the writer and the bohemian-aesthete hero—that Beckett's early work attempted to confront, and that surrealism attempted to develop into a method of composition, automatic writing. To a certain extent, Barthes's structuralism reinvents and elaborates the circular avant-gardist dilemma that had posed language as both blocking and providing access to the real.

The antinarrative analysis of narrative presents a closed circle of thought: structuralism showed that narrative was nothing but an abstract set of codes, functions, actants, moods, and so forth, only in order to then valorize a type of writing that (according to Barthes) extracted, denied, or exposed these things as mystifying. Narrative cause and effect, and the representation of the psychological person, Barthes claimed, rested on a "logical fallacy" ("Introduction" 94). This antagonism toward depicting the willfully acting individual has its complement in poststructuralism's claim that individual agency (for example, in both Barthes's and Foucault's rejection of the category of the author) is an insignificant factor in understanding cultural processes. As Anthony Giddens has argued, structuralist and poststructuralist theories were flawed because they were "unable to generate satisfactory accounts of human agency" (211). In general, for writers like Foucault or Lévi-Strauss, Giddens argues, "not only does history have no overall teleology, it is in an important sense not the result of the action of human agents. . . . That 'history has no subject' can readily be accepted. But Foucault's history tends to have no active subjects at all. It is history with the agency removed. . . . Moreover, that reflexive appropriation of history basic to history in modern culture does not appear at the level of the agents themselves" (214).

The extraction of agency in the structural study of narrative is not, however, only the manifestation of a linguistically based methodology hostile to "Cartesianism and to every philosophy . . . that treats [individual] consciousness as a datum upon which the foundations of claims to knowledge may be established" (Giddens 206). Like Beckett's work, with which it has been closely associated, the critique of narrative ideology was an expression, in the postwar decades, of a perceived crisis in the meaning and possibility of individual agency; in this sense, the structuralist polemic against narrative mimesis shared an allegiance with Beckett's fiction. Yet Beckett never achieved, nor intended to achieve, the structuralist-inspired call for "narration itself." The vanguardist stance of critics like Barthes and Goldmann led them to a contradictory celebration of the agency of the experimental writer, and his or her reader, which depended on denying that individuals in the social world were conscious, meaningful actors. Beckett's carefully constructed tension between *story* and *discourse,* in contrast, expresses the dilemma of agency as a relation of reader, writer, and the value of narrative mimesis, just as his parodies of philosophical and aesthetic precepts, and the decorum of the social world to which they belong, express a deep ambivalence about the function of high art. The tension between *story* and *discourse* in *Molloy* is also a tension between two views of what a novel is: a communicative narrative mimesis bound up with a faith in human agency, no matter how damaged, or a text; a tension that also posed the writer as both a social actor and an impersonal, immaterial transcriber of ordering principles.

The shift in Beckett's fiction—from the self-contradictory defense of inaction in the interwar years to the postwar narrative experimentation where the paradoxical absence of meaningful individual action is rooted in the absence of a mediating community, and expressed as a disruption of the ability to tell stories—is indicative of the development of his work in general. World War II is not only a stark chronological marker in Beckett's life and career—he was thirty-four when he joined the

Resistance—but it marks a set of changes in his vision of literary art. It was as if Benjamin's storyteller, the purveyor of wisdom and experience, had returned from some unimaginable void, to inform his listeners that the conditions of their existence had dissolved, and that he could not, in telling the story of its dissolution, find any explanation for his ability or his willingness to speak.

VI

A Contest of Nightmares:
The Unnamable and *1984*

"Incomprehensible Uneasiness" in the Void

In his first postwar stories, the nouvelles, and the first novel of the trilogy, *Molloy*, Beckett developed a new narrative perspective and a new social content. Abandoning the ironic omniscience of his interwar writing, and transforming the actively passive bohemian-aesthete protagonist into the consciously contradictory, eloquently communicative voices of vagrant and bourgeois, terrorized subject and paralyzed agent, Beckett had fashioned a strikingly innovative form of fiction, a disturbing and hilarious novelized storytelling that constantly undermines its own pretensions to offer a "moral." In *Malone Dies*, the second novel of the trilogy, Beckett experimented with a similar but ultimately less effective narrative perspective. The first-person narrator Malone, alone, approaching paralysis and death and confined to a bed in what seems to be a public institution for the indigent, describes his own pathetic condition and tells stories—"neither beautiful nor ugly . . . calm . . . almost lifeless, like the teller" (2)—about an impoverished family and an insane asylum. These stories-within-a-story deteriorate and intermingle with the frame story of Moran's own isolated demise. Compared to the paradoxical voices in *Molloy* and the interplay of its two sections, the novel seems static; closer, in some parts, to a relatively conventional dramatic monologue, in others, to the schematic oppositions in *Watt*. There is a simplification of the theme of the charitable institution, drawn from the earlier nouvelles, and an overreliance on the tired metaphor of the asylum, harking back to *Murphy*. Some years later, writers such as Camus, with the judge-penitent narrator of *The Fall*, and Fuentes, with the deathbed confession of the narrator in *The Death of Artemio Cruz*, would more successfully exploit the static, self-pitying monologue, primarily because they used it in conjunction with a geopolitically specific historical context, something that Beckett was never willing—or able—to provide.[1]

In *The Unnamable*, however, the last novel of the trilogy, Beckett pushed the narrative form he had created in the nouvelles (and extended in *Molloy*) in a new and extreme direction. Beckett had presented his earlier narrators' loss of identity (and consequently, the emphasis on the text) as a reaction-formation to a rejecting-rejected social world. *The Unnamable* begins with a first-person narrator already removed from any social or material context whatsoever. Neither beggar, isolated wanderer, nor moribund invalid, the narrator's only defining feature seems to be his uncertainty about who and where he is, and his relationship to the words he is uttering:

Where now? Who now? When now? Unquestioning. I, say I. . . . Can it be that one day, off it goes on, that one day I simply stayed in. . . . Perhaps that is how it began. You think you are simply resting, the better to act when the time comes, or for no reason, and you soon find yourself powerless ever to do anything again. No matter how it happened. It, say it, not knowing what. Perhaps I simply assented at last to an old thing. But I did nothing. I seem to speak, it is not I, about me, it is not about me. These few general remarks to begin with. What am I to do, what shall I do, what should I do, in my situation, how proceed? By aporia pure and simple? Or by affirmations and negations invalidated as uttered, or sooner or later? (3)

The preoccupation with agency and the contradictory status of the voice, important features of the earlier postwar works, become in *The Unnamable* the preconditions for the obsessively meticulous account of abstract conflicts about language and identity that make up the substance of the novel. The questions are simultaneously mimetic—the voice of a consciousness in crisis—and rhetorical; Beckett is making up a story by *asking* where, who, when, how to proceed, rather than by providing answers. The opening of the novel is, in part, a not-so-oblique reference to Beckett's self-consciousness about his own writing since the nouvelles: "affirmations and negations invalidated as uttered, or sooner or later" is a good description of one of the organizing principles of the narrative method he began to develop in 1945. What has been termed the novel's emphasis on intertextuality—the narrator's references to the characters of Beckett's earlier fiction, from Murphy to Molloy—is also a sign of this self-consciousness. Similarly, one of the novel's central motifs is the narrator's anxiety-ridden obsession with the authenticity of the voice, his longing to "find a voice of my own, in all this babble" (84) and his struggle against "their language" which "they have crammed me full of to prevent me from saying who I am" (51). The narrator's compulsive anxiety about narrative procedure seems to refer, abstractly but intentionally, to Beckett's uncertainty about his own experiments in fiction.

There are two contrasting implications of the narrating perspective constructed in *The Unnamable*. On one hand, the narrator's crisis of self-definition is an image of problems about writing that Beckett himself is experiencing. The intertextual references invite the reader to make an identification between narrator and author; in fact, because the narrator is first and foremost an abstract, nameless "I" obsessively concerned with language and voices, the author-narrator identity is the *only* identity suggested. When Beckett cites the first line of his first postwar story, "The End," or makes reference to *Molloy*, it's in the manner of an author complaining about his own work; in this case, chastising himself, futilely, for being unable to take the themes of domination and poverty seriously:

For what I am doing is not being done without a minimum of mind. . . . The master. I never paid him enough attention. No more perhaps either, that old trick is worn to a thread. I'll forbid myself everything, then go on as if I hadn't. The master. A few allusions here and there, as to a satrap, with a view to enlisting sympathy. *They clothed me and gave me money,* that kind of thing, the light touch. Then no more. Or Moran's boss, I forget his name. . . . But to investigate this matter seriously, I mean with as much futile ardour as that of the underling, which I hoped was mine . . . no, that never occurred to me. (33) (emphasis added)

On the other hand, in contrast to this self-reflection about writing, Beckett exploits to a greater degree than in earlier works those resources of written language that interfere with language's referential and mimetic capacities, to emphasize instead contradiction, paradox, and "aporia." As one commentator put it, by "constantly contradicting his own utterances and self-projections he [the narrator of *The Unnamable*] evokes the fleeting notion of a subject at the vanishing point" (Schwab 133). From this perspective, the narrator appears as a device through which Beckett explores the relationship between language and concepts of the individual, the self and "subjectivity" (Schwab 131). Viewed one way, then, Beckett's innovation in the last novel of the trilogy tends to emphasize *writing* as an inherently contradictory activity and the narrator as emblematic of the writer's troubled situation. Viewed another way, the novel emphasizes the *narrator* (the "I" or the "subject") as a contradictory entity and writing as a means of exposing traditional "philosophical and empirical notions of the subject" as absurd or self-invalidating (Schwab 137). The title of the novel embodies this contrast: "unnamable" may refer to a writer's problem—how to find a name for such a radically innovative novel—or it may refer to a linguistic-philosophical problem about the relation of identity to language. Throughout the novel, Beckett poses the narrator as both *author,* struggling against a set of conditions that he experiences but cannot understand, and abstract *subject,* struggling against linguistically bound definitions of the self. At times, Beckett lets this double status stand as a blatant contradiction: "How, in such conditions, can I write, to consider only the manual aspect of that bitter folly? I don't know. I could know. But I shall not know. Not this time. It is I who write, who cannot raise my hand from my knee. It is I who think, just enough to write, whose head is far" (17-18).

    This contrast of author and discursive subject, writer and object of writing, is refracted through the theme of "words" and "silence." Words are liberating, but only when the narrator senses, or hopes, that the words he utters are his own; words are also a force of domination, part of an ominous linguistic determinism. The narrator refers to his own disordered testimony as "the terror-stricken babble of the condemned to silence" (94); but this babble may only be a reflection of the narrator's nonempirical existence: "I'm in words, made of words, others' words . . . this dust of words, with no ground for their settling" (139). Images of imprisonment reinforce the sense that the narrator is trapped by this double condition, both speaking subject and discursive slave: the narrator registers his psychic situation as "motionless" (5), "condemned" (19) in a prisonlike "void" (17), a place of "uniform suffering" (112) and "terror" (88); at times, he imagines there is a "collar, or ring, of cement" (62) encircling his neck. He feels himself "a wordless thing in an empty place, a hard shut dry cold black place, where nothing stirs, nothing speaks, and that I listen, and that I seek, like a caged beast born of caged beasts born of caged beasts"(138).

Similarly, silence is a state of condemnation and, at the same time, a means of escaping the prison house of language. "What I speak of, what I speak with, all comes from them. It's all the same to me, but it's no good, there's no end to it. It's of me now I must speak, even if I have to do it with their language, it will be a start, a step towards the silence and the end of madness" (50–51). The contrast between narrator as author and narrator as subject is thus bound up with the variable values of silence and language (words, voices, speech, writing). This double view of language as both determining and liberating consciousness is part of Beckett's inheritance from the interwar avant garde, a contradictory aesthetic attitude that, as I have discussed, he had integrated into his earliest fiction and criticism. In *The Unnamable*, however, Beckett sets up the conflicting views in order to emphasize the contradiction itself, over and above any conviction that language either imprisons or liberates. The narrator describes the occasion of his narration as a response to an impossible situation; in turn, his response generates blatant contradiction: "The search for a means to put an end to things, an end to speech, is what enables the discourse to continue" (15).

If, during the interwar years, Beckett was unaware of the contradictions inherent in avant-gardist notions of language and consciousness, by the time he finished the trilogy he seems to have become obsessed by them. Characteristically, Beckett manages this obsession by playing contrasting attitudes against one another. No matter how much the struggle over voices and words in the novel—or between the "I" and the "they," between "me" and "my master" (30)—resonates with the value of radical individual freedom, the image of what might be gained by detaching identity from logos is bleak and angry:

> Ah a nice state they have me in, but still I'm not their creature, not quite, not yet. . . . Not to be able to open my mouth without proclaiming them, and our fellowship, that's what they imagine they'll have me reduced to. . . . But I'll fix their jibberish for them. I never understood a word of it in any case, not a word of the stories it spews, like gobbets in a vomit. My inability to absorb, my genius for forgetting, are more than they reckoned with. Dear incomprehension, it's thanks to you I'll be myself, in the end. Nothing will remain of all the lies they have glutted me with. And I'll be myself at last, as a starveling belches his odorless wind, before the bliss of coma. (51)

The narrator rails against their "lectures" and "words," only to realize there is no alternative. To be oneself, to find one's own voice, Beckett tirelessly reiterates, would be no better. The vanguardist fantasy of a psychically authentic language is powerless to undo the language of conformity, convention, and enforced "fellowship." "I shall have to speak of things of which I cannot speak," says the narrator, summing up the introductory paragraph of the novel. "And at the same time I am obliged to speak. I shall never be silent. Never" (4). The "never" carries the weight of both resistance and resignation. Throughout *The Unnamable* Beckett seems to insist that struggling and capitulating, at least in avant-gardist literature, amounts to the same thing.

Even though dominant views of *The Unnamable* in academic criticism insist that Beckett's text entirely effaces the referential function of narrative, becoming an exercise in "pure textuality" (Schwab 167), they nevertheless recognize, often unconsciously, the mimetic and referential aspect of the novel. For example, Gabriele Schwab (whose 1994 essay, cited above, is one of the most careful analyses of this type) claims that *The Unnamable* presents us with an "exhaustion of literary subjectivity" (132) in which "negation is used to subvert the very foundations of language and subject" (158). However, she continually refers to the narrator as "he." The narrator's undeniable maleness (which no critic seems to question) means that Beckett's text mimics the voice of a particular, gendered person. In fact, the narrator is not only male, he is also European, educated, a bourgeois. In some places, the narrator assumes a genteel, familiar tone: "I say what I'm told to say, that's all there is to it, and yet I wonder. . . . I don't feel the jostle of words in my mouth, and when you say a poem you like, if you happen to like poetry, in the underground, or in bed, for yourself, the words are there, somewhere, without the least sound, I don't feel that either" (133). In other places, he violently rejects his bourgeois origins, but in a typically bourgeois, masculinist fashion. Thus, telling one of his "stories" (in which he switches back and forth between third and first person) about the grotesque demise of his family, the narrator sums up: "I appear as upset at having been delivered so economically of a pack of blood relations, not to mention the two cunts into the bargain, the one for ever accursed that ejected me into this world and the other, infundibuliform, in which, pumping my likes, I tried to take my revenge" (48).

While the embedded story's imagery is surreal, its cruelty absurdly intensified—"stamping under foot the unrecognizable remains of my family, here a face, there a stomach" (49–50)—the relation to a masculinist literary tradition in which women appear as mother and whore, as vehicles of men's entrapment in conventional society and, consequently, as objects of men's aggression, is obvious. No matter how much Beckett short-circuits the ability of language to evoke an objective world, he equally evokes the culturally specific perspective from which this "subversion" of communicative norms is mounted. What constitutes the innovative power of the novel is not its status at "the cutting edge of contemporary explorations of language and subjectivity" (Schwab 131), but rather Beckett's self-conscious construction of a narrator whose obsessive struggle against the language of social order and identity never loses the cultural specificity characteristic of the genre.

Beckett ensures this specificity in two ways. First, he articulates the narrator's anxiety and guilt in terms of the midlife crisis of a bourgeois man, an intellectual or a professional. The narrator exhibits a masculinist repression of emotion, a complacent fear of change, an overriding desire for order, a sense of individual powerlessness, and a suspicion that his existential dread is nothing more than liberal guilt, a compensation for his ashamed awareness that he has never really experienced suffering at all. Secondly, Beckett parodically refracts attitudes about the social function of literature through images of the narrator, the "bright boy of the class" (125), as a victim of a good, middle-class upbringing. It is from this perspective that Beckett explicitly mocks the pretension that the voice is an impersonal creation or a purely textual construct: "But my dear man, come, be reasonable, look, this is you, look at this photograph, and here's your file, no convictions, I assure you, come now, make an effort, at your age, to have no identity, it's a scandal" (125).

While humanist critics have eschewed the structuralist-inspired emphasis on textuality, they have likewise ignored the cultural specificity of Beckett's voices.[2] Perhaps the underlying reason such critics have overemphasized the universal quality of Beckett's fiction is that Beckett shows how the claim of universality is also the expression of those who fear losing the social position necessary to maintain particular cultural tastes as unchanging principles of judgment.[3] In one of the novel's most effective passages (on pages 6–9), the narrator's description of his situation in the prisonlike void exposes both his fear of emotive affect and the need to believe himself the perspectival center of his universe, even though he realizes there are no grounds for such a belief. The passage begins:

> I have always been sitting here, at this selfsame spot, my hands on my knees, gazing before me like a great horn-owl in an aviary. The tears stream down my cheeks from my unblinking eyes. What makes me weep so? From time to time. There is nothing saddening here. Perhaps it is liquefied brain. Past happiness in any case has clean gone from my memory, assuming it was ever there. If I accomplish other natural functions it is unawares. Nothing ever troubles me. And yet I am troubled. Nothing has ever changed since I have been here. But I dare not infer from this that nothing ever will change. (6–7)

Intense sadness can only be admitted with the insistence that nothing is wrong; the sensate body is objectified, so fearful is the narrator of losing his sense of stability. Beckett configures the narrator's anxiety as a fixation on order. Just as he insists that "all has proceeded, all this time, in the utmost calm, the most perfect order" (7), Beckett turns the narrator's admission of denial—"Nothing ever trouble me. And yet I am troubled"—into a formula whose ritualistic repetition serves to quell his psychic disorder: "So I have no cause for anxiety. And yet I am anxious" (18); "So there is nothing to be afraid of. And yet I am afraid" (20).

In his attempt to understand his surroundings, the narrator summons forth an obstinate self-complacency. The passage continues:

> I owe my existence to no one. . . . These notions of forbears, of houses
> where lamps are lit at night, and other such, where do they come to me
> from? And all these questions I ask myself. It is not in a spirit of curiosity.
> I cannot be silent. About myself I need know nothing. Here all is clear.
> No, all is not clear. But the discourse must go on. So one invents
> obscurities. Rhetoric. (7)

Any emotion or intimate memory that might disrupt the order is immediately reined
in by the narrator's nervous compulsion to keep talking. In turn, utterance becomes
the narrator's means of denying responsibility for the "conditions" in which he finds
himself. Self-reflection becomes an occasion not for critical thought but for reinforc-
ing one's devotion to the status quo:

> From the unexceptional order which has prevailed here up to date may I
> infer that such will always be the case? I may of course. But the mere fact
> of asking myself a question gives me to reflect. It is in vain I tell myself
> that its only purpose is to stimulate the lagging discourse, this excellent
> explanation does not satisfy me. Can it be I am the prey of a genuine
> preoccupation, of a need to know as one might say? I don't know. I'll try
> it another way. If one day a change were to take place, resulting from a
> principle of disorder already present, or on its way, what then? That
> would seem to depend on the nature of the change. No, here all change
> would be fatal. (8)

The narrator suspects a "principle of disorder" in the lights he sees: "What is there so
strange about them, so wrong? Is it their irregularity, their instability, their shining
strong one minute and weak the next" (7)? Momentarily, he considers the possibility
of his own part in the problem: "They are perhaps unwavering and fixed and my fitful
perceiving the cause of their inconstancy" (8). He is tempted to give up thinking of
himself in the privileged perspective of the center; he admits, in any case, that his
views are narrowly "fixed": "I like to think I occupy the center, but nothing is less
certain. In a sense I would be better off at the circumference, since my eyes are always
fixed in the same direction" (8). But reflection on the possibility of his own relation to
the disorder only leads him back to the complacent admission/denial that something
is wrong. The passage ends:

> It is equally possible, I do not deny it, that I too am in perpetual
> motion. . . . In which case there would be no further grounds for my
> complaining about the disorder of the lights, this being due simply to my
> insistence on regarding them as always the same lights and viewed always
> from the same point. All is possible, or almost. But the best is to think of
> myself as fixed and at the center of this place, whatever its shape and
> extent may be. This is also probably the most pleasing to me. In a word,

no change apparently since I have been here, disorder of the lights
perhaps an illusion, all change to be feared, incomprehensible uneasiness. (9)

Beckett's method here is to reify abstractions by dissolving the distance between
elemental compositional choices of novel writing, such as narrative perspective, and
the narrator's psychic state of "incomprehensible uneasiness," his fear of being, as it
were, decentered. The rejection of the principle theme-forms of modernism, from the
device of the interior monologue to the narrative space of the metropolis, that Beckett
began in the nouvelles culminate in *The Unnamable*'s aspiration to reject perspective
altogether. Only a hypothetically perspectiveless form could mimic the incomprehen-
sibility and futility of individual action, a theme that had been part of Beckett's social
vision since "Dante and the Lobster." This perspectival void is an ideal; it cannot be
achieved, but it can be represented. The narrator emotionlessly complains that his
"very eyes can no longer close as they once could . . . no longer look away, or down,
or up open to heaven, but must remain forever fixed and staring on the narrow space
before them where there is nothing to be seen, 99 percent of the time. They must be
as red as live coals. I sometimes wonder if the two retinae are not facing each other"
(17).

     This is Beckett's image of the author in the void: blinded by his constant
vigilance, radically uncertain about the authenticity of his voice, believing in the
power of neither words nor silence, rejecting both submission to an anonymous they
and faith in an autonomous self, insisting without cause that he occupies the center of
the universe, anxious and troubled though claiming there is nothing wrong, weeping
without emotion, fixated on absolute order and fearing all change, self-complacent
though he understands nothing of the world around him. The abstract void is itself
part of the image's content. The narrator's anxieties are both a response to the
condition of having no means of referring himself to the world and a response to
questions—"I. Who might that be?" (68)—whose answers, *when posed in a void,* can
only wind up in hyper-self-conscious aporia. Compelled to face nothingness, the
narrator is aghast at finding that it is the existential space itself which generates, rather
than expresses, dilemmas about existence. In *The Unnamable,* the void provides no
clue of what a self stripped of its historically contingent identity could possibly be;
rather, the void is a place where critical consciousness, the awareness of one's own
relation to problems like suffering and disorder, becomes nothing but a defensive fear
about losing one's place in the center.

The Flâneur in a Jar

For Beckett, the void—beginning with his first published novel, in the chapter on
"Murphy's mind"—had always meant a place where the struggle to imagine a relation
between art and society, between inner mind and outer reality, resulted in aporia. In

The Unnamable, Beckett drew on two strands of his previous work to provide the necessary dynamic contrast with the void's negation of social content. One strand, the less effective one, is evident in the novel's master-servant theme, which harkens back to *Watt.* In this vein, the narrator complains that he has "spoken for his master" or perhaps "a whole college of tryants" (249). The master has given him "a pensum, at birth perhaps, as a punishment for having being born." To say the pensum is to be released, but the narrator has no clue what the pensum is. It might be an admission of guilt, or "might it not rather be the praise of my master, intoned" that will "obtain his foregiveness" (30–32). The other, more vivid, strand provides the link to the rejecting-rejected social world: Belacqua and the grocer in "Dante and the Lobster," Murphy in mercantile London in *Murphy,* the beggar on the street corner in "The End," Molloy passing through the gates of the city, Moran pondering his relation to the "anonymous organization" of agents. In *The Unnamable,* with its more extreme attenuation of social content, the existential dilemma is provoked not by the confrontation between the world and the liminal hero, but by the void itself. In turn, the void is parodied when Beckett projects the narrator outside the anxiously imagined "order" of nothingness and into the street; that is, into relation with the narrative perspective of the modern novel. Consistent with the self-critiquing attitude of the entire novel, Beckett begins the episode, the narrator's "last story," with a summary of the reduction of the narrating figure in his own fiction, from the nouvelles to *Malone Dies:*

> But at the period I refer to now this active life is at an end, I do not move and never shall again, unless it be under the impulsion of a third party. For of the great traveller I had been, on my hands and knees in the later stages, then crawling on my belly or rolling on the ground, only the trunk remains (in sorry trim), surmounted by the head. . . . Stuck like a sheaf of flowers in a deep jar, its neck flush with my mouth, on the side of a quiet street near the shambles, I am at rest at last. If I turn, I shall not say my head, but my eyes, free to roll as they list, I can see the statue of the apostle of horse's meat, a bust. (55)

While the narrator in the void responds to the terrifying vagueness of his situation, the narrator in the street is rather hilariously oppressed by a familiar, everyday world. Indeed, Beckett's Parisian colleagues might have recognized the spot of the narrator's enjarment, on the "Rue Brancion" (77) across from the Vaugirard abattoirs not far from where Beckett once lived. While the image is classically surrealist (the seedy Parisian street was a favorite surrealist backdrop), the narrator in his jar considers himself the antithesis of avant-gardist provocation:

> Though not exactly in order I am tolerated by the police. They know I am speechless and consequently incapable of taking unfair advantage of my situation to stir up the population against its governors, by means of burning oratory during the rush hour or subversive slogans whispered,

after nightfall, to belated pedestrians the worse for drink. And since I have lost all my members, with the exception of the onetime virile, they know also that I shall not be guilty of any gestures liable to be construed as inciting to alms, a prisonable offence. The fact is I trouble no one, except possibly that category of hypersensitive persons for whom the least thing is an occasion for scandal and indignation. But even here the risk is negligible, such people avoiding the neighborhood. . . . From this point of view the spot is well chosen, from my point of view. (55)

This particular "point of view" is one Beckett had been developing since the nouvelles. The beggar on the street corner, with his expressionless masklike face, was a parody of both liberal guilt and communist demands for a didactic art; Molloy, in his confrontation with the police, both an affront to decency and a self-pitying revolt against "systematic decorum." In *The Unnamable,* the refracted image of the author-in-society is absolutely harmless, stripped of arms, unable to offend, provoke, or violate. His masculinity, too, survives only as a reminder of what once had power but is now impotent. Every possibility of social disruption is neutralized:

And even those sufficiently unhinged to be affected by the spectacle I offer, I mean upset and temporarily diminished in their capacity for work and aptitude for happiness, need only look at me a second time . . . to have immediately their minds made easy. For my face reflects nothing but the satisfaction of one savouring a well-earned rest. . . . And alone perhaps the state of my skull, covered with pustules and bluebottles, these latter abounding in such a neighbourhood, preserved me from being an object of envy for many, and a source of discontent. I hope this gives a fair picture of my situation. (55–56)

Beckett builds up this grotesque figure, the vestigial remains of the modernist flâneur, to debunk the aesthetics of provocation and shock, even though other parts of the novel are clearly intended to disturb. As one earnest commentator put it, "it would be dishonest to pretend that its [*The Unnamable*'s] anguish did not cause discomfort in us, that its hatred, grief and misery did not make it somewhat unbearable to read" (Fletcher 179). Beckett's own brand of postwar vanguardism, his aesthetic of failure and his disdain for representational art (discussed below), was always accompanied by an undercutting self-criticism. In such a vein, Beckett makes his tale of the narrator-in-the-jar a parodic commentary on the prosaic function of art in everyday life. The shocking "*merdre*" spewed out by Alfred Jarry's infamous Ubu at the turn of the century has now become garden compost:[4]

Once a week I was taken out of my receptacle, so that it might be emptied. This duty fell to the proprietress of the chophouse across the street and she performed it punctually and without complaint, beyond

an occasional good-natured reflection to the effect that I was a nasty pig,
for she had a kitchen garden. . . . I realized darkly that if she took care of
me thus, it was not solely out of goodness. . . . It must not be forgotten
that I represented for this woman an undeniable asset. For quite apart
from the services I rendered to her lettuce, I constituted for her establish-
ment a kind of landmark, not to say an advertisement. . . . That she was
well aware of this is shown by the trouble she had taken to festoon my jar
with Chinese lanterns . . . And the jar itself, so that the passer-by might
consult with greater ease the menu attached to it, had been raised on a
pedestal at her own expense. It is thus I learnt that her turnips in gravy
are not so good as they used to be, but that on the other hand her carrots,
equally in gravy, are even better than formerly. The gravy has not varied.
This is the kind of language I can understand, these the kind of clear and
simple notions on which it is possible for me to build, I ask for no other
spiritual nourishment. (56–57)

This is the counterpart to the narrator in the void, the abstract "I" raging against
"their" words. The language of authenticity the narrator has been searching for all
along turns out to be, provisionally at least, the chatter of the petit bourgeois; his
search for "what to do" is fulfilled by the demands of the chophouse: "I represent for
her a tidy little capital" (57), he is proud to announce. In a festooned jar, raised on a
pedestal, the narrator is an emblem of a domesticated avant garde whose shock
techniques were developed in tandem with the techniques of advertising and
propaganda.

The episode is also a domestic comedy which deteriorates into a grotesque cry
for communication and companionship, growing more pathetic with the narrator's
increasing loss of "point of view." Most of the time, the proprietress neglects to cover
the hero in bad weather. "I have tried to make her understand, dashing my head
angrily against the neck of my jar. . . . I let my spittle flow over, in an attempt to show
my displeasure. In vain," he explains; "we made a balls of it between us, I with my
signs and she with her reading of them" (58). His head and torso wither in the
elements and the "woman, displeased at seeing me sink lower and lower," fills his jar
with sawdust and fixes his head in a cement collar (61–62). His vision severely
restricted, he can no longer observe his shadow at "the hour of the aperitif" when
people pause to read the menu, a "joy, for which my part I should have thought
harmless, and without danger for the public" (73). He becomes fearful that his
"protectress" will cease caring for him. When the people passing by no longer notice
him, the only outside evidence he has of his own existence are the dogs who piss on
his pedestal and the flies swarming around his rotting torso: "The flies vouch for me,
if you like, but how far? Would they not settle with equal appetite on a lump of shit?"
(75).

By the end of the episode these images, both absurd and evocative of physical
torture, begin to dissolve with the narrator's suspicion that his story is just another

device by "them" to distract him from his search for authentic speech-silence. In desperation, he turns to the woman as the only hope of validating his humanity:

> She loves me, I always felt it. She needs me. Her chophouse, her hus-
> band, her children if she has any, are not enough, there is in her a void
> that I alone can fill. . . . There was a time I thought she was perhaps a
> near relation, mother, sister, daughter, or suchlike, perhaps even a
> wife. . . . This woman has never spoken to me. . . . Never an affection-
> ate word, never a reprimand. For fear of bringing me to the public
> notice? Or lest the illusion should be dispelled? . . . The moment is at
> hand when my only believer must deny me. . . . something has changed.
> It is not a night like other nights. . . . The sawdust no longer presses
> against my stumps, I don't know where I end. I left it yesterday, the street,
> the chophouse, the slaughter. . . . There will never be another woman
> wanting me in vain to live, my shadow at evening will not darken the
> ground. (78–80)

With the loss of compassion comes the dissolution into the void, the dissolution of *story* into *discourse*. Beckett presents the stories the narrator tells himself as distinct from his abstract, aporia-ridden existence in words. "And I see myself slipping, though not yet at the last extremity, towards the resorts of fable. Would it not be better if I were simply to keep on saying babababa, for example, while waiting to ascertain the true function of this venerable organ [i.e, the voice]?" (28), he asks himself when in the void. In *The Unnamable* the emphasis on *text*—on the geopolitically placeless void, on the act of narrating itself, on words—is most pro-nounced because stories, once a comfort for Beckett's protagonist-narrators, now appear as the master's tool, as a trap. To tell a story about one's life outside the void is to capitulate to "them," but to allow them to tell stories about you is even worse. "Mahood," a name the narrator uses when referring to himself as a product of language, appears as an emissary from them; a figure who has "represented" the narrator "in the midst of men" (12) and "usurped" his name, "the one they foisted on me, up there in their world" (13):

> It was he told me stories about me, lived in my stead, issued forth from
> me, came back to me, entered back into me, heaped stories on my
> head. . . . It is his voice which has often, always, mingled with mine, and
> sometimes drowned it completely. . . . When he was away I tried to find
> myself again, to forget what he said, about me, about my misfortunes,
> fatuous misfortunes, idiotic pains, in the light of my true situation,
> revolting word. But his voice continued to testify for me, as though
> woven into mine, preventing me from saying who I was . . . it will
> disappear, one day, I hope, from mine, completely. But in order for that
> to happen I must speak, speak. (29)

By the end of the novel, however, the pointless struggle to wrest away a self-identical voice from the "babble" wears down the narration to a chaotic, breathless chain of phrases, while stories seem to be the narrator's last defense: "There was never anything to be got from those stories, I have mine, somewhere . . . it will be the end, of this hell of stories . . . perhaps I'll curse them yet, they'll know what it is to be the subject of conversation . . . then I'll let down my trousers and shit stories on them, stories, photographs, records, sites, lights, gods and fellow creatures." (130).

The only binding element in this manic accumulation of contradictory fears and hopes about stories and words, the only constant in the anguished clash of "affirmations and negations," is the sense of struggle itself—narrative is reduced and abstracted to its primary element. For struggle to exist, there must be at least two sides, there must be a decisive feature of the novel that wrests consciousness away from the solipsistic void, if only in order to contest, futilely, the solipsistic fallacy. For Beckett, the critical consciousness that fuels the sense of struggle is the antithesis of linguistic determinism or solipsism, or even the aesthetic sphere itself:

> My understanding is not yet sufficiently well-oiled to function without the pressure of some critical circumstance, such as a violent pain felt for the first time. . . . For others the time-abolishing joys of impersonal and disinterested speculation. I only think, if that is the name for this vertiginous panic as of hornets smoked out of their nest, once a certain degree of terror has been exceeded. . . . And sometimes I say to myself I am in a head, it's terror makes me say it, and the longing to be in safety, surrounded on all sides by massive bone. (87–88)

"Critical circumstance," rather than "the time abolishing joys of impersonal and disinterested speculation," ultimately define expression, no matter how chaotic or formless. The status of this critical consciousness is radically ambivalent, like everything else in the novel. But the sense of struggle, evident in every line, grows more intense as the "uneasy" sentences break down into a threadbare logic of phrases whose compulsive repetition alone propels the exhausted voice. There are images, toward the end, of solidarity and defeat in the face of domination: "Enormous prison, like a hundred thousand cathedrals, never anything else any more from this time forth . . . those are words, it speaks of a prison, I've no objection, vast enough for a whole people. . . . I must be there already, perhaps I'm not alone, perhaps a whole people is here, and the voice its voice, coming to me fitfully, we would have lived, been free a moment" (172). There is also a grotesque sense of anomie, the feeling that individual freedom without limitations imposed by a moral community is unbearable: "Yes, we must have walls, I need walls, good and thick, I need a prison, I was right, for me alone, I'll go there now, I'll put me in it" (173). The narrator begins to hear nothing but the echo of his own self-hatred and guilt: the voice is a "confession," an "indictment," it is "accusing"—"I want to be punished. . . . I want to go, give myself up, a victim is essential" (175). The source of the guilt, it seems, has been from the very beginning the narrator's awareness of a squandered resource. "Possessed of nothing but my voice, the voice, it may seem natural, once the idea of obligation has been swallowed, that I should interpret it as an obligation to say something" (31). The expressive voice, once considered a gift bestowed upon the poet by the muses, has become a horrible burden in postwar Paris.

The famous final phrases of the novel terminate, of course, in affirmation:

> You must say words as long as there are any. . . . Perhaps they have
> carried me to the threshold of my story, before the door that opens on my
> story, that would surprise me, if it opens, it will be I, it will be the silence,
> where I am, I don't know, I'll never know, in the silence you don't know,
> you must go on, I can't go on, I'll go on. (179)

This affirmation of the ability to use one's gift, no matter how painful, is also remarkable when we consider it comes from a writer who had already written eight books of fiction and was still, at the time of writing, virtually unknown. Beckett's entanglement with the contradictory cultural politics of the interwar period had led him to a narrative form fashioned out of nothing but those contradictions, laid bare and carried out to exhaustion. The affirmation at the end of *The Unnamable* is a sign of Beckett's awareness that, at last, he had found a way of overcoming his devotion to a vision of aesthetic modernism that denied the connecting, mimetic, communicative function of literature, but that he had done so without compromise, without taking up an alternative position that would, in turn, deny art its insistence on freedom of expression.

The Reinvention of the New and the Aesthetic of Failure

Beckett finished *The Unnamable* (in French, *L'Innomable*) in January of 1950. Although Beckett had, by then, a minor reputation, mostly among fellow writers in Britain and France, he was still unable to find a publisher for *Watt* or any of his longer postwar fiction. *Molloy* had been rejected by six publishers. Finally, in November 1950, the entire trilogy was accepted by Editions de Minuit, a struggling postwar publishing house looking for new experimental writing.[5] *Molloy* (in French) was published in March of 1951, *Malone Meurt* in October. *En attendant Godot*, which Beckett had written in late 1948 as a "relaxation" from the rigorous composition of the trilogy (qtd. in Bair 381), had its world premiere in Paris in January 1953; *L'Innomable* was published in July of that year. In 1955, the English version of *Molloy* came out. *Waiting for Godot* was performed in London later that year and in Miami and New York in early 1956. In April of the same year, in one of the first pieces about Beckett published in the United States, Kenneth Rexroth remarked, somewhat wryly, that "the European reception of Beckett in the last couple of years . . . has been dizzying. He has become an international public figure like Lollobrigida or

Khrushchev" (325). Within the span of five years, beginning around 1951, Beckett had gone from being an obscure writer in his midforties to an international literary star.

Beckett's entrance into the arena of world literature marks the end of the most important phase of his career. Though Beckett would continue to publish shorter plays and prose pieces, and one more book-length fiction at the beginning of the 1960s, nothing he wrote before 1945 or after 1950—with the exception of *Endgame,* begun in 1955—had the impact of the work he produced in the five years after the war. Beckett himself, just at the moment when he began to gain worldwide attention, recognized the uniqueness of this period. As he put it in an interview in May, 1956, in the *New York Times,* "I wrote all [*sic*] my work very fast—between 1946 and 1950. Since then I haven't written anything. Or at least nothing that has seemed to me valid. . . . In the last book—'L'Innomable'—there's complete disintegration. . . . The very last thing I wrote—'Textes pour rien'—was an attempt to get out of the attitude of disintegration, but it failed" (qtd. in Graver 148).

In one respect, this statement is part of the guarded public persona Beckett began to cultivate in the late 1950s, the self-effacing, inscrutable yet matter-of-fact utterer of postwar pessimism. Nevertheless, there is a good deal of truth in Beckett's suggestion that his postwar aesthetic of disintegration and failure, while only beginning to gain critical recognition in the late 1950s, was already a thing of the past. While his later theater pieces could plausibly be viewed within the development of performance art in the 1960s and '70s, around the time Beckett published his next book-length work of fiction, *Comment c'est* (1961; English version, *How It Is,* 1964), there was already a new set of cultural developments, especially in the genre of the novel, that seem distant from Beckett's reworking of the European modernist tradition. To cite only a few of the novels that, from the 1950s to the early '60s, seemed to initiate a new "school" or lend prestige to a previously marginal one: the beat movement, with Kerouac's *On the Road* (1957); the Afro-American novel, with Ellison's *Invisible Man (1952);* the feminist novel, with Lessing's *The Golden Notebook* (1962); the Latin-American "boom" novel and "magical realism," with Carpentier's *Los Pasos Perdidos* (1953) and Rulfo's *Pedro Páramo* (1955); the postcolonial novel, with Achebe's *Things Fall Apart* (1958); the "angry young man," with Sillitoe's *Saturday Night and Sunday Morning* (1958); and the *nouveau roman,* with Robbe-Grillet's *Les Gommes* (1953).[6]

Among the authors involved in these various trends and movements, it was only Alain Robbe-Grillet who claimed Beckett's writing in support of his own vision of literary renewal. Many critics since have viewed the trilogy and the novels of Robbe-Grillet, Saurraute, and Sollers as closely related literary experiments that heralded the postmodern metafiction of the 1960s and '70s. In Robbe-Grillet's writings which promoted a number of postwar works, including Beckett's, gathered under the rubric "*nouveau roman,*" Beckett appears as a direct descendant of Flaubert, Proust, Kafka, and Joyce. For Robbe-Grillet (born in 1922; first novel published in 1953) and others of his generation, the aspiration to develop a radically new fictional paradigm involved the creation of a canon of avant gardist *écriture,* positing as its first principle an historically evolving, ever-increasing rejection of the conventions of bourgeois realism. The new novel, Robbe-Grillet argued, was the culmination of this break from tradition; it entails "a rejection, finally, of every pre-established order" (*New* 73). Inevitably, Robbe-Grillet's call for a "revolution" and "rebirth" in art vis-à-vis the novel (17) repeats many of the gestures of earlier avant-garde movements. My purpose in briefly considering Robbe-Grillet's writing of the 1950s is to extricate Beckett's work from the new vanguardism of the postwar decade and open up another, more appropriate context for understanding the experiment brought to completion in *The Unnamable.*

Like the manifesto writers of the early twentieth century, in *For a New Novel* (a collection of essays published separately between 1955 and 1963 and revised for book publication) Robbe-Grillet emphasizes both the importance of the "new" and a faith in art's power to transform society: "The term *New Novel* . . . is merely a convenient label applicable to all those seeking new forms for the novel, forms capable of expressing (or of creating) new relations between man and the world" (9). In turn, he attacks the regressive institution of letters: "We must make no mistake as to the difficulties such a revolution will encounter. The entire caste system of our literary life (from publisher to the humblest reader, including bookseller and critic) has no choice but to oppose the unknown form which is attempting to establish itself" (17).

Robbe-Grillet's vision is predicated on a set of oppositions that run parallel to earlier modernist and avant-gardist distinctions: the revolutionary impact of "presence" vs. the bourgeois value of "Signification (psychological, social, functional)" (21), message/content vs. form/style—"the genuine writer has nothing to say. He has only a way of speaking" (45). Not coincidentally, it is in relation to the value of aesthetic autonomy that Robbe-Grillet comes up against the same contradictions Beckett himself faced in the early essays on Proust and Joyce. Having already linked the new novel to "revolution," Robbe-Grillet goes on to distinguish his project from directly political writing. His rejection of Sartre's "obsolete" notion of "commitment" (34) is couched in terms reminiscent of Beckett's 1929 defense of Joycean aesthetic autonomy: "The *necessity* a work of art acknowledges has nothing to do with utility. It is an internal necessity, which obviously appears as gratuitousness when the system of references is fixed *from without:* from the viewpoint of the Revolution, for example, as we have said, the highest art may seem a secondary, even absurd enterprise. . . . The work must seem necessary, but necessary *for nothing*" (45; emphases in text).

On one hand, Robbe-Grillet wants to restore a vanguardist claim for revolutionary art; on the other hand, he advances a notion of aesthetic autonomy not unlike turn-of-the-century aestheticism; an aestheticism against which, as Peter Bürger and others have argued, the historical avant garde mounted its project to connect art, everyday life, and politics. At times, Robbe-Grillet seems to take a directly anti-avant-gardist stance: "we must now, once and for all, stop taking seriously the accusations of gratuitousness, stop fearing 'art for art's sake' as the worst of evils" (38). At other times, he employs a positive notion of the "avant garde," but its meaning is restricted to an opposition with mass culture. "The word 'avant-garde' . . . despite its note of impartiality, generally serves to dismiss . . . any work that risks giving a bad conscience to the literature of mass consumption. Once a writer renounces the well-known formulas and attempts to create his own way of writing, he finds himself stuck with the label 'avant-garde'" (26). Ultimately, Robbe-Grillet can only reconcile the values of aesthetic autonomy and revolution through a formula so vague it approaches meaninglessness: "Let us, then, restore to the notion of commitment the only meaning it can have for us. Instead of being of a political nature, commitment is, for the writer, the full awareness of the present problems of his own language, the conviction of their extreme importance, the desire to solve them *from within*. Here, for him, is the only chance of remaining an artist and, doubtless too, by means of an obscure and remote consequence, of some day serving something—perhaps even the Revolution" (41; emphasis in text).

There is, however, a deeper contradiction underlying Robbe-Grillet's attempt to outline a revolutionary yet autonomous, "for itself alone," literature (12). As in Beckett's early writing, Robbe-Grillet's sense of aesthetic autonomy is bound up with a celebration of conscious artistic labor at odds with the avant garde's celebration of unconscious, automatic creation. He recognizes "the primary role taken . . . by a creative consciousness, by will, by rigor. Patient labor, methodical construction, the deliberate architecture of each sentence as of the whole book—this has always played its part. . . . Critical preoccupations, far from sterilizing creation, can serve it as a driving force" (11–12). While Robbe-Grillet encourages the conscious agency of the writer, he condemns the agency of the hero. As I have discussed, theories of narrative discourse starting with Barthes's advanced the contradictory proposition that the effacement of the representation of individual, motivated actions (equated with the conventions of realism) resulted in a more active mode of reception; the political meaning of *écriture* lay in its opposition to the passive consumption characterizing capitalist mass culture. Similarly, for Robbe-Grillet, one of the "obsolete notions" (25) that the new novel does away with is "character" or "hero"—the purposively acting, culturally specified individual. *Character* stands for the representation of an "individual" with "a proper name," "parents," "heredity," and "a profession" (27). Robbe-Grillet claims that "the great contemporary works" of Camus, Kafka, Faulkner, and Beckett reject the category of character by denying their fictional personae the preestablished social coordinates which might imbue them with "enough individuality to remain irreplaceable, enough generality to become universal" (28). For Robbe-Grillet, this rejection is historically motivated. "The novel of characters," he claims, "belongs entirely to the past, it describes a period: that which marked the apogee of the individual" (29). "The present period," he continues, "is rather one of administrative numbers. The world's destiny has ceased, for us, to be identified with the rise and fall of certain men" (29).

In this postindividual world, "the novel seems to stagger, having lost what was once its best prop, the hero" (29). Without a hero, "to tell a story has becomes strictly impossible" (33). But Robbe-Grillet is quick to point out that in the new novel things do "happen": "Just as we must not assume man's absence on the pretext that the traditional character has disappeared, we must not identify the search for new narrative structures with an attempt to suppress any event, any passion, any adventure" (33). The key difference between the bourgeois, individualistic, hero-bound story and the new novel turns out to reside in the power of the new writer to invent, to act with total freedom. The bourgeois novelist constructs a narrative out of "prefabricated schemas . . . [a] ready-made idea of reality . . . an entire rationalistic and organizing system, whose flowering corresponds to the assumption of power by the middle class. . . . Since the intelligibility of the world was not even questioned, to tell a story did not raise a problem. The style of the novel could be innocent" (31–32). In contrast to the bourgeois novelist's naive faith in a representable social world, the modern writer, starting with Flaubert, stands for pure invention, "he invents quite freely without a model. . . . Modern fiction . . . asserts this characteristic quite deliberately, to such a degree that invention and imagination become, at the limit, the very subject of the book" (32). "Each novelist," Robbe-Grillet claims, "each novel, must invent its own form. No recipe can replace this continual reflection. The book makes its own rules for itself, and for itself alone" (12).

Robbe-Grillet's vanguardist faith in the new novelist's ingenuity is quite obviously a reflection of bourgeois society's most cherished value, the autonomous individual's capacity for self-creation.[7] His advocacy of the new novel entails, as well, the normative liberal insistence on freedom of expression, threatened by both "the extreme Right" and the "the extreme Left" (167). Like many intellectuals of his generation, vanguardist and humanist alike, Robbe-Grillet is worried that art is losing its special status in a world of mass communication. "In order to succeed," he writes, "the New Novel asks the public to have some confidence, still, in the power of literature, and it asks the novelist to be ashamed no longer of producing it" (167). Rather than provide any new insight into questions of agency, autonomy, or the relation of mass culture and high art, Robbe-Grillet is even more contradictory than the manifesto writers of the past. His impulse to claim art's revolutionary power is upheld by a notion of aesthetic autonomy that undercuts art's power to effect anything except art. The conscious, rational, original agency of the writer appears only to the extent that the social world appears dominated by passivity and a stultifying "order"; Robbe-Grillet's vision demands that the critical, individual writer deny the hero the ability to interpret his or her world in an individual or critical way.

Although Robbe-Grillet mentions Beckett throughout as an exemplar of key principles of the new novel, Beckett's critical remarks in the late 1940s and '50s emphasize an entirely different awareness of the values of modernism and the avant garde.[8] Consider, for example, one of Beckett's most well-known statements from the 1956 interview:

> The Kafka hero has a coherence of purpose. He's lost but he's not spiritually precarious, he's not falling to bits. My people seem to be falling to bits. Another difference. You notice how Kafka's form is classic,

it goes on like a steamroller—almost serene. It *seems* to be threatened the
whole time—but the consternation is in the form. In my work there is
consternation behind the form, not in the form. . . . Joyce is a superb
manipulator of material—perhaps the greatest. He was making words
do the absolute maximum of work. There isn't a syllable that's super-
fluous. The kind of work I do is one in which I'm not master of my
material. The more Joyce knew the more he could. He's tending toward
omniscience and omnipotence as an artist. I'm working with impotence,
ignorance. I don't think impotence has been exploited in the past. . . . I
think anyone nowadays who pays the slightest attention to his own
experience finds it the experience of a non-knower, a non-can-er. . . .
The other type of artist—the Apollonian—is absolutely foreign to me.
(qtd. in Graver 148–49)

While vanguardist and academic critics alike were constructing a model of modernism running from Flaubert to Beckett, Beckett himself hoped to distance his work
from the achievement of high modernism. For Beckett, the Apollonian control
exercised by writers like Joyce and Kafka is an inappropriate goal for the postwar
writer. As he put in a 1961 interview, "To find a form that accommodates the mess,
that is the task of the artist now" (Driver 219). The writer appears neither as creator
of a new reality nor agent of revolutionary change, but as someone caught up, with his
audience, in a world Beckett characterizes as a "buzzing confusion," a "mess."

In the interviews Beckett gave when his work began to gain recognition, he set
his project apart from notions of aesthetic autonomy dependent on the artist's "omniscience and omnipotence." In his major postwar aesthetic statement, the
"Dialogues" with art critic Georges Duthuit first published in 1949, Beckett expressed his belief that art is always a response to its "occasion," even if the artist's task,
at present, is to express the "increasing anxiety of the relation itself" between art and
social reality. One-dimensional views of Beckett as high modernist aesthete, neovanguardist poetic revolutionary, or phenomenological philosopher, views which
Beckett himself quietly disavowed, have led critics to misread this statement.[9] One
major study goes so far as to adduce parts of the "Dialogues" to claim that Beckett's
"entire canon" is informed by "unremitting efforts to find a literary shape for the
proposition that perhaps no relationships exist between or among the artist, his art,
and an external reality" (Dearlove 3). On the contrary, the "Dialogues" demonstrate
Beckett's interest in reimagining aesthetic autonomy in a manner that does not
uncritically reiterate the ideological oppositions of the 1920s and '30s.[10]

Presumably based on conversations about modern painting between Beckett
and Duthuit, the three brief "Dialogues" were transcribed by Beckett alone and are
characterized by ironic asides that serve to make Beckett (referred to as speaker "B.")
appear as an ineffectual, oversensitive spokesman for an idiosyncratic view of art. At
the same time, Beckett seems serious about his praise of artistic failure. The meaning
of the "Dialogues" resides both in Beckett's pronouncements and in the logic of the

exchange between and B. and D. (Duthuit); indeed, the dialogue form suggests that Beckett's statements ought to be understood not as the oracular credos critics have taken them to be, but as provisional responses embedded within an ongoing argument about modern art.

Beckett begins with the painter Tal Coat, whose work he considers "a thrusting towards a more adequate expression of natural experience. . . . By nature I mean here, like the naivest realist, a composite of perceiver and perceived, not a datum, an experience" (101–102). Beckett considers art that attempts to explore *only* "experience" as belonging to the past. When D. objects to B.'s dismissal of Tal Coat, B. responds: "I agree that . . . Matisse . . . as well as . . . Tal Coat, have prodigious value, but a value cognate with those already accumulated. . . . The only thing disturbed by the revolutionaries Matisse and Tal Coat is a certain order on the plane of the feasible" (102–103).

In the context of this dismissal of "experience," which Beckett views as a development of realism, Beckett makes his most often-quoted critical statement. This "plane of the feasible," D. responds, is the only plane there can be. B. agrees, but he nevertheless advocates an art that is "weary of pretending to be able." Instead, B. prefers "the expression that there is nothing to express . . . no power to express, no desire to express, together with the obligation to express" (103). On one hand, this is a denial of modernism's basic value, the demand for ceaseless innovation, the search for the new. On the other, however, the statement does suggest a new aesthetic project, a form of expression arising out of the tension between the "obligation to express" and the awareness that art no longer serves any vital function. The tension between an antimodernist denial of art's power and a vanguardist impulse to envision a new art is evident throughout the "Dialogues." While these two attitudes threaten to cancel each other, Beckett nevertheless retains two positive values, both of which suggest a relationship between the artist and society. Art, for Beckett, is neither self-referential nor reality-creating: it is rooted in the need or responsibility to communicate, the "obligation to express."

Rather than form the endpoint of the "Dialogues" (as its quotation by critics, often out of context, suggests), this statement appears in the first dialogue. Beckett goes on to consider what kind of art might appear once the aspirations of modernism have lost their meaning. The second dialogue is on the painter Andre Masson, one of the original members of the surrealist group in the early 1920s who, at one time, had publicly supported the communist party. D. remarks that in the past Masson had been concerned with "the creation of a mythology; then with man, not simply in the universe but in society," but that now his concern is "inner emptiness." To this thumbnail sketch of the cultural politics of the interwar years B. responds that although he is "little familiar with the problems" Masson "set himself in the past" and which "have lost for him their legitimacy," he nevertheless feels "their presence not far behind these canvases veiled in consternation" (109). For B., Masson's work is more acceptable than Tal Coat's, but still seems mired in aesthetic concerns which are no longer valid. While D. maintains that Masson wants to reduce these problems "to nothing," he points out that there is still a positive "rehabilitation" in his work. Anticipating B.'s objection to this, D. asks, "But how can Masson be expected to paint the void?"

Beckett responds, "He is not. What is the good of passing from one untenable position to another? For B., the void is part of an obsolete aesthetic vocabulary. Masson appears not as an artist of the void but one "literally skewered on the ferocious dilemma of expression" (110). When D. points out that even in Masson's desire to reduce aesthetic problems to nothing, he "has to contend with his own technical gifts, which have the richness, the precision . . . of the high classical manner," B. agrees that this "throws light on the dramatic predicament of the artist" (111–12). For B., the artist's technical ability is now itself a problem; it interferes with the "dream of an art" which ultimately expresses a crisis in the function and capabilities of the aesthetic sphere.

In the third dialogue, on Bram van Velde, Beckett draws a link between B.'s idiosyncratic statements on art and the admission that art is always an expression of its historical situation, of the artist's "predicament." For B., van Velde, in contrast to Tal Coat and Masson, "is the first to accept a certain situation and to consent to a certain act." D. asks him to clarify and B. repeats his formula: van Velde, "helpless, unable to act, acts, in the event paints, since he is obliged to paint." "Why," asks D., "is he obliged to paint?" B. can only respond: "I don't know."

At this point, through D.'s questions, B. is backed into a corner. The result of this situation, D. asks skeptically, "is art of a new order?" B. responds defensively: "Among those whom we call great artists, I can think of none whose concern was not predominantly with his expressive possibilities, those of his vehicle, those of humanity" (120). D. interrupts: "One moment. Are you suggesting that the painting of van Velde is inexpressive?" B. answers "(A fortnight later) Yes." (120). D. considers this proposition absurd. B. attempts to defend himself in two ways. First, he defines inexpressive art as art that strives to be "independent of its occasion"; second, he claims that while other artists have tried to free art from any outside concern, "van Velde is the first whose painting is bereft, rid if you prefer, of occasion in every shape and form, ideal as well as material."

D. considers such a view tautological and, without acknowledging so, more or less repeats B.'s own formula from the first dialogue: "But might it not be suggested, even by one tolerant of this fantastic theory, that the occasion of his painting is his predicament, and that it is expressive of the impossibility to express?" (121). D. chastises B. for his inconsistency and, when B. suggests he should give up trying to explain, D. presses him to go on. B. accedes by claiming that his own view is not, it turns out, really descriptive of van Velde's project: "How would it be if I first said what I am pleased to fancy he is, fancy he does, and then that it is more than likely that he is and does quite otherwise?" What follows is the longest continuous passage in the "Dialogues," perhaps the closest thing Beckett ever offered to an explanation of his postwar view of art. He begins:

The realization that art has always been bourgeois, though it may dull
our pain before the achievements of the socially progressive, is finally of
scant interest. The analysis of the relation between the artist and his
occasion, a relation always regarded as indispensable, does not seem to
have been very productive either, the reason being perhaps that it lost its
way in disquisitions on the nature of occasion. (124)

"Occasion" is here specified as art's status in bourgeois society. "Socially progressive"
art (perhaps an allusion to Masson's communist phase) which causes B. pain, is like all
art embedded in bourgeois society. To realize this, B.'s remark suggests, might miti-
gate its achievement. In the end, however, the social status of art is "of scant interest,"
not because it is unimportant, but because analyses of art that focus on "the relation
between the artist and his occasion" lead more to a description of social context, "the
nature of occasion," and less to a consideration of aesthetic qualities. Far from a
rejection of the importance of social context, Beckett seems to be arguing that
aesthetic works cannot be explained by merely exploring the social forces to which
they respond. As if trying to correct, rather than reject, a socially informed view of art,
B. insists on a dialectic approach:

It is obvious that for the artist obsessed with his expressive vocation,
anything and everything is doomed to become occasion, as is apparently
the case to some extent with Masson. . . . But if the occasion appears as
an unstable term of relation, the artist, who is the other term, is hardly
less so, thanks to his warren of modes and attitudes. The objections to
this dualist view of the creative process are unconvincing. (124)

If the social context or occasion of art is always changing and developing historically,
then so too are the artist's attitudes toward his vocation. Thus, the relationship
between the terms, between artist and occasion, can never be settled. The implication
is that artistic attitudes develop according to an autonomous logic that has an unfixed
but inevitable relation to social and historical change. B. goes on to develop this
dialectical notion of aesthetic autonomy by projecting the duality onto the work
itself. The "occasion" is also the content of the work of art, which B. refers to
ironically as the "ailment"; the artist's "modes and attitudes" is the form, which B.
refers to as the "manner":

Two things are established, however precariously: the ailment, from
fruits on plates to low mathematics and self-commiseration, and its
manner of dispatch. All that should concern us is the acute and increasing anxiety of the relation itself, as though shadowed more and more
darkly by a sense of invalidity, of inadequacy, of existence at the expense
of all that it excludes, all that it blinds to [*sic*]. The history of painting,

here we go again, is the history of its attempts to escape from this sense of failure, by means of more authentic, more ample, less exclusive relations between representer and representee. (124–25)

For B., the changing relationship between art and its occasion can be traced in the changing relationship between form and content, a relationship characterized by an "acute and increasing anxiety." What interests Beckett is not so much modern art's increasing attention to formal matters; rather, he sees the project of modern art most clearly as a crisis residing in the relationship between formal concerns and the occasion which provides or allows art a content. Thus, modern art's attempt to create "more authentic . . . relations between representer and representee" appears as a response to the art of the past's "failure" to relate these two aspects of the creative process.

This "dualist view," according to which art's expressive power always appears in relation to its occasion, must be abandoned, however, when Beckett makes his case for "art of a new order." On one hand, he claims that "van Velde is the first to desist from this estheticised automatism, the first to submit wholly to the incoercible absence of relation, in the absence of terms or, if you like, in the presence of unavailable terms" (125). On the other hand, B. immediately recognizes that, in light of his own previous remarks, this is just another sign of the changing relationship between a new aesthetic attitude and a new context:

> I know that all that is required now, in order to bring even this horrible matter to an acceptable conclusion, is to make of this submission, this admission, this fidelity to failure, a new occasion, a new term of relation, and the act of which, unable to act, obliged to act, he makes, an expressive act, even if only of itself, of its impossibility, of its obligation. I know that my inability to do so places myself . . . in what I think is still called an unenviable situation, familiar to psychiatrists. (125–26)

Beckett's vanguardist impulse, to formulate a "new order" of aesthetic autonomy and detachment, is kept in check by his own awareness of art's historical development and the artist's "obligation to express." The "Dialogues" end not with an affirmation of an art "bereft . . . of occasion in every shape and form," but with B.'s self-deprecating admission that he is unable, or unwilling, to try to reconcile his self-avowedly contradictory view. D. gently reminds B. of his intention to supplement his view of van Velde with a consideration that it "is more than likely" that van Velde "is and does quite otherwise":

> D.—Are you not forgetting something?
> B.—Surely that is enough?
> D.—I understood your number was to have two parts. The first was to
>   consist in your saying what you—er—thought. This I am pre-
>   pared to believe you have done. The second—

B.—(Remembering, warmly) Yes, yes, I am mistaken, I am mistaken.

B.'s final words in the "Dialogues" leave the issue of art's communicative and referential qualities entirely open. It is a question, Beckett suggests, that is not the artist's responsibility to answer, but only to express.

Just as the vanguardist claims made by Robbe-Grillet have little in common with Beckett's ambivalent critical remarks, the concerns of his fiction are emphatically distinct from Beckett's postwar work. Robbe-Grillet's first novels are characterized by three principal features: a dispassionate, omniscient, and oracular narrative voice; intricately organized plots (the investigation of a political crime in *The Erasers* and the events surrounding the murder of a young girl in *The Voyeur*) arranged in a series of overlapping scenes whose causal and temporal relations are left intriguingly open; and a depiction of individuals unknowingly caught up in a series of fixed events which seem to determine their fate over and above their wills or desires.

These features are consistent with the tradition of the modern novel. In *The Erasers*, Robbe-Grillet combines the sensational plot elements of the popular crime novel—the male hero, the alienated detective, moves through the city looking for clues, a paradigmatic modern narrator/observer—with a mythical structure, evident in the novel's allusions to the Oedipus legend.[11] The protagonist of the novel, the investigator Wallas who winds up committing the murder he thinks he is investigating, seems little more than a "pawn" or a "mere agent of the plot" (Britton 68). The olympian detachment of the narrator's descriptions and pronouncements—"Things take their immutable course. . . . The perfectly adjusted machinery cannot hold the slightest surprise in store" (19)—serves to focus the reader's attention on the tightly organized manipulation of an otherwise stereotypical detective plot.[12] The figure of the detective, however, is what actually supplies the model for the narrative perspective of the novel. The detective is, first and foremost, the detached walker in the city:

> Wallas likes walking. In the cold, early winter air he likes walking straight ahead through this unknown city. He looks around, he listens, he smells the air; this perpetually renewed contact affords him a subtle impression of continuity; he walks on and gradually unrolls the uninterrupted ribbon of his own passage, not a series of irrational, unrelated images, but a smooth band where each element takes its place in the web. . . . It is of his own free will that he is walking toward an inevitable and perfect future. (47-48)

Wallas's observations become a "ribbon" or "web" where the "series" of images takes on a meaningful configuration; in this sense, he is like Robbe-Grillet's idea of the novelist as a creator of reality. But Robbe-Grillet distances Wallas from the narrating intelligence by making Wallas's sense of order only an "impression," and his "free will" an illusion in the face of an "inevitable and perfect future" that only the narrator-writer knows. The narrative perspective in *The Erasers* is a variation of the observing, detached walker in the city. The double experience of alienation and potential freedom evoked by the metropolis, so pervasive in modern literature, is figured as a contrast between the hero's illusory free will and the omniscient, oracular mode of narration. The difference between earlier, modernist constructions of this perspective and Robbe-Grillet's lies in the degree to which the sense of autonomy and freedom becomes associated exclusively with the formal manipulation of the material, while the hero, lacking interiority or subjectivity, is only capable of an illusory sense of participation in what befalls him.

The content of Robbe-Grillet's novels is not, as some might argue, arbitrary in relation to the narrative form. No matter how much his novels purport to subvert the conventions of the bourgeois novel, their appeal is intimately bound up with an articulation of masculinity pervasive in modern culture, high and low: urban aliena-tion, emotional detachment, aggressive sexuality, and violence. While *The Erasers'* narrative innovations are constructed through the elements of the detective novel, *The Voyeur,* Robbe-Grillet's second novel, centers on the rape, murder, and mutilation of a young girl and the lonely wandering of Mathias, a traveling salesman who may— or may not—have committed the crime, but who is fascinated by the image of the victim's ravaged body. As Susan Suleiman observed in regard to his later novel, *Project for a Revolution in New York,* Robbe-Grillet seems to view "fantasies of mutilation, rape, torture, and murder," staples of the "porno-detective novel," as cultural myths or *données* that the contemporary writer freely chooses to "deconstruct" in the service of "cultural demystification" (57–58). As Suleiman's reading confirms, "far from deconstructing male fantasies of omnipotence and total control over passive female bodies, *Projet* repeats them with astonishing fidelity" (65–66).

Robbe-Grillet's early novels consistently uphold the observational, masculine perspective that, as I have shown, Beckett explicitly strove to parody and minimize. Beckett's insistence on impotence and failure are further signs of his distance from the aesthetic ethos driving the foundational works of the *nouveau roman.* My point is not to argue that Beckett's work is more innovative than Robbe-Grillet's, but to demon-strate the inadequacy of the formalist reading of Beckett, as modernist and avantgar-diste par excellence, that Robbe-Grillet himself promoted. Extricating Beckett from the ideological oppositions of the interwar period, and their postwar mani-festations—signification vs. presence, readerly vs. writerly, the bourgeois author vs. the writing subject—points to an alternative cultural context in which to consider Beckett's postwar masterpieces of failure. The neovanguardism of the 1950s was largely the invention of intellectuals who came of age professionally in the postwar decade; in contrast, the decisive formative period for Beckett was the late 1920s and the 1930s. This links him, in a number of ways, to George Orwell, who perhaps more than any other writer of Beckett's generation struggled, during and directly after the war, with the question of art's relation to politics, and whose most famous novel,

1984, offers a bleak obituary of the cultural politics of the first half of the twentieth century.

Nightmare of Commitment: Orwell's "Inside the Whale" and *1984*

In 1946, shortly before he began work on his last novel *1984*, Orwell wrote that "*Animal Farm* was the first book in which I tried, with full consciousness . . . to fuse political and artistic purpose into one whole. I have not written a novel for seven years, but I hope to write another fairly soon. It is bound to be a failure, every book is a failure, but I know with some clarity what kind of book I want to write" (qtd. in Crick 1). Orwell's sense of failure and his clarity of purpose as a writer in the 1940s were closely linked. For Beckett, failure signaled an ambivalent attitude toward aesthetic achievement; for Orwell, literary failure seemed inevitable, because history had burdened the writer with obligations antithetical to aesthetic ends. "The invasion of literature by politics was bound to happen," he wrote. "We have developed a sort or compunction which our grandparents did not have, an awareness of the enormous injustice and misery of the world . . . which makes a purely aesthetic attitude towards life impossible. No one, now, could devote himself to literature as single-mindedly as Joyce or Henry James" (qtd. in Williams, *Orwell* 31).

There are deep-seated parallels in the paths that led Orwell and Beckett to their visions of failure in the late 1940s. Like Beckett, Orwell wrote the works for which he became internationally famous in the aftermath of the war; like Beckett, he began his career in the late 1920s in Paris and London, faced with a set of difficult choices. Well-educated sons of middle-class families, both Beckett and Orwell had entered a polarized literary culture which demanded that the writer justify his choices. As Raymond Williams put it in regard to Orwell, "He was living . . . at a time and within a class in which the whole practice of writing was problematic. . . . In the confident middle class . . . writing was thought of as an impractical secondary activity . . . [unless] the impractical activity had practical effects: that is to say, made money. . . . At the same time a growing minority of the same social class made a related but apparently opposite abstraction in reaction to this. . . . The 'writer,' the true writer, had no commercial aims, but also, at root, no social function and, by derivation, no social content. He just 'wrote'" (30–31).

Under the pressures of the period, Orwell's choice "was in the other direction from that emphasis of the twenties. . . . He chose content before form, experience before words" (32). Orwell himself, however, saw this choice as forced; in a different era, he claimed, he would have written "ornate or merely descriptive books . . . [but] as it is I have been forced into becoming a sort of pamphleteer" (qtd. in Williams 33). The tension between the kind of writer Orwell might have become and the kind of writer history had "forced" him to be, his uncertainty about whether a literature "invaded" by politics ceased to be literature at all, informs his best writing. Most of

Orwell's important work, Williams observes, "is about someone who gets away from an oppressive normality. . . . Yet it would be truer to say that [it] is about someone who tries to get away but fails." Orwell "felt, simultaneously, that the flight was necessary but also useless" (39). Orwell's sense of artistic failure, as he so acutely expressed after the war, and the failure of his heroes—especially the failure of Winston Smith, the hero in *1984*—are two aspects of a single vision.

Uselessness, passivity, the futility of struggle and failure—these are hardly emphases one would expect from a writer who chose the path of commitment in the 1930s. But by the beginning of the 1940s Orwell, like Beckett, was compelled to reassess the literary orthodoxies and choices of the past. That Orwell and Beckett had made seemingly opposite choices is only part of the story; what is more important is that both ended up struggling against the implications of those choices; both sensed failure as the inevitable outcome of the polarization itself and made failure the focus of their postwar work. The 1940 essay "Inside the Whale" is a direct account of Orwell's rejection of the cultural politics of the 1920s and '30s. What is most striking in this rejection is that, at a moment of severe historical crisis, Orwell is provoked into a defense of aesthetic autonomy; or rather, a version of aesthetic autonomy that Orwell pieces together out of the failures and ruins of the interwar period; like Beckett's notion of inexpressive art, Orwell's essay articulates literary value as a refraction of failure, of "the *impossibility* of any major literature until the world has shaken itself into its new shape" (50; emphasis in text).[13]

Orwell's view of the historical crisis and his understanding of the normative value of autonomy, as freedom of individual expression, are linked at the most general level. "What is quite obviously happening," he writes, "is the break-up of *laissez-faire* capitalism and of the liberal-Christian culture. . . . Almost certainly we are moving into an age of totalitarian dictatorships—an age in which freedom of thought will be at first a deadly sin and later on a meaningless abstraction. The autonomous individual is going to be stamped out of existence. But this means that literature . . . must suffer at least a temporary death. (48)

From this perspective, Orwell reassesses the literature of the preceding decades. First, he tries to work through the principal opposition of the period. "At bottom it is always a writer's tendency, his 'purpose', his 'message', that makes him liked or disliked. . . . And no book is ever truly neutral. Some or other tendency is always discernible" (24). His grouping of writers is typical: Joyce, Eliot, Lawrence, Lewis, and the like on one side, the "Auden-Spender group" on the other. But he quickly points out the grouping is inadequate: "Lawrence and Eliot were in reality antipathetic, Huxley worshipped Lawrence but was repelled by Joyce . . . and Lewis attacked everyone in turn" (25). What the writers of the twenties share is not a way of writing but a general attitude, a "pessimism" and hostility "to the notion of 'progress'" (25–26). Even more so, in these writers' works "there is no attention to the urgent problems of the moment, above all no politics in the narrower sense. . . . When one looks back at the twenties, nothing is queerer than the way in which every important event in Europe escaped the notice of the English intelligentsia" (27).

Orwell mocks the more pretentious characteristics of the 1920s. "In 'cultured' circles art-for-art's-saking extended practically to the worship of meaninglessness," he wrote; "even to be aware of [a book's] subject matter was looked on as a lapse of taste" (27–28). But "the best writers of the twenties," he adds, "did not subscribe to this doctrine, their 'purpose' is in most cases fairly overt, but it is usually a 'purpose' along moral-religious cultural lines. Also, when translatable into political terms . . . the tendency of all the writers in this group is conservative" (28). In contrast, the tendency of the Auden-Spender group was articulated in more or less direct political terms. Orwell (never mentioning his own work in reference to this group) sympathizes with their "leaning towards Communism" (30). "By throwing 'pure art' overboard they have freed themselves from the fear of being laughed at and vastly enlarged their scope. The prophetic side of Marxism, for example, is new material for poetry and has great possibilities" (31). Yet Orwell's main point is that the politically left writers of the '30s failed both to further social progress or to produce vital literature. Compared to the "very varied origins" of the writers of the '20s, "nearly all the younger writers fit easily into the public-school-university-Bloomsbury pattern" (31). While promoting egalitarianism, "Marxized literature has moved no nearer to the masses" (32). Most, Orwell claims, took up the cause of communism during "the period of anti-Fascism" without understanding or really caring about the reality of the Communist Party in Spain or the Soviet Union. Young writers searching "for something to believe in" found in Communism "a Church, an army, an orthodoxy, a discipline" (35). For Orwell, who had dedicated his career to socially responsible, left-leaning prose, this overview of the 1930s carries a sweepingly harsh judgment. "On the whole," he writes, "the literary history of the thirties seems to justify the opinion that a writer does well to keep out of politics. . . . Any Marxist can demonstrate with the greatest of ease that 'bourgeois' liberty of thought is an illusion. But . . . without this 'bourgeois' liberty the creative powers wither away. . . . The atmosphere of orthodoxy is always damaging to prose, and above all it is completely ruinous to the novel, the most anarchical of all forms of literature. . . . The novel is practically a Protestant form of art; it is a product of the free mind, of the autonomous individual. No decade in the past hundred and fifty years has been so barren of imaginative prose as the nineteen-thirties" (39).

By the middle of the essay, Orwell has come to an impasse, with the conservative or "reactionary outlook" (28) of the twenties coming off no better than the left orthodoxy of the thirties. His position allows for no positive alternative; as such, it is close to where Beckett winds up in the "Dialogues." According to Beckett's schema of the duality of the creative process, "inexpressive" art must be, despite its attempt to "fail," an expression of its "occasion"; his ideal form of art, he tacitly admits, is self-contradictory. For Orwell, "no book is ever really neutral. Some or other tendency is always discernible"—this is one of the major points of his essay. But the overarching tendencies of the past two decades are invalid: "progress and reaction," he declares, "have both turned out to be swindles" (48). Obliged by history to be a political writer, rejecting high modernism and committed writing, viewing extant political positions as invalid—all of this under the pressure of an historical crisis that would seem to call for decisiveness—Orwell is left with two inadequate alternatives: declare literature obsolete, or identify some mode of literature whose tendency manages to avoid the impasse he has so emphatically described.

Ultimately, Orwell risks self-contradiction rather than choose between the end of literature or the invention of some at-present unrealizable neutrality. Like Beckett, he attempts instead to refashion a belief in aesthetic autonomy out of the failures of the past. Surprisingly, Orwell singles out Henry Miller, author of *Tropic of Cancer,* as "the only imaginative prose writer of the slightest value" of the past decade. Miller functions in the essay as a symbol for the overall crisis: his "importance is merely symptomatic" (50). Like the Joyce-Eliot group's works, Miller's novel "about American deadbeats cadging drinks in the Latin Quarter" ignores politics in an irresponsible manner: "A novelist who simply disregards the major public events of the moment is generally either a footler or a plain idiot" (10). Like *Ulysses,* it is one of those novels that "create a world of their own" and that "opens up a new world not by revealing what is strange, but by revealing what is familiar" (11). Orwell describes *Tropic of Cancer* as both modernist masterpiece, displaying "a feeling for character and a mastery of technique that are unapproached in any at all recent novel. . . . [Miller] drag[s] the *real-politick* of the inner mind into the open" (13), and antiaestheticist, journalistic realism: "What Miller has in common with Joyce is a willingness to mention the inane, squalid facts of everyday life. . . . But there the resemblance ends. As a novel, *Tropic of Cancer* is far inferior to *Ulysses.* Joyce is an artist, in a sense in which Miller is not and probably would not wish to be. . . . Miller is simply a hard-boiled person talking about life" (15).

Miller's passivity and acceptance are, for Orwell, the signs of a quasi-populist, purposeless purpose: "To accept civilization *as it is* practically means accepting decay. . . . But precisely because . . . he is passive to experience, Miller is able to get nearer the ordinary man than is possible to more purposive writers. . . . It is a voice from the crowd . . . from the ordinary, non-political, non-moral passive man" (18–19). Miller creates an autonomous literature, individual and free from orthodoxy, by giving in to defeat and terror. "To say 'I accept' . . . is to say that you accept concentration camps, rubber truncheons, Hitler, Stalin" (17). Happily, Miller embraces the role not of the "propagandists" but the "victims" (18). Orwell describes this negative, detached attitude as a form of modernist mimesis which discloses how badly things have turned in Europe. "At this date," he writes, "it hardly needs a war to bring home to us the disintegration of our society and the increasing helplessness of all decent people. It is for this reason that I think that the passive, non-co-operative attitude implied in Henry Miller's work is justified. . . . No sermons, merely the subjective truth. And along those lines it is still possible for a good novel to be written" (47).

Paradoxically, the future of the novel, the literary form most closely bound up with liberal democracy, depends on a passive acceptance of the destruction of its own conditions. Like Beckett's skepticism about the agency of the writer, Orwell's contradictory praise of the passive attitude is both part of his social vision and a critical response to the cultural politics of the interwar years. For both writers, passivity and failure are never aesthetic credos, but indications of a crisis in literature's relation to the social world in which they write. For this reason, despite all his praise, Orwell must in the end deny Miller's status as an artist: "But do I mean by this that Miller is a 'great author', a new hope for English prose? Nothing of the kind. Miller himself would be the last to claim or want any such thing" (49). Miller's autonomous stance, "completely negative, unconstructive, amoral," is both the source of his integrity and the sign of a pervasive failure. *Tropic of Cancer*'s "importance is merely symptomatic. . . . It is a demonstration of the *impossibility* of any major literature until the world has shaken itself into its new shape" (50).

Like "Inside the Whale," *1984* projects into the future a fatalism rooted in the cultural and political failures of the past. The novel has been read as an anticommunist tract, a Swiftian satire of both communist and capitalist bureaucracy, a prophetic dystopian fantasy, and a despairing expression of Orwell's deteriorating health.[14] Orwell himself viewed it as a "fantasy, but in the form of a naturalistic novel" (qtd. in Crick 20). While the novel seems to belong to "a tradition of documentary realism of didactic or reformist intent" directed at the widest possible audience (Crick 107), its underlying logic was anchored in Orwell's conviction that although politics and art were incompatible, he was nevertheless obligated to bring them together. If *The Unnamable* evoked a nightmarish, interiorized world wrought out of the contradictions of modernism, *1984* evokes its counterpart, an objectified nightmare of political commitment.

Orwell's struggle with the idea of a politicized literature appears, in *1984*, as the struggle of the protagonist Winston Smith, a writer for Ministry of Truth, against a totalitarian social order.[15] Both the extreme narrative perspective of the novel and its central theme of a consciousness-controlling, centralized culture industry against whose language, images, and concepts Smith struggles to gain a sense of independence are, like *The Unnamable*'s extremely reduced perspective and its narrator's struggle to find a voice, formulated out of the cultural-political impasses of the interwar period. *1984* is narrated by an omniscient, critical voice that could not possibly exist under the conditions the novel describes. In turn, Smith's struggle is presented in terms of an act of critical, individuated writing that begins to free him from "the prevailing mental condition . . . of controlled insanity" (344) created through the techniques of Newspeak. Indeed, Newspeak itself, and the centralized cultural production of Oceania reflect both the vanguardist aesthetics of the interwar period and the critique of mass culture that was a formative subtext of modernism.

In his first book, *Down and Out in Paris and London* (1933), Orwell had created an autobiographical first-person narrator who lives among the poor and sympathetically describes the conditions of their lives. Yet the narrator, who never identifies himself or his own social background, tacitly admits that he is observing from the outside; he can never really experience the social degradation he is describing: "The man who really merits pity is the man who has been down from the start, and faces poverty with a blank, resourceless mind" (180). The premise of the book— that hands-on experience guarantees the integrity of a description of a social inequality that is foreign to both the author and the reader—is always in tension with the need to observe and explain from an objective, critical perspective: "I wish," the narrator remarks when recognizing the limitations of his experiential perspective, "I could be Zola for a little while" (64). While Beckett took the problem of subjective perspectivalism, already latent in his early fiction's depiction of "seedy" solipsism, to its ultimate, self-contradictory conclusion in *The Unnamable,* Orwell took the tensions between the naturalist-observer and realist-participant perspectives of his interwar writing to an equally extreme conclusion in *1984.*

In his 1956 essay "History as Nightmare," Irving Howe defended the extremity of the novel's form. Howe saw *1984* as both the culmination of the development of the modern political novel and its negation: "In a sense, it is a profoundly antipolitical book, full of hatred for the kind of world in which public claims destroy the possibilities for private life" (239). But Howe defends the book precisely because it expresses so clearly how the political trends of the twentieth century could lead to "a nightmare in which politics has displaced humanity and the state has stifled society" (239). Howe's defense echoes Orwell's own conflicted attitude toward politicized literature. "It is a remarkable book" he claims, but "whether it is a remarkable novel or a novel at all, seems unimportant. . . . The last thing Orwell cared about when he wrote *1984,* the last thing he should have cared about, was literature" (236–37). Complaints that the book's language is flat, its characters lacking in "psychological specification" and its plot deficient in "dramatic incident," Howe claims, ignore the extent to which Orwell's vision of politics demanded a new form. "The whole idea of the self as something precious and inviolable is a *cultural* idea . . . a product of the liberal era; but Orwell has imagined a world in which the self . . . is no longer a significant value, not even a value to be violated. . . . The book . . . posits a situation in which these categories are no longer significant. . . . About such a world it is, strictly speaking, impossible to write a novel, if only because the human relationships taken for granted in a novel are here suppressed" (237–38).

While Robbe-Grillet's call to rid the novel of "obsolete" categories such as "character" entails a neomodernist demand for aesthetic autonomy, Howe's view of *1984* sees the destruction of liberal society as the correlative to the inadequacy of the novel of individuated characters. Taken together, these two views suggest how Orwell's and Beckett's most extreme novels center on the same concerns. In both novels aesthetic and individual autonomy appear as values, but only in relation to a situation in which social and psychic autonomy have been destroyed. While Beckett sought to mimic, in the narrative form, the consciousness of the writer whose sense of autonomy is ruined and who desperately seeks to find a self-identical voice, Orwell sought to represent the social conditions under which autonomy is destroyed. Both projects necessitate an extreme perspective, one that either disturbs the reader's ability to understand the narrative as a coherent representation of anything at all, except the inability to speak and tell coherently, or one that affords the reader the critical and historical objectivity that the protagonist Smith, and everyone else in the novel, is denied.

The extremity of these perspectives also created problems, a sense of failure registered by both the authors and their readers. If Beckett's hypothetical perspectivelessness greatly distanced *The Unnamable* from any direct link to novelistic mimesis, making the last book of the trilogy seem the most radically self-referential and meaningless of Beckett's major works, then Orwell's extreme outer perspective made *1984* read, for many, like a sociopolitical tract, rather than a work of fiction. Parts of the novel, like the appendix on "The Principles of Newspeak" and the excerpts from "the book," are indeed written in the form of the political essay. As Williams points out, Orwell had difficulty integrating these documents from a totalitarian future into a novel whose plot was characteristic of Orwell's earlier fiction, the story of Smith's nascent critical awareness and the failed attempt to escape a cruel, oppressive social order.

Orwell's difficulty in integrating the narrative and essayist aspects of the novel are indicative of the perspectival tension. On one hand, the narrator has total knowledge, from beyond any position within it, of the world he is describing: "Newspeak was the official language of Oceania and had been devised to meet the ideological needs of Ingsoc. . . . The version in use in 1984 . . . was a provisional one. . . . It is with the final, perfected version, as embodied in the Eleventh Edition of the Dictionary, that we are concerned here" (417). On the other, the narrator speaks as if the world described is a projection of his, and his audience's, present experience: "Newspeak was founded on the English language as we now know it, though many Newspeak sentences, even when not containing newly created words, would be barely intelligible to an English-speaker of our own day" (418).

This tension is indicative of Orwell's experiment with an untried form, an aspiration to convincingly represent a world in which the ability to think critically or objectively has been destroyed. At times, this condition is described, from the outside, with an intensity equal to the descriptions of psychic terror, from the inside, in *The Unnamable:*

> It was as though some huge force were pressing down upon you—
> something that penetrated inside your skull, battering against your
> brain, frightening you out of your beliefs, persuading you, almost, to
> deny the evidence of your senses. . . . Not merely the validity of experi-
> ence, but the very existence of external reality, was tacitly denied by their
> philosophy. . . . And what was terrifying was not that they would kill
> you for thinking otherwise, but that they might be right. . . . If both the
> past and the external world exist only in the mind, and if the mind is
> controllable—what then? (225)

Along with this set of themes, Orwell built into the structure of the novel "intricacies of deception and betrayal" (Williams 99) which render the representation of "external reality" unstable. What appears at first as Orwell's historical projection, in the excerpts from the rebel Goldstein's book, turns out, in the story of Smith's struggle, to be an elaborate deception, written by the Inner Party torturer O'Brien, who claims that the book is nonsense (384).[16] But the fact that "the book" is a deception, part of the party's reign of terror and its destruction of science and humanist culture, does not invalidate it as historical projection.[17] Authorship, writing, and the instability of language are central concerns in *1984*—concerns which reflect, both intentionally and implicitly, Orwell's critical ambivalence toward the cultural politics of the preceding decades.

To an extent, Orwell's vision of the destruction of autonomous writing, literary and historical, leads to an unintended parallel between Orwell's descriptions of Oceania and the party's own cultural production. Consider, for example, the passage from the child's textbook, written by the party to indoctrinate the young:

> In the old days (it ran), before the Glorious Revolution, London was not the beautiful city that we know today. It was a dark, dirty miserable place where hardly anybody had enough to eat. . . . But in among all this terrible poverty there were just a few big beautiful houses that were lived in by rich men who had as many as thirty servants. . . . These rich men were called capitalists. They were fat, ugly men with wicked faces, like the one in the picture . . . dressed in a long black coat and . . . a top hat. This was the uniform of the capitalists, and no one else was allowed to wear it. The capitalists owned everything . . . and everyone else was their slave. . . . If anyone disobeyed them they could throw them into prison. . . . The chief of all the capitalists was called the king. (219)

Orwell included this in the novel for obvious reasons: it shows the party's distorted invention of history and its self-evident lies about London further stir Smith's distrust of everything but his own experience. It also links the capitalism of the past to Oceania: the Inner Party is an elite who live far from the cramped squalor and social decay of Smith's London. But this linkage creates a problem. The narrator's descriptions of the impoverished life of ordinary party members and "proles" on one side, and the life of the elite on the other, seem to repeat the fairytale simplifications of the party's lies and distortions. Consider, in comparison to the child's textbook, the scene where Smith finally works up the courage to visit O'Brien at home:

> It was only on very rare occasions that one saw inside the dwelling places of the Inner Party, or even penetrated into the quarter of the town where they lived. The whole atmosphere of the huge block of flats, the richness and spaciousness of everything . . . the white-jacketed servants hurrying to and fro—everything was intimidating. . . . The passage down which

[the servant] led them was softly carpeted, with cream-papered walls and white wainscoting, all exquisitely clean. That too was intimidating. Winston could not remember ever to have seen a passage way whose walls were not grimy from the contact of human bodies. (301–302)

The double status of "the book," as historical projection and ideological distortion, is repeated, apparently unintentionally, in this doubling. Orwell is forced, through the extremity of his vision, to write in a mode that the novel itself mocks as false. This type of almost unavoidable simplification is emblematic of the problems inherent in Orwell's aspiration to write a novel about a world that, as Howe put it, is nothing but politics. The simplification and overlapping are also indicative of Orwell's view of writing and language, presented most directly in Smith's double status as a writer.

The novel begins with Smith's first act of rebellion—his attempt to write down, in a secret, forbidden diary, "the interminable restless monologue that had been running inside his head" (162). Although constantly under surveillance in his shabby apartment, Smith manages to find a space of privacy "outside the range of the telescreen" in a "shallow alcove . . . which, when the flats were built, had probably been intended to hold bookcases" (161). The alcove that was once a bookcase; the outlawed paper Smith is about to write on, "a peculiarly beautiful book . . . [with] smooth, creamy paper, a little yellowed by age . . . of a kind that had not been manufactured for at least forty years"; the furtively obtained pen, "an archaic instrument, seldom used even for signatures"; the "dose" of cheap gin he gulps down and the crumpled cigarette he lights before he begins to write (160–62)—these are all symbols of the alienated writer in his room and stand in opposition to the tools of Oceania's centralized culture industry, such as the "speakwrite" that Smith employs in his job of revising the historical record (188) and the "novel-writing machines" of the "Fiction Department" (268).

In the world of the novel, any individual expression, no matter what its intention, is considered subversive and severely punished. Orwell presents Smith's diary not as a statement of reasoned political opposition, but rather as isolated self-expression, and thus antithetical to Oceania's official culture. In the process of its composition, Smith uncovers a repressed awareness through a technique canonized by the avant garde, the suspension of conscious will:

> For some time he sat gazing stupidly at the paper. . . . It was curious that he seemed not merely to have lost the power of expressing himself, but even to have forgotten what it was he had originally intended to say. For weeks past he had been making ready for this moment, and it had never crossed his mind that anything would be needed except courage. The actual writing would be easy. All he had to do was to transfer to paper the interminable restless monologue that had been running inside his head, literally for years. . . . The seconds were ticking by. He was conscious of nothing except the blankness of the page in front of him. . . . Suddenly

he began writing in sheer panic, only imperfectly aware of what he was
setting down. (162–63)

What Smith actually writes is a spontaneous, chaotic description of the violent,
propagandistic war film he had seen the night before and the audience's agitated
response. Smith's automatic writing both brings forth the programmatic images that
were always "battering against your brain" and constitutes the attempt to escape
them. "Winston stopped writing. . . . He did not know what had made him pour out
this stream of rubbish. But the curious thing was that while he was doing so a totally
different memory had clarified itself in his mind" (164).

The memory brought to consciousness involves a further act of spontaneous
expression. Smith works as a writer at the Ministry of Truth which manufactures the
mass culture, from newspapers to pornography, through which the party pacifies the
population of Oceania and "manipulate[s] public opinion" (335). The awakened
memory centers on the "Two Minutes Hate," a televised form of ritualistic propaganda intended to arouse hatred against the enemies of the party and the nation,
especially the political apostate Emmanuel Goldstein. Smith remembers how, seated
in the midst of his fellow workers who began to express "uncontrollable exclamations
of rage" (167), he found himself

> shouting with the others and kicking his heel violently against the rung
> of his chair. The horrible thing about the Two Minutes Hate was not that
> one was obliged to act a part, but, that it was impossible to avoid joining
> in. Within thirty seconds any pretence was always unnecessary. A hid-
> eous ecstasy of fear and vindictiveness, a desire to kill and torture . . .
> seemed to flow through the whole group of people like an electric
> current. . . . And yet the rage that one felt was an abstract, undirected
> emotion which could be switched from one object to another. . . . Thus,
> at one moment Winston's hatred was not turned against Goldstein at all,
> but, on the contrary, against Big Brother, the Party and the Thought
> Police; and at such moments his heart went out to the lonely, derided
> heretic on the screen, sole guardian of truth and sanity in a world of lies.
> And yet the very next instant he was at one with the people about him.
> (168)

Smith's visceral response to the Two Minutes Hate is, in part, an articulation of the
complex response to mass culture during the early twentieth century, the simultaneous fascination with and fear of the power of popular media, especially photography
and film, and the recognition of their inherently ambivalent nature. The form of the
"Hate," in which Goldstein's face changes into a sheep's face, then melts into the face
of an enemy soldier, eventually transforming into the reassuring image of Big Brother
(169), evokes cinematic experiments like photomontage which, while intended by
avant-garde artists to liberate the imagination, might just as well be used as propa-

ganda to instill hatred and manipulate consciousness. Smith, alone in his refugelike alcove, remembering the morning's events and distancing himself, intellectually, from the visceral effects of the film, manages to express his most authentic feelings:

> His eyes refocused on the page. He discovered that while he sat helplessly musing he had also been writing, as though by automatic action. And it was no longer the same cramped awkward handwriting as before. His pen had slid voluptuously over the smooth paper, printing in large neat capitals—
> DOWN WITH BIG BROTHER
> DOWN WITH BIG BROTHER
> DOWN WITH BIG BROTHER (171–72)

Momentarily, Smith panics at this concrete manifestation of an active opposition to the party; he is tempted to tear out the page and give up the diary altogether. He realizes that the significance of his action lies not in the written object, but in the process that created it. "He had committed—would still have committed, even if he had never set pen to paper—the essential crime that contained all others in itself. Thoughtcrime" (172).

This process, which leads Smith from a nascent critical consciousness toward an active opposition, follows a familiar cultural logic: writing as self-expression stands in opposition to the conformist power of mass media; the will-less spontaneity of writing by "automatic action" breaks through socially conditioned modes of thought; tapping into the innermost mind, the "skull" as Orwell's narrator calls it, leads to a revolutionary perception of "external reality." Smith's struggle with language, which works both against and within the mass-cultural images of hate, forms a counterpart to the cultural productions of Ingsoc that "dislocate the sense of reality" (343) and strip thought of all critical capability. Smith's diary entry, with its propagandistic climax of repeated anti-party slogans, is a negative image of Newspeak and "doublethink," the party's principal cultural innovation and its most effective means of social control.

Just as Orwell invests Smith's writing in the alcove with a range of modernist images and attitudes, Newspeak is imagined in terms of a vanguardist literary movement. Smith's friend Syme, a "delicate" intellectual philologist (199–200) who works in the Research Department compiling a new edition of the Newspeak dictionary, exalts in the "new" and the radical rejection of tradition: "By 2050 . . . all real knowledge of Oldspeak will have disappeared," he advises Smith. "The whole literature of the past will have been destroyed. Chaucer, Shakespeare, Milton, Byron— they'll exist only in Newspeak versions, not merely changed into something different, but actually changed into something contradictory of what they used to be" (202). Syme extols the beauty of the conceptual destruction of an antiquated bourgeois morality: "We're destroying words—scores of them, hundreds of them, every day. We're cutting the language down to the bone. . . . It's a beautiful thing, the destruction of words." He admonishes Smith for lagging behind the linguistic innovations that will shape the future: "You haven't a real appreciation of Newspeak, Winston. . . . Even when you write it you're still thinking in Oldspeak. . . . In your heart you'd prefer to stick to Oldspeak, with all its vagueness and its useless shades of meaning. You don't grasp the beauty of the destruction of words" (200–201).

Doublethink, the conceptual basis of Newspeak, is described in terms of negation and aporia. The disruption of normative, communicative reason, celebrated in the 1950s as a liberating écriture, is presented by Orwell in the context of propagandistic manipulation:

> His [Smith's] mind slid away into the labyrinthine world of doublethink. To know and not to know, to be conscious of complete truthfulness while telling carefully constructed lies, to hold simultaneously two opinions which canceled out, knowing them to be contradictory and believing in both of them; to use logic against logic, to repudiate morality while laying claim to it. . . . That was the ultimate subtlety: consciously to induce unconsciousness, and then, once again, to become unconscious of the act of hypnosis you had just performed. Even to understand the word "doublethink" involved the use of doublethink. (186)

As Syme puts it to Smith, "the whole aim of Newspeak is to narrow the range of thought. In the end we shall make thoughtcrime literally impossible, because there will be no words in which to express it" (201). This formulation's proximity to Beckett's famous statement in the "Dialogues"—"nothing to express, nothing with which to express, no power to express"—is emblematic of how Beckett's and Orwell's postwar visions overlapped, how each hoped to break down, from opposite but corresponding sides, the conceptual bases of the opposition between commitment and autonomy. For both writers, the opposition itself was the ultimate failure; a failure they could evoke, but could not move beyond.

The Unnamable ends with a contradictory, tenuous affirmation of the obligation to write, despite the narrator's suffering and the impossibility of ever disengaging his own voice from the punitive language of his masters; *1984* ends with a grotesque parody of the committed writer. Tortured into submission, Smith accepts as truth the self-contradictory slogans imposed on him by an "anonymous" (193) authority. His body (not unlike those of Beckett's deteriorating heroes) a "rotting," hairless "bag of filth" (394), he at last takes up the "stump of pencil" his torturers have given him and writes out the orthodoxies of the Inner Party—Freedom is Slavery, two and two make five, God is Power (398)—struggling to block out the vestigial awareness of "arguments that contradicted them" (399). Affirmation is the sign of total defeat: "He accepted everything" (398).

Epilogue
Engagement, Écriture, Autonomy: The Displacement of Politics in Postwar Critical Theory

> The notion of the art work as critique actually informs some of the more thoughtful condemnations of postmodernism, which is accused of having abandoned the critical stance that once characterized modernism. However, the familiar ideas of what constitutes a critical art (*Parteilichkeit* and vanguardism, *l'art engagé,* critical realism, or the aesthetic of negativity, the refusal of representation, abstraction, reflexiveness) have lost much of their explanatory and normative power in recent decades. This is precisely the dilemma of art in a postmodern age. (Huyssen 182)

During the interwar years when Beckett began his career, the rise of fascism, the consolidation of the Soviet revolution, the economic crises of the 1930s, and the expanding potential of mass media, photography, and film determined, to a great degree, how writers understood the relationship of art and politics.[1] As the political situation became increasingly polarized with the approach of war, ideas about the role of the writer in society became narrowly, antagonistically polarized. But the most insightful cultural critics of the period, themselves inevitably caught up in the polarization, continued to argue for the relative autonomy of art, even as they insisted that art could no longer remain politically neutral.

A case in point is Walter Benjamin's "The Author as Producer," originally delivered as a lecture at the Institute for the Study of Fascism in Paris in 1934. Benjamin hoped to persuade his left/communist audience that only a formally innovative art, like Brecht's epic theater, could be effectively progressive in the current political climate. The function of conventional "so-called left-wing literature," with which his audience was no doubt familiar, was "to wring from the political situation a continuous stream of novel effects for the entertainment of the masses" (*Reflections* 229). "The tendency of a literary work can only be politically correct if it is also literarily correct" (221), Benjamin argued. The self-conscious development of new artistic techniques would lead writers to "observations that provide the most factual foundation for solidarity with the proletariat," to see themselves not just as artists but as "producers" (236). If the writer understood his work not only in terms of its "political line," but equally in terms of its mode of organization, technique, and

161

reception, then his writing would appear to him as work and the process of writing as production; the writer could then join cause with the proletariat not as an intellectual specialist, as in bourgeois society, but as a fellow worker. In turn, the effects of revolutionary technical innovations, such as montage or Brecht's "interruption of action," would turn "readers or spectators into collaborators" (233).

When viewed in historical perspective, Benjamin's lecture is remarkable in two respects. First, it constructs a model of cultural politics through a metaphorical (Benjamin calls it "dialectical") linkage between progressive or radical political ideas and innovations in aesthetic form and technique.[2] In this sense, for example, avant-gardist techniques of collage are "progressive" in relation to realist or naturalist techniques of relatively uniperspectival representation. But for Benjamin progressive art did not, on its own, contribute to political progress. Like political tendency, progressive technique was a necessary but not sufficient condition for critical art. Truly progressive art, for Benjamin, necessitates both aesthetic autonomy—the writer's freedom to consider writing primarily in terms of form and technique—and a commitment to progressive political ideas. Because Benjamin linked these two requirements metaphorically, his view of critical art is open to much interpretive debate; it has also been read as an attack on aesthetic autonomy, a call to subordinate subjective expression to a utopian, collective program.[3] Second (and related to this metaphorical construction of cultural politics), in this essay and others, Benjamin set the agenda for some of the most influential ideas about cultural politics in the postwar decades, from notions of the political potential of aura-breaking popular cultural forms to Barthes's notion of the writerly in which passive reading is transformed into active "production."

The politicization of art in the interwar period left a problematic legacy for the postwar generation of writers and theorists. The idea that *all* art had an overarching, fixed political valence—reactionary or progressive, bourgeois or revolutionary—now seemed axiomatic. But with the defeat of fascism, the increasing awareness of the totalitarian and imperial aspirations of the Soviet Union, and the beginning of the postwar economic boom with its new consensus among labor, management, and government, the tendencies of the interwar period were becoming meaningless.[4] In the wake of this historical change, new paradigms of cultural politics took shape. While Benjamin had tried to link aesthetic autonomy and politics through the metaphor of progressive technique, in postwar Europe one side of the linkage—the idea of progressive aesthetic form—was promoted to the status of a fully developed theory; "tendency," in turn, became detached from organized political parties or practical political struggles.

Sartre's notion of engaged art, as expressed in *Literature and Existentialism* (originally published in 1947), was perhaps the most influential starting point for renewed debates about literature and politics. In many respects, Sartre seems to be reiterating the 1930s' call for commitment. Making a distinction between poetry and "writing," Sartre demands that the writer "utilize" language for a purpose. "The writer is a *speaker;* he designates, demonstrates, orders, refuses . . . persuades" (19).

For Sartre, writing is a form of action which must have a definite, worthwhile purpose in relation to "a system of transcendent values" (22–23). As in earlier attacks on "formalism" or art-for-art's-sake, questions of style, technique, and beauty are unimportant; "Style should pass unnoticed. . . . Words are transparent. . . . In short, it is a matter of knowing what one wants to write about" (25–26). Through the conscious choice of subject matter and the intention to persuade through an instrumental language, the writer makes his primary concern questions such as, "What aspect of the world do you want to disclose? What change do you want to bring into the world by this disclosure?" (23).

Sartre does not, however, identify these changes or disclosures with the same specificity as did the thirties' writers who took up antifascist, socialist, or communist positions. Instead, Sartre focuses first on an abstract, universal "appeal to freedom." Developing a rudimentary reception theory, Sartre argues that writing and reading are two sides of a single action. "Reading is directed creation" (45); "the writer appeals to the reader's freedom to collaborate in the production of his work" (46). Sartre's theory of engagement, his existential categories of freedom and choice, are presented first and foremost as free floating and individualistic, and not bound up with social or political forces:

> The belief which I accord the tale is freely assented to . . . the characteristic of aesthetic consciousness is to be a belief by means of engagement, by oath, a belief sustained by fidelity to one's self and to the author, a perpetually renewed choice to believe. . . . Reading is a free dream. . . . The reader's feelings are never dominated by the object, and as no external reality can condition them, they have their permanent source in freedom. (50–51)

It is only in the last part of the book, "For Whom Does One Write," where Sartre attempts to relate these abstractions to an "external reality" and a specifically political notion of freedom. Not surprisingly, this is the most difficult part of the book. To some degree, Sartre follows a familiar, quasi-Marxist argument against modernist "negativity and abstraction" (148–49): with the rise of bourgeois society after the French Revolution, the writer sees himself more and more in opposition to the values of modern society, yet at the same time "it was the bourgeoisie alone which maintained him and decided his fame" (123). The writer lives "in a state of contradiction and dishonesty"; he ideologically opposes and castigates the class whose interest he actually serves. Unwilling or unable "to leave it and try out the interests and way of life of another class," the writer instead makes writing into an autonomous, self-reflexive, formalist game. He withdraws, values "solitude" and abandons the communicative function of writing (123); by the twentieth century, the most creative aestheticist, modernist, or avant-garde writers aim for the "heightened artificialism" of Des Esseintes, or "a concerted destruction of language" and "nothingness" as in Mallarmé (130). The modern writer, from Flaubert to the surrealists, is a contradictory "rebel, not a revolutionary," who serves as an "accomplice" for the bourgeois classes: "It was better [for society] to keep the forces of negation within a vain aestheticism, a rebellion without effect; if they were free, they might have interested themselves on behalf of the oppressed classes" (135).

Sartre, however, must deviate from this historical account of the writer in bourgeois society in order to maintain that "the essence of the literary work is freedom totally disclosing itself as an appeal to the freedom of other men" (151). Sartre's logic is somewhat tortuous, but his conclusion is clear: the writer's freedom is incomplete, unrealized, unless he makes a communicative, concrete appeal to all people (his "virtual" public), not just to the bourgeois class (his "actual" public). The writer must make a "negation of formalism" (154), which is nothing but a sign of his contradictory status as "rebel," and communicate to the "sum total of men living in a given society" (155). The writer helps create a "classless" society by making his work an "appeal to freedom" directed at all men, whose awareness of freedom is awakened and strengthened through their "free" act of constructive reading. While "different forms of oppression" have hid "from men the fact they were [in essence] free," the engaged writer reveals to them their freedom and participates in their liberation (151–56).

What emerges in Sartre's attempt to fuse a Marxist political teleology to a belief in an existential notion of freedom is a view of the writer not as a person embedded in class society, but as one who has, by the very choice of becoming a writer, already reached the condition toward which others, his readers, must struggle: "No one is obliged to choose himself as a writer. Hence, freedom is at the origin. I am an author, first of all, by my free project of writing" (76). An author, for Sartre, is a symbol not of class conflict but its resolution. Having no conception of the engaged writer as a social actor among other social actors, Sartre actually poses the writer as the person who has no relation to class society at all. From his already-realized essential freedom the writer can then choose to realize it more fully by appealing to all men; men who unlike the writer live under particular social constraints that "hide" their freedom from them.

The problem this raises is evident in the examples Sartre chooses, from the "jew" (76) to the "negro" writer Richard Wright (77–80) to his later championing of Frantz Fanon.[5] As other parts of his book make clear, Sartre knows that those who "choose" to become writers are for the most part not from oppressed classes or groups; writing is a bourgeois profession. His formula comes close to tautology: the writer's freedom is predicated on the fact that he is already in a social position that leaves him relatively free to develop a career, be it as a writer or anything else. Sartre actually needs examples of writers who, living under forms of palpable social oppression, choose writing as a way of fighting oppression—their own and that of people who share their social status. In the end, Sartre's theory cannot address the situation of the European bourgeois writer at all. And this is one sign of the postwar historical shift: his own freedom no longer threatened by fascism or pressured to conform to the dictates of a specific "political line," the engaged European writer living in a relatively democratic society begins to understand cultural politics only in relation to others. His engagement, his integrity, is guaranteed by the oppression of "others," of black Americans, Jews, colonial subjects, and so forth. His own, actual relation to the institutions of bourgeois society—to what the committed writer of the thirties might call the mode of cultural production—remains unexamined.[6]

The most influential response to Sartre's manifesto in French is Barthes's 1953 *Writing Degree Zero*. As Susan Sontag points out, Barthes's book is so "terse and unconcrete" that it seems as though "Barthes were depending on his reader's familiarity with the generous development of the terms of the debate provided by Sartre" (*WDZ* xi).[7] I have already discussed Barthes's understanding of modernism and his rejection of "narration." Here, I only want to point out how Barthes poses the idea of écriture in opposition to Sartre. If Sartre modified the interwar idea of tendential writing into an abstract engagement between the writer's freedom and the unrealized freedom of the oppressed, Barthes hypostatizes the metaphorical linkage between avant-gardist experimentation and revolutionary or utopian politics. For Barthes, all articulated political programs, and all writing that poses itself as communication, are themselves inherently oppressive. He begins his attack on commitment by claiming: "Writing is in no way an instrument of communication" (19). For Barthes, writing is always imagistic, "symbolic, introverted, ostensibly turned toward an occult side of language" (19). He sees all attempts at "political writing" to be the imposition of order, a sign of "power" (20). Since, for Barthes, "the content of the word 'Order' always indicates repression" (26), any writing that claims to represent or argue for a political or social order is ultimately repressive: "In the present state of History, any political mode of writing can only uphold a police state" (28).[8]

Barthes's conviction that there can be no positive notion of order whatsoever leads him to advocate a "mode of writing" that, like earlier avant-gardist programs, seeks to reject "bondage to a pre-ordained state of language" (76); that approaches "an ideal absence of style" (77). While Barthes offers various evocations of what this writing might look like or how its "form as an instrument is no longer at the service of a triumphant ideology," these evocations are all necessarily in a negative form: "The new neutral writing takes its place in the midst of all those ejaculations and judgments [of journalism, bourgeois or engaged writing] without becoming involved in any of them; it consists precisely in their absence" (77). The emptying of content that Sartre saw in the rise of modernism, and which he considered the sign of the writer's contradictory stance toward a bourgeois public, Barthes sees as "disengaging" (76) literature from the oppression of "order." To empty writing of all conventions is a utopian project: "The search for a non-style or an oral style, for a zero level or a spoken level of writing is, all things considered, the anticipation of a homogeneous social state" (87). The belief that linguistic and discursive conventions determine political consciousness, always implicit in Barthes's early work, leads him to equate the vanguardist rejection of conventional, narrative literature with political emancipation: "Literature becomes the Utopia of language" (88). While Sartre had to sidestep the problem of the engaged European writer's relation to his own social context, Barthes posits a transcendent position for the writer, as the term *zero-degree* suggests; a position emptied of any productive relation to the organization of his or her own social world or literary tradition.

Adorno's advocacy of aesthetic autonomy is another influential response to Sartre. Perhaps the most fundamental distinction between Adorno, on the one hand, and Sartre and Barthes, on the other, is that Adorno places the writer's position in society at the center of his ideas about progressive literature. As he claims in his polemic with Sartre, the 1962 essay "Commitment," "an emphasis on autonomous works is itself sociopolitical in nature" (318). For Adorno, the political significance of literature lay neither in a communicative appeal from writer to reader nor in the writer's ability to transcend an oppressive order through a "neutral" writing. Rather, because the writer is bound up in the social processes of modern society—most importantly, for Adorno, the commodification of culture and the encroachment of instrumental reason over all forms of human interaction—the writer opposes these sociopolitical forces by constructing an aesthetic rationality or counterlogic predicated on what Adorno calls "a determinate negation of meaning" (316).

Although Adorno's ideas about autonomy and negation echo earlier aestheticist and modernist concerns, he understands aesthetic values not only "in opposition to society" (*Aesthetic* 322) but as themselves produced by developments in the modern institutions of art and culture. His objection to Sartre rests not on Sartre's political intentions, but on his naivete about how contemporary culture functions. Sartre's emphasis on content and communication is, for Adorno, perfectly in sync with the requirements of both conservatism and the "culture industry," which cynically turns a profit from images of human suffering that assuage the bourgeois viewer's guilt. "Commitment in itself," Adorno writes, "remains politically multivalent so long as it is not reduced to propaganda. . . . Cultural conservatives who demand that a work of art say something join forces with their political opponents against atelic, hermetic works of art" ("Commitment" 302). For Adorno, the critical work of art must confront, in its form and "social content," the instrumental reason dominating social relations, and must counter the underlying formal principles of the products of mass culture, which he sees as the degradation of a potentially egalitarian art.[9]

Adorno's understanding of critical art is embedded in his understanding of aesthetic autonomy, most fully explained in the unfinished *Aesthetic Theory.*[10] For Adorno, aesthetic autonomy means three interrelated things: a sociohistorical development; art's ideological self-conception; and a value, a feature of modern art that Adorno defends and advocates. First, aesthetic autonomy is a thoroughly historical category: "Autonomy, art's growing independence from society, is a function of the bourgeois consciousness of freedom, which in turn is tied up with a specific social structure. Before that, art may have been in conflict with the forces and mores dominating society, but it was never 'for itself'" (320). The autonomy of art, like the autonomous individual, is part of the development of capitalism and secular society; the idea of art as a sphere of free, unfettered expression exists only in relation to its institutional status in bourgeois society. But what this also means is that, in becoming free from ties to religion, prescriptive ethics, or private patronage, art becomes integrally connected to impersonal economic forces and the domination inherent in the social hierarchies of capitalism.

This leads to the second aspect of autonomy, art's ideological self-conception:

> Politically progressive critics have accused "art for art's sake" . . . of fetishizing the concept of the pure, self-sufficient work of art. This indictment is valid in that works of art are products of social labour. . . . Prior to any analysis of what they express, art works are ideological because they . . . posit a spiritual entity as though it were independent of any conditions of material production, hence as though it were intrinsically superior to these conditions. In so doing art works cover up the age-old culpability that lies in the divorce of physical from mental labour. (323)[11]

The more that capitalist relations determine social relations, the more art posits itself as separate and opposed to society. In positing itself as separate from a prosaic, unjust reality, art denies its own historical relation to the bourgeois society to which it owes its freedom and blindly reiterates underlying social hierarchies.

For Adorno, however, art can only oppose the domination inherent in modern society by intensifying its autonomous status, not denying it. Adorno argues that only the most thoroughly autonomous art is effectively political. Since, for Adorno, domination results from the increasing rationalization of society, art can only resist by developing its own form of noninstrumental, aesthetic rationality. Any attempt in art to communicate a politically progressive message—that is, to subordinate the work's autonomy to an instrumental intent—merely serves to integrate art into the overall logic of capitalism. Thus, "determinant negation" means the process by which the critical writer, by virtue of his position within society, shapes his work through a dynamic reaction to the everyday experience of the world that capitalism and rationalization create: "Works of art that react against empirical reality obey the forces of that reality" ("Commitment" 314).

This is not a transcendent position, but it is an explicitly paradoxical one. Since for Adorno communicative norms are bound up with instrumental rationality, "authentically" autonomous art reacts to those norms and deforms them or renders them self-contradictory. On one hand, Adorno seems to imply that truly political literature, which completely and integrally dismantles the logic of mass culture and instrumental reason, would be nearly incomprehensible. But, on the other, Adorno wants to retain art's communicative function. He insists that the *determinate* negation remains meaningful because, as in the works of Kafka, Beckett, or Joyce, it retains the "imprint" of the dehumanizing norms it resists. As he admits, "no firm criteria can draw the line between a determinate negation of meaning and a bad positivism of meaninglessness" (316). In other words, a nonsensical (for example, Dadaist poetry) or wholly noncommunicative literature simply has no force; total disengagement from the conventions of mainstream literature and communicative language amounts to resignation rather than resistance.

It is not coincidental that Adorno planned to dedicate *Aesthetic Theory* to Samuel Beckett.[12] For Adorno, Beckett was perhaps the only postwar writer who was able both to articulate "the negation of meaning in an aesthetically meaningful way" (Wellmer 96) and serve as an emblem for the paradoxical situation of art in Europe "after Auschwitz." While Adorno's, Sartre's, and Barthes's ideas about what constitute a critical art were posed polemically in opposition to each other—explicitly and implicitly—I have tried to show that Beckett's fiction actively tried to overcome such oppositions. For, in Sartre's sense, Beckett's work does take up an identification with the oppressed; in Barthes's sense, it does seek to neutralize its own relation to the order of narrative convention; in Adorno's sense, it does actively recreate, in a negative way, a reified, instrumental consciousness. To some degree, Beckett indirectly incorporated aspects of all these ideas of a critical art. If anything links Beckett's work more closely to Adorno than to other postwar theorists, however, it is both writers' awareness of the writer's (and the critic's) inextricable entanglement with the social order his work presumes to oppose.

In the postwar theorization of a critical art, politics became an abstract entity, less and less tied to political parties, organized movements, or institutional arrangements of power. Instead, politics existed in relation to an "inner" freedom, to an idealized "absence" of order, to a subjective negation of an objectively oppressive world. Partly, these abstractions no doubt stemmed from a deep and understandable pessimism about European enlightenment traditions in the wake of the barbarism unleashed during World War II. But equally important during the period Beckett became famous—when ideas about existential freedom, écriture, and negativity were becoming fashionable in European and American intellectual circles—were the newly invigorated struggles of women, black Americans, colonized people, and other groups hitherto denied political subjectivity; struggles which inaugurated a new understanding of cultural politics. The abstractions and paradoxes about art and politics issuing from postwar Paris, Frankfurt, or New York were themselves a sign that politics—direct, urgent, and palpable in everyday, lived experience—was being taken up elsewhere.[13]

NOTES

Chapter 1. Entering the Literary Field

1. *Watt* was not published until 1953; for the circumstances of its publication, see Bair, 431–34 and Knowlson, 355–58. Both Knowlson and Bair give vivid accounts of Beckett's literary "anonymity" (Knowlson 350) prior to the popular success of *Godot* in the early 1950s. Cronin reports that after its first five years in print, *Murphy* had sold less than one hundred copies (362).

2. He had also tried translating and literary journalism, with modest success and even less financial reward. See Knowlson, 243–72, for Beckett's inability to make a living as a writer.

3. I use the term *literary field* as Pierre Bourdieu defines it, as "a space of objective relations between positions—between that of the celebrated artist and that of the avant gardiste, for example." According to Bourdieu, "by analyzing the literary field as a space of positions corresponding to a space of homologous aesthetic positions we are able to transcend the opposition . . . between internal readings and external analysis and at the same time preserve the benefits and requirements of two approaches traditionally considered irreconcilable" ("Flaubert's" 544); for a systematic theory of the literary field see Bourdieu's *The Field of Cultural Production*.

4. Two recent studies offer a more balanced assessment of Beckett's early writing. In *Beckett before Godot* (1997), John Pilling, working within the formalist tradition of Beckett scholarship, attempts to lay out the "very variety of modes, registers, and genres observable [in Beckett's work] between 1929 and 1949." In a comprehensive sweep of almost all Beckett's pretrilogy writing, Pilling probes "how and why a problem presented itself" within each individual work, "and whether or not it was, or could be, satisfactorily (if only temporarily) solved" (3). Pilling's formalist and phenomenological categories do not, however, veer significantly from the canonical high-modernist view of Beckett. More relevant to my concerns is Tyrus Miller's *Late Modernism: Politics, Fiction, and the Arts between the World Wars* (1999), published as I was completing the final revisions of this book. Miller offers a reading of Beckett's interwar criticism and fiction, especially *Murphy*, within a consideration of a group of writers—Wyndham Lewis, Djuna Barnes, and Mina Loy—whose works exemplify a particular cultural moment, an "apparent admixture of decadent and forward-looking elements" which have no "clearly defined place in the dominant frameworks of twentieth-century criticism." Miller correctly argues that "the double life of this significant body of writing—its linkage forward into postmodernism and backward into modernism—has not, by and large, been accounted for" (7). Working

169

through many of the same critics of modernism as I do—Adorno, Benjamin, Bürger, Jameson, Moretti, and George Orwell (though, significantly, not Raymond Williams)—Miller likewise addresses several of the same central issues of the cultural politics of the late 1920s and 1930s. However, while we both agree that "Beckett came to call high modernist poetics into question" (170), our views fundamentally diverge to the extent that Miller, like so many Beckett scholars, links Beckett too closely both to poststructuralism—in "Proust," Miller writes, Beckett "delineates a rationale for modernist literature similar to that later articulated by Michel Foucault" (172)—and to a nascent postmodernism described primarily in terms of metafiction (see his discussion on p.12; my objections to this model of postmodernism are discussed in detail in chapter 3 of this book). More specifically, Miller claims that "as late as 1934" Beckett "reaffirms the heroic ethos of high modernism" (174) in his critical writing, and that, while "articulating a coherent modernist *critical* position" he was "working to sabotage its functioning in his own fiction" (176). My analysis in this chapter, in direct contrast, shows how Beckett's interwar criticism and fiction both display a mutually informing incoherence, especially in regard to Beckett's contradictory allegiance to modernist, aestheticist, and avant-gardist cultural values. Ultimately, Miller resorts to the type of negative description of Beckett's work that is characteristic of modernism's own vanguardist pronouncements: an "aesthetic of entropic decay, deformation, debasement, and disfiguration" (184). Miller's book is an exciting contribution to our reassessments of twentieth-century culture; my disagreements with him are particular to his incongruous inclusion of *early* Beckett into a canon of *late* modernism. As Miller himself admits, "a more comprehensive development of this idea [of Beckett's rejection of high modernism] . . . will have to await further discussion of Beckett's whole body of writing, a task beyond the limited scope" of his book's chapter on Beckett (170).

5. In the discussion that follows I accept, for the most part, Peter Bürger's distinctions among aestheticism, modernism, and the "historical avant garde," as he explains them in his influential *Theory of the Avant Garde*. Bürger's claims about the specificity of the avant-garde movements of the early twentieth century provides the best framework for understanding Beckett's relation to the vanguardist artists and ideals of his immediate cultural milieu. This might not be the case for other writers of the period. For a good survey of how Bürger's theory measures up to other classic accounts of the avant garde, especially in regard to British culture, see Josephine Guy's *The British Avant Garde: The Theory and Politics of Tradition*.

6. As Miller puts it, the essay on Joyce "careens from pedantry to snarling polemic, between scornful detachment and the enthusiasm of the true believer" (170). Pilling calls "Proust" "an explosive exercise in self-definition" and links its eccentric style to Beckett's decision to give up his brief academic career as lecturer at Trinity (36–37).

7. Nadeau cites the invention and elaboration, in the early 1920s, of a rigorous "automatic" method of composition as constituting surrealism's decisive break with dada (79–84).

8. Levenson's *A Genealogy of Modernism* provides an insightful discussion of the formation of such oppositions.

9. Knowlson discusses Beckett's excitement about dada and surrealism when he first arrived in Paris in 1928, which led him to do translations of works by Breton, Eluard, and Crevel (65, 113).

10. See Seigel's *Bohemian Paris* for an excellent history of both the actual lives of artists and "bohemians" and the symbols that served to define bohemia as a cultural space in which to explore and reconcile the contradictions arising from the processes of modernization in nineteenth-century urban Europe.

11. Pilling sees only a negative, parodic relation between Joyce's *Dubliners* and Beckett's early stories (95). See Miller (183) and Harrington (66–72) for other possible interpretations of the conflicted overlap between Joyce's and Beckett's short fiction.

12. As Beckett put it in a letter complaining about the trying process of writing *More Pricks than Kicks*, "it is all jigsaw" (qtd. in Pilling 97).

13. "*Ulysses*," Moretti argues, "caused a deep split within the development of European literature and particularly, the novel: this much was immediately clear. Less clear was . . . the link between this split and the rupture that occurred in the functioning of capitalist societies at the turn of the century" (182). Moretti hopes to demonstrate the "structural homology" (190) between, on one side, the historical "crisis" of liberal capitalism in England, and, on the other, the aesthetic logics and ideological implications in the works of British high modernism. Here, I focus on only one side of this theoretical "homology"; appreciating Moretti's observations on features of Joyce's and Eliot's work does not require accepting the causal premises of the larger argument.

14. As Menand notes concerning Eliot's remarks on the mythic method, the idea "seems to be parodied by the footnotes to his own poem ["The Wasteland"]. . . . Modernist literature holds many funds of irony to mock its own prescriptions" (113). The task is thus not to decide whether or not modernist writers' explicit aesthetic programs match their works of art, but to describe how the attitudes informing the aesthetic programs shape literary works in ways their authors may not intend.

Chapter 2. Contact with the Outside World

1. Information about Beckett's life and publishing history in this chapter is drawn from Bair, chapters 9, 10, and 11; Cooke, pp. 7–12; Graver and Federman, pp. xiii–xx; and Knowlson, chapters 8 through 11.

2. After the war a French publisher, Georges Duthuit, bought the defunct *transition* from American Eugene Jolas and renamed it *transition 48*. Beckett did several unsigned translations for the journal but no longer published original work in it.

3. See, for example, Dylan Thomas's negative review of the novel in *New*

English Weekly: Beckett "has not yet thrown off the influence of those writers who have made 'Transition' (*sic*) their permanent resting place. . . . If I do not straight-forwardly praise his new book . . . for its obvious qualities—of energy, hilarity, irony, and comic invention—then it is [Beckett's] fault: he should never try to sell his bluffs over the double counter. I must say that 'Murphy' is difficult, serious and wrong" (republished in Butler 12–13).

4. Valentine Cunningham's encyclopedic *British Writers of the Thirties* provides vivid descriptions of the heated debates and ideological divisions of the decade. See also Samuel Hynes's *The Auden Generation* for an account of the decade's explicit social and political problems and Herbert Lottman's *The Left Bank* for an account of the various alliances among the communist party, French writers, and diverse antifas-cist movements.

5. One of the most extreme leftist literary figures of the decade, Christopher Caudwell, considered these choices superficial—what was necessary was an entirely new relation to the "bourgeois" institution of art: "Most bourgeois artists are at present treading the road of alliance [with the proletariat]—Gide in France, Day Lewis, Auden, and Spender in this country—and many of the surrealists have signed the same treaty. Such an alliance can only be an 'anarchist alliance.' . . . They often glorify the revolution as a kind of giant explosion which will blow up everything they feel to be hampering them. But they have no constructive theory—I mean as artists: they may as economists accept the economic strategies of socialism, but as artists they cannot see the new forms and contents of an art which will replace bourgeois art. . . . Of course this anarchic position of the contemporary bourgeois artist is only a variant of the old tragedy of bourgeois revolt" (318–20). In effect, Caudwell's position implies the most overarching opposition of all: "art" as opposed to some new, as yet unimagined proletarian creative activity whose forms and function would correspond to a transformed world.

6. See Lottman, p. 64, for the Soviet critique of Malraux's novel. In *The Culture of Redemption* (pp. 102–109) Leo Bersani makes a similar point about Malraux's contradictory expressions of Marxist determinism and individual choice. As both Lottman's and Cunningham's surveys of the decade point out, the high value placed on individuality in art and culture by British and French writers was a major source of tension between "fellow travelers" and Soviet party officials.

7. The most recent, and most sobering reassessment of the legacy of the troubled association between writers and communism in France can be found in Tony Judt's *Past Imperfect: French Intellectuals, 1944–1956.*

8. The review, entitled "Intercessions by Denis Devlin," was reprinted in 1984 in a collection of Beckett's miscellaneous writings, *Disjecta,* and is now part of the Beckett canon.

9. Beckett had repeatedly attacked the poetry of the Celtic Revival: "These are the antiquarians, delivering with the altitudinous complacency of the Victorian Gael the Ossianic goods," he wrote in a review titled "Recent Irish Poetry," published originally in *The Bookman* in 1934 under the pseudonym Andrew Belis (reprinted in

Disjecta 70). See Harrington, pp. 28–34, for an assessment of Beckett's position on the Revival, from the perspective of the Irish literary community.

10. Radek was condemned as a Trotskyite in the Moscow "show trials" of 1937 and sent to Siberia. He died, by the official Soviet account, at the hands of a fellow exile, in 1939.

11. See Cunningham, pp. 299–300, and Lottman, pp. 62–67, for the importance of the Soviet Writers' Congress for Western leftist writers. The redacted proceedings of the congress—Radek's speech was one of the main events—was quickly translated and published in Britain in 1935.

12. See Susan Suleiman's *Subversive Intent* for an account of how avant-garde writers retained and exploited middle-class values concerning male dominance.

13. Declan Kiberd interprets this scene as a "spoof on the socially committed literature of the thirties" and "an attack on the notion of the inherent dignity of work" ("Samuel" 126) that is rooted ultimately in Beckett's Protestant beliefs about the value of self-reliance; see also the chapter 26. "Religious Writing: Beckett and Others" in Kiberd's *Inventing Ireland.*

14. See Ellman, p. 709; for Beckett's antifascist sentiments, see Knowlson, chapters 10–13.

15. Bair's biography was the standard source of information for Beckett's life from its publication in 1978 until 1996, when Knowlson's "authorized" biography *Damned to Fame* appeared. Knowlson diverges from Bair's insistence on Beckett's apoliticism during the German occupation (see pp. 278–80). I focus here on Bair's account because it typifies the way Beckett's work has been drained of its social content. See Christopher Prendergast's review-essay of Knowlson's book, and Cronin's 1997 *The Last Modernist,* for an account of where the later biographies both fail and succeed in making plausible links between the life and the works.

16. See Judt's chapter "Resistance and Revenge" for the postwar creation of the myth that "all but a tiny majority of the French people were in the Resistance or sympathized with it" (45). Beckett downplayed his own participation in the Resistance; he was recruited into the cell named "Gloria" by his friend Alfred Péron, who was later arrested by the Gestapo and died as a result of his imprisonment in a concentration camp; see Knowlson, pp. 273–90.

17. Williams gives a good description of the interwar avant garde in this respect: "For in each of these cases, though in interestingly different ways, an old language had been marginalized or suppressed, or else simply left behind, and the now dominant language either interacted with its subordinate for new language effects or was seen as, in new ways, both plastic and arbitrary; an alien but accessible system which had both power and potential yet was still not, as in most earlier formations, however experimental, the language or the possible language of a people but now the material of groups, agencies, fractions, specific works, its actual society and complex of writers and game players, translators and signwriters, interpreters and makers of paradoxes, cross-cultural innovators and jokers. The actual social process, that is to say, involved not only an Apollinaire, a Joyce, an Ionesco, a Beckett, but also,

as Joyce recognized in Bloom, many extempore dealers and negotiators and per-suaders" (*Politics* 78).

18. See Hobsbawm's *The Age of Empire,* chapter 6, for an account of the right-wing invention of the linguistic-ethnic definition of nation in the late nineteenth century.

19. See Seigel's *Bohemian Paris.* See Janet Wolff's *Feminine Sentences,* especially the chapter "The Invisible Flâneuse," for a discussion of women artists' restricted access to the urban public spaces which constituted much of the subject matter and social perspective of bohemian modernism and the avant garde.

20. Thus the need the Nazis felt for mounting several "degenerate" art exhibits across Germany which offered the public concrete interpretations of the works of many avant-garde and modernist artists, usually presenting them as signs of mental illness, sexual perversity, moral weakness, and antipatriotic treason. See Stephanie Barron's *"Degenerate Art": The Fate of the Avant Garde in Nazi Germany.* As one visitor to the *Entartete Kunst* exhibition in Munich in 1937 described it: "The visitors were practically forced by the installation and the accompanying texts to despise the art and the artists. And this reaction was praised as the proper attitude of 'true' Germans who should not be misled by those who wanted to destroy 'true' art" (Barron 43).

21. For similar interpretations, see Steve Dubin's argument in *Arresting Images* about the "culture wars" of the 1980s in the United States; see Jauss, pp. 42–45, for Flaubert's trial over morality in *Madame Bovary;* see Gagnier's remarks, in *Idylls of the Marketplace,* on the reception of *Dorian Gray* and the persecution of Oscar Wilde.

22. Poststructuralist-informed critics like Connor view Beckett's use of per-mutation and repetition as a means of subverting stable meanings in order to disengage writing from the repressive restrictions of narrative order. But a device like repetition is in itself meaningless and can be used equally to reinforce monolithic meanings, as in advertising and propaganda.

23. The novel has many other elements: extensive parodies and verbal bur-lesques of Catholic intellectuals, prudishness, bureaucracy, and the Celtic Revival, and simple word play both clever—as with the names of the twins Art and Con (101)—and cheerfully infantile, as in Watt's "Ot bro, lap rulb, krad klub" (165). As a whole, however, these elements are subordinate to, and a refraction of, the central concerns with ambiguity and the extremes of a radically noncommunicative style.

24. See *Disjecta,* p. 172.

25. See Harrington for an interpretation of the novel that focuses on its possible antecedents in Anglo-Irish literature, from *Tristram Shandy* and "A Tale of a Tub" to the "Big House" novel.

26. In *The Predicament of Culture* James Clifford draws interesting parallels between surrealism and ethnography in the first half of the century, comparing "their way of taking culture seriously, as a contested reality—a way that included the ridiculing and reshuffling of its orders" (121). In *Vision and Design* Bloomsbury art critic Roger Fry used a quasi-cultural-anthropological approach to justify modernist aesthetic autonomy through reference to the arts of tribal Africa. For provocative

discussions about the intellectual affinity between modernist ideas of culture and the rise of professional anthropology, see Stocking's *Race, Culture, and Evolution* and the essays edited by Stocking in *Romantic Motives.*

Chapter 3. Rewriting Modernism in the Nouvelles

1. Throughout this chapter I use the term *modernism* to mean somewhat different things in different contexts. Here, I refer to the conventional notion of literary modernism, which would include Joyce, Pound, Woolf, Eliot, Kafka, along with dada, futurism, surrealism, etc. Elsewhere, I make distinctions among the "historical avant garde," "aestheticism," "Joycean modernism," etc., in order to stress the differences within modernist works and writers. The manner in which Beckett experienced and understood these works and writers does not necessarily correspond to either the conventional views of modernism or the more recent reevaluations of modernism, as in Bürger and Williams. For a comprehensive view of modernism that focuses on the central value of the "new," see Marshall Berman's *All That Is Solid Melts into Air.*

2. See Nadeau, part two, for a description of the first surrealist experiments with, and ideas about, automatic writing, dreams, the unconscious, etc., beginning in 1923; see his chapter 14 for the split, along cultural-political lines, between Aragon and Breton after Aragon's participation in the Second International Congress of Revolutionary Writers in Kharkov. See also Breton's reference to the "social face" and the "poetic face" of the controversy surrounding Aragon's famous poem "Red Front" (reprinted in Nadeau 296).

3. Whatever other motives Beckett may have had for beginning to write primarily in French, and whatever other effects such a change entailed, two practical concerns seem dominant. First, like a number of international writers, such as Borges or Gombrowicz, he self-consciously severed his relationship to any definitive notion of a national literature. Secondly, and independently of the first more ideological motive, was the fact that his reception by the English-reading public had been abysmal. Censored in Ireland, ignored for the most part in England, unknown in the United States, he looked to the French intellectual and artistic community as his new public. See Hill (40–58) for a poststructuralist and psychoanalytic discussion of how the simultaneous existence of French and English versions of Beckett's postwar fiction contributes to the destabilizing of identity in his work; see Fletcher (94–99) for how Beckett used French as a way of simplifying his style and making his writing more direct and emotively satirical. I deal here only with Beckett's English versions of the nouvelles. The discrepancies and minor changes between the two versions do not affect my readings or general argument.

4. Beckett wrote five fictional works in French before he began *Molloy* in 1947: "La Fin" (originally titled "Suite"), "*L'Expulsé*," "*La Calmant*," "*Premier Amour*," and *Mercier et Camier.* These were eventually translated as "The End," "The Expelled,"

"The Calmative," "First Love," and *Mercier and Camier.* Of these, Beckett was originally only interested in publishing three—"The End," "The Expelled," and "The Calmative," the definitive French versions of which appeared together in the 1955 volume *Nouvelles et textes pour rien.* Many years later, after he had become a world famous author, he published, in French and English, the other two works. In this chapter I focus on the three nouvelles that Beckett saw as representative of his best work and which he wished to have published immediately. See below, in this chapter, for why only the first half of "Suite" ("La Fin") was published in *Les Temps modernes.*

    5. For example, in Conrad's *Heart of Darkness* or E. M. Forster's *A Passage to India.*

    6. David Lloyd has attempted to read the contradictions about authenticity in Beckett's fiction as "an aesthetic of nonidentity . . . [which] equally writes out the inauthenticity enforced upon the colonized subject" (55). For Lloyd, this is a sign of Beckett's critical rejection of the Celtic Revival's "fetishization of national identity" (50) in which "Irish nationalists reproduce in their very opposition to the Empire a narrative of universal development which is fundamental to the legitimation of imperialism" (46). Lloyd's reading of Beckett is both too narrow and too broad. On one hand, for this type of analysis one would have to understand Beckett's rejection of "authenticity" in relation to ideologies of nationalism in general and not only in the context of colonization, since Beckett understood himself in the context of European modernism and the avant garde. On the other, Lloyd's argument rests on an internal contradiction: if Beckett really does reject all forms of "identity," then there is no compelling reason to read him in an Irish context. Lloyd implicitly assumes that because Beckett was born in Ireland, he is an Irish writer; Beckett himself (unlike Joyce) had no interest in being an Irish writer and throughout his works he parodies such a notion. Lloyd has to create Beckett as an authentic Irish writer (Lloyd himself admits his reading is "strained" [41]) in order to show that Beckett then rejects Irish authenticity. It would be more accurate to say that Beckett rejected the notion of national literatures altogether and occasionally wrote about his relation to Ireland in the context of such a rejection. See Williams (*Politics* 77–80) for a discussion of how immigrants and exiles from all over Europe were separated from national languages and literatures and contributed to an international avant garde whose project in-volved the search of a transnational language of form. For other views of Beckett's relation to Irish identity, see Harrington, Kiberd's *Inventing Ireland,* and Deane's *Celtic Revivals* and *A Short History of Irish Literature.*

    7. As Wilde put it in the preface to *Dorian Gray:* "We can forgive a man for making a useful thing as long as he does not admire it. The only excuse for making a useless thing is that one admires it intensely. All art is quite useless" (4). For the Marxist roots of Adorno's modernist theory of art's functional "uselessness" see Lunn's *Marxism and Modernism* and Brenkman's *Culture and Domination.*

    8. See Judt for a comprehensive analysis of French intellectuals and commu-nism in the postwar decade; see also Lottman (231–37) for the strained relations

between Sartre's *Les Temps modernes,* Camus's *Combat* (and many other leftist literary journals that dominated French intellectual life) and the Communist Party from the end of the war until 1949.

9. See Bair 353, Fletcher 96, Cronin 366, and Knowlson 325–26, for accounts of the curious half-publication of "La Suite" in *Les Temps modernes.*

10. See Bakhtin's "Epic and Novel" in *The Dialogic Imagination* for a now-classic account of the relationship between epic and novelistic modes of narration.

11. The critical literature on the metropolis and modernism that informs my argument begins with Simmel's 1903 essay "The Metropolis and Mental Life" and Walter Benjamin's interwar writings on Baudelaire, Paris, and surrealism. Some important contemporary accounts can be found in David Harvey's *The Urban Experience* and *The Condition of Postmodernity,* Berman's *All That Is Solid Melts into Air,* Williams's *The Country and the City,* Jukes's *A Shout in the Street,* and Moretti's "Homo palpitans: Balzac's Novels and Urban Personality" in *Signs Taken for Wonders.*

12. Kenner's phrase, the "Cartesian centaur," nicely evokes the tensions between modernist and archaic figures and longings in the story. See Kenner, pp. 117–32, for his clever discussion of this and other related images in Beckett.

13. This theme-form could be traced in modern fiction from novels such as Flaubert's *Sentimental Education,* which begins with Frédéric's chance sighting of Madame Arnoux, to the avant-garde exultation of chance, male sexuality, and "amour fou" in *Nadja.* See Suleiman (101–10) for an analysis of the way Breton constructs a concept of self around the conjunction of aimless wandering, chance, and the figure of the woman.

14. For example, in Harvey 1989, Suelieman 1990, Appiah 1992, and, most recently, Tyrus Miller's *Late Modernism,* 1999 (see chapter 1, note 4, above).

15. The others are Robbe-Grillet, Fuentes, Nabokov, Coover, and Pynchon. Obviously, though apparently unaware of it, McHale is limiting his discussion to a dominant male modernism. I discuss Robbe-Grillet's relation to Beckett in chapter 6.

16. About Foucault's relationship to the philosophical and discursive norms guiding the self-critique of modernity, see Habermas's *The Philosophical Discourse of Modernity,* pp. 336–67, and Nancy Fraser's *Unruly Practices,* pp. 35–54.

17. See Anthony Giddens essay "Structuralism, Post-Structuralism and the Production of Culture" for a discussion of how some of the constitutive contradictions of poststructural thought can be traced back to Saussure's distinction between *langue* and *parole.*

18. See Habermas's "The Incomplete Project of Modernity" for a critique of poststructuralism in this regard; see the volume edited by Dorothy Ross, *Modernist Impulses in the Human Sciences,* for a variety of views on the interrelations of social philosophy and modernism from 1870 to 1930.

19. See Huyssen, p. 213, for why he thinks Foucault's arguments are irrelevant to postmodernism and merely reverse without critical effect the "very ideology that invariably glorifies the artist as genius." In my view, Foucault's essay is both useful and contradictory.

20. Huyssen goes on to view the postmodernism—American and European—of the 1970s and beyond as unfolding in an historical context that lacks the political aspirations of the 1960s. He also constructs a narrative of decline, cooptation, random eclecticism, and collage that resembles the formalist accounts of the postmodern against which he inveighs: the "1970s seems to be characterized . . . by an ever wider dispersal and dissemination of artistic practices all working out the ruins of the modernist edifice . . . supplementing it with randomly chosen images and motifs from pre-modern and non-modern cultures as well as from contemporary mass culture" (196). In this he fails to obey his own insights about the danger of nostalgia.

Chapter 4. Molloy (one): Molloy, the Subject

1. Beckett's "charcoal burner" evokes the landless peasantry whose livelihood, often dependent on access to forests and unclaimed land, was threatened by the encroachment of the bourgeoisie into all parts of Western Europe by the early twentieth century. For a fascinating account of the violence attending such a confrontation, see Hobsbawm's *Primitive Rebels*.

2. For example, Connor (1988), Hill (1990), Trezise (1990), and Begam (1996).

3. Roland Barthes's *Writing Degree Zero* (originally published in 1953) was one of the earliest and most influential statements of the anti-interpretive stance.

4. Knowlson reports that when Adorno met Beckett in 1961 and told him that the name Hamm in *Endgame* was derived from "Hamlet," Beckett replied, "Sorry, Professor, but I never thought of Hamlet when I invented this name" (428). What Adorno did not know, however, was that in the midst of working on *Fin de partie* (the original French title), Beckett decided to reread all of Racine's plays; Beckett claimed that his new understanding of Racine changed his perception of what might be done in the contemporary theater. Thus, Adorno's insight about Beckett's conscious attempt to transform the principles of classic European tragedy was sound. Beckett's suggestive working title for the play, the rejoinder to Adorno notwithstanding, was "HAAM" (*sic*) (see Knowlson, pp. 383–84).

5. The debate between Lukács and Adorno is well represented in *Aesthetics and Politics* (by Adorno et al., with commentaries by Jameson); see also Lunn, pp. 272–79, and Arato about the polemical nature of Adorno's view of Beckett.

6. See Connor, pp. 56–57, for a discussion of how the network of differences and similarities in the two narratives create an unsolvable hermeneutic problem. Connor views the relation between the two parts as a problem in intertextuality; see Hill for a similar view of the Molloy-Moran relationship as "aporetic doubling" (68).

7. See, for example, Brooks, chapter 9, and Menand, pp. 101–13, for interpretations of *Heart of Darkness* that relate the frame to Conrad's self-understanding as a novelist; for Cather's analogous use of narrative framing, see my essay "From Romance to Kinship: Tradition and the Autonomous Woman in *My Antonia*."

8. See, for example, Ford Madox Ford's "On Impressionism," Pater's essay on "Style," Conrad's preface to *The Nigger of the "Narcissus,"*, the concluding sections of Proust's *Le Temps retrouvé*, Henry James's "The Art of Fiction," and Woolf's "Modern Fiction."

9. Pater's essay on "Style" in *Appreciations* is one of the clearest statements of this opposition between scientific fact, on one side, and literary imagination, sense, and intuition on the other.

10. See Paul Davies' essay "Three Novels and Four *nouvelles:* giving up the ghost be born at last" for an extended consideration of Jungian motifs in Beckett's fiction.

11. See Bakhtin's *Rabelais and His World,* chapter 6, "Images of the Material Bodily Lower Stratum" for his influential discussion of how such images function in literature and popular culture as expressions about institutionalized authority.

12. See above, chapter 3, note 6, for views on Beckett's relation to Irish "identity."

13. In *Molloy* Beckett evokes and mocks the full range of meanings attached to the ideas of discrimination and distinction, from artistic appreciation to bodily comportment. Bourdieu's *Distinction: A Social Critique of the Judgment of Taste,* offers an encyclopedic sampling of the symbolic vectors that create social hierarchies of taste.

14. See Fletcher, p. 138, for similarities between Swiftian and Beckettian satire in this regard.

15. See also Levenson's chapter on "Consciousness" for a discussion of some of the constitutive tensions in the modernist view of subjectivity.

16. There were, of course, other critical traditions which sought to understand modernist innovation in terms of the representation of everyday, social life. See, for example, the last chapter of Auerbach's *Mimesis* (first published in 1946) on Woolf's *To the Lighthouse.*

17. While not well known in the United States, Barrès was an influential figure in both artistic and political circles in *fin de siècle* France. See Seigel, pp. 278–89, for an account of Barrès as novelist and political publicist for the rightwing opposition to the liberal parliamentarianism of the Third Republic.

18. For a typical view of Forster as outside the modernist canon, see Tambling's "Introduction" in *E. M. Forster,* pp. 2–4. Malcolm Bradbury's influential essay *"Two Passages to India: Forster as Victorian and Modern"* makes an interesting argument about the tension between modernist and liberal-humanist values in Forster's last novel.

Chapter 5. Molloy (two): Moran, the Agent

1. This is Brian McHale's influential view, discussed in chapter 3.

2. There are alternative terms, such as *statement* and *utterance,* or a tripartite story-plot-discourse, as in Brooks. See Ricoeur (vol. 2, chapters 2 and 3) for the genesis and implications of these analytical distinctions for the study of narrative.

3. See Noah Isenberg's *Between Redemption and Doom,* pp. 127–27, for similarities between Benjamin's concept of community in "The Storyteller" and Tönnies influential opposition of *Gemeinschaft* (traditional community) and *Gesellschaft* (modern civil society)

4. The celebration of laziness and a principled indifference to work is, of course, a common theme in much modern fiction. Henry Miller's *Tropic of Cancer* (written in the 1930s when he and Beckett were both living in Paris) is perhaps the classic interwar statement of this archetypical bohemian attitude. See Ihab Hassan's *The Literature of Silence* for a comparison of Miller and Beckett; see also "Inside the Whale" (1940) for George Orwell's guarded celebration of Miller's apotheosis of passivity, in the face of the inadequacies of both high modernism and the socially engaged writing of the 1920s and '30s (discussed below in chapter 6).

5. See Hill, pp. 23–26, on oxymoron as a key Beckettian trope.

6. As Barthes put it: "Structurally, narrative shares the characteristics of the sentence without ever being reducible to the simple sum of its sentences . . . a narrative is a long sentence just as every constative sentence is in a way a rough outline of a short narrative" ("Introduction" 84).

7. "Every narrative," Ricoeur claims, "presupposes a familiarity with terms such as agent, goal, means, circumstance, help, hostility, cooperation, conflict, failure, etc., on the part of its narrator and any listener" (I, 55). For Ricoeur, narrative discourse is a linguistic, rhetorical recoding of already meaningful and ordered human activities. Stories are built up from a "preunderstanding" or "practical understanding" of "the domain of action" (I, 55); "If, in fact, human action can be narrated, it is because it [action] is always already articulated by signs, rules and norms. It is always already symbolically mediated" (I, 57); "What is resignified by narrative is what was already presignified at the level of human acting" (I, 81).

8. This quality of blocked or frustrated positive meaning was central to Adorno's reading of Beckett and his argument against Lukács's critique of modernism; see Adorno's "Reconciliation Under Duress," especially pp. 160–68.

9. Brooks uses a Sherlock Holmes story by Conan Doyle to demonstrate the "overt" manner in which "plot" transforms "discourse" into "story" (23–36); Barthes uses Ian Fleming's *Goldfinger* and Agatha Christie's *The Sittaford Mystery* to exemplify how conventional narratives transform "sequence" into "causality" and conflate "personal" and "impersonal" modes ("Introduction" 109–24).

10. In *The Political Unconscious,* Jameson's argument depends on accepting that the resolution of a "real contradiction" can only be articulated in a nonimaginary way through an historical master narrative of class struggle and reification.

11. See Bakhtin's essay "The Problem of Speech Genres" for a critique of formalist linguistics which, in part, informs my own perspective here.

12. In this regard, see Ricouer's comments on why, in Beckett and other

innovative modern writers, "the dissolution of the plot has to be understood as a signal to us to cooperate with the work, to shape the plot ourselves. . . . Frustration cannot be the last word. The reader's work of composition cannot be made completely impossible" (vol. 2, 25).

13. Appiah offers an excellent critical overview of modern and traditional views of agency and causation in this regard; see pp. 122–33 in *In My Father's House: Africa in the Philosophy of Culture.*

14. As Genette admitted, it was Barthes's concept of the writerly that implicitly organized his derivation of the categories of narrative discourse from Proust: "Everything underlying Proustian narrative in the direction of interference and repetition was an element of transgression of classical norms and therefore a factor of valorization" (*Revisited* 27–28).

Chapter 6. A Contest of Nightmares: The Unnamable *and* 1984

1. See Abbott's "The Writer's Laboratory: Samuel Beckett and the Death of the Book" in *Diary Fiction: Writing as Action* for a consideration of the book within the tradition of epistolary or diary-form novels. While Abbott sees *Malone Dies* as a crucial step in Beckett's development as an experimental writer, the innovations it incorporates seem to come at a cost; as he puts it, "*Malone Dies* is, in effect, an extension of the principle of the boring [diary] entry to the entire novel" (193).

2. Fletcher sees the narrator as "a universal figure" (182); for Deane, the "orphic voice" in the *Unnamable* expresses an "inertia . . . [which] is metaphysically, not socially, dictated" (*Short History* 190); Frye characterizes the book as an "hypnotic voice, muttering like a disembodied spirit at a séance" (24; in Bloom, ed., *Samuel Beckett*).

3. In a similar vein, critics who wish to see Beckett's work, and especially *The Unnamable,* as "an anti-Enlightenment critique of humanism that rejects the idea that the cogito provides the ground of all knowledge" (Begam 149) overemphasize the overlap of cultural and cognitive claims to universalism. There is nothing in Beckett's writing that rejects the admission of universally valid rules of argumentation; in fact, many passages in *The Unnamable* make a devastating case against cultural and psychological universalism through adducing and weighing evidence. The Enlightenment that Beckett reputedly rejects always had a tradition of self-critique; the aesthetic sphere's critique of technological and social modernity could only have developed within the Enlightenment's ideals of free expression and universal human rights. See Ernest Gellner's *Reason and Culture* for an eloquent discussion of why claims to cognitive and cultural universalism cannot be equated.

4. See Shattuck's chapter on Jarry, "Suicide by Hallucination," in *The Banquet Years* for a description of the outrage the play's premiere instigated, starting with its very first word, an obscenity to which Jarry had added an extra letter (usually translated as "shite" or "shrit"). Shattuck also reports the famous response of the

young W. B. Yeats, who was in the audience on opening night: "After Us the Savage God" (209).

5. See Knowlson, pp. 340–42.

6. For some good surveys of these developments in the novel, see, for example, Hewison (England), Schaub (U.S.), Britton (France), Sinfield (Britain and Anglophone), and González Echevarriá (Latin America). Hobsbawm provides a provocative sweep of the era in the chapter "The Avant Garde Dies—The Arts after 1950" in his history of the "short" twentieth century, *The Age of Extremes*.

7. See Marhsall Berman's influential discussion of the centrality of the idea of individual self-development in the modernist intellect and imagination, especially chapter 2.

8. Robbe-Grillet claims that Beckett rejects character (28) and story (33), while valuing "presence" over "signification" in *Godot* (111–25).

9. See the interview reprinted in Graver (219) for Beckett's disclaimer of the relation of his work to Heidegger and Sartre.

10. Hill sees the *Dialogues* only in negative terms, as a refusal to convert "negativity" into a "differed positivity" (122); similarly, Rupert Wood comments that they display a "deconstructive logic" and "appear to recommend total capitulation" (12).

11. Beckett also used plot elements derived from detective fiction in the Moran section of *Molloy*, but in order to achieve a very different effect; parodied, deprived of all sensationalism, and removed from the metropolitan narrative structure central to the modern novel, Beckett's "agent" works against, rather than with, the narrative expectations aroused by the masculine detective. See Morrissette (3–5) for Robbe-Grillet's use of myth.

12. Britton provides helpful descriptions of Robbe-Grillet's fiction and the intellectual context in which the theory of the "new novel" emerged; see pp. 67–72 for her reading of *Les Gommes*.

13. See E. P. Thompson's "Inside *Which* Whale" for the historical background of Orwell's attack on the leftist politics of Britain in the 1930s. The weaknesses in Orwell's position that Thompson points out are, I believe, indications that Orwell ought to be read as a cultural rather than a political critic; that cultural-politics rather than historical-political analyses are his main concern.

14. Crick (92–105) provides a summary of the responses to the novel.

15. For some of the sources Orwell drew on in his understanding of totalitarianism as a highly centralized political regime that destroyed distinctions between public and private and dismantled the liberal-capitalist separation of the spheres of science, culture, law, and politics, see Steinhoff's *George Orwell and the Origins of 1984*.

16. See Williams (*Orwell* 98–99).

17. In *Orwell*, Williams also points out how many of the ideas laid out in "the book" are consistent with Orwell's nonfiction writing of the same period. He also discusses the possibility that Orwell, had he not been severely ill during much of the

time he was writing *1984*, might have tried to smooth over the tensions in narrative perspective.

Epilogue. Engagement, Écriture, Autonomy: The Displacement of Politics in Postwar Critical Theory

1. Even for a writer as resolutely suspicious as Beckett was of any direct tie among art, politics, and mass culture, the decade's cultural programs held an inevitable attraction; in the mid 1930s, Beckett wrote to Sergei Eisenstein at the State Institute of Cinematography in Moscow, in the hopes of studying film there. Apparently, his letter went unanswered (Bair 204–205; Knowlson 212–13).

2. Raymond Williams comments on the development of this type of linkage in *Marxism and Literature:* "Significantly, since the late nineteenth century, crises of technique—which can be isolated as problems of the 'medium' or of the 'form'—have been directly linked with a sense of crisis in the relationship of art to society, or in the very purposes of art which had previously been agreed upon or even taken for granted. A new technique has often been seen, realistically, as a new relationship, or as depending on a new relationship. Thus what had been isolated as a medium, in many ways rightly as a way of emphasizing the material production which any art must be, came to be seen, inevitably as a social practice; or, in the crisis of modern cultural production, as a crisis of social practice. This is the crucial common factor, in otherwise diverse tendencies, which links the radical aesthetics of modernism and the revolutionary theory and practice of Marxism" (163–64).

3. For example, as Arato points out in comparing Benjamin with Adorno, the essay "is also remarkable for its apology for the instrumentalization of art in the Soviet Union. To be sure Benjamin attacks artistic autonomy not in the name of administration but in the name of a collective, open, experimental, technically innovative political art form" (214).

4. David Harvey provides an excellent description of changes in the relationship among state, industry, and labor in the most advanced industrial nations from 1945 to the early 1970s. See *The Condition of Postmodernity,* pp. 119–88.

5. See his introduction to Fanon's *The Wretched of the Earth,* in which Sartre tries to identify with Fanon by warning his French audience (in which, awkwardly, he includes himself) that Fanon does not intend to speak to them, but only about them. Somehow, Sartre speaks for Fanon by claiming that Fanon, as a postcolonial, is rightly demanding that he, and he alone, can speak for himself.

6. See Judt, especially chapter 4, for his analysis of the many contradictions in Sartre's notion of engagement. "In the political context of postwar France," Judt argues, Sartre's call for intellectuals "to commit to opposing things as they are . . . pointedly inevitably in the direction of Marxism, and thus communism . . . was not because existentialism in its Sartrean guise was intrinsically sympathetic to Marxism; indeed, the two were logically incompatible" (83).

7. Sontag cites other evidence for how the book is shaped as a polemic against Sartre's influential formulations of the late 1940s; see pp. x–xvi.

8. Some of these hyperbolic statements appear as responses to Stalinism; see, for example, p. 24 and p. 73.

9. Adorno's clearest expression of his concept of "social content" is in the essay "Lyric Poetry and Society." See Huyssen, chapter 2, for a careful interpretation of Adorno's attitude toward mass culture.

10. Although Adorno was still working on *Aesthetic Theory* when he died in 1969, the book expresses ideas he had been developing since the end of the war. See the "Editor's Epilogue" to the English translation, pp. 493–98.

11. See Brenkman, pp. 59–76, for the importance of ideas about the social division of labor for Marxist cultural theory.

12. See the "Editor's Epilogue," p. 498.

13. This does not mean that artists and writers involved in such struggles did not also have to come to terms with the normative value of aesthetic autonomy; see, for example, the debates about the role of the "Negro Writer" among Ralph Ellison, Richard Wright, Langston Hughes, and James Baldwin (reprinted in Gibson).

WORKS CITED

Abbott, H. Potter. *Diary Fiction: Writing as Action.* Ithaca: Cornell UP, 1984.

———. *The Fiction of Samuel Beckett: Form and Effect.* Berkeley: U of California P, 1973.

Adorno, Theodor W. *Aesthetic Theory.* Trans C. Lenhardt. London: Routledge, 1984.

———. "Commitment." Trans. Francis McDonagh. *The Essential Frankfurt School Reader.* Ed. Andrew Arato and Eike Gebhardt. New York: Urizen, 1978.

———. "Lyric Poetry and Society." Trans. Bruce Mayo. *Telos* 20 (1974): 56–71.

———. "Reconciliation under Duress." *Aesthetics and Politics.* Trans. Rodney Livingston. London: NLB, 1977.

———. "Trying to Understand *Endgame.*" *Notes to Literature* Vol 1. Trans. Shierry Weber Nicholson. New York: Columbia UP, 1991.

Appiah, Kwame Anthony. *In My Father's House: Africa and the Philosophy of Culture.* New York: Oxford UP, 1992.

Arato, Andrew. "Introduction," Part 2. *The Essential Frankfurt School Reader.* Ed. Andrew Arato and Eike Gebhardt. New York: Urizen, 1978.

Auerbach, Erich. *Mimesis.* Trans. Wilard R. Trask. Princeton: Princeton UP, 1968.

Bair, Deirdre. *Samuel Beckett: A Biography.* New York: Harcourt, 1978.

Bakhtin, M. M. *The Dialogic Imagination.* Trans. Caryl Emerson and Michael Holquist. Austin: U of Texas P, 1981.

———. *Rabelais and His World.* Trans. Helene Iswolsky. Bloomington: Indiana UP, 1984.

———. *Speech Genres and Other Late Essays.* Trans. Vern W. McGee. Austin: U of Texas P, 1986.

Barron, Stephanie, ed. *"Degenerate Art": The Fate of the Avant Garde in Nazi Germany.* New York: Abrams, 1991.

Barthes, Roland. "Introduction to the Structural Study of Narratives." *Image-Music-Text.* Trans. Stephen Heath. New York: Noonday, 1988.

———. *S/Z.* Trans. Richard Miller. New York: Hill and Wang, 1974.

———. *Writing Degree Zero.* Trans. Annette Lavers and Colin Smith. New York: Noonday, 1968.

Barwise, John, and John Etchemendy. *The Liar: An Essay on Truth and Circularity.* New York: Oxford UP, 1987.

Beckett, Samuel. *Disjecta.* New York: Grove, 1984.

———. *Endgame.* New York: Grove, 1958.

———. *First Love and Other Shorts.* New York: Grove, 1974.

———. *How It Is.* New York: Grove, 1964.

———. *The Lost Ones.* New York: Grove, 1972.

———. *Malone Dies.* New York: Grove, 1956.

———. *Molloy.* New York: Grove, 1955.

———. *More Pricks than Kicks.* New York: Grove, 1972.

———. *Murphy.* London: John Calder, 1977.

———. *Proust and Three Dialogues with Georges Duthuit* (PTD). London: John Calder, 1965.

———. *Stories and Texts for Nothing.* New York: Grove, 1967.

———. *The Unnamable.* New York: Grove, 1958.

———. *Watt.* New York: Grove, 1959.

Begam, Richard. *Samuel Beckett and the End of Modernity.* Stanford: Stanford UP, 1996.

Benjamin, Walter. *Illuminations.* Trans. Harry Zohn. New York: Schocken, 1969.

———. *Reflections.* Trans. Edmund Jephcott. New York: HBJ, 1978.

Berman, Marshall. *All That Is Solid Melts into Air.* New York: Simon and Schuster, 1982.

Bersani, Leo. *The Culture of Redemption.* Cambridge: Harvard UP, 1990.

Bloom, Harold, ed. *Samuel Beckett: Modern Critical Views.* New York: Chelsea, 1985.

Bourdieu, Pierre. *Distinction.* Trans. Richard Nice. Cambridge: Harvard UP, 1984.

———. *The Field of Cultural Production.* Ed. Randal Johnson. New York: Columbia UP, 1993.

———. "Flaubert's Point of View." Trans. Priscilla Parkhurst Ferguson. *Critical Inquiry* 14.3 (1988): 62.

Bradbury, Malcolm. "Two Passages to India: Forster as Victorian and Modern." *A Passage to India: Modern Critical Interpretations.* Ed. Harold Bloom. New York: Chelsea House, 1987.

Brenkman, John. *Culture and Domination.* Ithaca: Cornell UP, 1987.

Breton. André. *Nadja.* Trans. Richard Howard. New York:Grove, 1960.

Britton, Celia. *The Nouveau Roman.* New York: St. Martin's, 1992.

Brooks, Peter. *Reading for the Plot.* New York: Vintage, 1985.

Bruck, Jan. "Beckett, Benjamin and the Modern Crisis in Communication." *New German Critique* 26 (1982): 159–71.

Bürger, Peter. *The Decline of Modernism.* Trans. Nicholas Walker. University Park: Pennsylvania State UP, 1992.

———. *Theory of the Avant Garde.* Trans. Michael Shaw. Minneapolis: U of Minnesota P, 1984.

Butler, Lance St. John, ed. *Critical Essays on Samuel Beckett.* Brookfield, Vt.: Scholar P, 1993.

Caudwell, Christopher. *Illusion and Reality.* London: Macmillan, 1937.

Clifford, James. *The Predicament of Culture.* Cambridge: Harvard UP, 1988.

Cohn, Ruby. "Foreword." *Disjecta.* By Samuel Beckett. New York: Grove, 1984.

Connor, Steven. *Samuel Beckett: Repetition, Theory and Text.* London: Blackwell, 1988.

Conrad, Joseph. Preface to *The Nigger of the "Narcissus."* Oxford: Oxford UP, 1984.

Cooke, Virginia, ed. *Beckett on File.* London: Methuen, 1985.

Crick, Bernard. Introduction. *1984.* By George Orwell. Oxford: Clarendon P, 1984.

Cronin, Anthony. *Samuel Beckett: The Last Modernist.* New York: HarperCollins, 1997.

Cunningham, Valentine. *British Writers of the Thirties.* New York: Oxford UP, 1988.

Davies, Paul. "Three novels and four *nouvelles:* Giving up the ghost be born at last." *The Cambridge Companion to Beckett.* Ed. John Pilling. Cambridge: Cambridge UP, 1994.

Deane, Seamus. *Celtic Revivals.* London: Faber and Faber, 1985.

———. *A Short History of Irish Literature.* London: Hutchinson, 1986.

Dearlove, Judith E. *Accommodating the Chaos: Samuel Beckett's Nonrelational Art.* Durham: Duke UP, 1982.

Dubin, Steve C. *Arresting Images: Impolitic Art and Uncivil Actions.* New York: Routledge, 1992.

Ellmann, Richard. *James Joyce.* Oxford: Oxford UP, 1982.

Federman, Raymond, and John Fletcher. *Samuel Beckett: His Works and His Critics.* Berkeley: U of California P, 1970.

Fletcher, John. *The Novels of Samuel Beckett.* New York: Barnes and Noble, 1970.

Ford, Ford Madox. *Critical Writings of Ford Madox Ford.* Ed. Frank MacShane. Lincoln: U of Nebraska P, 1964.

Foucault, Michel. *The Foucault Reader.* Ed. Paul Rabinow. New York: Pantheon, 1984.

Fraser, Nancy. *Unruly Practices.* Minneapolis: U of Minnesota P, 1989.

Frye, Northrop. *Fables of Identity: Studies in Poetic Mythology.* New York: Harcourt Brace, 1963.

Gagnier, Regenia. *Idylls of the Marketplace: Oscar Wilde and the Victorian Public.* Stanford: Stanford UP, 1986.

Gellner, Ernest. *Reason and Culture.* Oxford: Blackwell, 1992.

Genette, Gerard. *Narrative Discourse.* Trans. Jane E. Lewin. Ithaca: Cornell UP, 1980.

———. *Narrative Discourse Revisited.* Trans. Jane E. Lewin. Ithaca: Cornell UP, 1988.

Gibson, Donald B., ed. *Five Black Writers: Essays on Wright, Ellison, Baldwin, Hughes, and LeRoi Jones.* New York: New York UP, 1970.

Giddens, Anthony. "Structuralism, Poststructuralism and the Production of Culture." *Social Theory Today.* Ed. Anthony Giddens and Jonathan H. Turner. Stanford: Stanford UP, 1987.

Goldmann, Lucien. *Towards a Sociology of the Novel.* Trans. Alain Sheridan. London: Tavistock, 1975.

González Echevarría, Roberto. *Myth and Archive: A Theory of Latin American Narrative.* Cambridge: Cambridge UP, 1990.

Graver, Lawrence, and Raymond Federman, eds. *Samuel Beckett: The Critical Heritage.* London: Routledge, 1979.

Guy, Josephine. *The British Avant Garde: The Theory and Politics of Tradition.* New York: Harvester Wheatsheaf, 1991.

Habermas, Jürgen. "The Incomplete Project of Modernity." *The Anti-Aesthetic.* Ed. Hal Foster. Townsend, Wash.: Bay Press, 1983.

―――. *The Philosophical Discourse of Modernity: Twelve Lectures.* Trans. Frederick Lawrence. Cambridge: MIT, 1987.

Harrington, John P. *The Irish Beckett.* Syracuse: Syracuse UP, 1991.

Harvey, David. *The Condition of Postmodernity.* Cambridge: Blackwell, 1989.

―――. *The Urban Experience.* Baltimore: Johns Hopkins UP, 1989.

Harvey, Lawrence E. " *Watt.*" *On Beckett: Essays and Criticism.* Ed. S. E. Gontarski. New York: Grove, 1986.

Hassan, Ihab. *The Literature of Silence: Henry Miller and Samuel Beckett.* New York: Knopf, 1967.

Hewison, Robert. *In Anger: British Culture in the Cold War 1945–60.* New York: Oxford, 1981.

Hill, Leslie. *Beckett's Fiction in Different Words.* Cambridge: Cambridge UP, 1990.

Hobsbawm, Eric. *The Age of Empire.* New York: Vintage, 1989.

―――. *The Age of Extremes.* New York: Vintage, 1996.

―――. *Primitive Rebels.* New York: Norton, 1965.

Howe, Irving. *Politics and the Novel.* New York: Horizon, 1957.

Huyssen, Andreas. *After the Great Divide: Modernism, Mass Culture, Postmodernism.* Bloomington: Indiana UP, 1986.

Hynes, Samuel. *The Auden Generation.* London: Bodley Head, 1976.

Isenberg, Noah. *Between Redemption and Doom: the Strains of German-Jewish Modernism.* Lincoln: U of Nebraska P, 1999.

Iser, Wolfgang. *The Implied Reader: Patterns in Communication in Prose Fiction from Bunyan to Beckett.* Baltimore: Johns Hopkins UP, 1974.

James, Henry. *The Art of Criticism.* Eds. William Veeder and Susan M. Griffin. Chicago: U of Chicago P, 1986.

Jameson, Fredric. *The Political Unconscious.* Ithaca: Cornell, 1981.

Jauss, Hans Robert. *Toward an Aesthetic of Reception.* Trans. Timothy Bahti. Brighton: Harvester Press, 1982.

Jolas, Eugene, ed. *Transition Workshop.* New York: Vanguard Press, 1949.

Judt, Tony. *Past Imperfect: French Intellectuals 1944–1956.* Berkeley: U California P, 1992.

Jukes, Peter. *A Shout in the Street.* Berkeley: U California P, 1990.

Kenner, Hugh. *Samuel Beckett: A Critical Study.* Berkeley: U California P, 1968.

Kiberd, Declan. *Inventing Ireland: The Literature of the Modern Nation.* Cambridge: Harvard UP, 1995.

―――. "Samuel Beckett and the Protestant Ethic." *The Genius of Irish Prose.* Ed. Augustine Martin. Dublin: Mercier, 1985.

Knowlson, James. *Damned to Fame: The Life of Samuel Beckett.* New York: Simon & Schuster, 1996.

Levenson, Michael H. *A Genealogy of Modernism.* Cambridge: Cambridge UP, 1984.

Lippard, Lucy, ed. *Surrealists on Art.* Englewood Cliffs: Prentice-Hall, 1970.

Lloyd, David. *Anomalous States: Irish Writing and the Post-Colonial Moment.* Durham: Duke UP, 1993.

Lottman, Herbert. *The Left Bank.* San Francisco: Halo, 1991.

Lukács, Georg. "The Ideology of Modernism." *Marxism and Human Liberation.* Ed. E. San Juan, Jr. New York: Dell, 1973.

———. "Narrate or Describe." *Writer and Critic.* Ed. and trans. Arthur D. Kahn. New York: Grosset and Dunlap, 1970.

Lunn, Eugene. *Marxism and Modernism.* Berkeley: U California P, 1982.

McHale, Brian. *Postmodernist Fiction.* New York: Methuen, 1987.

Menand, Louis. *Discovering Modernism.* Oxford: Oxford UP, 1987.

Miller, Tyrus. *Late Modernism: Politics, Fiction, and the Arts between the World Wars.* Berkeley: U California P, 1999.

Moretti, Franco. *Signs Taken for Wonders.* Trans. Susan Fischer et al. London: Verso, 1988.

Morrissette, Bruce. "Surfaces and Structures in Robbe-Grillet's Novels." *Two Novels by Robbe-Grillet (Jealousy) and (In the Labyrinth).* By Alain Robbe-Grillet. New York: Grove, 1965.

"Murphy." Book Review. *Times Literary Supplement* 12 March 1938: 172.

Nadeau, Maurice. *The History of Surrealism.* Trans. Richard Howard. New York: Macmillan, 1965.

Orwell, George. *Down and Out in Paris and London.* New York: HBJ, 1993.

———. *Inside the Whale.* New York: Penguin, 1962.

———. *1984.* Oxford: Clarendon, 1984.

Pater, Walter. *Appreciations.* London: MacMillan, 1895.

Pilling, John. *Beckett before Godot.* Cambridge: Cambridge UP, 1997.

Prendergast, Christopher. "Il n'y a pas de Beckett." *Times Literary Supplement.* 14 November, 1996: 8–10.

Rabinovitz, Rubin. *The Development of Samuel Beckett's Fiction.* Urbana: U of Illinois P, 1984.

Radek, Karl. "Address at First Soviet Writers Congress." *Problems of Soviet Literature.* By K. Bukharin et al. Westport Conn.: Greenwood, 1979.

Rexroth, Kenneth. "The Point Is Irrelevance." *The Nation.* 14 April 1956: 325–28.

Ricoeur, Paul. *Time and Narrative.* 3 vols. Trans. Kathleen McLaughlin and David Pellauer. Chicago: U of Chicago P, 1984.

Robbe-Grillet, Alain. *The Erasers.* Trans. Richard Howard. New York: Grove, 1964.

———. *For a New Novel.* Trans. Richard Howard. New York: Grove, 1965.

———. *The Voyeur.* Trans. Richard Howard. New York: Grove, 1958.

Ross, Dorothy, ed. *Modernist Impulses in the Human Sciences 1870–1930.* Baltimore: Johns Hopkins UP, 1994.

Sartre, J. P. *Literature and Existentialism*. Trans. Bernard Frechtman. Secaucus: Citadel, 1972.

———. Preface. *The Wretched of the Earth*. By Frantz Fanon. Trans. Constance Farrington. New York: Grove, 1963.

Schaub, Thomas Hill. *American Fiction in the Cold War*. Madison: U Wisconsin P, 1991.

Schwab, Gabriele. *Subjects without Selves*. Cambridge: Harvard UP, 1994.

Seigel, Jerrold. *Bohemian Paris*. New York: Penguin, 1986.

Shattuck, Roger. *The Banquet Years: The Origins of the Avant Garde in France 1895 to World War I*. New York: Vintage, 1968.

Simmel, Georg. "The Metropolis and Mental Life." *On Individuality and Social Forms*. Ed. Donald E. Levine. Chicago: U Chicago P, 1971.

Sinfield, Alan, ed. *Society and Literature: 1945–1970*. London: Methuen, 1983.

Sontag, Susan. *Styles of Radical Will*. New York: Dell, 1967.

Steinhoff, William. *George Orwell and the Origins of 1984*. Ann Arbor: U Michigan P, 1975.

Stocking, George W. Jr., ed. *Romantic Motives: Essays on Anthropological Sensibility*. Madison: U Wisconsin P, 1989.

Suleiman, Susan Rubin. *Subversive Intent: Gender, Politics, and the Avant Garde*. Cambridge: Harvard UP, 1990.

Tambling, Jeremy, ed. *E. M. Forster*. New York: St. Martin's P, 1995.

Thompson, E. P. "Inside *Which* Whale?" *George Orwell*. Ed. Raymond Williams. Englewood Cliffs: Prentice Hall, 1974.

Trezise, Thomas. *Into the Breach*. Princeton: Princeton UP, 1990.

Wells, H.G. "The Contemporary Novel." *Henry James and H. G. Wells*. Eds. Leon Edel and Gordon N. Ray. London: Rupert Hart-Davis, 1958.

White, Hayden. *The Content of the Form: Narrative Discourse and Historical Representation*. Baltimore: Johns Hopkins UP, 1987.

Wilde, Oscar. *The Picture of Dorian Gray and Other Writings*. New York: Bantam, 1982.

Williams, Raymond. *The Country and the City*. New York: Oxford UP, 1973.

———. *The English Novel from Dickens to Lawrence*. New York: Oxford UP, 1970.

———. *Marxism and Literature*. New York: Oxford UP, 1977.

———. *Orwell*. London: Fontana, 1991.

———. *The Politics of Modernism*. London: Verso, 1989.

Wolff, Janet. *Feminine Sentences*. Berkeley: U of California P, 1990.

Wood, Rupert. "An endgame of aesthetics: Beckett as essayist." *The Cambridge Companion to Beckett*. Ed. John Pilling. Cambridge: Cambridge UP, 1994.

Woolf, Virginia. *The Common Reader*. New York: Harcourt, Brace, 1925.

Zola, Emile. *The Experimental Novel and Other Essays*. Trans. Belle M. Sherman. New York: Haskell House, 1964.

INDEX

A

Adorno, T. W., 6–7, 58, 80, 87, 166–68
aesthetic autonomy (*see also* Beckett and
  aesthetic autonomy), 11–13, 26, 29, 41,
  42–44, 80–81, 139–40, 142, 145–46,
  150, 152–53, 154, 156, 161–68
aestheticism, 4, 11, 13, 16, 25, 26–27, 82,
  98–100, 139, 151, 163, 166
agency, 14, 40, 48, 103–07, 117–23, 125,
  140–41, 152–53
Aragon, Louis, 29
Auden, W. H., 29, 32, 150–51
automatic writing, 11, 15, 48, 159
avant garde, the, 4, 13, 16, 24–25, 29, 34,
  43, 53, 65, 77, 80–81, 127–28, 132,
  139–40, 157, 161–68

B

Bair, Deirdre, 42–43
Balzac, Honoré de, 21, 61, 66, 117
Barrès, Maurice, 98, 100
Barthes, Roland, 2, 74, 76–78, 103, 116,
  118, 119–22, 140, 165–66
Beauvoir, Simone de, 60
Beckett, Samuel: and aesthetic autonomy,
  1–6, 11–13, 15–16, 35–36, 39–41,
  43, 45–47, 52, 97, 139, 142, 145–46;
  and audience, 7, 10, 28, 43, 49, 60, 73;
  and committed writing, 1–6, 30–32,
  35, 73, 82, 84–86, 95; on expression,
  3–4, 55, 93, 137, 143–45, 151; on failure, 3–4, 10, 133, 141–42, 146, 151,
  153; and Joyce, 2, 4, 11–13, 15, 24, 43,
  46, 52, 82, 97, 109, 142; and modernism, 5, 53–56, 59, 61, 74, 81, 87, 91,
97, 137, 138–39, 142, 143, 148, 153–
54; political convictions, 1, 42–43; as
postmodernist, 2, 5, 10, 63, 74–75,
78–79, 102–03; as poststructuralist, 2–
3, 5, 63, 86, 98, 126; on Proust, 11,
13–17, 52; publishing history and reputation, 4–5, 10–11, 24, 28, 93, 137–
38; on social hierarchy, 19, 39, 47, 85–
88, 96–97, 104, 106–07, 132; and
World War II, 1, 5, 28, 41–44, 49, 53,
122. Works: "The Calmative," 57, 64–
65, 68–73; "Dante and the Lobster," 8,
17–24, 34, 131, 132; "Dante ... Bruno .
Vico .. Joyce," 11–13; "Dialogues," 3,
142–47, 151, 160; *Dream of Fair to
Middling Women,* 8; "The End," 8, 54–
64, 95, 125, 132; *Endgame,* 6, 87, 138;
"The Expelled," 57, 67–68, 71; "German letter of 1937," 17; *How It Is,*
109–10, 138; "Intercessions by Denis
Devlin" (review), 30–32, 40; *The Lost
Ones,* 69; *Malone Dies,* 8, 57, 113, 124,
132; *Mercier and Camier,* 8; *Molloy,* 19,
39, 57, 71, 82, 83–97, 101, 102–16,
124; *More Pricks than Kicks* (*see also*
"Dante and the Lobster"), 8, 17, 19, 47,
65, 96, 107; *Murphy,* 4, 8, 27, 28, 29,
30–41, 44, 46, 47, 52, 65, 73, 84, 94,
96, 107–08, 124, 132; the nouvelles (*see
also under specific titles*), 53–56, 65–66,
73, 87, 91–92, 94–95, 101, 124, 132;
"Proust," 13–17; "Texts for Nothing,"
1, 54, 68–69, 79; *The Unnamable,* 5,
45, 57, 109, 124–37, 139, 153–55,
160; *Waiting for Godot,* 137; *Watt,* 5, 8,
42–54, 65, 84, 96, 124

Benjamin, Walter, 4, 64, 105, 123, 161–62
bohemianism, 19–20, 23, 34, 43, 55, 59
Bourdieu, Pierre, 169n. 3
Breton, André, 13, 17, 29
Brooks, Peter, 102, 113, 116, 117–18
Bürger, Peter, 26, 97, 98–101, 139

C
Camus, Albert, 69, 124, 140
Caudwell, Christopher, 172n. 5
communism, 30, 40, 53, 60, 133, 143, 145, 151, 163
Conrad, Joseph, 26, 88
Curtius, Ernst, 27

D
dada, 4, 16, 24, 26, 167
Dante Alighieri, 12
Descartes, René, 71
Devlin, Denis, 28, 30
Dickens, Charles, 13, 21

E
Eliot, T. S., 11, 25–27, 150
existentialism, 5, 131, 164

F
fascism, 29, 41, 43, 151, 162, 164
feminism, 56
flâneur, the, 67, 133
Flaubert, Gustave, 16, 117–18, 138, 141, 163
Forster, E. M., 101
Foucault, Michel, 1, 5, 74, 78–79, 81–82, 122
Frye, Northrop, 116
futurism, 4, 24

G
gender, 34, 72, 128, 133, 148
Genette, Gerard, 102–03, 116
Giddens, Anthony, 122
Goldmann, Lucien, 116, 118–19, 122

H
Harvey, Lawrence E., 42
Hill, Leslie, 42, 86
Howe, Irving, 5, 154
Huysmans, J. K., 59, 163
Huyssen, Andreas, 74, 79–83, 161

I
identity politics, 56, 168
impressionism, 13, 17, 91
Ireland, 4, 30, 41, 48, 94–95, 101, 176n. 6
Iser, Wolfgang, 86, 113

J
James, Henry, 26, 98, 149
Jameson, Fredric, 111, 116
Jarry, Alfred, 133
Jauss, Hans Robert, 22
Jolas, Eugene, 5, 28–29
Joyce, James (*see also* Beckett and Joyce), 4, 11–13, 15, 21, 25–27, 36, 53, 67, 101, 138, 149, 150, 167

K
Kafka, Franz, 4, 138, 140, 141–42, 167
Kenner, Hugh, 71

L
Left Review, 29
Lévi-Strauss, Claude, 111, 116, 122
Lewis, Wyndham, 30, 150
Lloyd, David, 176n. 6

Lukács, Georg, 56, 61–62, 74, 87, 117–18, 119

M
Malraux, André, 29
Márquez, Gabriel Garcia, 69
mass culture, 6, 24–26, 77, 80, 140, 141, 153, 157–58, 161, 166
Masson, André, 143–44, 145
McHale, Brian, 74–77
metropolis, the, 36, 54, 64, 66–69, 148
Miller, Henry, 152–53
Miller, Tyrus, 169n. 4
mimesis, 56–57, 63–64, 88, 98, 102, 110, 116–17, 122
modernism (*see also* Beckett and modernism), 24–27, 32, 43, 50, 55, 57–59, 65, 80–82, 87, 97–101, 142, 151–52, 159, 161–68
modernity, 57, 67, 69, 92
Moretti, Franco, 25–27, 66, 97

N
Nadeau, Maurice, 86
narrative and plot, 7, 66, 76–78, 101, 102–03, 107, 116–23
narrative form: in "The Calmative," 64–65, 68–70, 72; in "Dante and the Lobster," 18, 20–24; in "The End," 54–56, 59–61, 62–64, 66–67; in "The Expelled," 67–68; in *How It Is,* 109–110; in *Malone Dies,* 113, 124; in *Molloy,* 83–91, 96–97, 102–116; in *Murphy,* 29, 33–39, 41, 44, 107–09; in "Texts for Nothing," 68–69; in *The Unnamable,* 45, 109, 124–27, 131–34, 154–55; in *Watt,* 44–46, 49, 50–52, 54
nationalism, 43, 176n. 6
naturalism, 21, 23, 24, 61, 98–100, 154
novel, the, 6, 7–8, 27, 36, 56, 102–03, 111, 116–17, 147

O
Orwell, George: as Beckett's contemporary, 4–7, 148–150; on failure, 4–5, 29, 149–50. Works: *Animal Farm,* 149; *Down and Out in Paris and London,* 95, 153–54; "Inside the Whale," 150–53; *1984,* 4, 149, 153–60; "Why I Write," 4; "Writers and Leviathan," 149

P
Pater, Walter, 12–13, 16, 25
permutation, 38–39, 46, 50, 84–85
postcolonialism, 56, 176n. 6
postmodernism (*see also* Beckett as postmodernist), 74–81, 97, 102, 161
poststructuralism, 3, 5, 122
Pound, Ezra, 30
primitivism, 50, 55–56, 61
Propp, Vladimir, 103, 116
Proust, Marcel, 11, 13–17, 73, 117, 138

R
Rabinovitz, Rubin, 24, 42
Radek, Karl, 30–31
Rexroth, Kenneth, 10, 137–38
Ricoeur, Paul, 110, 113
Robbe-Grillet, Alain, 3–4, 5, 69, 76, 117, 118–19, 121, 138–141, 147–48, 154

S
Sartre, J. P., 2, 87, 139, 162–65
Schwab, Gabriele, 126
Simmel, Georg, 66
social content: in "The End," 56–61; in *Endgame,* 6; in "Dante and the Lobster," 19–21; in *Molloy,* 19, 88–97, 103–06, 111–16; in *Murphy,* 32–33, 36–38; in *The Unnamable,* 128–31, 132; in *Watt,* 47–48
socialist realism, 29, 30–31
solipsism, 38, 94, 98

Sontag, Susan, 86, 165
Stein, Gertrude, 53
stream-of-consciousness, 41, 109
Suleiman, Susan, 148
surrealism, 4, 13, 15, 16, 23, 29, 40, 53,
    73, 132, 143, 163

T
Temps modernes, Les, 5, 54, 60
Times Literary Supplement, 28, 29, 32
totalitarianism, 43–44
transition, 5, 26, 28–29, 43

W
Weber, Max, 57, 78
Wells, H. G., 98
White, Hayden, 113
Wilde, Oscar, 58, 59
Williams, Raymond, 6, 7–8, 15, 27, 36,
    43, 66, 74, 97–98, 149–50
Woolf, Virginia, 13, 24

Z
Zola, Emile, 24–25, 98–100, 117, 154